W9-AJO-973

ELYSIUM GIRLS

KATE PENTECOST

HYPERION
LOS ANGELES NEW YORK

First Edition, April 2020
10 9 8 7 6 5 4 3 2 1
FAC-020093-20059
Printed in the United States of America

This book is set in Adobe Garamond Pro/Fontspring
Designed by Phil Buchanan

Library of Congress Control Number: 2019945906
ISBN 978-1-368-04186-7

Reinforced binding

Visit www.hyperionteens.com

Logo Applies to Text Stock Only

TO MY STUDENTS (ALL OF YOU). I LOVE YOU, BUT YOU ALREADY KNEW THAT.

AND TO THE MEMORY OF KRISTIN IDLEBIRD, WHO SHOULD BE PUBLISHING BOOKS ALONGSIDE ME TODAY.

PART ONE:

ELYSIUM

CHAPTER 1

1935
10 YEARS
REMAIN.

They say that there was a big bang when the world began. When a whole lot of nothing exploded into everything. Some say that it was the one true god speaking, commanding the light and the water and the earth to all be. The end, from what I've read, doesn't seem too different. The sun will go supernova. Loud and violent. Or maybe, they say, it will be trumpets blown by angels made out of wings and eyes and wheels. Roars of beasts and leviathans. But that's all a lie. First of all, there isn't only one god. There are two Sisters—Life and Death—and their Mother, who presides over everything else. And the Sisters like to gamble against each other with things like time and space and human lives. And when our world ended and their Game began, it was silent and smothering as the grave.

I was six years old.

On April 14, 1935: Black Sunday, the dust rolled over the whole Oklahoma Panhandle, black and boiling, a thousand feet high, filling the sky and our eyes and our mouths and our lungs. Darkness. Suffocation. But what I remembered most was the silence, as though some divine power was watching us, holding its breath, waiting for our first moves. We had no way of knowing then that They were.

We crept out of our shelters, those of us who *had* found shelter, and what we saw terrified us. Our fields were gone, our farms were gone, and in their places was nothing but desert, gray dunes stretching over miles immeasurable. A still, waterless sea with only our town standing in the center. The dunes broke into ridges, canyons, cliffs we had never seen before, and among them lay the pieces of what had been. Cars lay covered; headstones were buried; cattle and horses lay dead, their lungs and stomachs filled with mud; and strange new creatures watched us from behind the dunes.

Some of us went out into it, to go to Boise City and see if they'd weathered the storm all right. But what we found was that there *was* no Boise City. No Dalhart, no Kenton or Felt or Texhoma. No sign even of the XIT Ranch that had spanned miles and miles in its own right. They were all simply *gone*, without the slightest trace that they'd ever been. And if you kept walking, even in the straightest of lines, somehow, you'd find yourself back where you started again. This world wasn't *right*; it wasn't natural. Now creatures like fire coyotes and carnivorous hordes of locusts roamed the desert, along with some things too terrible to even think of. And when we turned on our radios to listen for President Roosevelt's assurance that everything would be all right, we couldn't even hear static.

But it was only at sunset, when Death had her first say, that we realized how bleak our situation truly was. At first, we had thought it was a black roller, a dust storm rolling in from the north. But as we braced ourselves in the wreckage, the black dust stopped at the edge of town and went no farther. Then we saw what it was: soldiers, one hundred of them, all made entirely of black dust. Each of them stood eight feet high, and in the light of the full moon overhead, their shadows seemed to cut teeth into the sand. They had swords in their hands, swords made of jagged black stone, and our blood curdled in our veins as they called out for our leader.

The fathers of each family, farmers and cowboys alike, fell silent, looking at their empty, work-hardened hands. We looked to them, and for once, they had no answers. God had failed them. Hard work had failed them. Manhood had failed them. Then a woman stepped forward, an old, pale woman with tattooed hands.

"Bruja," I heard someone whisper. But I couldn't keep my eyes off her.

"I'll speak for this city," she said to the Dust Soldiers. "What do you want?"

Their leader opened a mouth like a well and spoke in a voice like grinding stones.

The Goddesses Life and Death have begun a Game. They have given you exactly ten years to build your city. No more, no less. During those years, you will put aside one-third of your crops for us every year. We will return at sunset on the final day to judge you. If we judge your society good and responsible, despite your difficulties, then Life has won, and your society will continue. If your society has been irresponsible, then Death has won the Game. And every man, woman, and child shall be slain.

"This is a wicked Game to impose upon us," the old woman said. "Haven't we suffered through enough already?"

But the Dust Soldiers did not—or could not—answer, and in the end, the old woman had no choice but to agree to the terms of the Game we had been entered into.

"Who . . . who are you?" a man whispered when the Dust Soldiers had gone.

"I am Mother Morevna," she said. "And if you listen to me, we'll get out of this mess just fine. But we will have to do things exactly as I say."

There was a murmuring among the crowd, then a nodding of heads. And then an acknowledgment: We had found ourselves a new leader.

That night, we gathered at the center of town and listened as Mother Morevna told us about the world we would make. Because, she said, we'd been given a chance to create a world that could be truly wonderful, truly prosperous. She said that we must band together—no matter our sex or color—or we would perish. She told us that we must build wells and irrigation systems, shelter, fields, and, most importantly, walls to keep ourselves safe from the desert creatures. We had to reinvent ourselves. And we did.

Cars proved useful once again: to be taken apart and used for scrap. And the old Case tractors . . . well, they had been the cause of a lot of our problems in the first place, hadn't they? They were the first things we used for the walls. Next had come possessions. Last had come the bodies of the fallen, and between dust storms, the walls rose around us, keeping us safe.

Until I, Sal Wilkerson, brought an end to everything.

1944
4 MONTHS
REMAIN.

My nose was broken, it was pretty clear. It was reddish-black and bruised, and twisted off to one side, and when I touched it, pain lit up my whole face. As I sat up on my perch on the top of the west wall, I tried to lessen the pain by counting the names carved into the walls below me. Behind each one of those names was a body, adding its height to our walls. Joanna Schutter, Gregory Farrell, Ludie Mae Fuller, Andrew Jackson LaGrange, Noemi Álvarez . . .

In cultivation class, Trixie Holland had *accidentally* hit me in the face with the backward stroke of her shovel, then made such a big show of being sorry that my classmates ended up consoling *her*. I tried, again, to breathe through my broken nose and felt a surge of anger as a big wad of blood slid down into the back of my throat. I hacked for a minute and spat it over the wall, into the desert, then wiped my nose again and wrote *Trixie Holland is a bitch* in blood on the mud brick beside me. Juvenile, sure, but it helped, if only just for a moment. Then I felt bad about it and wiped it away.

The walls were my sanctuary when Trixie and her girls tried

to follow me after school—which was getting more and more frequent these days. They'd hide behind houses, under windmills, in storm cellars. Then there'd be a "Hey, Sal!" and the running would begin. Sometimes they caught me and harassed me, tore my things. Sometimes I lost them. It didn't help that Trixie's was the reluctant family I was supposed to be staying with this season. They say it takes a village to raise a child. But that only works if the village wants her. And after everything that had happened, Elysium, Oklahoma, did not want me.

Oh, they'd been fine with me at first. Back when I was Sal Wilkerson, the poor little girl whose mother had died. But then I saw the rain, and that changed everything. Rain. I saw it on the horizon, coming toward Elysium in sheets, in curtains. Heavy rain. Miraculous rain, coming to end this Dust Bowl and save us all. I had seen it in the sky, felt it on my skin, believed it in my bones. And being a nine-year-old, I had told everyone. I went from orphan to Child Prophet, lifted on shoulders, gathered around, and petted and celebrated. "When will the rain come, Sallie?" everyone had asked. "Soon!" I'd told them. "The rain will come and everything will be all right!"

But the rain didn't come. And as the townspeople waited, I felt the tide turn against me. From Sal Wilkerson, the Prophet, I became Sal Wilkerson, the Liar. Sal Wilkerson, the Crazy Girl. Sal Wilkerson, the Girl Who Cried Rain. And instead of families wanting to take me in every season, they had to be forced to, bribed with more rations or work exemptions.

When the sun set and everyone went into their houses, I climbed down. I took my bucket out of its place under the toolshed at the base of the wall and started on my weekly journey. My dust mask thudded against my chest and my bucket against my thighs as I slinked quietly along the wall, toward the Dowsing Well. It was too dark to manage without touching the walls, and I felt the names go by under my fingertips. Susannah Halper, Lennie Rodríguez, John Rowe, all buried in the walls, plastered in with their faces turned out to the desert beyond.

I left the wall and slipped between the legs of the tower, moving quickly through the path I had made for myself, through the narrow spaces between the bare-plank houses. No one was outside except for Mr. Jameson, so I relaxed. Even though he was head of the guard, Mother Morevna's second-in-command, he always looked the other way when he saw me go by.

Mr. Jameson had been the one to oversee the building of the walls. He'd been the leader of the group that went out into the desert and had seen how everything had changed. He'd been one of the three men who'd made it back alive. He was strong and quiet and tough as an old boot, and I liked him. He of all people could commiserate, when his wife and son were back in Texas, somewhere outside the tiny, temporary world he'd been stuck in. If they were still alive. If a world even existed beyond the desert anymore.

He knew how I hated being shifted from family to family, about the lean-to I'd built against the northern wall to sleep under when one family had been particularly bad. He'd even put in a motion to let me live with him once. And when his motion was rejected on account of him being "too high on the food chain to be compromised," he'd spent his nights revamping an old chicken house for me to live in. It wasn't the same as a house, of course, but it was surprisingly good—better than staying with Trixie, at any rate—and I was grateful to him. It had wallpaper—the same kind anyone else had, anyway: newspapers and flour sacks. It had a lock and windows and a floor made of plank wood. It had a dresser salvaged from who knew where, and even a bed made of feed sacks and feathers, and it only smelled a little like chickens anymore. It wasn't much, but it was mine. And at least there I was alone because I wanted to be, not because I had to be.

"Why did you do this for me?" I'd asked him.

"My daughter is about your age" was all he'd said. I liked that he always said "is," not "was."

Now his hooded eyes flickered to my nose. "That girl been after you again?"

I thought about it for a second, trying to decide if it was more cowardly to say yes or no, then shook my head.

"Stepped on a rake," I lied.

"You sure it wasn't a shovel?" he said, his eyes serious under his old, sweat-stained Stetson.

"No, sir," I said finally. I was a lot of things, but I wasn't a tattletale.

He squinted at me, then gave me a nod and spat tobacco into an old peach can.

"Get on outta here, then," he said. "And if you have any more problems with rakes, you let me know, all right?"

"Yes, sir," I said. "Thank you, sir." And I slipped through the alley between his house and the Andersons' and made my way toward the Square.

• • •

I heard the hammers before I saw the work lights. Already, the circle at the center of town was being set up for Mourning Night.

About twenty young men were working. In the shadows of the old jail and Baptist church, they hammered and sawed. Some were hauling pieces of wood to the place where the bonfire would be, others had begun setting up the platform that Mother Morevna would stand on during the ceremony.

It was our most important holiday, a celebration of those we had lost during the year. In the evening, we would bring pictures of those who had died—and for those who hadn't ever had their pictures made, small belongings, like combs or snuffboxes or dolls. There were entirely too many toys last year.

Dust Sickness was everyone's greatest fear, the silent killer that crept through Elysium, taking whom it would. It was a lengthy, agonizing sickness you got from breathing in too much dust. Sometimes it could lay dormant for years, then rear its ugly head. It could take years to kill you, or months, or weeks, or days. Mother Morevna did what she could to protect us, covering the whole city in a spell that made dust storms roll right over us. We had faith in her and the magic that had saved us over and over. Still, we put on our dust masks just in case. And still, every year we wondered whose bodies would add to the height of our walls come next Mourning Night.

"Someone's breaking curfew," said a familiar voice. I froze.

When I turned, I saw Lucy sitting with her back against the wall, her hair in twists just visible under her vibrant kerchief. She looked at me, her face serious. She smiled as I let out the breath I'd been holding.

I tried to smile back, then held my hand to my face when my nose throbbed.

"What happened?" Lucy asked.

"Trixie has a mean aim with a shovel," I said, and because of my nose, "mean" sounded like "bean."

"Don't know why you don't punch her in the nose," she said. "I would."

I didn't doubt it. Lucy and her family had been sharecroppers at the farm next to ours, and I'd seen her give a boy a busted lip when he took one of her dolls. Even now, though Lucy was widely known as not only the most fashionable Black girl in Elysium, but the most fashionable girl period, everyone knew not to mess with her. Even the boys.

We hadn't spoken much growing up, but when the rain fiasco happened, she was the only one who had believed that I wasn't crazy. *Some people see things that others don't,* she'd said, and shrugged. I never forgot that. Or that when Trixie and her friends had been seen sneaking over toward my chicken coop, it had been Lucy who chased her away. I didn't have many friends, but Lucy was the closest thing I'd had to one in a long time, even if it was only because of our arrangement.

"What are you doing out here anyway?" I asked her. "You know I always get the water."

"Oh, don't worry," she said. "I'm waiting for my supply girl." Despite the law that stated that women should wear no makeup in order to conserve resources, Lucy had started her own underground cosmetics empire. She made subtle eye shadows and liners, mascaras, rouges. I, myself, had some of her mascara, packaged discreetly inside a corncob pipe she'd gifted me after noticing how pale my eyelashes were.

"She's bringing me these," said Lucy. "Of course, the Dowsing

Well water will come from you." She pulled a list out of her pocket and showed it to me.

Red clay (3)
Beetle wings (Japanese, Potato, Red)
Ink—nontoxic
Crayons
Beeswax

I gave it back to her, and we watched as the workers finished what was left of their job on the platform and shuffled over to the little spread-out handkerchief on which a few water rations (old Coke bottles filled with water) waited.

"Nobody suspects anything, don't worry," Lucy said, watching how nervously I was holding the bucket. "Least of all from you."

"I'm just a false prophet, after all. I couldn't be a thief too."

"Oh, brush that chip off your shoulder," Lucy said. "Besides, I don't think you can *steal* from an endless well."

"There are people who would argue with you on that one," I said.

"Well, crime or not, I'm glad you can do it, because without that water, I'd be sunk." Lucy squinted into the darkness and crossed slim, elegant arms. "Where is this girl? I've been out here for thirty minutes. She's supposed to be coming from the west."

"I'm headed west," I said. "You can come with me if you want."

Lucy's eyes darted toward the platform. The workers, satisfied for the night, wiped their brows and began to leave the clearing in twos and threes. Across the platform, the steeple of the Baptist church jutted up, taller than the windmills, and somehow whiter, its wind-battered cross stark against the sky. The round rose window—unbroken by the high winds—was dark like a closed eye. Mother Morevna was asleep.

"Okay," she said. "I've always wanted to see how you do it anyway."

• • •

Sequestered in the shadow of the largest windmill in Elysium, inside a makeshift mud-brick igloo, almost as big as a house, was what I'd come for. The Dowsing Well: the salvation of Elysium. Mother Morevna had divined it herself, and we'd built the walls around it: the holy water that would never run dry. Once a week, I came to the Dowsing Well to trade Lucy a bucketful of water for a week's worth of rations. That way, I wouldn't have to see Trixie or her aunt and uncle at all if I didn't want to.

I hugged my bucket close to me, and we sneaked over to the door.

It was locked, of course, but I pulled a hairpin out of my hair and went to work.

"Jesus," Lucy said. "You're a lock picker too?"

"Do you want this water or not?"

It clicked open, and Lucy and I went inside. It was dark without a lamp, so Lucy struck a match from her pocket. There on the cool ground was a circular door. I opened it and looked down into the circle of darkness. Even through my broken nose, I could smell the slightly mineral, sulfuric tang of deep well water.

I seized the nearby rope and pulley and attached my bucket.

Then I lowered it down into the darkness until I felt it hit water and sink. Then I pulled up, up, up, until it emerged from the darkness, full of cool water. I heaved it into my arms, and it sloshed against my dusty skin as I handed the bucket to Lucy.

She kept watch as I covered the hatch and locked the door.

"Shoot," Lucy said. "I left the rations back at my house."

"That's okay," I said. "Just bring them tomorrow."

"It's just toward the Square. Come with me and I'll give them to you. Unless you've got something important to do."

"Nah, I can come," I said.

We weaved back through the houses in the strip where the east and west sides met. We passed the little brick building where Mr. Truman lived and taught piano, then the little wood house where one of the German families ("them Krauts from down Shattuck" as a boy in my class had once said) made homemade schnapps. We passed the dust mask factory, the clothing factory, and, last, the enormous, stinking chicken coop, where the chickens slept fitfully, wondering if tomorrow would be the day they became dinner. All was quiet. All was still.

Suddenly, Lucy stopped.

I followed her gaze. There in the darkness lay a squarish plank-board house. Unlike the other houses, it had not been hung with Mourning Night banners. One window was broken. Bottles and dead weed-flowers sat, dusty and undisturbed, in front of the door.

The Robertson house.

No one talked about what had happened there four years ago, but it didn't matter. We all remembered. That was when everything had begun to go downhill. It all started when Mrs.

Rosales died and left her two girls in the care of their stepfather, James Robertson. He was a nice, smiling guard who was known for things like giving up rations to families with sick children and building houses for people who had never had houses before. And even though it was a shame that the Rosales girls' mother was dead, we couldn't imagine a better father for them.

The girls themselves, however, were a different matter.

Both of them were older than I was, fifteen and seventeen when I had been twelve, but I remembered them. Especially Olivia, the younger of the two. After her mother died, she began acting up at school, starting fights, stealing rations. She had often been seen going to and from the church—getting a talking-to from Mr. Jameson or Mother Morevna, probably. As for the older sister, Rosalita, she was rarely seen, even in those days. What was the point of a girl that slow going to school, after all? people said.

There hadn't been any crime at all in Elysium since the walls went up. Aside from my mother's death, the first six years of Elysium had seemed almost dreamlike. Everyone, no matter their color or gender, had gotten along. Everyone had believed in Mother Morevna's new, equal society, and if they hadn't, no one had dared say anything. But then, one morning four years ago, Mr. Robertson's corpse was found lying in the dust in the Square outside the church. He was spread-eagled, his throat slit. The words *¿Me oyes ahora?* had been scrawled around him, a bloody halo.

When guards went to the Robertson house, Olivia was holding her sister's hand in her own bloody ones, and weeping, "No te preocupes, Rosa . . . cálmate, aquí estoy, aquí estoy . . ."

And everything changed. There was a surge of ugliness. Fights sprang up between the races. There were threats, insults thrown in the streets. There was even talk of bringing back Whites Only areas, sending "Mexican" families out into the desert, and it had taken everything Mother Morevna and Mr. Jameson had to calm everyone again.

I remember hearing stories about how Olivia just sat across from Mother Morevna, silent and hard-hearted as a stone, with his blood still under her fingernails. In the end, it was decided: Olivia Rosales, the fifteen-year-old murderess, had to pay for her sins in the Desert of Dust and Steel.

I remember as they opened the doors to the desert. I remember how everyone gathered around the gate, how Rosalita cried out and drooled and had to be taken away to the hospital. I remember Olivia's black hair flying in the wind, her dark eyes wide with fear and anger. But the doors closed behind her anyway.

Rosalita remained at the hospital for a while, as little seen and ghostly as she had always been. When she died a year later, she was buried in the northeastern wall, at night, to avoid further scandal. Her name was carved into the outside of the wall as well as the inside, so that if Olivia was still out there somewhere, she could see. Their house was boarded up, and we all went back to our lives as well as we could, working ever onward, ever toward the goal we would be measured for in April. But the tension never completely went away. Crop production went down and unrest rose, simmering beneath the surface of Elysium. Especially in these last months before the Dust Soldiers' return, unease and blame lurked in shadows, smiles, handshakes. And that bloodstained house sat like a scar in the center of town, a constant reminder of the crime that had cracked our foundation. Even going near it made me feel sick.

"I dare you to go onto the porch," Lucy smirked.

"No!" I said. I glanced back toward the church, still visible from the shadows.

"I'll do it," Lucy said.

She crept toward the house, her shoulders bent, her dark skin gleaming in the torchlight.

Just then, the rose window of the Baptist church flared into light, its great round eye opening.

Mother Morevna.

"Shit!" we hissed together. Lucy leapt off the platform, and we ran off in the direction of the hospital, lugging the bucket as best we could together, water splashing against our dresses. No one chased us. No one came for us. But still, we felt Mother Morevna's presence like breath down our necks. And, behind us, the light in the rose window dimmed again.

• • •

By the time we got to Lucy's house, our arms and legs hurt and we'd spilled nearly half the water. But there was no helping it. Lucy took what was left into her house and brought the empty bucket back out to me.

"Here you go," she said, handing me a stack of food and water rations. "Thanks again."

"Lucy!" came a voice from the darkness. We turned.

Jane Cornett, a white girl a year younger than us, was standing in the dark a few houses away. She gestured to Lucy, then to her coat with its full pockets.

"There she is," Lucy said. "I gotta go. And if Trixie gives you trouble again, let me know, all right?"

"Sure," I said. "Night, Lucy."

"Night, Sal."

And like that, Lucy slipped into the shadows with Jane and disappeared.

I headed back across town with my empty bucket. Then I slipped behind Mr. Jameson's house to my chicken coop. I unlocked the door and let it swing open. Inside were my few things: my scavenged dresser full of clothes and shoes, my little box of pictures and mementos, my father's useless old radio, my bed. I crawled inside and set down my bucket, lit the kerosene lamp. On the wall just outside the window, close to the base, Mama's name flared into light: *MYRTLE WILKERSON.* As always, my heart twisted in on itself when I saw it. Before I could stop myself, I remembered her as she had been the last time I saw her, thin and pale, lying on her cot in the hospital, her forehead beaded with sweat, a rag beside her covered with mud and blood.

I shook myself and went through all the motions of going to bed in the Dust Bowl. I wetted the sheets that covered the windows, secured them over the frame. I washed up in the water trough close by, changed into sleeping clothes, ate a piece of stale cornbread. Then I lay on my back, my face away from Mama's name, trying not to think about Trixie, or Mama, or the rain that never came. And in the silence, I could have sworn I heard my radio, dead for nine years, begin to crackle.

• • •

In the place between worlds, Life sat, invisible and present as electricity, brooding on the Game, which was coming to its end. The young daemon She had called to Her hesitated just a moment before saying, "You called me, ma'am?"

Ten years have almost passed, and the scales are tipping against me, Life said. **But I will not give up to my sister so easily. Given her many advantages, I want to exercise one of my own: I am choosing my Wildcard.**

"I . . . don't understand," said the daemon in the darkness. "What do I have to do with that?"

It will be you, said Life. **I will make my own Wildcard, unlike my sister. I will fashion you a body, and you will go down to our Game board in the middle of the desert. Use your influence and tip the scales in my favor. If you're successful, you will be rewarded handsomely.**

"Really?" he asked. The darkness thrummed, and he knew it was a yes. It wasn't every day that someone was invited to go down, and certainly, *he* had never been chosen. And to have a body, a human body . . . it was like a dream!

"But . . . why did you choose me?" he asked.

I didn't, said Life. ***She* did.**

The Mother Goddess. The creator of everything that had been and everything that would be. She had chosen him. Him, over all the others. But why? What had he done to command Her attention?

"There has to be some mistake," the daemon started. "I'm not particularly special, or . . ."

But as he drew himself up, he found that he was taking shape. He grew taller, leaner, shifting between several possible faces, skin colors, heights, hats, sport coats, suspenders, shoes. He looked down, and his hands were pale, long-fingered. Round spectacles—cracked in one lens—appeared on his nose. In his hand, he held a suitcase. In his mind, there was a past, a name.

"Asa Skander," he said, and he knew it was right.

An odd form, said Life. **It is not what I expected, but it is what was in you, so I suppose it will do.**

A door appeared in the darkness, narrow, wooden, and just taller than the young man himself. It seemed to vibrate with possibility, and he knew that beyond it was the World.

Your mission is simple, She said, and there was a smell of petrichor in the air. **In keeping with the rules, you may not tell them outright what they must do, and you'll find you won't be able to. But I will give you something important, something that can turn the tides of the Game, and you must return it to its owner. That is your mission.**

Asa felt something in his hand. A small piece of amber with what looked like a cricket inside it.

"I don't understand," he said. "That's all?"

It is not for a daemon to understand, said Life. **Just worry about your mission. And keep in mind that Death's Wildcard can disarm your entire mission—unless you want to try disarming hers, which I would not suggest. Death has the advantage, after all, since all She has to do is create enough chaos to tip the scales.**

"Who is she?" Asa asked. "And what is her mission?"

I do not know, other than that she is unknowingly bent on destroying Elysium. I'm sure you will know her if you pay attention.

Fair enough, thought Asa, pocketing the amber piece. *I'm just along for the ride.*

The soles of his wing-tip shoes began to glow. He raised his foot and saw the designs on the bottoms: eyes, wheels, wings, lightning, the sun. They shifted under him, wiggled, changed, moved.

"What happens if I fail?" he asked.

The Sentinels will come and take back what is mine, She said. **You don't want that, do you?**

"No, ma'am," he said. "I surely do not." And with a deep breath, he stepped through the door and disappeared.

CHAPTER 2

3 MONTHS AND *29 DAYS* REMAIN.

Before Black Sunday, I'd never had a vision. But after the walls went up, the whole world had the feeling of an unseen storm about to creep up over the horizon. I smelled it in the air, felt it prickle my skin. It had been so real that a few times I'd run outside, my arms spread, my mouth open, convinced that rain would fall any moment, only to be met with dust and wind. But the truth was that I was strange long before the world of the Game began. Mama and Papa had thought I was funny, a little tomboy with her head in the clouds. *My strange girl,* Mama would call me. Her favorite story was how when I'd been born there had been blackbirds all over our roof. Not anyone else's roof. Just ours. She said they'd given me a blackbird blessing.

They'd read me books about knights and heroes, made up stories about inventive young girls who saved the day, and gradually I grew to understand that all these plucky young heroines were me in disguise. They both believed that I was special. And special people were born for a reason. Even after the accident that claimed Papa's life, even after our world ended and the walls started going up, Mama never stopped believing that my specialness, my *destiny*, would make itself known. That I would make a difference someday. And when I smelled rain on the wind for the first time and it didn't come, she didn't think I had lied about it. Not exactly. But she didn't believe it was real *yet*. She believed that I thought it was real. And to her, if I believed it, it wasn't a lie. I should have known that not everyone thought that way.

• • •

When morning came, I woke to a throbbing nose, filled with dust and dried blood. I washed up in the trough and got dressed in my shabby Sunday dress that was about two inches too short, and carefully shadowed my face with an old straw hat.

But as I was passing the hospital, a nurse appeared, Nurse Gladys Ann, on her way to open up the hospital, and she stopped in her tracks when she saw me.

"Sal Wilkerson?" she said. "Well, bless my soul! How are you doing these days?"

"Fine," I said. "Just . . . trying to get some errands run."

"I see," she said. She glanced at my face and saw my nose. "What happened? Somebody beat you up? Because if they did—"

"It's nothing," I said. "Just stepped on a rake."

"Well, next time you find yourself in a situation like that, you run away as fast as you can. There's no shame in running, you know. And stay out of unsafe areas. Wandering out on your own where no one can help can get you killed."

"Yes, ma'am," I said flatly. "I know all about that."

"Oh, Sal," said Nurse Gladys. "I didn't mean . . . That was different . . . You were just a little girl. And there's no running from a dust storm, Sal. You know that."

I opened my mouth to reply, but before I could, there was a crash from inside the hospital. A full bedpan was hurled against the nearest window and its contents splattered all down the glass.

I jumped.

From inside, I could hear the overnight nurses running down the hall, and a woman shouting in Spanish.

"Oh, Lord, what is it now?" said Nurse Gladys.

"Hold her down!" came a muffled voice through the window.

"I'm trying!" said another.

"Quick! The syringe!"

"¡HOY!" the woman shouted. *"¡Ella viene hoy!"*

"Hold her!"

Then there was a high, keening noise and she fell silent.

I glanced at Nurse Gladys. "Who is that in there?" I asked.

"Oh, just Miss Ibarra," she replied with a knowing look.

I'd heard about Miss Ibarra, though I'd never seen her myself. During the unstable time when Elysium was still reeling from Olivia Rosales's banishment, a young woman named Angélica Ibarra had gone absolutely insane when her fiancé had fallen from the west wall and broken his neck. She ran around town screaming and shouting and causing a ruckus until Mother Morevna had her sent to the hospital, where she'd been ever since. She was, possibly, one of the few people in Elysium that I pitied.

"She's an odd one, that girl," said Nurse Gladys. "Always seeing things that aren't there. People that aren't there. Of course, in a world like this, who's to know what's real and what's not? Still, she's crazy as a horsefly in a henhouse." She stopped, thinking of my rain visions maybe, and straightened herself. "Best not to talk about it. Now you'd better get on with your errands, Sal. And wash out that nose with salt water. It'll do you good."

"Yes, ma'am," I said. And with a glance at the closed window, she headed into the hospital.

A familiar tingle ran under my skin. *Dishonesty.* Ever since my first vision of the rain, I could feel it tingling like electricity the day before a dust storm. I didn't feel it every time someone was being dishonest, but when I did, it was unmistakable. I wondered for a moment what she could be lying about and why; then I shrugged and went on my way. This certainly wasn't the first time I'd been lied to.

• • •

I went into my little shack and did my best to distract myself with an old schoolbook. But it seemed that every word I read passed over me like a cloud.

I sighed and looked at my nose in the small hand mirror that had been my mother's. Still red and angry and obvious. *I can't go out looking like this,* I thought. Then the announcement blared overhead: Mother Morevna's voice, amplified with magic so that it rang out all over town.

"Attention, everyone! The ceremony is soon to begin! Please make your way to the center of town."

I groaned and pulled my hat back on, shutting my book. Outside, the night wind blew, but not harshly, and the dust only rose to my ankles. The banners hung from building to building, house to house, windmill to windmill, bright against the dark sky, and I followed them to the Square, where all the garlands met at the enormous pole that rose out of the platform in front of the church and jail. People from all over town were congregating on each side of the platform: white people on one side, and everyone else on the other, with buzzing tension in between.

Everyone faced the doors of the Baptist church, where Mother Morevna would climb up onto the platform and begin the ceremony. People slumped, and their suits and dresses wrinkled in the heat—we didn't have seasons anymore. Not in this world. Just endless, unbearable heat. One woman across from me was fanning herself with her wide straw hat. Many of them watched me out the corners of their eyes.

I pulled my hat lower, keeping my eye out for Trixie and her aunt and uncle. God, I hoped they didn't make me stand with them, though admittedly, there was a low chance of that. Glancing over my shoulders, I went to the shadow of the nearest windmill and stood there alone.

"Scoot over, criminal," said a voice. It was Lucy again, in a patterned feed-sack dress, her hair back in a brightly colored kerchief. Her eyelids shimmered slightly in the light.

"How'd your supply run go?" I asked, making room for her.

"All right. I gave Jane an extra blush for following us all the way back home." She looked at me. "I should have given you some concealer. Your nose still looks bad."

"Well, it's the thought that counts," I said, and she smiled.

I was thankful that I had someone to stand with. Mourning Night was always hard. The platform now held a small collection of photographs and a few other items. A pair of glasses, an old blue bottle, a bolt of fabric, something that glinted silver and was probably a thimble. These reminders of the dead were so grubby, so pitiful, that they tugged at the heartstrings of even the hardest in Elysium. There were only two toys that I could see: a dirty, one-eyed teddy bear and a turtle that someone had whittled out of a block of wood and painted. Yes, this was much better than last year. But what would next year bring? I had seen the frantic way the farmhands had worked, the textile mill ladies, the dairy farmers, the tanners. I had heard the grumbling. I had seen how much people had done without. But still, the question buzzed among all of us: *Would there be a next year? Who would win: Life or Death?*

Suddenly, the crowd quieted. Everyone leaned forward, and all that could be heard was a dog barking somewhere on the edge of town.

Then the church door opened and she appeared, the one who had saved us all. Mother Morevna seemed to demand attention, even though none of us had ever heard her raise her voice. She was elegant, fierce, powerful, everything I could never be, and the world seemed to stop for her. She wore a beautiful green dress, almost Victorian in modesty, but that seemed to whisper and move with a life of its own. A floral shawl was wrapped around her shoulders, even in the heat, and her hair was pulled back into a tight steel-gray bun. Her nose was like a hawk's beak behind half-moon glasses, her hands, covered in their strange black tattoos, hung at her sides. Everyone cheered when she drifted out to us. But she raised a hand and the crowd went silent.

"Dearest friends," she said, and her clear, sharp voice seemed to crackle with power. "We are gathered here tonight, on this anniversary of the Great Storm of 1935, to mourn the passing of our loved ones. But just as we have found a haven in the great experiment that is Elysium, our loved ones have gone on to their great reward. We remain strong and united, no matter what the future may bring."

Lucy shifted beside me, and I caught a whiff of her perfume—yes, perfume, though who knew where she'd gotten it; even in Elysium, Lucy always made it a point to smell nice.

". . . so while we grieve their passing just as we grieve our own in these threadbare days before the Judgment," Mother Morevna was saying, "we must be mindful of where we are, where they are: Elysium. A good, peaceful home for all."

The crowd began to applaud, but Mother Morevna held up her hand.

"Also, it is of importance that I announce tonight I will be choosing a Successor, a young person who will learn the ways of magic and diplomacy, so as to preserve the society we have created for future generations."

At this, there was a low rumbling in the crowd as everyone turned to the people near them to see if they could make any sense of it. A Successor? Successor with a big *S*—that's how she'd said it, right? She had never done anything like this before. But who here held the power that Mother Morevna did? Who here could ever hope to measure up to her?

I turned, scanned the crowd. Out of all my classmates, I couldn't think of many girls who were anything like Mother Morevna, who were so fearless and quick-acting and, well . . . magic. Lucy, maybe. She certainly had her own way of doing things, but magic?

Mother Morevna pulled her black pendant from her blouse—the one she had found the Dowsing Well with. She wound the chain around her hand once, then held it up, where it shone in the light. The pendant pointed straight out into the air, in the direction of the audience.

"And now," she said, "I will find her."

As we watched, Mother Morevna stepped down from the platform, holding the pendant out as it strained forward, against the chain like a dog on a leash, leading her. She walked several feet into the crowd, then stopped in front of Anna McComber, a red-haired white girl a year older than me. She looked over her shoulder at her mother; Anna's face was pale and terrified. Mother Morevna said something to the black pendant—I couldn't tell what—and it went limp again in her hand. Then she raised it over Anna's head. It hung still for a moment; slowly, it began to swing from side to side, and somehow I knew it meant no.

Mother Morevna looked at Anna for a moment, then moved on past her as the pendulum went taut again: a black arrow pointing into the crowd. Anna's mother gathered Anna up and held her close, but her eyes were on Mother Morevna.

Mother Morevna's pendulum led her farther, into the west side of the crowd. She stopped again, in front of a Black girl two years younger than me, Georgia Fuller. I saw a few older white men exchange glances as Mother Morevna held the pendulum over Georgia's head. I wondered if Lucy saw them.

"She's wearing my lipstick," Lucy said when Georgia turned her head away from the pendulum. "Petal Pink."

"Petal Pink doesn't look like that on me," I said.

"Not everything's for white girls," said Lucy.

The pendulum over Georgia's head swung back and forth, back and forth. Mother Morevna dismissed Georgia and moved on through the crowd for a few more feet before stopping at another girl. She held her pendulum over her head, then kept moving when the pendulum, once more, gave her a no.

"She's coming this way," Lucy said. And she was. My stomach lurched. Mother Morevna was moving through the crowd, her eyes following where her pendulum led. I could see the chain clearly now, straining, pulled by unseen magic. She was moving straight through the crowd, and as girl after girl was dismissed, my heart sped, and some small, faraway, daring part of it seemed to take on the rhythm of *what if, what if, what if?* What if, after all this time, after all the hurt and sorrow and humiliation, this was what I was destined for? What would people say then? But Mother Morevna stopped in front of someone else.

Lucy grabbed my arm.

Trixie Holland, next to her bulldog-faced aunt and uncle. Three rows up, in a yellow dress patched with flour-sack fabric. Unlike the other girls Mother Morevna stopped before, Trixie didn't cower or whimper. She gave Mother Morevna her wide smile, holding her broad shoulders back with the confidence of Roosevelt. *Oh no,* I thought, my nose throbbing as though it too was terrified. *This isn't good.*

Mother Morevna raised her pendulum over Trixie's head. I turned my eyes away. I couldn't watch. *Not Trixie,* I thought. *Not Trixie.* But even as I thought it, I knew that Trixie would make sense. She had all the qualities a leader needed, on the surface, anyway.

My stomach lurched again. I closed my eyes. I couldn't watch her be chosen. The Trixies of the world were always chosen. The mean, violent ones. The fight pickers, the hypocrites, the truly dishonest. But what did I expect? After all we'd all been through, it was stupid to think that anything could happen to us but the very worst thing.

Somewhere I heard Lucy's voice say, "Um . . . Sal?" but I barely heard her.

What would happen once Trixie was the leader of Elysium? Would she toss me out into the Desert of Dust and Steel, like Olivia Rosales? In my mind, it seemed that Trixie's shadow stretched over all of Elysium, her big hands grasping, her high voice laughing.

"Sal." Lucy tapped my shoulder. *"Sal!"*

"What?" I snapped.

But when I turned, it felt as though my stomach dropped out of my body altogether.

Mother Morevna was standing right in front of me, her black pendulum straining against its chain, pointing at my chest like an arrow.

"Sallie Wilkerson," she said, and her voice didn't echo like it had before. "Well, well. This *is* a surprise." Then she whispered to the pendulum, and it went limp in her hand. She raised it up, over my head, the black stone directly over me. My breath froze in my lungs.

It didn't swing back and forth. It didn't do anything at all. It hung still. Dead still. The crowd around me began to murmur, but Mother Morevna didn't move and neither did the pendulum.

My body was full of something that felt like ten thousand bees were making a home in my rib cage. It was unbearable. *Please,* I thought at the pendulum. *Please move.* The hairs on my arms, on my neck, began to prickle, and I closed my eyes as I realized what I already knew: *I want this. I want it to be me.*

Then I felt the electricity intensify, go somehow gold above my head.

There was a gasp in the crowd. Beside me, Lucy breathed, "Oh my God . . ."

I opened my eyes and looked up. Above my head, the pendulum was swinging in a broad, frantic circle.

"My new Successor, Sallie Wilkerson," said Mother Morevna, her magically amplified voice echoing from the walls of Elysium. Every eye was on me—me!—and before all those eyes, I felt so small. Was this a mistake?

Mother Morevna's claws were on my arm. "Stand up straight. Don't slouch."

I stood to my full, awkward height—just shorter than her, I realized for the first time.

"Now, come with me."

She pulled me through the crowd, and I saw face after shocked face as I passed. Trixie Holland looked about ready to explode from surprise.

We got to the platform, and Mother Morevna led me up onto it. In the bright light, I could see everyone in Elysium. And for the first time they could see—really *see*—me. I took a deep, shuddering breath and stood up straight like Mother Morevna had said.

"People of Elysium," Mother Morevna said. "Welcome Sallie Wilkerson, my new Successor."

There was a moment of stunned silence, a murmur of thought so loud I could almost hear it: the Girl Who Cried Rain? And then the people of Elysium, the people who had called me a liar, the indifferent and the pitying alike, slowly began to applaud. I stood there, pale as a fish's belly, my stomach threatening to turn itself inside out.

Then Mother Morevna's hand was on my shoulder, and she was beside me again.

"Sallie will begin her training immediately," Mother Morevna said. "Hopefully, her services will not be needed for a long, long time. But meanwhile, I am certain she will prove to be an excellent leader, worthy of your utmost admiration and trust."

It was a challenge to the crowd, I realized. She was challenging them on my behalf, daring them *not* to trust me—not to trust her.

"Do you have anything to say?" she asked me.

A speech? Now? I blanched. Public speaking was always my worst subject.

"I . . ." I started. "I would just like to say that . . ." *What would I like to say?*

But before I could finish, something caught my eye. A figure on top of the wall, small and quick. A child? A woman? I squinted. It turned, looked right at me. . . .

I began to hear it: the rain. *Not now, not now, not now* . . . I fought with everything in me. I fell to my knees, trying hard not to vomit. The wind seemed to roar as the rain approached. My nose filled with the smell of it. The last thing I heard before the vision rose up and took me was one of the guards shouting.

"The Sacrifice! We've been robbed!"

CHAPTER 3

The rain came like it always did, with a distant rumble that shook the base of my brain. It rolled in much like dust storms roll in. The sky was swollen and roiling; the entire dome of the heavens was so dark that the few trees standing inside Elysium seemed vividly green against the darkness. Then the horizon began to blur with falling rain. The desert began to look like an oil painting, ruined and bleeding as the rain came toward me, turning the dust to mud. It came in sheets, in curtains. Biblical rain, blowing my braids over my shoulders, soaking me to the skin. And as I stood there in it, my wet dress clinging to me, I lifted my arms up as though to welcome the rain home to this dusty, thirsty world, thinking as I always did, *Why can't this be real?*

• • •

When I woke later, I could still smell the rain for a few minutes. Then the pain hit. It always felt like I'd been thrown from a roof when I woke from seeing the rain. It was morning. But I wasn't in my shack. I was in a bed and wearing a white nightdress—old-fashioned in style. Here, there was no dust on the top of the covers, nor on the floor, despite the fact that there were no sheets over the windows or rags under the doors. But there was something familiar about the room. It had been my own Sunday school room, I realized, long ago. There had been a table in the middle, and Miss Willis had gathered us around it and made us read from the Bible, out loud, every Sunday.

"Hello . . . ?" I said. My voice sounded creaky and hoarse.

The voice that answered was as old and slow as a weather vane rusted stiff.

"Hey there, girl." Mr. Jameson was sitting in a rocking chair by the door, holding a cup of coffee in his weathered hands. The sight of him made me feel relaxed, despite myself. I wondered how long he'd been there.

"That must have been a bad one," he said. He handed me a plate covered with a napkin. I removed it. Toast. It had been buttered, and the butter had sunk deep into the hard bread.

"What happened after I . . . after I fainted?" I asked.

"We brought you here and put you to bed," he said. "Fortunately, the room was already waiting for you. Sal Wilkerson, the Successor to Mother Morevna." He smiled. "I'm proud of you, kid."

A ripple of excitement went through me. So it hadn't been a dream. This was real. I had really been chosen. Gingerly, I sat up, and without thinking, I touched my nose. It was straight and normal, not even a hint of tenderness.

"Mother Morevna fixed that for you," Mr. Jameson said. "Nobody can tell it's been broken anymore."

I looked around at the unfamiliar familiar room, so stark, so sterile.

"Everything's so . . . clean," I said.

"A lot better than that ol' chicken coop, huh?" Mr. Jameson said. "Mother Morevna prefers you to live here while you're in training."

"Training," I breathed, letting the smile I felt creep into my voice. I was really going to do this.

Mr. Jameson sighed and put his coffee cup down beside his chair. "I don't know if it's my place to tell you this, but . . . there's a little more to it than that. Mother Morevna's sick—not Dust Sick, mind you. Something about the liver. It could be that she dies before the Dust Soldiers come, which would leave us without anybody powerful enough to face them."

I felt the air go out of my lungs.

"So that's why she needs a Successor now," I said. "To face them if she dies before she can."

"I pressured her into it, to be honest," he said apologetically. "She's old and set in her ways, especially after . . ." He paused, redirected. "She had a few real bad experiences that have left her thinking she has to do everything on her own. She doesn't like for things to be out of her control. But even she can't ignore this possibility."

I didn't say anything. I couldn't. Fear began to bubble in my stomach. Of course she didn't want to give up her power, especially not to me, the false prophet who had caused such a ruckus all those years ago.

Mr. Jameson's eyes were gentle, concerned. "I'm sorry, kid. It's a hell of a thing to have to deal with: a game with unclear rules and unclear goals, and you leading everybody against it. But she chose you. You're the best option for this, whether you realize it or not."

The Game and the Dust Soldiers rose up in my mind, snuffing my excitement like a flame. I swallowed nervously, dry toast tasteless as a shingle on my tongue. But, I told myself, I was the one who had been chosen. It had to be for a reason.

When I looked back at Mr. Jameson, he was looking out the window, out over the walls, where a sliver of desert was showing. "Of course, after last night, we've got even more to deal with."

I remembered the cry then, just before I fainted. I remembered the shadow on the wall.

"Were we robbed last night?" I asked cautiously, in case, like the rain, it had all been "my imagination."

Mr. Jameson nodded slowly. "Unfortunately so."

I felt sick to my stomach all over again. "What did they take?"

"A lot, sad to say. It'll set us back about a month. Forty pounds of salt pork, twenty pounds of beef, four sacks of flour, six sacks of potatoes, six sacks of charcoal, five bottles of moonshine and two of schnapps. All from the Sacrifice building. But there's still time before the Judgment, and Mother Morevna laid a curse on anybody who steals from the Sacrifice, so we'll be finding their bodies somewhere around town pretty soon. Though it's strange. I can't think of a single person in Elysium who'd want to do something like that. Especially not now."

"And this was . . . this was while I was . . . ?"

"Yes," he said. "While we were making sure you were all right."

In my mind, I saw the shadow I'd glimpsed before the vision took me, the flash at the top of the wall, small, quick . . . familiar in some way. But sometimes I saw things before my episodes, shadows flitting in the corners of my eyes, so I said nothing.

Were my visions magic? I thought suddenly. And if so, what did they mean?

"It's not your fault," Mr. Jameson said. "But it is what it is, and we've gotta look it straight in the eye and deal with it." He picked his cup of cold coffee up off the floor and stood. "But that's my responsibility. All you're responsible for now is learning."

He stopped and looked at me for a moment, an odd expression on his face.

"What?" I asked.

"I was just thinking of your mama, how proud she would be," he said. "She always knew you were something special."

And despite all the fear, all the nerves, all the uncertainty, I couldn't help but smile.

• • •

In the desert, Asa Skander was alone. He had been barely a smudge at first, but now his lines had steadied and he had begun to cast a shadow. At first, the sensation of *sensation* had nearly overcome him, and he'd lain gasping on the dust until the sunlight dazzled his eyes into bright blindness. What a thing it was to go one's whole life, if life it could be called, without feeling anything, smelling anything, tasting anything, and then suddenly to have all the senses roar into being. He was struck by the grit of the dust, by the weight and drape of his clothes, by the dry heat of the sun and wind. He held his hand up into the light and let the goldenness slide over his palms and between his fingers. He tested out smiling, jumping. He tasted the dry, gritty air and felt grains of sand in his mouth. He bit his lip until he felt what must be pain and tasted his own metallic red blood, warm and thin in his mouth.

I am alive! he thought, and he felt his new heart speed in his chest.

He couldn't believe his luck. He had spent countless days throughout the eons looking down from the Between, watching humans. Most daemons watched during wars or plagues or disasters—some even had a hand in them—but Asa had loved watching their quiet moments more. *No human life,* Asa thought, *could ever really be called quiet.* He'd watched courtships and marriages and births; he'd seen sorrow and anger and death. He knew the names of many people, from tartan-skirted librarians in Lansing, Michigan, to tattooed warriors in Polynesia. He knew about burdensome taxes and the luxuries of wealth; he'd seen the jutting ribs of starvation and the heaping tables of excess. It all played out before him, an endless melodrama with an endlessly rotating cast, and he never ever tired of it. Now, with his own new, young, and capable body, he would get to be *part* of it. And though he privately wondered why he, a most unremarkable daemon, had been chosen—and by the Mother Herself!—Asa couldn't wait to begin.

He wiped wetness from his brow, and thin mud came away on his forearm. *Is this what it is to sweat?* He smiled. On a bit of wood with a rope were the six bags of wheat, which had appeared along with the makeshift sleigh they were on. He knew the plan: use them to barter for his entry to Elysium. They were a bit heavy, though. Was this what it was to work? He squinted into the distance. Over the ripples of heat, he could just make out the tall dark shapes of walls and windmill arms. Elysium. Not too much farther.

He heard a papery sound and glanced to his left. From the

ditch, three grasshoppers the size of terriers watched him, wondering, perhaps, whether or not to attack. He showed them his face—his real face, which was hidden behind this human disguise—and the grasshoppers sprang away in terror.

Hmph, he thought, and started moving. It was easy at first, but as his body grew heavier and more substantial, he began to sink into the dust. Even so, he walked on, passing automobiles, rusted, doorless, stripped of anything useful. Some had radios left in them, long dead, and these began to spark and sputter, crackling as he walked by, in reaction to the strong magic that clung to him. He stepped over half-buried fencerows, walls of tumbleweeds. He passed through the high-ribbed, tubelike skeleton of something like a giant snake, bleached by the sun. *Only about three hours,* he suspected.

But once he got there . . . then what? How was he supposed to do what he had been sent to do, exactly? Go to everyone in Elysium and show them the weird amber bug? That would take too much time. And what happened when he found the right person? He was sure that it indicated to them that they must change in some way. Humans, he had noticed, were oddly change-resistant, and if there was one thing they hated, it was a messenger. He'd seen how things like that had gone for a few people in the past, and it was almost uniformly Not Good. But She hadn't given him instruction. She'd just given him the bug and told him to go to Elysium, using the bags of wheat as his key to entry.

Then he thought perhaps that there was some sort of clue in the appearance and items that had been provided for him. He stopped and looked around, looked at his hat, at the suitcase that he carried with all its stickers and tags. He opened it and found one change of clothes, a book of card tricks, a harmonica, and . . .

"Magic supplies?" he said aloud. He cocked his head to one side. He saw something blue sticking out of his shirtsleeve, and when he pulled it, out came a seemingly unending string of colorful handkerchiefs.

"I'm a magician?" he said aloud, feeling his face crack into what must have been a smile. Simultaneously, he felt years of study, years of tricks, illusions, sleight of hand rush into his mind and take up residence there, like a flock of birds lighting in a tree. Then, again, he said, "I'm a magician!"

He was delighted. He'd watched magicians for centuries, marveling at their tricks, the miracles they seemed to create. How much joy and wonder they gave the people who saw them. It felt appropriate to Asa somehow. Was this what was inside him? Was this what he would be if he were human? Asa wasn't sure. So what could he do now? He thought. Then a new idea dawned on him: With this new human body, what *couldn't* he do?

• • •

The sanctuary had made me feel small in the past, but now it just felt . . . empty. No pews, no paintings of Jesus or banners or wall hangings. Those had all been taken down after the walls went up. There weren't any mandates about it or anything. Mother Morevna wasn't that kind of leader. But after all that had happened, it just felt so pointless, so silly. And so sad. Now all that was left was the stained glass, the bare, wooden floor, and an enormous stack of water rations waiting to be sent to the northeast families. Images of saints looked down from the windows with expressions of ecstasy or agony.

In the colored light, I paced to and fro, taking deep breaths and trying to keep my hands from shaking. The Dust Soldiers kept rising in my mind, but gradually, they were overshadowed by something else, by a strange, fiery eagerness that had rested in my stomach ever since Mother Morevna called my name. I thought of all the amazing things I had seen Mother Morevna do, realizing for the first time how I had always longed to be able to feel even an ounce of the power, of the confidence that seemed to float around her like perfume.

There was a sound of heels clicking, and I turned just as she stepped in front of the altar, straight-backed and stern, her black dress stiff and immaculate. My teacher.

This woman, said a voice in the most daring part of my mind, *this woman can teach me about what I can become. What I am meant to be.*

When she spoke, there was a sizzle behind her voice, like gunpowder. "I am sorry you are being forced into this position, my dear. Especially after our . . . *former difficulties.*"

I squirmed and felt my face grow hot, amazed by how much meaning she could fit in two words.

"Oh, yes, I was quite surprised that you were the one as well," she said, reading my expression. "But that is behind us, my dear. I bear you no ill will. You were a child, after all, and unsure of your own powers."

Powers.

"Um . . . thank you, ma'am."

"Jameson spoke to you, I take it," she said. "About my . . . *condition* and his worries about it?"

"Yes, ma'am," I said. "I'm sorry to hear about your health.

And I want you to know that I'm willing to learn anything you'll teach me. Anything that will help Elysium."

"I'm sure you are," she said. "Unfortunately, it won't be necessary."

"Ma'am?" I asked quietly.

She smiled a wry, pained sort of smile.

"Do you know why I created Elysium, child? Why it is the way it is?" She came toward me, and I could feel the energy, the magic, crackling around her. "I wanted to create a society where things like prejudice and inequality are stamped out, where groups of posturing, truculent men don't ruin everything. A society that is truly responsible for everyone. I have done so. I was there when the Dust Soldiers came the first time, and I intend to be there when they come again, to win this infernal Game and to connect Elysium to our proper world, once and for all. Unfortunately, events in the past have made me leery of sharing that responsibility with another." She paused. "Jameson was right about a few things. I believe the *visibility* of my having a Successor is important in order to bolster the people's faith in this difficult time, my health being as it is. That is all."

My heart sank. All my feelings of importance were dissolving like sugar.

"I do appreciate your enthusiasm," she was saying, "and you will be *recognized* as my Successor and enjoy all the privileges therein, but I simply cannot take that risk again." She paused, reading my expression. "You are disappointed. I'd have thought anyone would want to avoid dealing with the Dust Soldiers herself."

"I think I just . . . wanted to learn," I said. "If the . . . If *magic* is in me, it would explain a lot. The visions . . . and a lot of other things that have no other explanation."

"Well, certainly you're a witch, my dear," she said. "And, yes, your visions stem from your innate powers, whatever they may be. Does that make you feel any better?"

It should, I knew, but without knowing what power I had, without being trained to use it, what did it matter? Before I could stop myself, I heard myself say, "I think the idea of being trusted to make important decisions after all this time was . . . That was what I really wanted."

She was looking at me so intently, so calculatingly.

"I see," said Mother Morevna. "You meant to redeem yourself."

I nodded sheepishly, my eyes on the floor.

She regarded me with those steely, unblinking eyes, and deep within them, I saw a glint of sympathy. Mother Morevna opened her mouth to respond, but before she could, a guard, Willard, the Jeffries' oldest boy, opened the door.

"'Scuse me, Mother Morevna," he said, his hat in his hand, his rifle on his shoulder.

"What is it, young man?" Mother Morevna said.

"I'm sorry, ma'am . . . someone's knocking on the door. I think you'd better come talk to him."

This was surprising, but it wasn't shocking. It certainly wasn't the first time it had happened. Though we rarely saw them, even from the tops of the walls, we knew that there were other people in the desert, other survivors living like feral animals outside the walls, paying the price after they chose to stay on what was left of their homesteads rather than join Elysium. But our doors were always, always closed to them.

"Tell whoever it is that we've too many mouths to feed as it is," she said.

"I—I would have," the guard said, taking a step back. "But he says he's desperate. He's brought supplies to barter for his entry. Seems worthwhile, to be honest."

"Gifts?" she said. "From where? There are no fields, no places to grow crops."

"Like I said, ma'am, you'd better come talk to him."

Mother Morevna sighed. She hitched up her skirts and clicked away from me across the sanctuary. I stood where I was, awkward and confused in the multicolored light, my brain spinning with questions. Then, at the door, she turned to me and put her hands on her hips.

"Well?" she said. "Are you coming or will you just stand there idle?"

"Y-yes, ma'am!" I said, and ran to catch up with her.

CHAPTER 4

Mother Morevna strode to the great steel door, her skirts flicking up clouds of dust, and I trailed behind her, my handkerchief over my mouth. A crowd had gathered around the door, a semicircle of townspeople there to see the new curiosity out in the desert.

"Go home," Mother Morevna said to the crowd, and slowly, they moved back, glancing over their shoulders as they went. "Gawkers," said Mother Morevna under her breath. Then she turned to the guard. "Let me see him."

The guard nodded, and Mother Morevna took a step back as he opened the rusty peep slot in the steel door. Through it, I could see a pale, sunburned face.

"Oh, hello!" said the man behind the door. "Are you the leader of this establishment?"

"I am," said Mother Morevna. "Who are you and why have you come to Elysium?"

"Just a wayfaring stranger, ma'am, wandering through this world of woe. As the song goes, you know. Asa Skander's the name, and as for where I'm from, I suppose I'm from everywhere and nowhere."

He gave Mother Morevna a wink through the peep slot, but Mother Morevna was not amused.

"Where *exactly* are you from, and how did you come to be here?" she asked in a way that was more a warning than a question.

"I . . . uh . . . started up in Chicago, Illinois," he said. "Part of a family of traveling magicians. When my pa and I got stranded out here and he subsequently died, I had to fend for myself. So now, at the ripe old age of nineteen, I've taken up the family business out here in the desert, pulling rabbits out of hats and coins out of ears and scarves out of sleeves, entertaining whoever I can. Of course, you can't entertain everyone and now I'm . . . how shall we say . . . on the run? Fleeing from certain death?"

I grimaced. I'd heard stories of the people who had chosen to remain in the desert. They were supposed to be a nasty, lawless, bloodthirsty bunch, worse even than the creatures out there. A pang of pity went through me. But Mother Morevna seemed unaffected.

"I didn't ask for your life story," she said. "And as . . . entertaining . . . as you may be, I'm afraid we have enough mouths to feed as it is. Don't you understand that the Game is ending soon?"

"Yes, ma'am," he said. "Which is why I plan to pay my entry with this." He stepped back and gestured. "Six bags of the finest, most golden wheat to ever exist. I'm sure it'll add more value to your Sacrifice than twelve bags of the normal stuff."

"Have you verified this?" Mother Morevna asked the guards.

"Yes, ma'am," they said. "It's fine stuff. Like back in the old days."

Mother Morevna's brows were still furrowed.

"And what *else* do you have to offer us?" she asked.

"Well," said the boy on the other side of the door, "I can put on one hell of a magic show!"

Mother Morevna's lip curled. "Typical," I heard her mutter. "The first person to come offering help and it's some . . . *vagrant* run away from Barnum and Bailey's." She glanced at the door, a sour expression on her face. Then, surprisingly, she turned to me. "You wanted to be trusted with decisions," she said. "So I will hand this one off to you. What should be done about him?"

I paused. Never since the walls had gone up had we let anyone into Elysium. But this young man . . . there was something odd about him. Something that set my teeth on edge and sent an electric gooseflesh tingle through my skin. It felt almost the way deception did but not quite. Even through the door, I could tell that something was *strange* about him, different from anyone I'd ever met, and I couldn't tell whether it was good or bad. But still . . . I couldn't turn him away. Not when he had nowhere else to go. Not when I'd heard stories of the things that lived out there. Besides, I was curious.

"Well?" she said.

"Let him in," I said.

Mother Morevna looked at me for a moment, then nodded. She raised her hand, and the guard at the top of the gate pulled the lever. The door creaked open with a great metal groan, and I saw him for the first time.

He was young—only a few years older than me—tall and

bent-looking, all angles, like Harold Lloyd in that movie I'd seen over in Boise City before the walls went up. But this boy was scruffier somehow, wilder. He wore a dust-covered suit that once must have been brown, cut in an odd, old-fashioned way, and his equally dusty hat had a feather sticking out of the hatband. His suitcase was covered with labels, but all of them looked far older than he was. Waves of strangeness seemed to emanate from him like too much cologne, and there was something about the way that he moved . . . but for the life of me, I couldn't place it.

"Thank you for your kindness, ma'am," he said to Mother Morevna with a deep bow.

"For Sallie's kindness, you mean." She gestured to me.

The young man tipped his hat to me and said, "I'm much obliged, miss." His eyes, now that I was closer to him, were oddly yellowish in the light.

"I'm . . . uh . . . sorry you had to wait so long," I managed.

"It's just fine, Miss . . . ?"

"Sal," I told him. "Sal Wilkerson."

"Sal Wilkerson," he repeated. "My savior. Um . . . you ladies wouldn't happen to have a place where I could rest? I'm awful tired." He smiled and for a second I thought his teeth looked oddly pointed, but I looked again and they were just normal, very white teeth in a normal, very pleasant-looking smile.

"Certainly," Mother Morevna said. "Guards, would you kindly take our visitor to the jail? Give him a cell to spend the night in. Make him as comfortable as he can be, do you understand? I will be there soon to question him and make sure he's on the up-and-up."

"Yes, ma'am," they said.

"Much obliged, ma'am! Thank you!" he said, tipping his hat again.

They led him away, and as he passed me, Asa Skander tossed me something that glinted silver in the light. I caught it: A quarter? Who had any use for a quarter these days? I pocketed it and watched them take him.

"Want me to go with them, ma'am?" asked Mr. Jameson, leaning on his rifle.

"No," said Mother Morevna. "Let him sit for a while. You take Sallie back to the church. I'm afraid lessons for today will have to be rescheduled. Now that the door has been opened, I must resecure the wall and gate before I interrogate him." She didn't look at me as she said, "Thank you, Sallie. That will be all."

I tried to read her face, to see if she was pleased with me. Then she turned away and strode over to the steel door to begin whatever spells she was going to cast.

Was this some sort of a test? I wondered, my stomach dropping little by little. *And did I fail?*

"Come on now, girl," Mr. Jameson said, starting back toward the church. And as every eye in Elysium turned toward me, I had no choice but to follow.

• • •

The rest of the day dragged by agonizingly slowly. I rearranged things in my new room, putting away dusty flour-sack dresses and worn boots, moving furniture, opening the curtains and closing them and opening them again.

After lunch (chipped beef on toast—"shit on a shingle," as

Papa used to call it) was brought up to me by a dour, disapproving-looking woman named Mrs. Winthrop, I decided to take a walk, unable to stand the crampedness and the boredom anymore. I went out into the streets of Elysium as the sun was setting.

My eyes kept drifting over to the jail, where Asa Skander was being kept. Mindlessly, I reached into my pocket and fished out the quarter he'd tossed me and looked at it for the first time.

It was a simple enough quarter, worthless now, stained on the back with something that might have been blood. But then I flipped it over to the heads side and I saw something that made my heart leap to my mouth and stay there, speeding.

The date on the quarter was 1944. Nine years after our world ended.

This quarter had been made somewhere else—somewhere that still existed beyond the desert.

"Oh my God . . ." I breathed. I had to tell Mr. Jameson . . . or, better yet, Mother Morevna.

I ran toward the jail, slipping through the shadows, hoping to catch her. But when I reached the jail, two guards blocked my way.

"Mother Morevna's already gone," one of them said. "Says he's good to go as soon as we get him some lodgings."

"Oh." I fumbled with the quarter, then, thinking quickly: "She just had a couple of minor questions for Mr. Skander. She sent me down to . . . er . . . try my hand at interrogation."

The guards exchanged glances, wondering whether or not to believe me.

"Unless you doubt her word?" I added.

"Oh, no, of course not," said the guards, deciding they better not risk it. The shorter guard pushed the door open and held it for me. "Keep it short, though," he said. "We gotta be getting on home." And the door shut behind me.

The jail was small and dusty, with slightly crooked, framed daguerreotypes on the walls. There was only one cell. Inside, on a cot, sat Asa Skander. He grinned brightly when I came in.

"Ah, Miss Wilkerson," he said. "I didn't expect you back this evening." He gestured to a stool outside the cell, where Mother Morevna must have sat during the interrogation.

I sat down, my limbs too long for the short stool. Across from me, Asa Skander sat, one leg propped up on his other knee, as though his cell were a comfortable living room and I was a guest he'd invited over for tea. But the strangeness was still there, and the hairs on my arms had already begun to stand on end.

"So," he said. "To what do I owe this visit, my lovely benefactor?"

Taking a deep breath, I opened my palm and let the quarter shine in the dim light, heads up.

"Where did you get this?" I asked.

"Oh, that old thing?" Asa said. "I just . . . picked it up on the journey. I'm like a magpie, you know, always picking up shiny things."

I focused on him, tried as hard as I could, but I could feel no deception.

"But the world outside the desert," I said. "It still exists, then? We're not the only ones?"

"I assume so," he said. "To me this world seems like . . . like a cake under a glass dome. Separate, protected. It would have to be so the Game could happen, wouldn't it?" He blinked. "All conjecture, of course. I don't know."

I frowned. I hadn't felt anything different from his usual strangeness. He was being truthful.

"Look," I said. "If you are from outside the desert, Chicago or whatever since before the Game began, tell me. I'll keep your secret as long as you're not dangerous or anything. But I've got to know: What is happening? Is the Depression over? Has rain come to the Dust Bowl again?"

Asa Skander opened his mouth to speak; then he got a desperate look on his face and clutched his throat. He buckled forward, gagged, and white smoke billowed from his mouth, disappearing into the air.

Fear shot through me. I stood up, knocking over my stool, legs bent, ready to run.

Then Asa Skander coughed a few times, sat up, red-faced and shaking. He regained his composure as well as he could and smiled weakly.

"I . . . don't think I can talk about that," he said. "Something's . . . stopping me. I'm sorry."

"Why are you really here?" I asked when I caught my breath. "Who are you?"

Asa Skander looked at me with those strange yellow eyes.

"I am what I say," he said. "Just a magician looking for shelter. That's all. And Mother Morevna has already vetted me for entry. Please, just trust me. I'm not here to cause any trouble."

I focused on him, on the aura that seemed to gradually lessen the longer I was in the room with him. As strange as he was, as strange as the quarter in my hand was, I realized that there was not a *dangerous* feeling coming from him. Magician or not, he wasn't here to hurt us.

"I believe you," I said. "For now. But I think you know more than you say you do. And I'm going to keep my eye on you."

Asa Skander smiled.

"What?" I said.

"Nothing," he said. "That's what Mother Morevna said too." He stood and extended his hand through the bars. "I hope we can be friends someday."

I took his hand and shook it.

"I hope so too," I said. Then I put the quarter back in my pocket and slipped out of the jail.

CHAPTER 5

3 MONTHS AND *27 DAYS* REMAIN.

I was up at six the next morning, long before Mrs. Winthrop arrived with breakfast (honey and biscuits made with fine white flour), dressed and ready, the quarter from Asa in my pocket. And when the clock in the hall struck eight, I ran downstairs, scooted past the empty baptistery tank, and opened the door to the narrow stairway that led up to Mother Morevna's room in the attic of the church. My hands shook with nerves and black coffee. I took a deep breath and began climbing. Before I could even reach to knock on the door, Mother Morevna's voice from inside said, "Come in."

I opened the door, trying hard to seem like the climb hadn't winded me. The room was wide, and the pitched ceiling rafters hung with dried herbs, some familiar like sage, and some I'd never seen before. A twin-size brass bed lay in the shadows, simple and tightly tucked. Beside it was a bookcase so tall that it required a step stool, and filled with thick leather-bound books, many of them with titles written in a strange, jagged-looking alphabet. Across the room was another small door with a sign labeled *ROOF ACCESS.*

From a high-backed chair, silhouetted in the multicolored light of the rose window behind her, Mother Morevna sat at a desk with her hands folded, contemplating a stack of papers. I gulped.

"Mother Morevna?" I asked, stopping at the door. "Can I show you something? It'll only take a second."

Mother Morevna sighed. "I suppose. What is it, girl?"

I reached into my pocket and pulled out the quarter. I handed it to her heads side up so she could see the date. "Mr. Skander gave this to me, and I just thought you should see it." I waited for her reaction, waited for her to tell me that what I'd found was important. That she was wrong and my lessons would begin in earnest immediately.

"Hmmm," she said instead. "Another of these, eh?"

My heart dropped.

"The guards keep finding them on desert patrols," she said. "I believe them to be anomalies originating in the real world that exists beyond the desert."

She handed it back to me, and it sat impotent on my palm, even more worthless than before. Maybe I'd been too quick to jump to conclusions about Asa Skander, I thought. Maybe he really was only what he said. I shook myself mentally.

"Then the real world *is* still there," I said.

"Yes," said Mother Morevna. "The small world of the desert exists separate from it, a bubble of space and time and magic, until the Game ends and we either rejoin the outside world or continue in this one."

Rejoining the world . . . that would really be something. But even continuing in this one was better than the alternative. If the Game ended in our favor. I thought of the Dust Soldiers, of the sacrifice.

"Is there any way I can help?" I asked. "Any at all? After all, I am a . . . a . . ."

"A witch?" Mother Morevna said.

Witch. The word sent a thread of lightning up my spine. Images of blood sacrifices, of cauldrons at midnight, of flying broomsticks sprang unbidden into my mind. Images of women with power.

"Yes, ma'am," I said.

She looked at me for a moment, considering me. Then she sighed and gestured for me to sit down. Clumsily, I plopped down on the stool. Mother Morevna flicked her wrist, and with a gust of wind, curtains fell over all the stained-glass windows, leaving only the thin light of a few oil lamps to brighten the room.

"All right," she said. "The first thing you must understand is the power."

I nodded vigorously as though to say, *Yes, yes, tell me everything.*

"The power of the earth flows through everything, everyone. We are all connected to these powers in some way or another, and these powers eventually lead us to our specialties. I, myself, have a skill for laying trapdoor spells that can be quite complicated, indeed. All the spells outside my specialty, my coven sisters tattooed on my hands so I would never lose them, as was their way."

"Will I have to have tattoos?" I asked, looking at the many intricate lines and symbols that stretched across her wrinkled claws.

"No," she said. "It is still far too early for that. Any education, even witchcraft, must have a strong foundation in order to stand the test of time. You can worry about specialties later." She folded her hands. "For now, I suppose you can begin with runes. I have a workbook on Elder Futhark that you can begin tonight."

"Elder . . . what?" I asked, my excitement deflating a little bit.

"Futhark. Viking runes. One of English's roots is in Futhark, so when you get down to writing your own basic spells, that's likely what you'll use."

She went to the bookcase and pulled two books off the middle shelf, one a thin paperback and the other a book about the size of a King James Bible and probably older than Mother Morevna herself.

"Here," she said. "A runic workbook and *A History of Witches*. That should be enough. Now, that's it for today, I'm afraid. I must be about my duties."

What? Already? My heart sank. I hesitated, feeling the weight of my expectations drag my shoulders down.

"Have they been caught?" I asked. "The thieves, I mean."

"Not yet," Mother Morevna said, putting a pair of bifocal spectacles on the end of her nose. "Though we are looking into the matter, and we should be able to find them soon." She looked down at her stack of papers. "Now, please, my dear. I have quite a lot of work to do if anything is going to get done in that regard. I'll see you in a few days."

I wanted to ask if there was anything I could learn that might help catch the thieves, might help me feel useful. But Mother Morevna was already back into her stack of paperwork and didn't even look up.

". . . Yes, ma'am." I had barely said the words before the door closed itself behind me.

• • •

Four hours later, I was halfway through chapter two of *A History of Witches*. I'd read about water witches who divined with forked sticks in the Appalachian Mountains. I read about witches in Egypt and the Caribbean and Africa. I read about witches reading cards and smoke and tea leaves. I read about witches getting burned at the stake in Germany and England and hanged in Massachusetts, and somehow the author of *A History of Witches* had managed to write about all of these things in the driest, most boring way I could think of.

"Uggghhh," I said, rubbing my temples. "That's all I can do for today."

I put a scrap of paper into the book to mark my place and closed it. I felt bleary-eyed and lazy, and even after all that reading, I still didn't know how witchcraft had anything to do with *me* in particular.

I went to the bookcase to find a place wide enough for *A History of Witches*. There were seventy-three copies of the Cokesbury Baptist Hymnal, from back in the days when we had actually used them. I shoved the Cokesburys to the side and wedged *A History of Witches* in where I could.

But it wouldn't fit! Something was back there, a loose board or something. I took a few Cokesburys from the shelf and peered into the dark, dusty shelves. Then I saw it.

At the back of the bookcase, shoved far behind the rest of the books, was a small, leather-bound book no bigger than those pocket Bibles I'd seen in Boise City. I reached behind the other hymnals and pulled it out.

Squinting against the dust, I held it up and blew the dust

off the cover. There, in crisp gold letters, the title stood out: *The Complete Booke of Witchcraft.*

Must be one of Mother Morevna's books, I thought. She must have forgotten it was in here.

But when I flipped through it, the chapters were not dull or didactic. They were things like "Dowsing for Beginners," or "Quick Shortcuts to Spellcraft." And the scribblings in the margins were not in the tight, dark handwriting Mother Morevna had left in *A History of Witches.* This wasn't cursive at all. All capital letters, in pencil, writing notes about things like how to create lightning from a handful of dust and crushed seashells, or how to make light appear in your hand. And then, far toward the back, *how to breathe fire.*

New energy seemed to leap into my veins. This was something practical, something I could *use.* With this, I could prove that I *was* cut out for this. And extra study couldn't hurt, could it? Surely not, if there was even the remotest possibility that I'd be dealing with the Dust Soldiers in four months' time.

So I flung the Futhark workbook to the floor, did a few quick stretches, and spread out on the bed with *The Complete Booke of Witchcraft.*

I flipped through the introduction and landed on the second page.

" 'Chapter One: Practical Spells for Every Witch,' " I read.

Though many spells center on specialty, there are a few basic spells that can be mastered by almost any witch. First, IMBUED OBJECTS. In order to direct and focus her power, a witch may choose an object and imbue it with her essence. This will act as a conduit for her magic, strengthening her power. Usually, pieces of jewelry are best for this, as metal and stone are conductors of magical power.

Like Mother Morevna's pendulum, I thought. But I didn't have any necklaces or brooches, or even earrings. A pebble, maybe? No. That didn't seem special enough, unique enough.

But then I remembered. I went to my desk and opened the small wooden box that had been brought over from my shack. I opened it, riffled through, and after a moment I found what I was looking for. It was a normal penny at first, tails-side glance, two stalks of wheat surrounding the words *ONE CENT UNITED STATES OF AMERICA* and, above that, *E PLURIBUS UNUM.* I'd found it on the floor of the hospital room Mama had lived her final days in. At first I'd thought it was good luck, but when I turned the penny over to see what year it had been minted, instead of a heads side, there was just another back. Another tails. I had been disappointed at first. "This penny's broken," I had said. But I remembered the smile on her cracked, dirty lips. "It's got 'E pluribus unum' on it twice," she'd said. "So that's double good." "What does that mean?" I had asked. "It means 'From many, one.' "

It felt good, warm, right, somehow. *This will do,* I thought.

I went to the next step and read along to myself out loud.

" 'Take the object into your hand and focus on it. Memorize the object in your mind' . . . Okay."

I closed my eyes and did as the book said. I focused on how the penny felt in my hand, its coolness growing warm with my body heat. Then I opened one eye a crack and went on.

" 'Imagine all of your power, your energy, flowing from your head, to your chest, through your muscles, and into your object. When your object is full of your power, you will feel it vibrate.' "

I took a deep breath, in and out.

"All right," I said to myself. "Here goes . . ."

Then I closed my eyes again, tight, concentrating on the penny in my hand. I imagined myself full of energy, thought of the blackbirds, of the feeling of the rain on my skin. I imagined all of that flowing from my head, down into my chest, down through the muscles and veins and arteries of my arm, into my hand. And to my surprise, the penny began to grow warm in my hand, abnormally warm. Something was happening! But it hadn't vibrated yet. I kept at this for what felt like several minutes, the penny growing hotter all the while—beginning to burn my palm. Suddenly, the penny's heat faded and it gave a soft vibration, almost like a cat purring.

I opened my eyes. Though the penny was still dull copper, it now had a strange sort of glow about it. *I did it.* I held it in my hand, seeing it shine from the darkness between my fingers. My heart sped. This was magic—*my* magic. It felt more real, more true, more destined, than anything had ever felt in my life. And as I held the penny in my hand, I could feel the warmth of it, the power of it, coursing through my whole body like blood. I felt awake. Alive. Connected.

A connection to the world, Mother Morevna had said. *So this is what she meant.*

Mother Morevna. My heart sank. What would she think if she found out I'd disobeyed her—and on the very first day, no less?

From inside my palm, the penny glowed reassuringly.

"Mother Morevna doesn't have to know," I said to it. The penny seemed to glow brighter in response.

• • •

Across town, from his place on his cot, Asa Skander heard the door to the jailhouse open. There was a sound of footsteps, and Mr. Jameson, the sad-looking man from before, trudged into the light.

"You can come on out," Mr. Jameson said, taking a ring of keys from his pocket. "We got a place for you now, 'long as you agree not to cause any trouble."

"Just when I was getting used to my lovely abode." Asa grinned.

Mr. Jameson didn't answer; he merely unlocked the door and let it groan open.

"Come on, boy," he said, and Asa scrambled to his feet and followed him.

Outside the jail, the sky was clear and dark, and when he looked closely, Asa realized that the stars were *different.* Gone were Orion and Cassiopeia and the Pleiades, and in their places were patterns of stars that he'd never seen before. He had to give the Goddesses one thing: They were thorough.

Somewhere out in the night, something howled. Asa followed Mr. Jameson carefully, through winding lanes that separated the smaller houses toward the middle of the city, focusing on the glow of Mr. Jameson's lantern until he stopped abruptly.

"Here we are," Mr. Jameson said. "This is all we had on short notice."

The house was small and dusty, with a broken window in

the front, the porch littered with broken bottles, dried flowers, and dust. But the kerosene lamp on the porch had been lit and it made the broken glass sparkle in the orange light.

Asa was overjoyed. A human house of his own!

Mr. Jameson led him onto the porch, kicking bottles aside.

"Soon, you'll receive rations and all of that. We'll bring the paperwork by first thing in the morning." Mr. Jameson unlocked the door and opened it to reveal a rectangle of dusty darkness that seemed to Asa like it might be hungry. Mr. Jameson went into it, and Asa followed.

In the sphere of Mr. Jameson's lamplight, Asa saw that the people who lived in it before seemed to have been quite messy, indeed. In the kitchen, a chair had been broken and lay on its back with its legs in the air. On the green iron stove a cast-iron frying pan still sat, with the solidified frying grease turned to mud. The counters were practically caked with dust.

"There'll be plenty of time for you to clean it up later," Mr. Jameson said. "There should be a broom in one of the closets."

Mr. Jameson led him down the hallway, narrow and short, and it creaked as they passed through it. A bedroom lay just past the kitchen. Mr. Jameson pulled a match from his pocket and lit a lamp on a table by the door.

Down on the floor was a broad, dark stain.

Asa moved toward it, bent. One sniff confirmed his suspicions: blood. Old blood. And there was a feeling in the room . . . a darkness, but not the thrumming, pregnant darkness of Life. An ominous darkness, empty, gaunt, hungry. On the walls hung several crucifixes, suffering Jesuses (*Jesi? What was the plural form of Jesus, anyway?*) dying for sins innumerable. Beneath them, Asa saw that the walls too were spattered with dark bloodstains, set deep.

"What happened here?" Asa asked.

Mr. Jameson's wrinkles seemed to deepen in the lamplight. "That story's not for me to tell," he said.

Mr. Jameson shut the door, and Asa followed him down the hall. He opened the door to a second bedroom and lit a lamp on top of a white-painted dresser. The small room flared into light, and Asa realized that the family who lived here before him must have had daughters. There were two twin beds, leaning against opposite walls, but still very close together. They were separated by one bedside table and a rag rug so dusty that it sent up little gritty clouds when Asa stepped on it. The wallpaper was made of newspaper clippings.

"You could use this room for whatever you like," said Mr. Jameson. "An office, maybe. Or a sitting room. You can get rid of those beds whenever you like."

Asa opened the drawer of the bedside table. At first, he thought it was empty, but when he felt along the sides of the drawer, he felt a piece of paper. Gently, he pulled it from the drawer. It was a photograph of two girls on the steps of the church. One stood behind the other, her hands on the other's shoulders, looking distant and ghostly. But the one who was seated drew Asa's attention immediately. She wore an elaborate white dress that had a skirt with layers of ruffles, and held a bouquet of flowers. Her black hair had been woven into a bun, but wisps fell on her forehead and around her face. Her eyes were black and bright as she looked up at her sister.

Asa was instantly fascinated in a way that he did not

understand. He found it very difficult to look away from her. No matter how he tried, it was as though his eyes kept being dragged back to her smiling, upturned face. There was something about her. Something significant. But he didn't understand what. He had a sudden need to know who she was, what she was like. He flipped the picture around to the back. There, written in slanting, feminine-looking script, were the words *Quinceañera Olivia. Hermanas bonitas.*

Then he saw something that made him forget the picture all together.

Behind the bedside table, something had been scratched into the wall. *Muerte, ayúdanos, Muerte, ayúdanos . . . Help us, Death* over and over and over. And when he ran a finger across them, he was surprised to feel a tingle of power. He drew back as though he'd been burned. *Did that mean that one of these girls . . . ?*

"Well," said Mr. Jameson in the doorway. "I'll leave you to it, then. G'night."

And Mr. Jameson shuffled away, leaving Asa alone in the bloodstained house, wondering about the hermanas, and about what on earth he was supposed to do next.

A flash of movement caught his eye. On the wall to his right, there was a broken mirror framed in grimy white wicker. *Is that me?* Asa thought. He came closer and examined his new face.

He was even younger-looking than he expected behind those cracked spectacles—only a scant bit of dark stubble on his chin. *So this is me as a human,* he thought. He leaned close to the mirror and put his finger to it. The cracks began to mend, slowly, as though they were melting back together, and soon the mirror was smooth and whole again. *There, that's better.* Asa smiled, turning his face this way and that. *I look a lot like Harold Lloyd!* He thought of all the times he'd looked down and watched movies being made. *Not bad! Not bad at all.* He grinned like a jack-o'-lantern, then gave a pitiful frown, then lifted one eyebrow. He'd have to practice postures and facial expressions later.

Suddenly, he smelled mercury. The room went cold and dry. His bones felt as hollow as a bird's.

So you're the Wildcard, eh? The one my Sister built . . . came a voice at the furthermost corner of his mind. **She's twisting the rules, making Her own Card instead of just choosing one, and I don't like it.**

"I th-thought you two weren't allowed to see each other's Cards?" Asa stuttered. He felt a strange popping sensation. In the mirror, the lower half of his human face was gone. Instead, there were long, sharp black teeth, charred skin, a long, snakelike black tongue—his daemon face.

Wait a moment, said Death. **I know you. You're the young daemon always watching the earth from the edge of the Between. The one they call a human lover.** Death paused. **And our Mother chose you? Interesting. . . . What could She want with you?**

Death considered this for a moment. Then Her voice changed, became soft and soothing.

Are you enjoying your time as a human?

"I am just here to do my job," he said.

And what is that, pray tell?

"Just to find someone, and give something back to him—or her, I suppose—a-and leave."

Death's voice became soft and cooing, with barely an echo of the mercury-stained growl that it had been before. **Just like that? What a pity, to have to spend so little time in a form you've always been enamored of. Very cruel of my Mother to send you of all daemons here. Unfair, I think. And they say that I am the harsh one.**

There was a tickle in his mind then, almost a caress.

Well, I suppose I'll leave you, then, Human Lover. Spend what time you have wisely—what little of it you still have.

Then She leaked from his mind and left him alone. His face in the mirror snapped back to its human features. With shaking hands, Asa felt his nose, his mouth. He breathed a sigh of relief.

But Death's words had left their mark in his mind, a breadcrumb trail that he could not ignore.

It *did* seem unfair. To give him just a taste of humanity before wrenching him out of it, bringing him back, sadder but wiser. Why had the Mother done it, and why had Life agreed to it? Was it to teach him a lesson? To let him see that the grass was no greener on the other side?

Asa turned away from the mirror and began to pace the floor.

He knew what he *should* do: find the owner of the cricket in amber as soon as possible, finish the mission, and leave.

But that wasn't what he *wanted* to do. What he wanted to do was explore, to test out this new body, to *see* and *feel* and *hear* and *taste* and *touch* as humans did. He wanted to make friends, acquaintances, enemies. To laugh and shout and whisper and weep! He wanted to live a human life while he could. As Asa realized this completely, the yearning seemed to fill his every sinew, his every fiber, and he knew he was powerless to resist this new, intoxicating thing called humanity.

Asa reached into his pocket and took out the cricket in amber. In the low light, it shone like honey. Life's presence seemed to wind around it like vines.

He took a deep, steadying breath. Back in the Between, to disobey meant punishment. To disobey meant pain. And for the very worst offense, to disobey meant being ripped apart and scattered, atom by atom, through the universe, then feeling each atom fade to oblivion.

But this isn't the Between, Asa thought.

Rebellion was a new feeling, a very un-daemon-like one, and to Asa it felt nearly delicious. He cupped his hand over the amber cricket and put it into the drawer where he'd found the sisters' picture. *Out of sight, out of mind,* as the humans said. And just for a while. After all, what harm could it do?

CHAPTER 6

3 MONTHS AND *19 DAYS* REMAIN.

As the days went on, I was called to Mother Morevna's room for "lessons" three times. Each time, I was merely given a vague explanation of magic, handed some books, and practically pushed out of Mother Morevna's room afterward so that she could do whatever it was she did all day and I could serve my function of making everyone feel better. So much for being the Successor, I thought.

I had tried to follow her and find out what it was when she went out into Elysium, but either she saw me and vanished or she was too fast for me. So, dejected, I spent my days reading from the Booke or wandering Elysium by myself, wearing my new importance like a cloak while the other girls my age were in school—school I couldn't go to anymore because it would ruin the illusion that I was really learning something with Mother Morevna.

But no matter what the truth was, the way people talked about me had changed. There were no longer looks of disapproval on their faces, or pity. They were curious now. As though they'd been wrong about me all this time. People greeted me, even people I hadn't known before the walls went up, like the Speers, the Coxes, the Sanchez-Romolos. Even the man down at the Blue Moon, Elysium's only "café," said good morning to me now. One day, he even gave me two small fried pies.

"Take them for Mother Morevna," said the Blue Moon man. "Try to get me on her good side, will ya?" and he had winked and smiled a silver-toothed smile.

Like hell was I giving these pies to Mother Morevna, I thought. I wrapped them in a handkerchief and headed down into the west side, toward a row of clapboard houses where speckled chickens pecked at the grit. I was looking for one person in particular, who would hopefully be excused from school for lunch like the rest of the seniors. And sure enough, she was sitting on her front porch. Both her dress and the artfully tied kerchief she wore were the yellow of newly ripened corn. She was seemingly finished with lunch and just taking time for herself.

"Surprise," I said, handing one of the pies to her. "To make up for not being able to bring you water anymore."

"Thanks!" she said. "And don't worry about it. Normal water works fine anyway. What kind is this, cherry?"

"Apple," I said.

"Perfect." I expected her to just take the pie and send me on my way, but to my surprise, she scooted over and patted the porch beside her. We ate in silence for a few moments; then, after about half of her pie, Lucy wrapped it back in the napkin. "I'm gonna save the rest of it to give to Aunt Lucretia when she gets back from the ration office. She loves apple pie even more than I do."

"I think you told me her name once," I said. "Lucretia?"

"Yep. I'm named for her. She's strong as an ox. She's gonna live to be three hundred at the rate she's going." Lucy laughed. "If we make it through the rest of this year, of course."

A silence fell, like it always did when anyone mentioned the coming end of the Game.

Then she turned to me and said, "So how's it going, being the Successor and all?"

I shrugged and took another bite of pie.

"That bad, huh?"

"I thought it would be okay at first," I said, surprised at myself for being so forthcoming. "I mean, she allowed me to decide about letting in Asa Skander. But she doesn't want me there. She doesn't even want a Successor, I don't think."

"Well, to your credit, he's a good magician," Lucy said. "All the kids love him."

I thought of him, Asa Skander, how strange he felt, how something about him made my hair stand on end. Of the smoke I'd seen billow from his mouth. Then I thought of the quarter in my pocket. An anomaly.

"Maybe Mother Morevna can't let you help her with whatever she's doing because it would take too long to teach you at the moment," Lucy said.

"I'm pretty much teaching myself right now," I said, thinking of the penny glowing in my pocket. I told Lucy about how in only a matter of days, I had learned several basic, typeless spells—though I left out the part where I ransacked my room doing so.

I told her about the spell I learned that sent a knee-high whirlwind careening around my room (scattering my Futhark pages and spell ingredients to high heaven). I told her about how I learned to create fire—just enough to light a candle for now—with a pinch of pepper and a motion like blowing a kiss, and burned the corner of my blanket black. And, the most useful one so far, I told her how I'd learned to cast a spell on my shoes that made them quiet, even on the hardwood floors of the church.

"Sounds pretty impressive to me," said Lucy. "I can't do any of that."

"Yeah, but I feel like such a fraud," I said. "I mean, there are only three months left until the Dust Soldiers come, and here I am, making tiny whirlwinds and quiet shoes. I wish I could do something to help catch those thieves, you know? Since they were only able to steal from us because I was seeing the rain again."

"Maybe that's what you should do," said Lucy. "Catch the thieves. Prove that you're worthwhile even if she doesn't think so right now. I mean, you *were* chosen. Surely there's some kind of spell you can learn that'll help you."

I thought about this. There were all kinds of spells in the Booke: spells for blocking light, spells for making the wind blow, spells for making fire in your hand, and spells for looking into mirrors and seeing other places like you were looking through a window. Maybe I couldn't catch the thieves with one of these spells. But surely I could use one of them to *help* catch them. After all, two witches were better than one, right?

There was a familiar clanging sound a few streets away.

"Well, that's the end of lunch," said Lucy. She got up and brushed off her skirt. "Don't worry, Sal. She'll come around."

"Let's hope so," I said.

"She will if you keep trying and do your best. Don't be so

negative." She straightened her kerchief and dabbed on a bit of lipstick. "Thanks for the pie," she said with a smile. Then she set off toward the school, and I headed back to the church and the five pages of unfinished Futhark on my desk, the penny in my pocket glowing just a little brighter.

• • •

That night, after dinner, I pulled the Booke out from under my pillow, flipping to the place I'd left off the night before.

DOWSING: also known as divining. A form of divination employed for the finding of objects, elements, or spirits. Though some types of witches are stronger dowsers than others, dowsing can be done by most types, to some degree. All that is needed is an Imbued Object.

I pulled my penny out and held it in my hand, where it thrummed quietly, simmering with my own unidentified magic.

First, you must form a method of communication with your Object. Simply ask it to show you yes and no. Then use these commands to find lost objects. Dowsing is something that can only be perfected through trial and error, so practice is vital to its success.

All right, I thought. *Here we go.* I took the penny in my hand and asked it, "Um . . . could you show me a yes?" To my surprise, it gave one short pulse of power in my hand. My heart raced. *I was communicating with it.*

"What's a no, then?" I asked, sitting up on the bed.

It pulsed twice, two bumblebee buzzes in my hand.

I asked it a few questions, just for practice. Am I a girl? (Yes.) Do I have black hair? (No.) Are there three dresses in my closet? (Yes.) And every time, the thrum of magic was strong and sure and effortless. Dowsing, unlike the other spells I'd attempted, was coming easily to me.

If used as a pendulum, an Object can indicate direction as well as any dowsing rods, I read.

I remembered how Mother Morevna had found the Dowsing Well, how she had taken the black pendulum and it had pointed to exactly the place the Well stood now. I remembered how that same black pendulum had pointed at me out of everyone in Elysium. The tiny whirlwind and the flames and the quiet shoes were fun, but Dowsing was something that had real, practical use. I fumbled through my chest of drawers until I came out with a piece of twine. This I tied around the penny and hung around my neck, a sad, cheap imitation of Mother Morevna's pendant.

"Show me left," I told it, and it swung immediately to the left.

"Now the right," I said, and it swung to the right.

"Um . . . how about north?" I asked, and, sure enough, it swung outward toward the north, holding itself outward from my chest.

"Can you . . . can you find the thieves?" I asked, my voice soft and hesitant.

Suddenly, the penny shot straight out from my chest, straining its twine like a bloodhound on a leash. It pointed toward my door as though leading me, pulling me downstairs.

"What, really?" I asked it. "You can find them?"

It thrummed once. Yes.

My heart sped. *I can do this,* I thought. *I can really do this. I can find them. And then she'll have to take me seriously.* I tore open the curtain and looked outside. The sky was clear and dark over the walls, and one by one, I saw the lamps in the windows of each house wink themselves out. I threw a dress on over my nightgown and put the Booke in my pocket. I pulled on some stockings and slid into my boots. I sneaked downstairs, boots magically quiet over the planks, and went out into the night, the penny around my neck softly pulling me onward.

• • •

Through the empty streets, I followed the penny as it led me this way and that, toward the northeast. It pulled me forward, glowing brightly in the dark, and eagerly I followed. But just as we approached the wall, the penny started to go wild. It began to move in short, hesitating jerks, first one direction, then another, as though it were confused. As though it had lost the scent. Then it stopped altogether and dropped against my chest, where it hung still. It didn't move again.

"I thought you said you could find them?" I asked it, but it was quiet and dull against my chest.

It was worth a try, I guess, I thought. But the more I thought of dowsing to find the thieves, the more foolish I felt. Surely Mother Morevna had already tried this. It was pretty obvious, after all. Besides, she was a much better dowser than I was. And what was I supposed to do? Go outside the walls?

I shuddered, thinking of all the things that were supposed to live out there. But part of me, a part of me that I'd never been able to talk sense into, was curious. What all did live out in the desert? What horrible, unseen creatures had been created just to populate the world of the Game? We'd all heard stories of fire coyotes—once I'd even seen their glow and heard their howls on the horizon. But what else was there? In the back of my mind, I remembered the shadow on top of the wall on Mourning Night, just before the vision of the rain came.

What if . . . ? I thought suddenly. *What if Mother Morevna and Mr. Jameson were wrong? What if the thief was someone from outside the walls? Someone still out in the desert?*

We all knew that there were people in the desert. Very, very few people, but they were there, farmers who had chosen to stay with their land, mostly, although what child in Elysium hadn't heard stories of the terrifying cannibal men who roved among the wreckage in the desert? What if one or more of these people had grown brazen after Asa escaped them? What if they planned to attack?

I had to go back and tell Mr. Jameson. But as I squinted into the darkness, I saw his porch light was off. *He must still be in his office,* I thought. I headed back toward the church, toward its sharp black shape jutting into the sky. Nearby was the hospital, the second-tallest building in Elysium, a second monolith looming in the dark. But as I watched, a light came on in the hospital office.

Only the overnight nurses were supposed to be there, in the wings with the patients. Why was someone in the office?

I heard footsteps and, without thinking, ducked into the shadows of a nearby windmill. A man was walking toward the steps of the hospital, where one of the nurses opened the door and held it for him. I couldn't tell who the nurse was, but the man's Stetson hat was as distinctive as my blond braids. In his arms he held what looked like a stack of water rations.

"Well, if it isn't Sallie Wilkerson," said a voice that sent a flash of fear up my spine. I turned and Trixie Holland was standing there with another girl from school, Mae, one of the ones who had chased me only a week before Trixie broke my nose. "I'd say I missed seeing you at home, but that would be a lie in so many ways."

The penny around my neck began to grow hot against my breastbone. I took a step back.

"Your nose looks better," Trixie said, coming up to me and looking me up and down. "And look at you! You're clean. Looks like you finally learned how to take a bath."

"Leave me alone," I said, my hands balled into fists.

Trixie put up her hands. "Lord, I was just making conversation. You going to magic me into the ground or something?" She laughed and took out a homemade cigarette. "We were just out here catching a smoke. We didn't expect to run into the *Successor* herself."

Mae smirked, her already lit cigarette glowed.

"Mother Morevna's teaching you all kinds of magic, huh?" Trixie said.

"That's not what I heard," said Mae. "Mrs. Winthrop told her son that Sal's just been sitting around, reading. She says that Sallie can't even *do* magic."

"Awww, how sad," said Trixie. "Imagine being made to feel special all of a sudden only to find out that you're not. You must have really believed it this time, huh? I feel for you, Sallie. I really do."

"I *can* do magic," I said.

"Let's see some of it, then," Trixie said. "Turn Mae into a mouse!" They laughed uproariously at the very thought.

I wanted to turn them both into mice and their cigarettes into traps. But I couldn't.

"What's that around your neck?" Mae asked. She pointed at the penny. I took a step back.

But Trixie came forward and pushed my braids out of the way.

"Awww, would you look at that?" she said. "Sal's made herself a necklace like Mother Morevna's! How sad. How pathetic!"

Before I could do anything, Trixie reached out and grabbed the penny, to pull it off my neck and throw it into the dust, probably. But the second she touched it, Trixie's whole body went stiff. Simultaneously, a wave of nausea rolled through me. *Not the rain . . . not right now . . .*

But the rain was not what came next.

"Trixie?" Mae said.

Trixie's eyes were wide in shock. Then they went white.

The darkness was rising over my own vision. And suddenly . . .

Something was wrong. I was not myself. I felt disembodied, a ghost floating in a house that wasn't my own. A small, brown-haired girl was sitting under a kitchen table, watching a man shouting through a doorway. This was Trixie, I realized. Trixie right after the walls went up . . . and the man who was shouting was her father, now dead like my own.

"Get your fat ass up, Molly!" he yelled. "It's always something with you. Always making something up. Headaches, fevers, back pains . . . you'd better get your ass up, or I swear to God . . ."

Trixie's mother said something from her bedroom, and her father went in. There was a struggle, and he dragged Trixie's crying mother out into the kitchen and shoved her into a chair. Trixie scooted farther back, out of reach, against a box of water rations, half-empty. All of them had a black smudge at the corner, which I'd never seen before.

Trixie's father bent down and sniffed her mother as she wept in her chair.

"I don't believe this. You're drunk. You're blind drunk, and I'm

out there working all day—all day, Molly! To try and get out of this place! To try and feed our goddamn kid!"

Trixie sobbed, then quieted herself as well as she could. But her father had heard her. He bent down and in a gentle voice said, "Are you okay down there, honey? Are you okay down there in all that dust?"

Trixie raised her arms and let herself be picked up like a baby, though I knew somehow that she was seven. Her father brushed the dust off her face and hair, then turned back to her mother, sobbing and slumped in the chair.

"She's got dust all over her, Molly! She's gonna get Dust Sickness. She's gonna get Sick!" he shouted. "And . . . ! And . . . !"

He turned to Trixie. "Have you eaten?"

Trixie shook her head.

He turned back to Trixie's mother.

"Dammit, Molly! What good are you? I can't even trust you to keep the dust out of my house or off my kid! I'm covered in it all day, breathin' it in, feelin' it scratch the skin right off my arms. All day, Molly! While you're here, saying you've got headaches when what you've got is a belly full of booze! Can't even keep this shit out of my goddamn house!"

"That's enough!" Mae's shout broke like thunder over the memory. I felt Mae wrench the penny out of Trixie's hand, and immediately, I woke from the memory as though cold water had been thrown on me.

"What the hell did you do?" Trixie hissed. There were tears in her eyes. "What the hell did you do to me?!"

"I don't know! I—I didn't mean to!" I took a step forward, but Trixie pushed me away.

"Want me to hit her?" Mae asked, her eyes on me, sounding somehow meek and threatening at the same time.

"Nah . . ." said Trixie, wiping tears away with her fist. "Mother Morevna will have our hides. Come on, Mae." And with Mae following like a confused puppy, she disappeared into the night, a trail of cigarette smell following her.

I had seen into Trixie's past, somehow, and it had not been a pretty one. Both her parents, dead now of Dust Sickness. But how had I done it? And what exactly had I done?

I looked over toward the hospital, but the light had gone out, and Mr. Jameson was gone. Quickly, I headed back to the church, thinking of nothing but the memory, what had happened leading up to it, what that meant—if it meant anything.

I tiptoed over the hardwood floors as quietly as I could. But as I approached the stairs, I saw a sliver of light cutting across the hallway: There was a light on in Mr. Jameson's office. I had to pass through it to get back up the stairs. I took a deep breath and darted over it, quiet as a shadow in my spelled shoes. But as I did, Mother Morevna's voice stopped me just on the other side of the light.

". . . she must be monitored to be useful."

"This whole thing makes me sick to my stomach," Mr. Jameson said. "And to have her right above me while I work?"

Who? Me? I thought. But I wasn't above him. . . .

"Would you rather her . . ." Then her voice faded and came back again. ". . . on the walls with the guards?" asked Mother Morevna. "No, it's best for us . . . keep her close. At least until we catch them."

"What happens once we catch 'em?"

"We shall see when we do so," she said. "Until then . . ." Her voice quieted again, too quiet for me to hear the rest.

I could tell that the conversation was drawing to a close. I slipped up the stairs and down the hall. But just before I snuck back into my room, I noticed something odd.

The door across from mine, the one that had always lain empty, now had a padlock.

CHAPTER 7

3 MONTHS AND 18 DAYS REMAIN.

The next morning, through the window, I watched Asa Skander set himself up a soapbox and a sign: *ASA THE GREAT! MAGICIAN EXTRAORDINAIRE!* I watched the crowd gather around as he performed all the usual magician fare. Colored handkerchiefs from his sleeves. Coins from ears. And all the while the workmen applauded. It was shocking, really, how well he seemed to be fitting in. I'd expected him to be blamed for the robbery, but the opposite was true. He was well-liked, and no one seemed to have anything bad to say about him. I was a different story. Who knew what rumors might be going around about me today, after what had happened with Trixie? I thought of Trixie's eyes, blank white, her body rigid. . . .

"I *said*, what is the difference between spodomancy and haruspication?" Mother Morevna's voice snapped me out of my daze.

"Sorry!" I said. "Spodomancy is . . . telling the future with soot? The patterns and so on?"

Mother Morevna nodded. "And haruspication?"

"Telling the future with . . . animal bones?" I asked.

"Entrails, not bones," she said, peering over her reading glasses at me, half-interested. After all, this test was only pretense. Only to appease me and Mr. Jameson.

"Entrails, then," I said.

She grimaced, her wrinkles deepening around her eyes and mouth as she gritted her teeth and put a hand to her abdomen.

"Are you all right?" I asked.

"It's the . . . illness," she said. "It'll pass . . . in a . . . moment."

And it did. After a few minutes, her wrinkles smoothed, and gingerly, she sat up straight.

"I beg your pardon," she said. "I just . . . have a lot to deal with as of late. The Sacrifice and the thieves and all that nonsense. Now then, where were we?"

"Actually, Mother Morevna . . ." I ventured. "I have a question. About the thieves."

"Yes?" Mother Morevna raised her impatient gaze to meet mine.

"Are you sure they're from here in Elysium?" I asked. "Because I . . . I think that maybe they're not. They might not be, I mean."

Mother Morevna was silent for a moment, but when she spoke, it wasn't to address my question. "What's that around your neck?" she said, an edge to her voice.

I realized too late that my penny, my Imbued Object, was hanging out of my blouse.

"It's . . . uh . . ." I fumbled. "It's nothing. I was just doing a little . . . extra research—"

"Let me see it," she said. Obediently, I did. But having her hold it and examine it, I felt strangely exposed, vulnerable, powerless.

She looked at the penny again, then at me. "Now, what all have you taught yourself behind my back?"

"Er . . . not much, ma'am," I said. "Just . . . um . . . a wind spell, a fire spell, and a . . . a little bit of dowsing."

Mother Morevna rose to her feet. "Come," she said. She strode across the room and opened her door. She led me down the stairs, and I followed her, trying not to step on her long green skirts.

"Show me," she said when we reached the sanctuary. "The fire spell. Show me."

She reached into her pocket and pulled out a pinch of dust. She put it and the penny in my hand and took several steps back, watching me intently.

Faintly, I heard Asa Skander's voice outside. *"Pick a card! Any card!"*

I took a deep breath and put the pinch of pepper to my lips.

"Entflammt!" I said, and blew. A tongue of flame the size of my palm leapt out into the air. It burned there above the ground for a few seconds, then burned to ash and drifted to the floor.

"The accent was wrong," said Mother Morevna. "It is Ent-*flahm*-t. Try it again, the right way. Keep your back straight. Blow hard."

I stood still, my heart pounding. A tiny spark of anger lit and began to spread in my mind. What right did she have to demand me to do magic like this, to correct my pronunciation, when she couldn't be bothered to teach me in the first place?

I put the pepper to my lips, and, focusing all my energy, all my frustration, all my anger on the spell, I said, "Entflammt!" and blew.

Immediately, there was an orange flare of heat and light. I nearly fell backward as fire rocketed outward from my mouth and hand, like a circus fire-breather. It hung there in the air, a tongue of flame almost as big as me. Then it began to dwindle, until it was only a solitary shred of ash drifting to the dust at my feet. I turned to face her, my eyes as steely as hers.

Mother Morevna's brows were furrowed, her wrinkles deep. My magic had impressed her, I could tell. But not in the way I wanted. I wanted her to welcome me into the fold, to really teach me like I knew she could. But the look on her face was one of concern. She opened her mouth to say something to me, but before she could, a high, screeching sound wailed out over Elysium.

Sirens.

Fear scraped the bottom out of my stomach, made my breath come in spurts as the old panic rose inside me. A dust storm.

"Go and seek shelter, Sallie." She pulled a cloth dust mask from her pocket and put it on. "Go," she said, her voice muffled. Then she turned on her heel and strode out of the room, her skirts billowing behind her.

Every part of me was telling me to run, to hide, to seek shelter. *No,* I thought. *I want to see how to do this.* I tried to calm my breathing. With shaking hands, I put my dust mask on and followed her.

Dust storms didn't come as frequently as they used to, about once a month now, but my fear of them never lessened. Every time I heard the sirens, every time I heard the rumble of dust, it was as though I was nine again, out in that field, seeing Mama running toward me on one side and the dust on the other.

Out the window, everyone was going into the dust storm preparations like automatons: goggles on, dust mask on, stockings up, neck covered, sleeves down. I saw guards climbing from their towers to take shelter, the cowboys bringing their cattle to the barn, men and women running inside, shutting their windows, stuffing rags under their doors. All of them glanced fearfully back toward the church, waiting for Mother Morevna to come out and perform her spell to keep us safe. Beyond the walls, an enormous horizontal line of dust advanced, dark and ominous. Dust Dome was a spell we all knew. It covered the whole city, keeping the dust from flowing in and smothering or infecting us. But it only went as far as the walls. My palms sweated, my mouth was dry.

Just then, there was a sound from upstairs, in the room across from mine: a frantic, wordless shouting, a scratching at the walls, the sound of someone throwing themselves against the door.

I almost screamed and ran for cover in my room, but I saw Mother Morevna turn the corner and I darted after her, trying not to listen as the person in the room pounded at the door.

When I caught up to her, Mother Morevna was in the Dust Room. In a bin, there were four packages in plain brown paper, marked *STORM*. She reached and took one, unwrapping it deftly and tossing the twine in the corner. As she unwrapped each item, I tried to take note of it as well as I could from a distance.

She took out three chicken eggshells and smashed them, then put them in her pocket. What followed was an envelope labeled *seashell dust*, a handful of tawny fur, and a tiny vial of what looked like blood.

From the shadows, holding my hands over my ears, I watched her pour the small vial of rabbit blood onto her steady wrinkled hands. Then she turned and walked out into the vacant streets, her hands filled with bloody fur and eggshells and dust. I followed from a distance, the panic threatening to squeeze my heart to a pulp. The air was growing painful with static electricity, cold, taut, as it always did when a dust storm approached. I tried my best to stand up straight, but my legs shook, my knees seemed to bend against my will, and one thought drummed through my brain: *run, run, run, run, run.*

With her eyes closed, Mother Morevna took the ingredients into her hands and raised them outward. She took her hands and clasped them together, crumbling the eggshells, smearing it all with the blood, rubbing it all together between her long, bony palms. The tattoos on her hands seemed alive.

"PULVAREM FIRMAMENTUM!" Mother Morevna shouted, raising both fists and letting the wind whip the mixture out of her hands, leaving her bloody-palmed and defiant in front of the storm full of the glow of power.

There was a great thrum of magic that went up from her. Up toward the sky. And just as the dust started to slip over the walls, it was sent upward, outward, away. It flowed over Elysium as though we were inside an overturned glass bowl, looking safely up at the sky.

Dust Dome.

My heart was beating so fast it almost hurt. *We're safe,* I had to tell myself. *It's over. We're safe.*

But it wasn't over. Mother Morevna winced. Her eyes closed; she gritted her teeth, and she crumpled like a leaf, clutching her abdomen. There was a loud crack as her head hit the concrete porch.

"No!" I shouted, running out too late to catch her. "No, no, no! Mother Morevna!"

But she was unconscious.

All the fear, all the panic rose inside me again. *Oh, God, what do I do? What do I do?*

Then I heard a woman scream. The clear dome of magic over the city began to crack like an egg. The spell was breaking.

I have to fix it! I thought. *I have to!*

My hands were shaking as I stood up again. A long fissure was growing in the spell Mother Morevna had cast. I had to mend it somehow. I had to cast the spell again. Frantically, I gathered bits of fur and eggshells from the ground, dropping them, and trying to pick them up again. *Please,* I thought. *Please, please, please.* I closed my eyes and tried to ground myself in the feeling of the ingredients in my hands. The coyote fur was soft; the eggshells were sharp and small; the seashell dust seemed to thicken into a paste with the blood. I willed my panicked brain quiet and focused on the outcome, the spell I'd seen so many times before. . . .

I raised my hands like she had done, tried to clear my mind, to make the magic happen.

Come on, come on! But my penny was cold. Above me, the crack widened again. People began to scream and run back to their houses, securing their dust masks on. My heart raced; my hands were clumsy. I couldn't breathe. I had to run for cover.

"Sal!" said a voice. Asa Skander was there on the steps beside me.

"Get back to your house!" I shouted over the wind. "Put your mask on! Shut your doors!"

"What are you going to—" Asa started.

But I didn't have time to talk to him. I had a city to save. Desperately, I willed all my magic into my red-stained hands and screamed into the storm, "PULVAREM FIRMAMENTUM!"

There was another, weaker pulse of magic. *Please, please, please.*

Miraculously, the cracks in the spell began to heal themselves, to draw back together.

But then they stopped. Tendrils of dust came howling down with the wind. The crack lengthened, a big dark lightning bolt in the fabric of the spell. The dust grew thicker, its roaring sounding like a hundred freight trains at once, plunging us into darkness as it blocked the sun. The people ran for cover. The spell was failing. I wasn't strong enough. Soon the dust would cover all of us like it had Mama so long ago, and with it would come the Sickness. I tried to stand, tried to shoulder the weight of it, straining against the wind and the force even as my breath began to come in gasps and my legs began to shake. The roar of it was overwhelming. It rose in me and drowned out everything else, even the beating of my own panicked heart. My knees buckled, and I felt myself fold. I crumpled down onto the steps next to Mother Morevna, my hands over my head, my brain blank with fear, waiting for the dust to swallow me whole like the monster it so resembled.

But there was someone standing over me: Asa Skander, facing the crack in the spell as the wind whipped his coat back.

"What are you doing?" I croaked.

"Helping," he said. He put his hand up, closed his eyes, and I felt the sudden, unmistakable pulse of very strong magic. Magic without words or spell components.

There were exclamations in the street. People were pointing

upward. Above us, the cracks in the spell began to knit themselves back together. The two halves of the dome drifted toward each other like a continent re-forming, tectonic plates about to collide. Then they connected and melded together, seamless and whole as a clear glass bowl over us. Beyond it, the storm flowed silently over us, its angry darkness impotent beyond the border of Asa's magic.

"How—" I gasped. "How did you—"

But a great cheer went up then. The people of Elysium poured from their houses, shouting their delight and relief. A man and woman began dancing, their dust masks at their chests again. And over everything, a new cry rose up among the gathering crowd: "Asa! Asa! Asa! Asa!"

• • •

Asa was pleased with himself for helping, but Sal Wilkerson looked confused, almost angry. That didn't make sense. Who would be angry at receiving help?

Mr. Jameson appeared soon with nurses from the infirmary, telling everyone to get back, get back, so he got back, into the crowd, where his back was slapped and his hand shaken and questions were asked of him.

"You can do real magic too?"

"Are you a witch too, boy?"

"Thank God you're here! 'Bout time we had us a *man* who could do magic!"

There was a tingle in his mind, and he knew what Life would say to him.

Show them! Show them the object! Finish the job!

But it was in the drawer. Perhaps he could go back and get it? But then Asa felt a lengthening, a sharpness in his mouth. *Oh no!* he thought. *My teeth!* He knew without looking that his facade was slipping. He'd never used that much magic at once before. Soon his hands would lengthen into claws. His back would bend itself into its natural position. His skin would grow scaly and sharp. It would all be over. He opened his mouth to speak, to tell them he had to be off, that he wasn't feeling well, but a plume of white smoke slipped out.

The crowd gasped.

I've got to get out of here! Asa thought. Clapping his hand over his mouth, he pushed through the crowd and ran behind a nearby chicken coop. Then he disappeared altogether, leaving the townspeople to gasp at the mystery of it all.

He reappeared back in his house, his chest heaving and his teeth almost too big for his mouth. Too weak to stand, he crawled into the bloodstained bedroom, feeling his human form unraveling like a poorly knitted sweater.

I shouldn't have done that, he thought as his hands became claws and his scaly skin shredded his shirt before he could get it off. *I shouldn't have meddled.*

He would have considered this more, but he heard the footsteps of many pairs of shoes crunching in the street, then plunking across his porch. A crowd had assembled. There were knocks at the door.

He didn't answer. A few minutes later, a man said, "Probably real tired after all that. We need to leave him be."

Asa sat still as a stone until all of them left, one by one, trudging away into the darkening evening. He waited until it was dark, then looked outside. There were several sets of footprints in the dust on his porch, and five plates of food, wrapped carefully in rags and dishtowels, and only a little gritty.

Thank you for saving us, said a note on a plate of biscuits. *We appreciate all you did for us today,* said a note that came with a roast chicken. "'We'd love to get to know you better, friend,'" Asa read aloud from the final note, which had come with a pound cake on a scratched milk-glass platter.

You still have time, said a crackling, mercury-scented voice in his mind. **Enjoy yourself here. Make some friends! It's not like you had any back in the Between.**

That was true. Asa had always been the odd daemon out. Never a kind word did anyone speak to him there. But here . . .

It was a lot to think about. The more he put his mission off, the bigger the risk he took. Life could strip him of his essence, shred him like ribbons and leave him flapping like bloody rags in the firmament.

But what was his existence without seeing and hearing and smelling and tasting? He was enamored with it, even just the small bits he had seen so far. Perhaps there was something to what the other daemons said, that there was a toxin in the air of the Earth that made you hungry, made you want more and more and ever more. That made you want to go rogue and take over a human's body just to stay (they didn't talk about those daemons much—that was what made one a demon, after all, rather than a daemon).

It was a lot to think about. So Asa, too tired to give the

matter the consideration it deserved, merely decided to ignore his thoughts for now. He unhinged his jaw like a snake, swallowed the pound cake in a single gulp, and lay down on the floor to sleep while his human body repaired itself.

CHAPTER 8

3 MONTHS AND *18 DAYS* REMAIN.

I sat up with Mother Morevna as best I could, but after the spell, my bones felt like sand and my blood like water. A nurse came in then, walking carefully around the pentagram on the floor, probably for fear of turning into a salamander. Her name was Ada Speer, and she was one of the younger, nicer nurses.

As I watched her check Mother Morevna's pulse, her hands seemed so plump and healthy next to Mother Morevna's. In her white nightgown, it was suddenly obvious how frail and thin Mother Morevna was. How mortal. And this mortality hit me like a hammer and left me reeling.

"She's going to be all right," said Nurse Ada. "It'll take some time, but she'll be all right."

"She says she's sick," I said.

"She is . . ." the nurse admitted. "But she's a pretty tough old witch—" Nurse Ada's eyes widened. "I—I'm sorry," she said. "I didn't mean—"

"Will she make it to . . . will she make it to the ten-year mark?" I heard myself ask.

"We'll see," said Nurse Ada. "If she rests and doesn't push herself too hard, maybe. And now that we have that magician around—maybe things will be easier for her—and you, of course. Another witch couldn't hurt, after all."

Asa Skander. Another witch. The witch who had stopped the storm when I couldn't. There was certainly more to him than met the eye. . . .

The air grew thick with silence. Then we heard a loud crash and a wail from the second floor: the room across from mine.

"Poor Miss Ibarra," she said. Then she turned to me. "It's so good of Mother Morevna to take interest."

"What?" I asked. "Miss Ibarra?"

"Mother Morevna didn't tell you she was coming?" said Nurse Ada. "Perhaps not. But we're glad she decided to take her. There was only so much that could be done at the hospital."

I wasn't sure what to think. This was the patient who had visions, who threw bedpans at windows. Why would Mother Morevna possibly want her here?

Nurse Ada soon gathered her things and left but just before she closed the church door behind her, she turned and handed me what looked like a small stack of postcards folded in half.

"This was in Mother Morevna's pocket when she fell," said Nurse Ada. "Just some water rations, but they're Dowsing Well ones, so I figured just in case."

I looked down at the folded rations, puzzled. What did Mother Morevna need rations for? We had all we needed at the church. I unfolded the papers. There were five of them in all. Good for a month. All of them seemed to have a black smudge at one corner, but it was probably a misprint. She was most likely going to take them to the office or something before the storm hit. I'd give it back to her later.

• • •

For the next three days, the doors and windows of the Robertson house were closed and shuttered. Asa Skander was nowhere to be found. Not on his soapbox, not walking around, exploring Elysium. But he was never far from my thoughts. What he had done, how he had essentially had to jump in and save me, had humbled me more than I cared to admit. And something like anger was steadily growing inside me. *Simple magician my eye!* And what's more, the townspeople had just . . . accepted him? Just like that. And how long had he had magic, anyway? Was he a witch too? Could men even *be* witches? There was something funny going on. And whatever the case, I wasn't about to let him humiliate me again, not after I had worked so hard and endured so much. I had been chosen, after all, and despite my reputation, despite Mother Morevna, despite everyone, I was the Successor. And I was going to be ready for that role if it killed me.

Then there was the matter of the thieves. So while Mother Morevna convalesced, I practiced my magic in case they attacked again. In case I needed to act. I practiced channeling energy, finding things that were lost, breathing fire. My brain hurt from constant practice with runes and sigils. My fingers hurt too and were often caked in the various dusts that I needed to cast certain spells. There was a greater fire spell that I learned that burned my fingers black when I miscast it.

I was still wiping the soot from my hands when I went

downstairs and saw Lucy, pretty and well-dressed as always, but carefully makeupless, waiting outside Mr. Jameson's office.

"Been burning something?" she said. "You smell like smoke."

"Fire spell," I said, wiping my hands again. "I can do all kinds of things now. I can make a whirlwind, a giant flame, and . . . Wait, why are you here?"

She shifted in her seat.

"I'm here to fill out a water ration request form," she said. "My aunt Lucretia is coming down with Dust Sickness, we think. We need to change her water from the normal well to the Dowsing Well. We're hoping it might still be early enough to fight it off."

"Oh no," I said, thinking how frivolous my spellwork must have sounded. "I'm so sorry, Lucy. I haven't seen Mr. Jameson, or else I'd go get him for you. Do you . . ." I dropped my voice to a whisper. "Do you want me to break in for you? I will if you want me to."

"That was fine back then, but you're the Successor now," Lucy said. "What kind of friend would I be if I risked your reputation like that?" My heart jumped a little at the word "friend." Is that what we were now?

Lucy sighed. "I'm probably waiting around for nothing, anyway. I hear Jameson doesn't even grant these requests to white people. But still. Sometimes I wish someone would just *lose* some extra ones close to the house. Then I could just pick 'em up and not feel like I was stealing."

But someone *had* lost some.

"Wait a minute!" I said. "Stay right there!" I shot up and ran as quietly as I could upstairs, tiptoeing past the locked door to my own room, where the stack of water rations the nurse had given me was still sitting on my bedside table. I grabbed it and ran back down to Lucy.

"Here," I said, shoving the rations into her hands. "Take these."

"Jesus, Sal! Where did you get these?" She looked at them like each one was a hundred-dollar bill. "This is enough for more than a month!"

"Just take them," I said. "They're for one person too, so they should be fine for your aunt. And this makes up for me not being able to get water for you myself anymore."

"Are you sure?"

I hesitated. Mother Morevna had dropped them, but I reminded myself, they couldn't have been hers. She had probably been on her way to Mr. Jameson's office herself and forgotten. And Lucy's aunt had Dust Sickness. How could I refuse her after what had happened to Mama?

"Yeah," I said. "I'm sure."

Lucy suddenly threw her arms around me and held me in the sweetest-smelling hug I'd ever had. "Thank you," she said. "So much." Then the hug was over, and Lucy stuffed the rations into her bag. "You don't know how much this means to my family. You're the real miracle worker, Sal. Not Asa Skander."

Asa Skander. All the warmth and pride went out of me like air from a balloon.

She rolled her eyes. "Asa this, Asa that. People acting like he's some kind of messiah, here to help heal the Sick and lead us out of the desert. You'd think they'd have learned their lesson by now. People are even slacking off in their duties, thinking he'll save us all. They only got fifteen barrels of corn done yesterday. Fifteen when they should be getting fifty."

So it was worse than I thought. If people thought of Asa as a messiah, what must they think of me? How would they ever see me as anything but a weak, scared false prophet now? And if they were banking on a miracle, how would we ever harvest enough to please the Dust Soldiers?

"People love a mystery," she said almost apologetically. "But you did half that spell. And I'll make sure to tell everybody what a good job you're doing."

"Thanks," I said. "Really."

"Well, I'd better get going," she said. "Try not to worry about Asa. Everything will sort itself out. You know, you should go see him. Go and talk it out."

"Maybe I should," I said. My penny thrummed against my breastbone. "Maybe I will. It couldn't make things worse, I guess. Thanks, Lucy." I stood there for a moment, unsure of what to do. Hug her goodbye? Wave? I felt like I needed to do something. "Well . . ." I said finally. "See you later, I guess."

"Wait a minute," she said, grabbing my wrist. She pulled me back and stopped me in front of her, looked up at me in a scrutinizing sort of way that made my heart give a sudden, strange thud. Then she reached up and tucked a piece of my hair behind my ears.

"There you go, girl." She smiled. "Pretty as a picture."

Then, with a flounce of her bright flour-sack skirt, she turned and headed back out into the streets, leaving me fighting back a blush.

No one had ever called me pretty before.

CHAPTER 9

3 MONTHS AND *15 DAYS* REMAIN.

Asa had been hiding for three days—far longer than it had taken to rebuild his body. He had lain there, half-corporeal on the bloodstained floor, unable to think or feel, and when he woke again, his stomach was nearly turning itself inside out with hunger. He rose gingerly and ate a pound of raw salt pork rations in one gulp. He followed this with six eggs, shells and all, and drank nearly a case of water rations before he stopped to catch his breath.

Asa went to the bathroom, washed up, and pulled on a clean set of clothes. In the mirror, he looked thin, wan, used up. He didn't feel 100 percent better, but he ran a comb through his hair anyway and put on his spectacles with the shattered lens. Magic was no joke. It regenerated, of course, but he would have to pace himself better next time. And on top of all of it, the people of Elysium just wouldn't leave him alone.

When he opened his door the morning after the dust storm, there had been a crowd of people on his doorstep.

"Can I help you?" Asa asked.

But they'd all begun speaking at once, shouting, clamoring as they pushed forward.

"Help us, please!" they cried. "Use your magic!"

"My daughter is Dust Sick!" one woman said, grabbing his hand and squeezing it in hers. "Can you please come and see her? Come and heal her!"

"I'm sorry, ma'am." Asa pulled his hand from hers. "But I . . . My magic doesn't work like . . ."

"We know what you can do!" she shouted. "You can do what even Mother Morevna can't! You've been sent to help us all! To get us out of this mess!"

"I—I don't know about that, ma'am!" he said. "I'm just a magician! I—I can do a little magic here and there, but I'm just a magician! I—"

But the crowd didn't want to see a trick. They wanted real magic. Powerful, impossible magic. They wanted a way out of this terrible, miserable Game, once and for all.

"Help us!" shouted a man in the crowd. "Lead us out of this desert! We believe!"

"We believe!" they chanted. "We believe!"

Everyone was so close. Too close. Asa sent a pulse of magic and sent them staggering. Then he ran back inside and shuttered all the windows, locked the doors. Terrified, he crawled under the kitchen table and waited for the people to leave. For the next two days, he'd barely moved, except to slink to the kitchen to eat and make coffee. And though the crowds had dwindled to only one or two visitors per day, there had been a number of letters and notes slipped under his door, no doubt requesting some kind of supernatural aid he had no authority to give.

So when he heard someone knock on his door, Asa held his breath and waited for whoever it was to go away.

"I know you're in there," said a female voice. "And you and I need to talk."

Uh-oh, Asa thought. *Maybe if I slip out the window?*

"It's Sal Wilkerson," the girl said, getting irritated. "The one who let you in! So return the favor!"

He supposed she was right. Asa crawled out from under the table and went to the door. He opened it a crack and looked outside. Sal Wilkerson was standing on the porch with her hands on her hips, looking unhappy.

"Is anyone else out there?" he asked, eyes darting. "Are they looking for me?"

"If you mean the crowd of people standing around your soapbox, yes," she said. "But they're not around right now. I guess I scared them off. So let me in. We need to talk."

"Oh, thank goodness," Asa said. "If you're coming in, hurry." He opened the door, and Sal hesitated for a second, looking past him into his dark, bloodstained house; then she darted inside.

She looked around, her expression a mixture of curiosity and horror.

"So what brings you around here?" Asa said, doing his best to slick his hair back down. "What do you need to talk to me about? More questions about quarters? Or maybe nickels or dimes?"

"Obviously you weren't honest with me before, so I'm going

to ask you outright, one more time: What is going on? Why did you really come here?"

"Like I said at the gate and in the cell, I am stuck here." Asa crossed his arms as he'd seen humans do when they were being obstinate. "That's it."

"Fine, don't tell me," said Sal. "But know that you've made my life way more difficult than it had to be. Running up there and fixing everything—"

"Are you . . . *mad* at me?" Asa asked. "For saving you?"

"Yes," Sal said. "And, I mean . . . no. But—"

"I just wanted to help," Asa said. "You needed help and I thought I was doing the right thing and . . ." A sudden, awful thought. "Did I do something bad?"

"It's not that it was *bad* bad. It's just . . ." She paused, looking for the right words. "It's not what it's supposed to be, you know? I don't know if you know about my past, but I've been through a lot. And it's a really big deal to me that I'm the Successor. That I got the chance for people to trust me again. And then you came along, and you're new and powerful and . . . you have no idea how hard I worked only for you to come in and undo so much all at once."

"But you're the Successor!" Asa protested. "Surely the people see you as that."

"That's what I'm supposed to be," Sal said. "And I've been working so hard to be what they need me to be. What *I* feel like I need to be. But here, people have one impression of you and you stay whatever that is in their minds forever. It takes a miracle to change minds here." She looked at Asa. "And when you saved me, it kind of undermined all that. It made me look bad and it made you look . . ."

"Like a threat," Asa groaned. "A threat to your power. Oh no . . . I've disrupted everything."

That's why the people of Elysium were at his door. They were looking to *him* as their leader now and not who they were supposed to be looking to. He had really messed things up this time.

"That's the last thing I intended," he said. "I'm not here to try and . . . and usurp anybody's power! I'm just trying to figure things out right now. Make the best of my situation. And I don't want everyone at my door, thinking I can do miracles! I don't want this! What can I do?"

Sal blinked. "So you're not some messiah sent to lead us out of the desert?"

"Of course not!" said Asa. "I'm as shocked as you are!"

Sal took a moment to digest this; then finally she spoke.

"Look," said Sal. "I believe you when you say you didn't intend to disrupt Elysium or whatever. But the damage has been done. Mother Morevna's authority and mine have been undermined, and I know what that's like. When the people think there's some way out of here, they stop focusing. When the people aren't focused, they can't be productive, and if they can't be productive, we can't produce enough for the harvest, and if we don't, then everybody dies." She took a deep breath. "And it's my job as the Successor to help make sure that doesn't happen."

It was a very bleak picture, indeed. Asa felt something that must be regret, maybe mixed with a little bit of shame, wash over him.

"So what do we do?" Asa asked.

"We have to find a way to set things straight again so we can get back to . . . what we're really supposed to be doing."

"Sounds good to me," Asa said. "But how do we do that?"

"I don't know," said Sal. "But we've got to figure something out. Soon."

They sat there at the table for a few tense, awkward moments. Then Sal got an odd look in her eyes and said, "You don't have any books here, do you?"

"I sure do!" he said. He bent and picked up his corner of the kitchen table and pulled out the worn, bent paperback book he'd been using to level it. "I took this out to try and read it the other day, but . . ." He shrugged. "I'm more of an F. Scott Fitzgerald type, I think."

Sal held the filthy book by its corner, looking at its cover. "*Brothers of the Western Sage*," she read, raising a skeptical eyebrow. She shrugged. "Well, it's better than nothing, I guess."

She put the book down on the table, then spilled some salt from the saltshaker into her hand. A feeling of electricity began to surge around her. Magic, Asa knew. He leaned forward to get a better look.

"What are you doing?" he asked.

"Rhapsodomancy," she said. "Mother Morevna told me about it once. It's a kind of divination where you ask a question, then open a book, and whatever line you put your finger to answers your question. Or it's supposed to. I've never tried it before."

She looked down at the book. "Here goes nothing," she said. She closed her eyes and dropped a pinch of salt over the book. Asa felt a strong surge of magic, heard her whisper something under her breath. Then the book's pages began to turn, flipping faster and faster, until the book suddenly stopped its page riffling and fell open. The magic ceased its surging, and Sal opened her eyes. Then they looked down at the open book together. There on the page was a black-and-white illustration of two cowboys in the street, hands hovering over their gun belts, with a quote beneath it.

"'. . . and the two of them took to the dusty streets to settle things the cowboy way,'" Asa read.

He paused, feeling a little sorry for Sal. "Well . . . I thank you for trying, I suppose, but the two of us are anything but cowboys. Maybe *Frankenstein* next time? Or *Moby Dick*?"

But Sal's eyes were alight with an inner flame that was a little intimidating.

"The cowboy way . . ." she said softly. "Of course." Suddenly, she pulled another, tiny book from her pocket and opened it, riffling through its pages. "Aha!" she said. "I thought I'd seen that somewhere! It's perfect!"

"What?" Asa asked, feeling suddenly nervous. "What's perfect?"

"A duel," Sal said, her eyes glowing. "We can have a duel!"

Asa's mind was suddenly filled with images of cowboys facing each other in dusty streets, crying "Draw!" and shooting, falling to the ground to lie twitching as their blood sank into the dust.

Asa gulped. "Well, you see, I'm kind of a . . . er . . . conscientious objector when it comes to guns. . . ."

"No, I mean a *Witches'* Duel," she said. "'A Witches' Duel is a time-honored way of settling disputes between witches when there does not seem to be another alternative.'" She read on a little ways, then said, "'Despite its name, a Witches' Duel, is not necessarily deadly and is over when one witch has displayed her dominance over another. . . .' You see? It's perfect."

"So you just want to . . . to duel out in the street?" Asa said.

"No," Sal said. "I want to fake a duel. I want to rig the duel so I win. Then the people will see that I'm the stronger witch and maybe they'll leave you alone."

Asa considered this. A duel was one thing, but a fake duel was another. A fake duel was a performance, just like his magic shows. Harmless. Entertaining. He nodded.

"I'll do it," he said. Then he had a sudden, sobering thought. "Won't Mother Morevna object to something like that?"

Sal furrowed her brows and went quiet. Mother Morevna. She gave the impression of a woman who liked to be in control. And she certainly wouldn't allow something like a duel to happen on her watch.

"I'll see what I can do," Sal said finally. But the fire in her eyes hadn't gone out. "You just wait for word from me, all right?" she said. "And thank you."

And with that, Sal rose from the table and headed back outside, leaving Asa in his kitchen, holding his cowboy book, wondering what on earth he'd just gotten himself into.

• • •

The light went on in Lloyd Jameson's bedroom—the light that would only come on if Miss Ibarra was doing as expected and the whole idea wasn't some magical flimflam. Jameson rolled out of bed and pulled on some trousers. He snugged into his boots and pulled his shotgun down from its spot on the wall. His jaw was set. His eyes were grave. He did not look at the photograph of his wife and daughter, standing in front of their ranch in Amarillo. He did not.

But he did look up at the church, at the window where Miss Ibarra was wide-awake and shouting to wake the dead. Across the hall from her, he saw a light come on in Sal's room. He saw Sal, carrying a kerosene lamp, head out into the hall, probably to try and comfort the woman. That would be like her. Then, through the hall window, he saw Mrs. Winthrop come up the stairs and shoo Sal back into her room. After a moment, the kerosene light went out. But Sal wouldn't be asleep. Not after that. He sighed. He'd have to tell Sal about her one day. But not today.

Mr. Jameson strapped his rifle onto his back and looked out into the night. Making his breaths and boots as quiet as he could, he pushed open his door and slipped out into the dark streets. From his place in the night, he scanned the walls, looking through narrowed eyes for something, anything out of the ordinary.

And then he saw it.

Up on the wall, a shadow moved. It was smaller than a man, larger than a child. Familiar. And it too was good at moving quietly. It had scaled the wall with a rope and pulled the rope up behind it. Then it secured the rope on the lip of the wall and crawled down. Were there more? Jameson felt like there were—there had to be. No one could survive in the desert alone. But if there were, they didn't follow. This shadow, solitary, slipped down the wall. Then it pulled the rope free, caught it, and coiled it around its torso. As it turned, Jameson could see that it had a dark bandanna around its face and a satchel on its back. It looked one way, then another, then darted directly under a guard tower and hid in the shadow of a nearby house.

Jameson looked up at the guard tower. The guard, young Joe McPherson, was asleep and drooling, his arm dangling down at his side. Jameson almost cussed him; then he saw the others. All the other guards in all the other towers—or at least all the ones Jameson could see—were fast asleep. A dreamy blue silence had fallen, hanging around each tower like a low cloud.

"Goddamn magic," Jameson muttered. That's what it had to be, after all. Only magic could do something like that. And this wasn't good. This complicated things. He loaded his shotgun and followed the shadow.

It slid from dark place to dark place, weaving through streets and under clotheslines. Jameson followed at a distance, watching to see what it did. It kept moving, past the church and toward the building that housed the sacrifice to the Dust Soldiers.

Just like the guards in the towers, the guards placed at the front of the doors were slumped down, asleep in the dust. *A damn powerful spell,* Jameson thought, *to work over such a distance.* The shadow slipped between them soundlessly, pulling the keys from the pocket of the one on her right—the shadow was a *her* now, he knew—and fitting the key neatly into the lock.

It clicked and the shadow disappeared into the yawning darkness, shutting the door behind her. For a moment there was a glow under the door—Mother Morevna's trapdoor spell, perhaps. Then it went dark again. She'd gotten past the circle somehow.

Jameson slunk closer. He had options. He could trap the thief inside the building—there was only one way out, after all. That would be the easiest thing. Perhaps the smartest thing. But it somehow didn't seem fair. And if the thief was who he thought she was, it didn't answer any of his questions. No, he would see what she did.

He sat still, holding his gun out of sight, watching the guards snooze, their breaths stirring little puffs of dust. Then the door opened, and the thief emerged. She adjusted her bandanna and shrugged her satchel over her shoulder. It had weight now; there was something in it. She looked down at the guards, put the key back into its respective pocket, and slunk onward into a shadow across from Jameson. She looked over her shoulder, toward the hospital, its many-eyed form dark in the night, then slunk onward, back through the path she had taken.

She moved faster, running now, as quietly as possible. Shadow to shadow to shadow, and Jameson followed, keeping his careful distance. She ran to the base of the lowest wall, threw the rope up and over. She pulled until the hook stuck in place under the lip of the wall.

Jameson put his rifle to his shoulder.

She began to scale the wall, the sack slung over her back. She climbed, her eyes on the sleeping guards, who had begun to twitch and shift in their sleep. The spell was almost used up. She was nearly to the top.

Jameson closed one eye, looked down the barrel, focused. Pulled the trigger.

The bag on her shoulder ripped open, spilling its contents. The girl held on fast to the rope, paused for just a moment to see if she'd been shot. Then she scrambled to the top of the wall, grabbed the rope, and threw herself over, back out into the desert.

Down the barrel of his gun, Jameson watched her go; then he left the shadows to see what had fallen from her bag.

A few seemingly random things lay broken and spoiled in the dust. Cakes of cattle salt, a busted jar of honey, garlic, homemade vinegar, tea leaves. Any of these things wouldn't have been strange, but all of them together made Jameson narrow his eyes. Medicine. *She was going to make medicine. So that meant that Mother Morevna's curse had worked the first time: It had made someone sick. But why hadn't this one fallen ill? Was this a different robber?*

He heard the slapping of boots against the dust. "We . . . we've been robbed!" panted one of the Sacrifice guards. "Again! I . . . I don't know how, boss, I promise!"

"No, we haven't," said Jameson. He pointed to the debris on the ground.

"Wh-where is the thief?" asked the guard, confused eyes darting and white in the darkness.

"Don't worry," Jameson said, his eyes on the wall where she'd disappeared. "She'll be back."

CHAPTER 10

3 MONTHS AND 14 DAYS REMAIN.

When I woke, light was filtering in through the curtain, and my head ached from too little sleep. But the Booke was open to the place where I had left it, and the penny gave a thrum of encouragement. Quickly, I dressed and put the Booke in my pocket. When I stepped outside to head to the bathroom, the room across from mine was as quiet as ever. I gave the door one last glance, then started down the stairs, my boots magically silent. Then the sound of voices from the sanctuary stopped me.

"They got magic," Mr. Jameson was saying. "That's how they get in. They put the guards to sleep and just slip in—right past that magic circle of yours. I'm telling you, they got some real magic, and not like before, when—"

"As intrigued as I am about this fact, I am more interested in why you allowed one of them to escape when you had a clear chance to catch her."

I crept down the stairs until I could see them. Mother Morevna was walking back and forth in front of an enormous stack of water rations and marking things on a list.

"I didn't let her steal anything," Jameson was saying. "And besides, they'll be back."

"And what makes you say that?"

"One or some of 'em are sick," Mr. Jameson said. "The things she was stealing, they're all ingredients for medicine I've made myself out there."

"Seems the trapdoor spell took hold, then," Mother Morevna said. "Pity it didn't get all of them."

Trapdoor spell.

I vaguely remembered reading something about trapdoor spells further back in the Booke. They could be set up from anywhere, but they relied on a Master Stone that you charged your power into. Multiple spells could be charged into one Master Stone too, or so I'd read. These were Mother Morevna's specialty. I wondered how many more trapdoor spells were laid around the city, how many I walked over every day.

"But it got at least one of 'em good, and they must be desperate to save them if they're risking coming back now." He cleared his throat. "This might be our chance."

"What are you suggesting?" Mother Morevna asked.

"I'm suggesting that we make it easy for them to come back if we want to catch them. We gotta give them the opportunity."

Mother Morevna paused, considered this. I began to back away.

"Sallie," Mother Morevna said. "Come out here. I'd like to talk to you. Jameson, you may go."

"Yes, ma'am," Mr. Jameson said. "But just think about it, ma'am." He tipped his hat as he passed me in the hallway.

Mother Morevna stood there in the light, her eyes and cheeks looking more hollow than ever. When she spoke, it seemed that even her voice creaked with weariness.

"After the events of the dust storm, I must admit, I am not all that I should be," she said. "I suppose it is fortunate that you have been taking matters into your own hands up until now."

My heart gave a single jackrabbit jump. Was she admitting that she had been wrong not to really train me? But I could tell by the steeliness of her eyes that this was a very serious matter. She went on.

"I have heard all about this Asa Skander business," she said. "How he finished the spell for you after I fell unconscious. I must admit, I did know he had a bit of magic power when we interrogated him—sometimes this happens with men, though it is rare—but I did not estimate it to be to such a degree, and this troubles me. Have you spoken to him since?"

"Yes, ma'am," I said. "People are hounding him now. They won't leave him alone. He's locked himself in the Robertson house and won't come out."

"A bit fed up with celebrity, is he?" Mother Morevna said. "A shame, I'm sure. But this young man is proving to be more trouble than he's worth. We cannot afford for production to drop lower than it has already."

We, she was saying. *We* and not *I.* "I think I found a way to solve everything," I said. Nervously, I told her about the duel, about our plan to have him throw the duel in my favor. And, surprisingly, Mother Morevna listened intently. When I reached the end of my explanation, I could see that cunning spark she usually wore in the place of the weariness that had been there before.

"And you're certain that he'll go through with it?" she said finally.

"Yes, ma'am," I said. "I think he's prepared to do anything right now. If we made it a big event, maybe we could make the whole town believe."

She was trusting me. Despite the fact that Asa had been the one to cast the spell, she was finally trusting me. I wanted to do more, to prove that I could be everything she ever needed, to prove that she did need a Successor. That she did need me. Then a sudden, dangerous thought came to me.

"We could use the same event to catch the thieves," I heard myself say. She turned to me and I faltered. "I—I couldn't help overhearing that we needed to give them a reason to come. And since they last came during a big, public event, I thought . . . why not kill two birds with one stone?"

Mother Morevna raised her cold gray eyes to mine, her expression unreadable.

"That is brilliant," she said.

My heart thudded in disbelief. "It is?" I said, still reeling. "Th-thank you."

"Yes." She rose, a fire in her eyes that I hadn't seen before. "Go to the Robertson house and inform Asa Skander that the two of you have approval for your duel," she said. "And don't tell him about the trap element. That is to remain between us, do you understand?"

"Yes, ma'am," I said. And feeling as though I was walking on air, I headed to the Robertson house.

• • •

The sun was setting over the walls as Lucy Arbor sat on the steps of the hospital. The rest of her family was inside, standing around Aunt Lucretia's hospital bed, but Lucy couldn't make herself go in. She couldn't see her aunt like this. She had seen Dust Sickness take its grip on many people since the walls went up, and it was always jarring and terrible. But never was it so terrifying as when it bent the features of someone you loved, when they coughed and their handkerchief came away covered with bloody mud. She knew now how Sal must have felt. How she still felt, because now that she had gotten a taste of this pain, there was no forgetting it.

She pulled out the water rations Sal had given her. Five trips to the Dowsing Well in all, and still Dust Sickness had crept up and grabbed her aunt by the throat.

Lucy wiped a tear away with a subtly manicured hand.

She could still pull through, Lucy told herself. Though as far as she knew, no one ever had. They'd just managed to stay alive longer than anyone thought, depending on how much Dowsing Well water they'd been given.

The door opened behind her, and she scooted to one side as Mr. Jameson, sad-faced as ever, walked down the stairs and out of the hospital. He had a stack of papers in his hand: water rations for the Dust Sick. A lot of good it was doing anybody. Miguel at school had said that Dowsing Well water didn't do anything different from normal water, that that was just something people hoped for so they could feel better. And now, despite the rations in her hand, the ones straight from Sal herself, Lucy was beginning to believe him. She turned the stack of rations over in her hand, looking at the smudges on their corners. So regular and uniform, almost like they'd been put there. And this other paper that had come with them, she thought, scanning a finger down the column of symbols. What was it?

But before she could think too much about it, there was a crackling of magic, and Mother Morevna's voice boomed over all of Elysium.

"I would like to make an announcement. On Wednesday evening, on the twenty-fifth, ten days from tonight, a very special event will be hosted outside the church. A Witches' Duel between newcomer Asa Skander and our own Successor, Sallie Wilkerson."

Lucy looked up.

"The duel will be friendly in nature, an exhibition of magical talent and skill to bolster and amaze in these final few months before our Judgment. Attendance will be mandatory. Thank you."

There was another crackle and the announcement ended. Sal? In a duel? Lucy couldn't imagine that. Not even a friendly duel. Sal was too shy and awkward for that kind of thing, she always had been. Come to think of it, Lucy had never seen Sal stand up to anybody, much less in front of the whole town. That had always been her job, though she wasn't sure if Sal knew. Lucy had protected Sal more times than she could count. And now what a sight it would be to see Sal, the girl who was bullied by Trixie Holland, the Girl Who Cried Rain, throwing magic in a duel! Even though her heart was still weighed down with worry, Lucy almost smiled. Then her mother called her back inside.

Aunt Lucretia needed more water.

CHAPTER 11

3 MONTHS REMAIN.

The next ten days flew by in a rush of dust and blood and flames. Every day, I practiced with Asa in the sanctuary of the church, and every night, I practiced by myself on the roof. He had an odd style with magic, a theatrical flourish that was nothing like the calm elegance of Mother Morevna's magic, nor the wild desperate flailing of mine. The spells we choreographed were fiery, showy, loud, and impressive to watch. And as the days wore on, we grew good at them. Still, nervousness rose in my stomach like bile, and on the night before the duel, it was all I could do to keep myself from vomiting into the washbasin. Once more, I looked over the carefully choreographed order of spells Asa and I had worked out over correspondence. Just to be sure.

A—light beam (miss S by 5").
S—counter w/dust wall.
A—raise ground.
S—avoid (jump left), send whirlwind.

A—let whirlwind pick up, throw. Land and send fire projectile.
S—block fire projectile, send back to A.

Finale:

A—pretend to be burned.
S—"heal" A.
A—congratulate S.

According to the order of spells, Asa would attempt some weak magic, which would miss me. I would throw him a dust spell, he'd counter, then I'd throw him around a bit with my wind spell. Then he'd pretend to be angry and throw a fire spell at me when I "wasn't looking," and I'd turn just in time to send it back to him. This was the piece we considered most carefully. He had to throw magic at me when I wasn't looking so he could stop seeming like a nice guy and seem more like . . . well, a heel. I'd whirl around, send the spell back to him, and he would pretend to be hurt by it. Then I, the benevolent Successor of Elysium, would say a few magic-sounding words, and he'd "heal" himself, giving me all the credit, and we'd both leave happy.

Two birds with one stone.

I stood and paced the room. Then I stopped in front of the standing mirror. My new spell components belt and all its pouches hung from my waist like a gun belt. A gun belt that held the dusts and feathers and shells I would need for spell casting, rather than six-shooters.

"Looks like we're settling things the cowboy way," I said to my reflection. But Mother Morevna said that all witches wore these for duels. Asa would have one as well.

I reached into my pouch and pulled out a bit of white dust.

"Ventus proiectum," I whispered, and blew the dust from my fingertips as though I were blowing a kiss. A small, very powerful blast of air scattered the papers from my desk all around the room. I smiled. I'd pick them up later.

From books of Mother Morevna's, I'd learned to use my flame spell as a projectile, like a flamethrower, to create a whirlwind powerful enough to send someone flying into the air, and, most importantly, to create a shield of dust that stopped or slowed nearly anything. I felt completely drained and usually threw up after practice every morning, but even I had to admit that what I'd learned was pretty impressive. Why then did it feel like rabbits were running around and around in my belly?

I heard a loud noise from the hallway, a thudding, then shouting. Miss Ibarra across the hall was at it again. It sounded like she was jumping in there, jumping and shouting.

"¡Ella vendrá!" She shouted happily. *"¡Ella vendrá esta noche! ¡Ella vendrá esta noche!"*

I opened my door.

About this time, I heard footsteps and turned. This time it was Mother Morevna standing there in her long black nightgown, looking like the very Grim Reaper in the dark hallway.

"Get back in your room, Sallie," she said. "You've got a big day ahead of you tomorrow."

"Why is she in there?" I heard myself ask, emboldened maybe by Mother Morevna's newfound approval of me.

"I am helping treat her visions," Mother Morevna said. "Now get to your room. We will discuss this tomorrow after the duel. Do as I say!"

She took a key from her pocket and unlocked the door. The shouting grew louder when she opened it. Inside it was dark, but I saw the vague shape of a young woman silhouetted against the window.

"Now, now, now, dear," Mother Morevna was saying. "That's quite enough."

Moments later, Miss Ibarra stopped shouting. She just went silent. I stood with my eye at my door, but I couldn't see anything in the dark hallway. I pulled the door shut, listening to Mother Morevna's footsteps down the hall and down the stairs again. When I heard her in her room above me, I opened my door again.

"Hey," I whisper-shouted at the closed door across the hall. "Are you all right in there?"

No answer.

"My name . . . er . . . me llamo? Or estoy? . . . *Soy* Sal Wilkerson," I tried again, trying to remember all the Spanish I could from grade school. "¿Cómo estás?"

Again, silence. I stood in the hall for a few moments more, but the woman in the room across from mine did not stir. After a few moments, I went back into my room and shut the door behind me, trying as hard as I could to focus on tomorrow or magic or sleep. But when sleep finally came, it was fitful, and tinged with the faraway smell of rain.

• • •

Lloyd Jameson sat in his chair on his front porch, trying not to think of the duel tomorrow. He spat—*plink*—into his peach can and went over it again, searing the guards' and *decoy* guards' posts into his mind. This was not, after all, a simple event, and he felt heavy with the weight of Mother Morevna's expectations. Tomorrow would be the day, he was sure of it. The day he had to put an end to those thieves, once and for all, no matter how he felt about it.

It had surprised him that Sal had thought of the plan. It was so unlike the timid, guilty-looking girl he'd been helping all these years. But if he thought about it, really thought about it, he had seen how much the girl had been mirroring Mother Morevna. He'd seen her begin to walk taller, affect some of the prim elegance Mother Morevna had when she moved, had seen her begin to grow cunning.

Jameson sighed and let himself think of his own family, his own daughter back in Texas. She'd be tall like him, maybe. Blond, like Sal. Would she remember his face? he wondered. He hadn't forgotten hers. But it seemed like her features and Sal's features had begun to bleed into each other a little, blend a little in his mind, until he couldn't be sure he was remembering his daughter correctly or not. He shook himself. This damned place with all its dust. He shouldn't even be here. He should be back in Texas. And if they ever got out of this godforsaken desert, Texas was the first place he'd go. Hell, even when Oklahoma had been what it was supposed to be, it was not what Texas was. Not to him. But he supposed that when one was born in Texas, raised in Texas, that Texas-ness never left. It was his reality.

He spat again into his peach can. He couldn't allow himself to think like that for too long. Reality now was endless cracked sand, skeleton cars half submerged in the dust, stripped of anything useful. Air-rippling heat, endless thirst. And the creatures . . . he shuddered.

The fire coyotes, with their earth-blackening flames, were the first to spring to mind, always. But there were so many more things out there, strange things, things that Jameson dreamed of so often that he tried not to sleep. The tar-like black blobs he'd seen, skittering across the sand on little pale fingers. The pale, three-foot-long worms that passed beneath the soil and built cone-shaped nests like ant lions, surfacing only to eat the scorpions or horned toads that fell into them. The shadows that rippled in between the heat waves and disappeared, waiting, into one's own shadow, to leap up and pull a man down into the sand, down to death. There was no hope beyond the walls. This he knew better than anyone. And if there was no hope beyond the walls, what did that mean for everyone inside the walls? Was it only a matter of time? Were they fooling themselves thinking they could ever escape a place like this with their lives and souls intact? Jameson just didn't know.

Six o'clock. Less than twenty-four hours until the duel.

Above him, the banners snapped in the night wind. It was gaudier than any Mourning Night he'd ever seen. And with the announcements blaring over the desert—*"A reminder that on Wednesday evening, everyone is expected to be in attendance at the duel," "A reminder that the duel will begin promptly at six," "A reminder that the searchlight on the northwest side is broken, please do not fear on the night of the duel"*—he was certain that all the hullaballoo had not escaped the thieves' attention. Half of him hoped that the thieves would recognize it as the threat that it was and not dare to show their faces.

But just as that hope crystallized in his mind, the light came on. Miss Ibarra was awake. And if she was up and shouting, throwing herself against the walls, that could only mean one thing: The thieves had gotten their message. They were going to climb those walls, right in front of his rifle.

"There's no stopping it now," Mr. Jameson murmured, his voice heavy with disgust. Then, with a final glance up at the night sky, Mr. Jameson emptied his peach can and went back inside.

CHAPTER 12

2 MONTHS AND 29 DAYS REMAIN.

Outside, the pennants fluttered to and fro, faded but cheerful against the dull sky. It was so overcast that barely any sunset orange showed through. If I didn't know any better, I might have thought that it meant rain. But I did know better, and as I stood at the window of the sanctuary, looking out, I went over the order of mine and Asa's spells, my hands moving along with the words.

But something felt off. Was it that my dresses were tighter than usual from all the good food I'd been having? Or maybe because my hair was out of its usual braids and up into a bun to keep it from catching on fire? My penny lay against my breastbone, thrumming with magic or my nerves, or both. But this was it. There was no going back.

Nervously, I looked outside.

A poster on a nearby wall proclaimed: *SAL WILKERSON VS. ASA SKANDER. 6:00 Wednesday evening.*

Fifteen minutes from now.

The fight of the century! I thought, imagining the two of us with boxing gloves and him with ketchupy fake blood to squirt when I socked him in the jaw. But boxing was one thing. Magic was another. And the rest of it . . . the trap . . . only made everything more nerve-racking.

But Mother Morevna knew what she was doing. No, I thought, *I* knew what *I* was doing. And this time, neither of us would lose.

All around the walls, the white stones Mother Morevna had laid waited, smeared with their mixture of cats' blood and herbs, ready for her to say the word that would activate the trapdoor spell. To contain rather than to sicken this time. From there, the guards hanging just out of sight would descend and capture the thieves. They'd go to jail and we'd hold them there until after the Dust Soldiers had come, at which time we'd figure out something to do with them. Even if we had to stop the duel to do it, we'd come out looking good in the end. Trustworthy. Like good protectors.

Outside in the cleared-off space, the workmen were spilling Morton salt to make the circle that Asa and I would "duel" in. Mother Morevna appeared then from the upper floor. The woman in the room across from me had been absolutely crazy this morning. She'd thrown things against the wall and shouted in gleeful Spanish. *¡Hoy! ¡Hoy!* Once or twice I even heard her throwing herself against the door, trying to escape. Then Mother Morevna, darkly elegant in her best dress, had gone up a few minutes ago and the room went silent.

"She's asleep and will be asleep until morning," said Mother Morevna, coming to stand beside me at the window. She looked out at the banners and ribbons, her face wrinkled with disdain. She didn't mention Miss Ibarra again.

"With any luck, we'll be through with this spectacle in an hour or two; then we can go on with business as usual," she said.

"Business as usual," I murmured in agreement, straightening my back and drawing myself up to her height.

Outside, the people were trickling in from all sides of town, dressed as well as they could be. They stood in twos and threes, congregating animatedly, and even Mother Morevna couldn't ignore the buzz of excitement in the air. I knew then that many of the people would have come whether the duel had been mandatory or not.

Mr. Jameson walked by with three guards. He talked to them beneath the shadow of a windmill; then they scattered, heading up into their towers to wait. It was almost six o'clock. The dancers had already arrived and were getting ready for the jarabe tapatío number that they hadn't gotten the chance to do at Mourning Night. The choir could be heard in the distance, behind the chicken houses, warming up with the third verse of "Shall We Gather at the River?"

Asa appeared then, soundlessly, shuffling out from between two houses as though he had just materialized out of thin air. He was wearing a gray linen suit and striped bow tie. His glasses slipped to the end of his nose as he read the sheet of paper he was holding in front of him. He'd attempted to slick his hair down, but it was fighting its way up again, especially in the back, giving him the look of a rooster who had woken up and decided to become a rather paranoid-looking boy. He came to the back door of the church and knocked quietly, looking over his shoulder for would-be miracle seekers out to tackle him to the ground. Mother Morevna opened the door for him, and I could have sworn I saw him shudder once before entering the church.

"Good evening to you, Mr. Skander," Mother Morevna said stiffly. "It is good to see you looking well."

"Same to you, ma'am," he said. Then he nodded to me. "Sal."

"I trust that the two of you will not vary from the order that you have given me and Mr. Jameson, correct?" she said to both of us, her eyes flicking from Asa to me to Asa to me again.

"Yes, ma'am," we said together.

"Good," she said. "Perhaps we can get all of this cleared up once and for all."

We looked at each other, both equally nervous. Mrs. Anders came to the door then and knocked.

"We need a wind spell, ma'am," she told Mother Morevna. "The wind is low, and it keeps blowing the choir girls' skirts up."

"I'll be out in a moment," she said, sending Mrs. Anders away. She turned to us. "I'll leave the two of you to it. Do not do anything that differs from the plan, do you understand?" Here she looked at Asa. "Tread carefully, Mr. Skander. Tread carefully."

He gulped.

"Yes, ma'am," he said. Mother Morevna gave us one last look and went out to see if the choir was ready.

"Jeez, she's scary," said Asa, breaking the silence that had fallen between us. "I'm so nervous. I keep going over the list over and over."

"I barely slept last night," I told him. "I just went over all the spells."

"Can't be too well-practiced, eh?" Asa said. He took a deep breath and closed his eyes. "I almost wish it would start just so

I could get out of here. I feel hot under the collar. . . ." Then he squinted out the window. "What are those guards doing?"

The other guards—the real guards—were getting into their leather harnesses. One by one, they were raised to dangle beneath the lip of the wall, just out of sight, their guns in their hands. I saw one of them give Mr. Jameson a thumbs-up.

"Extra security," I told Asa. "In case the thieves try anything."

"It looks almost like you expect them to," Asa said.

"You can't be too prepared."

I tried to sound nonchalant, but the fact is that the trap made me nervous. It had been my idea, but now, seeing the guards with their rifles in hand, I wondered if it had been the right thing to propose. If it was the right thing to do. They had only been coming in for medicine last time, after all. . . .

The door opened, and Mother Morevna came back inside.

"It will begin in just a moment," she said. "Wait until I introduce the two of you."

"Yes, ma'am."

"Last but not least," she said, "here."

At first, I wasn't sure what she had given me. Then I nearly gasped.

It was one of the white stones for her trapdoor spells, like the one the thieves had triggered, and the ones she'd laid around the base of the wall to catch them today. If she was giving me one of these, did that mean that, finally, she trusted me as a witch? As her Successor?

"If something goes wrong today," she said. "If the thieves manage to get past Jameson, the guards, and myself, and you find yourself needing to undo one of my trapdoor spells, all you must do is smear the stone with your own blood and command it: 'Set it right.' Or, more accurately, 'Setzen Sie es richtig.' I find that my spells respond best to my family's original language."

"Setzen Sie es richtig," I said.

"Good," she said. "Now keep that in your pouches where no one can bother with it."

The people were all here now, all gathered outside the church. Everyone in Elysium: Black, white, brown, young, old, fat and thin. They stood together in front of the church, all around the circle of salt, looking on eagerly. One man even had a bag of peanuts. From under the nearest guard tower, behind the audience, Mr. Jameson pulled a white handkerchief from his pocket and blew his nose. The signal.

Mother Morevna opened the door and took the stage. The oil lamps around the circle lit themselves, and in the light that came dancing up at her, she looked mystical and ancient.

"Friends, it is so good to see you all here tonight," she said, her voice magically amplified. "I have the privilege now to open tonight's ceremonies and to introduce two of the finest young witches in Elysium."

The crowd applauded like people used to at football games or basketball games back before the walls went up. Like we were the event of the season. Mother Morevna raised her hands to quiet them.

"It will be a riveting event, I'm sure," she said, her eyes flickering up to the dark place on the northwestern wall, where the thieves would surely come. "But before we get to that, let's hear from Elysium's Mexican heritage dancing troupe, Las Mariposas!"

Seven little girls in yellow dresses took the stage, and their mothers pushed their way to the front of the crowd. The white-haired guitar teacher, Mr. Ramirez, strummed once, twice on the guitar, then launched into a fast, thumping song as the little girls flounced here and there, vibrant and smiling in their layers of fabric.

Suddenly, Asa leaned over and said, "You wouldn't happen to know who this belongs to, would you?"

He opened his pocket and something small and golden winked out at me from the bottom. A cricket suspended in amber.

"I . . . er . . . found this a while back, and I think somebody may have dropped it," he said. "It . . . uh . . . looks like it might be valuable."

"To a little boy who collects marbles or something, maybe," I said.

Outside, the girls smiled and spun in their frills.

"Sure . . ." said Asa. "I just, you know . . . want to make sure it gets back to its rightful owner is all." His yellowish eyes had a strange gleam to them, a seriousness that I hadn't seen before.

"That's nice of you, I suppose," I told him. "But we kind of have bigger fish to fry right now."

"Yes, but . . . I *really* want to get this back to the person it belongs to," Asa said. He seemed agitated somehow, nervous, as though the real matter on his mind was this trinket and the duel itself were an afterthought. "You're sure you haven't met anybody who's misplaced something like this?"

Was this really what he was worrying about right before the duel that could change so much for us? "I don't know if you know," I said, "but I'm not exactly Miss Congeniality around here."

He went quiet, looking even more nervous than ever. And nerves weren't good for duels.

"Okay, okay," I said. "If you want to find the owner of the thing, how about you show it right after I'm declared the winner? Everybody will be there. They're bound to see it then."

A change seemed to come over Asa then. His agitation melted like an ice cube, and he said, "That's a really good idea, Sal! Really good!" He clapped his hands once in triumph and turned to me excitedly, "And then . . . it'll all be over!"

"Yep . . ." I said, thinking once more how odd he was. "Then it'll all be over, all right."

Before I knew it, the little girls did a low curtsy and, after a few final chords from the old man with the guitar, bounced offstage and back to their mothers, who hugged them and straightened the flowers in their hair.

Mother Morevna stepped forward then to introduce the children's choir and Mrs. Anders. As they took the stage, their skirts seemed almost pulled downward against the wind. I looked at Asa. He wiped his palms on the front of his pants and dabbed at his forehead with a handkerchief.

"We're gonna be fine," I told him. "Just do it like we did all this week."

"Then we can return the cricket," Asa said.

"Jesus, what is it with you and this thing?" I hissed. "But sure. Then you'll find the owner of the cricket and I'll have everyone's faith and we'll . . . we'll go on with our lives."

The choir finished the last screechy notes of "On the Jericho Road," and the crowd clapped politely. Then Mother Morevna walked to the middle of the salt circle.

"And now," said Mother Morevna, "the moment we have all waited for. First, I will call forth a young man who needs no introduction: Asa Skander!"

"Go!" I whispered, and pushed him out the door.

The crowd applauded wildly when they saw Asa. There were even a few whistles here and there. He adjusted his glasses and looked sheepishly out at the audience, then took his place at the far left side of the circle.

"Second, my Successor, a gifted young witch with the will to take on any challenge, Sallie Wilkerson!" she boomed.

I took a deep breath and plunged through the door.

The crowd cheered but not nearly as loudly as they had for Asa. I felt my face grow hot. Across the circle Asa tipped his hat to me, looking even more like Harold Lloyd than usual.

"Ladies and gentlemen," Mother Morevna was saying, "I would like to remind everyone that in a Witches' Duel, the rules are quite similar to a wrestling match. One is only down if he or she stays down beyond the count—in this case to seven—so you may see these two young people fall and rise numerous times before we have a winner. But it is all perfectly safe, and by the end of what I hope is a spectacular event, we shall know, once and for all, who is the strongest young witch in Elysium, fitting to lead us as the game we're in continues: the magician, or the Successor!"

And with that, she bowed out of the circle and took her place beside the church. There, she would watch the match, but more importantly, she would watch the walls for the thieves' arrival.

I squared off, facing Asa from the far right side of the circle.

And we began.

First, Asa sank into a dramatic stance, put his hands out,

and from them he sent a beam of light toward me. The crowd whooped with delight.

I leapt to the left, and it missed me by a matter of inches, then fizzled into nothingness at the edge of the salt ring. My penny glowed. I reached into my far left pouch and pulled out a handful of black roller dust. I whispered the command and threw it into the air. Just as I had practiced it so many times, it thickened and lengthened into an opaque black wall surrounding me. The crowd shouted and hooted.

Asa sent a couple more weak light beams that ricocheted off the dust wall and fizzled out at the salt line. "Come on! Try something else!" someone yelled. Then, right on schedule, he raised the ground beneath me. It rumbled, split as the crowd gasped. Then one side of the split raised three feet in the air, and the other lowered, knocking me off my feet. My dust wall dissipated as my body fell through it. But just as we planned, I jumped back up just in time to catch the remainder of the dust wall and spin it into a whirlwind. It grew and grew between the two of us. Gasps went up in the crowd, and the people fell back. Then Asa pretended to be sucked into the swirling black vortex. Carefully, I tossed him to and fro inside the circle, my whirlwind shaking him like a dog shakes a toy. In the audience, Trixie Holland pouted in a way that meant I was more impressive than she wanted to admit. I smiled.

The guards suspended beneath the lip of the wall were moving. Sure enough, there were shadowy silhouettes on the wall, six of them, flitting across from the dark place where the spotlight had been deliberately disabled. Small, slight shadows like the one I had seen on Mourning Night. In their towers, the decoy guards were all sound asleep, bewitched with a sleeping spell just as Mr. Jameson had guessed, their guns hanging useless at their sides.

But beneath the walls, the real guards hadn't been touched by the spell. They were alert, and their guns were trained on the shadows as they began to descend into Elysium one by one, a rope of small black ants slipping down the wall. Underneath the windmill, Mr. Jameson flapped his handkerchief twice.

I saw Mother Morevna reach for the stone in her pocket. I saw the thin sparkle of her containment spell crackle overhead, an invisible dome of magic. Then she pulled out her own handkerchief and pretended to cover her nose with it.

I gave Asa another shake or two with my whirlwind and tossed him to the ground. He landed, crumpled, and as the crowd shouted, he rose to his feet, clutching his arm. Now would come the fire projectile. He'd send it at me, I'd send it back, and then it'd be over for both of us. Across the circle, Asa's eyebrows rose ever so slightly.

Are you ready? he was asking.

Nearly imperceptibly, I nodded.

Asa raised his hand, palm outward toward me. I felt his energy grow stronger, vibrate. A jet of fire shot out at me from his hand, grew into a thick log of flame. I grabbed the handful of dust and threw it into the air, whispering it into action. Under the windmill, Mr. Jameson nodded, turned, and flapped his handkerchief again. The guards began following the thieves as they slunk, silent, through the streets and back toward the Sacrifice building. I stood up just slightly taller to see.

Then everything went wrong.

The fire ricocheted off my shield of dust, but instead of flying back toward Asa, it went up, into the sky—straight up, impossibly up. Parting the clouds. Then it disappeared, leaving the clouds dark and angry and boiling overhead.

An eerie silence fell.

Then someone pointed.

"Look!"

The fire was coming back down, bigger and brighter than it had been before. It descended like a comet, over the church, over the garden, straight toward the Sacrifice building. There was a deep, earth-shaking boom of impact, the sound of metal tearing, wood breaking.

Oh God . . .

Then came the *bang bang bang* of gunshots followed by screams. The thieves.

The crowd panicked, began to scatter. Smoke and dust rose around them, in a cloud, thick, choking. I felt someone grab my hand—Asa.

"What's happening?" he said. "Did *I*—" he asked. "Did *you*—"

We jumped off the platform and started to run. Asa shouldered his way through the crowd, and I stayed close behind him until he stopped and I collided with his back.

"Get some water!" someone cried.

Above the cloud of dust, flames rose, huge and angry, cracking wood, whisking away black tar paper. The smell of burning food rose above it all. People ran and shouted. Buckets of water sloshed. Smoke rose into the billowing sky, unbelievably black.

The Sacrifice building was burning.

"This . . . this isn't supposed to happen . . ." he breathed.

My breath came in gasps. *What have I done? What have we done? What went wrong?*

In the light of the flames, I could see black lumps on the ground. The guards lay, some unconscious, some bleeding. Mr. Jameson was rising from the dust, his head bloody but unbowed. I didn't see any of the thieves. But . . . several ropes had been flung up over the nearest wall. A line of blood smear followed one rope, and through the smoke I could see a gaping, shimmering rip in Mother Morevna's spell at the top of the wall. They had escaped. They had escaped, and the Sacrifice building was on fire.

Asa's face was half-orange in the firelight. "I didn't mean to!" he spluttered desperately, grabbing my shoulders. "I didn't mean to, Sal, I swear it!"

But I couldn't say anything. I could only stand and watch as townspeople ran to the Dowsing Well and back, trying to douse the fire. But the flames were all-consuming. There was a horrifying sound, a crackling roar. Then the Sacrifice building collapsed in on itself, the flames mushrooming into the sky. Forty feet high now and still climbing, fueled by homemade liquors and dried wheat and everything else we owed the Dust Soldiers.

The Dust Soldiers.

We would all be killed. Everyone. And all because of me.

I swayed on my feet. Bile rose in my throat.

"What do we do now, Sal?" Asa asked. "What do we do?"

I didn't know. I didn't know, and a crowd was assembling around us, dark and angry, familiar faces suddenly featureless with rage. I wanted Mama. I wanted Mother Morevna. Where were they?

"You!" a voice said, sharp and accusatory. I turned and recognized the man from the Blue Moon. And he was pointing at us.

"This is all y'all's fault!" he shouted.

A murmur went up over the crowd. *They did it. It's their fault.* The murmur became a rumble.

"Hang them!" someone in the crowd yelled. Then two more people joined in. "Hang them! Hang them!"

There was nowhere to go, nowhere to run. They had encircled us on all sides. Surely they would kill us. Where was Mother Morevna? Where was Jameson?

"No," Asa was saying. "No, no, no, no, no, no, no . . . it's not supposed to happen this way . . . I can't . . . I can't do this!"

Then, suddenly, he disappeared. Just *vanished* from behind me as though he had never been there at all, leaving me alone to face the crowd.

The people gasped, then seemed to grow even angrier. "Coward!" someone cried. "Come back and fight like a man!" But they didn't look for him. They had me, and I couldn't disappear.

The circle was closing. There were ropes in people's hands, panic and anger in people's eyes.

"Mother Morevna!" I shrieked. "Mother Morevna! Please help!"

Then I saw her: a lone, elegant shadow silhouetted against the flames. But she didn't come to me. She didn't turn and take my hand and tell me she had a plan for us, that it was going to be all right. Instead, when she spoke, her voice was as hard as obsidian.

"You have doomed us," she said.

"But Asa—" I started.

"It doesn't matter whose magic it was," she said. "Someone must pay for this."

An angry shout went up in the crowd, "Hang her! Hang her!" but Mother Morevna put her hand up and the crowd went silent.

"I will not see hangings in this city," she said. "We have not grown so barbarous as that." Her eyes flickered to mine. She reached behind her neck and took off her black pendant. She held it out over her hand in front of me.

"No . . ." I heard myself sob. "Please . . ."

But all I could do was wait for my judgment.

At first, the pendulum hung still in the air, its gold chain catching the light. The crowd was completely silent, and all I could hear was the sound of the timbers snapping in the fire.

Please stay still, I thought. *Please . . .*

But very slowly, very slowly, it had begun to swing. It gained momentum and speed, and everyone could see its direction: back and forth.

"A pity," she said, stepping away from me. "You were becoming such a good witch."

I choked back a sob.

"Sallie Wilkerson," she said, her silhouette dark and jagged as she walked in front of the flames. "You are hereby banished from the City of Elysium, never to return. From this day forward, you must travel the Desert of Dust and Steel without protection, without love, and without pity. May the Gods have mercy on your soul."

"Please!" I cried. I reached out and grabbed her hand. Mother Morevna's eyes went out of focus. A wave of nausea rose inside me, just like it had when I saw Trixie's memory. Like it did when I saw the rain. Voices rose in my mind. *For a moment, I was a girl in a plain black dress, drawing something in the dirt, pricking her finger and drawing blood to make the crops grow taller. I heard a man yelling something in another language, dragging the girl away as she cried out that she meant no harm. . . .*

Mother Morevna broke out of my grip, her eyes wide with anger and disbelief, as though she were truly seeing me for the first time.

Then she looked at Mr. Jameson. "Get her out of my sight," she said. And she turned and walked into the darkness.

Mr. Jameson looked at me, his face sad and powerless.

"I'm sorry, Sal," he said.

"No!" I cried, but the crowd was already coming toward me. They surged forward, grabbed my arms and shoulders, lifted me up. Trixie herself was carrying my left arm, clamping it hurting-tight. I struggled, but they held my wrists together, pulled my hair, as they carried me through the city and to the steel door.

"No!" cried Lucy, fighting her way to the front. "Sal!"

"Lucy!" I screamed. But she was swept away by the crowd.

The great doors were pried open. The creak of the hinges was barely audible over the shouts and the hoots and the cries for blood. It was open, the desert black and bleak in front of me.

"No!" I cried. "You're making a mistake! Please!"

Then they hurled me into the air. I fell hard on the ground, pain shooting through my side.

"So long, *Rain Girl*!" someone spat. And the door closed, leaving me in utter darkness.

Sobbing, I lay in the dark sand where I had fallen, crumpled in the shadow of that great closed door, and wept. Alone.

• • •

After the doors had closed and the people had gone back to their homes, Lloyd Jameson surveyed the damage. Nothing was left. The Sacrifice building was nothing but a smoldering pile of ash. The thieves had escaped back into the desert—though he'd shot one of them in the shoulder himself. Two of his guards had been wounded. Asa Skander was nowhere to be found. And Sal Wilkerson . . .

But Mother Morevna was right. Someone had to pay for all their deaths. Should it have been Sal, though? A surge of disgust ran through him. He spat on the ground, his tobacco leaving a dark stain in the dust. Now Sal was gone, and he hadn't been able to help her. Everyone might as well be gone. All thoughts of Texas, of his ranch, of his wife and his daughter, were gone now, blown away like Oklahoma topsoil, irretrievable as rain.

"I can't believe it . . ." a voice said. He turned. Lucy Arbor, the girl everyone knew was selling makeup, was standing there in the dark, staring at the door Sal had been carried through. "They just . . . threw her out like that."

"Were you a friend of Sal's?" he asked. "Sal never seemed like she had many friends."

"Yeah," Lucy said. "Since we were little. She was kind to me, even before Elysium. Can't say the same for everybody, you know."

Lucy looked at the great, closed door. She wiped away what might have been a tear. Then she turned to a little boy behind her, her brother probably. "George, you need to head on back to the hospital. Aunt Lucretia needs her bedtime story."

The little boy wasn't listening. Instead, he was picking something up off the ground. Something small, golden. A marble maybe.

"George!" she said.

"I'm going! I'm going!" said George. Then he stuffed the marble in his pocket and headed off toward the church. Lucy, however, stayed there, staring at the door like she could look through it and see out into the desert beyond. "I'll miss her," she said finally.

"Me too," said Mr. Jameson.

The two stood in silence for a moment more, listening to the crackling of the dying conflagration.

"What are we going to do now?" asked Lucy, her voice quiet with fear and sadness. "They're coming back in just a couple months' time. . . ."

"I don't know," said Mr. Jameson, staring into the embers. "I just don't know."

PART TWO:

THE DESERT OF DUST AND STEEL

CHAPTER 13

2 MONTHS AND *28 DAYS* REMAIN.

I didn't sleep at all the first night in the desert. I couldn't. The terror fell on me as soon as the doors closed, and all the stories of creatures, of cannibals, of god-knew-what rose in my mind like dust clouds until I was so smothered with fear I could barely breathe. In the end, I was able to gather enough of my wits to crawl into a ditch and pull a tangle of tumbleweeds over me for camouflage. And all night, all around me, the creatures of the desert made themselves known. The air was dusty and sharp, full of growls, screams, cries. I could barely think. All I could do was sit awake, listening, watching the dark for movement, my hand near my components belt, ready to run or fight.

The next morning, when the light filtered through the tumbleweeds, I climbed out of the ditch, gritty and filthy and bruised, and looked out at the desert in the day. Unbelievable miles and miles of dry, cracked earth, with jagged stones spiking up in the distance and pools of mirage just beginning to waver. That endlessly big sky like a bell jar over it, making me feel smaller than ever. A line from a poem at school jumped into my mind and stuck there. *The lone and level sands stretch far away.* The reality of my situation, the guilt, hit me like a sledgehammer, knocking me to my knees. It had really happened. I had really brought the end down on all our heads, on Lucy, on Mr. Jameson, on everyone. It beat painfully next to my heart: *my fault, my fault, my fault.* And after last night, I was too worthless to them to even be allowed to try to fix it. For the first time in my life, I was really, *truly* alone.

I sat there among the tumbleweeds and cried until my rib cage felt like it had been scraped hollow. Then, when my tears had left muddy rivers down my cheeks, I felt resilience spark, catch fire somewhere in the hollowness. *I'm not going to let this be the end.*

The thieves, the cannibals, the creatures. All of them had to be able to find a way to survive out here. They had to eat. They had to drink. There must be something out here, something to live off of, something of value. And if I wanted to live long enough to have a chance of figuring out what I could do to fix everything—of maybe even finding a way out of this desert—I had to look for it myself.

I looked out over the horizon of the strange, alien desert that had once been fields. The high mesas, the jagged peaks of red stone, miniature mountains making lakes of shadows beneath them. The picked-over skeletons of rusted cars stuck up out of the ground here and there. The remains of fencerows cut across portions of the land. But in the distance, Black Mesa and Robbers Roost were visible, unchanged despite the scenery that surrounded them, looking much closer than they actually were. And if I remembered them, maybe I could use them to find my way.

Quickly, I took an inventory of what I had with me. I had my dust mask. I had the belt of spell components, still full. I had

The Complete Booke of Witchcraft in my pocket. Surely, with all this, *and* the penny to help guide me, I could find some food or some shelter.

But the most important thing now was to find water, and that I knew I could do.

I took my penny necklace off and held it by the twine.

"Water," I told it, and after a moment, it pulled straight outward, pointing into the Desert of Dust and Steel.

"All right," I told it. "Let's go."

• • •

I followed the penny for hours, over sunbaked rocks, the stubbly remains of fields turned into dunes, a plain filled with boulders, and still it strained and pulled against the twine that held it. By the time the penny led me to the side of a limestone plateau, the sun was so high and direct overhead that my shadow had all but disappeared under me. I stopped and looked up at the plateau, tall and unyielding before me. I wiped my forehead and mud came off on my arm.

"What, you want me to go over it? Under it?" I asked the penny. "Because I can't go through it." But the penny strained onward, ever forward. And sure enough, when I reached out, I found a crack between two rocks: a pathway leading to somewhere inside the plateau—somewhere with light streaming in at the end.

"Is it safe?" I asked the penny. It buzzed once. Yes.

Gulping with my dry throat, I crawled into the crack. It was narrow—so narrow, I had to edge sideways at times, feeling the dust and pebbles scrape off onto my clothes. I edged onward, foot by foot toward the light until I nearly stumbled out into a small, sandy clearing.

"Fancy meeting you here!" said a voice.

I spun around, my hand on my belt, the word *Entflammt* on my lips. There, sitting on a rock to my left, looking like the world's scruffiest Harold Lloyd impersonator, was the last person I expected or wanted to see.

"Asa?!" I nearly shouted.

"Sal," he said, tipping his hat to me. "I was just in the neighborhood and—"

"You son of a bitch!" I shouted. *"You left me there!"* I grabbed a rock and threw it at him.

"Ow! Stop it!" He put his arm up.

I threw another rock.

"Hey, cut it out!"

"No!" I pelted him again. "You left me there to die!"

"Look," said Asa. "I'm sorry! It was just getting a little tense back there and I thought—"

"'*Every man for himself!*' is what you thought!" I shouted. "Of all the *slimy, spineless* . . . You're not even good enough to be called a worm, you . . . *worm*!"

"I get it, I get it," he said. "But let me explain . . ."

"I don't have time for that," I said. "I have to get out of here, and that's what I'm going to do. See you in hell. Never mind—we're already here! Now, if you'll excuse me."

"Did you still want the water?" he said. And my throat was so hot and dry that I turned to him without thinking. In his hand, miraculously, he held a bag of rations.

"Where did you get that?" I asked. "Did you steal—"

"No, no, no," Asa said quickly. "That old cowboy, Mr. Jameson, rode out here on a horse in the middle of the night last night and left them here. But these rations have got your name on them." He rotated the burlap sack and, sure enough, the name *SAL WILKERSON* was written on it in smudged black charcoal. "I haven't touched anything inside."

Mr. Jameson. I remembered his sad, shocked face as they dragged me away, the surge of betrayal I'd felt when he hadn't stood up for me. And now he was doing his best to make sure I didn't die out here. Somehow, the world suddenly seemed a little better.

"Well, give it here," I said, reaching for the bag. "And thank you for not touching anything in it. I at least need to make sure I don't die of thirst before I either fix everything or find a way out of this desert."

"There really isn't one," Asa said, and his voice sounded so sure, so serious that I looked up at him despite myself. "You're wasting your time. I promise."

"How do you know that?" I asked, narrowing my eyes. "What all *do* you know?"

"Look, I wasn't completely honest with you before . . . and I don't know how much I can say now, but—"

Then something about him shifted. Changed before my eyes. The lower half of his face was suddenly, terrifyingly different. His nose was more of a snout, but the end of it was gone, replaced by a sort of dark hole, like a horse's skull. His teeth were long, black, and needle-sharp, and a snakelike black tongue lolled downward.

My body went cold and stiff, my mind trying its hardest to reject what I was seeing. I stumbled and fell onto my backside, scrambling backward, spluttering.

"What?" Asa asked, his eyes puzzled above the rest of the monstrosity.

I fumbled with my pouches, pulling out a handful of crossroads dirt.

"D-don't come any closer!" I said. "I've got enough pepper here to roast you alive!"

"What do you mean?" he said. "Why are you so scared all of a . . . ?" Asa put a hand to his face; then the human part blushed. "Oh! Oh, I'm sorry. I don't . . . quite know what happened there. . . ."

He moved his hand over his face, and there was a flicker of electricity. Then his face went back to its normal, human shape. "Don't worry. I won't hurt you."

"What . . . what was . . . ?" I gasped.

"My real face," Asa sighed. "I . . ." He choked for a moment, searched for words. "I failed. So it's harder to maintain the illusion now."

My back was against the wall. But the crack through which I'd crawled was only a yard away. Slowly, I began to inch toward it.

"Don't come any closer!" I said. "I'll burn you to a crisp!"

"Humans are so distrustful," he said, with a tone in his voice that was both disappointed and pitying. "Come on, let's talk it out like civilized . . . beings. I'll tell you what I can. Then, if you want, you can burn me to a crisp."

He was looking at me. I froze, my hand full of pepper.

"So let's address it," he said over steepled fingers. "I am what you might call a . . . d—" He choked, then tried again. "A d-d—" He used his fingers to make horns on his head.

"A *demon*?" I gasped. "You're a *demon*?!"

He shook his head emphatically. "No, those are the evil ones. I'm . . . I've got an *ae* instead of just an *e*. The ancient Greek kind, you know? Inhuman messengers between people and the Gods. Like the voice that spoke to Socrates!" Smoke started to trickle from his nose again. "Completely . . . neutral!" he gasped.

"But you're not a voice! You have a body!" I paused. "Is that body even yours or did you . . . possess it?"

"No, no, no, no. Of course not." He knocked against his chest, pulled at his hair. "This was created especially for me. It just . . . takes a lot of magic to keep it together."

"Who made you? God? The . . ." I gulped, inched just a step closer to the crack. "The Devil?"

"I'm from the ones who built it all, who set everything in motion, here to influence the . . ." He gagged. A trickle of smoke ran out of his nose. "The G-G . . ." He took a deep breath and rasped, *"The Game!"*

He doubled over, choking. Smoke began to pour from his mouth, his nose, his eyes.

It stunned me for a moment; then I realized: This was my chance. Like a flash, I was gone, back through the crack as fast as I could shimmy.

"Sal!" he shouted. "Where are you going?"

"Entflammt!" I sent a stream of fire at him and he staggered. I wrenched myself through the crack in the plateau and started running. I ran and ran across the hard, baked earth, into the wind and grit, until I jogged to a stop, sides heaving, in a pool of my own shadow. I looked behind me. Asa—whatever he was—was nowhere to be found.

But when I turned back, he was right there, in front of me, as though he had materialized from the dust itself.

"Like I was saying—" he said. But I was already backing away.

"Don't come near me!" I gasped, digging in my pouches again. "I mean it!" I took another step back.

"Sal!" he said, eyes wide. "Watch where you're—"

But before he could finish, I felt a painful grip around my ankle and looked down. A hand made of shadow was wrapped around my ankle. I jerked and kicked, but it was no use. It pulled downward on my ankle, and my foot sank into the hard earth as though it were water. The shadow thing was pulling me down, down into the very earth itself. Before I knew it, I was waist-deep into my own shadow, losing sensation as I went.

My pouch was too deep in the shadow to reach. I scrabbled on the ground for anything, anything I could use to cast a spell, to free myself. Then I saw a multicolored rope—a rainbow of handkerchiefs tied together—in the dust.

"Grab on!" shouted Asa.

I grabbed the rope of handkerchiefs, and Asa pulled. The shadow thing tightened its grip around my ankle and pulled back. Asa groaned and strained, and just when I thought my leg would be pulled completely from its socket, the shadow creature loosened its grip just enough for my waist and hips to be pulled out of the shadow. I released the rope with one hand and reached into my pouches.

"What are you doing?" Asa cried. But I was moving fast, reaching for the crumbled robin's eggshells in my farthest pouch. I grabbed a pinch of ground eggshell, took aim at the shadow creature, and flicked it beneath me. *"Lichtfleck!"* I shouted.

Light flared, and I heard a muffled shriek as the shadow creature detached itself from my shadow. Then the claws left my ankle, and I scrambled over to Asa. A dull spot slightly darker than the soil rocketed away back toward the boulders, seeking safety in their shade.

"That light spell was good thinking," Asa said, pulling his scarf rope back and tucking it into his sleeve. "You all right?"

"I'm fine," I said, my muscles still tensed. ". . . Thanks. Now leave me alone, because you're terrifying."

"Sal, will you *please* listen to me?" he said. "I am not your enemy. I swear it. I am here to help Elysium. I'm here to try and make things better!"

"Fine job you did of that," I said. "And why should I listen to you? You're the whole reason I'm out here. Besides, what can you even say without spewing smoke all over the place?"

"I . . . I don't know," he said. "I can't write it, either, or my hands stops working. I just wish I had a way to show you what was in my head; then you'd understand."

Something clicked in my mind.

"Give me your hand," I said.

"What?"

"Just do it. Give me your hand."

"All right, all right." Asa extended his hand as though he were giving a handshake. I took it.

I thought of Trixie and Mother Morevna and squirmed. I had only ever done this by accident before. But maybe, just maybe, I could do it on purpose this time. I shut my eyes and concentrated on the power, the magic, the question *What is the truth?*

And to my surprise, the magic channeled itself, responded.

Darkness and nausea rose up. Across from me, Asa's eyes turned daemon again and rolled back, and then the both of us were gone, gone into the vastness of Asa's mind. . . .

At first, there was nothing but darkness, boundless, huge. My nostrils filled with the smell of mercury and blood one moment, and water and green grass the next. All around was the sensation of others with me—not people, not animals, but other things—moving in the darkness. And somehow I knew that I—that Asa—was one of them.

My ears suddenly boomed with the sound of radio static, amplified a thousand times. Then I saw what looked like a young man—Asa—switching appearances as quickly as an electric light turns on and off and on again. Different suits. Different hats. Glasses. No glasses. Blond hair. Black hair. Dark skin. Fair skin. Gradually he became the Asa that I knew, the Harold Lloyd–looking one.

His shoes began to glow—there were symbols on them, moving and twisting as though they were alive. I could feel the joy, the excitement welling in his heart. Then something golden appeared out of the darkness, a tiny, quarter-sized speck of gold: the cricket in amber he had had at the Witches' Duel. Importance seemed to bleed from it like ink in water. He reached out his hand for it and put it in his pocket, promised to do his duty as a Wildcard, and suddenly I knew. I KNEW everything. Then there was a door that seemed to be made of light. He moved to step through it, but just as he did, a female voice boomed out, loud as a thunderclap.

This is not meant for you! Begone!

My head was suddenly racked with pain. It threatened to explode like a watermelon with a firecracker inside. *Wake up! Wake up! Wake up!* I commanded myself. But the pain worsened. Still I fought it, and just as the pain grew almost unbearable, I felt myself slipping away, out of my trance, back into myself.

I felt my hand come unstuck from his. I gasped for breath, then coughed and choked, curls of white smoke leaving my mouth and disappearing into the air.

So it was true, all of it.

"That was crazy!" Asa said. "It's like I was living it all over again! Like— Sal! Your nose is bleeding!"

I wiped my nose and a long, dark line of blood came off on my forearm. "I—I'm fine," I said. I wiped it off on my dress, leaving a thin rusty stain on my skin. "Was it the truth, Asa?" I asked. "Was what I saw real?"

"Yes!" Asa said. "Completely and utterly real! And that magic! I've never felt magic so strong!"

"That voice . . ." I said, putting a hand to my aching temple. "Was that . . . ?"

"That was Life," said Asa. "And She didn't seem too pleased with you seeing that. . . . I'm surprised She didn't do more."

"And you—" I coughed. "You're a Wildcard. . . . She built you to . . . save us?"

"To try to win the Game for Her side," said Asa. "Death has a Card too, somewhere out here."

My head throbbed again. I saw the cricket in my mind again, so golden and important in the darkness.

"And that cricket thing . . . you were supposed to return it to its owner, and that's what was supposed to help us. That's why you were so eager to find the owner at the duel."

"But I failed," he groaned. "Completely and utterly. I had everyone's attention for days and weeks and even an assembly and, still, I managed to mess it all up. The cricket is gone, Sal.

Lost. Sometime during the duel, I must have dropped it, and now I don't know what to do. And then burning the Sacrifice . . . it really couldn't have gone worse."

"So it *was* you?" I said. "You destroyed the Sacrifice? All this time I thought it was me, accidentally aiming a little higher. . . ."

"I don't know," Asa said. "I assume so. But I don't know how I would have messed it up that badly. My magic shouldn't have been able to leave the salt circle, just like yours . . . unless . . ."

"Unless what?" I raised an eyebrow.

"Death, that's what!" he shouted. "She's been trying to sabotage me this entire time. She must have filtered in some magic of Her own. Yes . . . yes, that's where the smoke came from! Because there's no reason for Life to do something like that."

"I thought you were sent by Life?"

"Daemons are neutral," said Asa. "Even though Life made me, they can both interfere if they choose. Does that make sense?"

"No," I said.

"Well, I don't know how to explain it any better," he said. "All I know is that if it doesn't get made right again, I'll be taken apart, shredded, my particles scattered across the firmament until I vanish as though I'd never been!"

"And without the Sacrifice . . . without the cricket . . . we don't have much of a chance of winning, do we?" I asked, my heart sinking.

Asa sighed. "From here, we've got two choices: to wait for the end of the Game—which will go to Death now, I'm sure—and be killed, or . . ." He paused, licked his dry lips. "Or we could hope for some sort of miracle, I guess."

"No," I said. "There's got to be a way to fix everything."

"How do you know?" Asa asked.

I was quiet. I wasn't sure how I knew, but I *knew*. It tingled under my skin like deception, like there *was* a way to fix this, even now. There had to be.

"I just know," I said finally. "There's a solution to this. It can be fixed."

"And how exactly do you propose we do that from where we are now?" he asked, gesturing to the great, empty expanse around us.

"If it's such an inconvenience, don't come." I shrugged. "Lord knows you're not my favorite person—or whatever you are. But it seems like if you don't fix this you're in just as big a mess as I am. So are you coming with me or not?"

He extended his hand to me. "Partners?" he asked. "For now?"

"Partners for now," I said, and I shook it.

He turned and looked over the vast, cracked plains and rocky crags. "But . . . uh . . . where *are* we going, anyway?"

"Only one way to find out," I said. I brushed myself off and took my penny in hand. Closing my eyes, I whispered to it. "Just . . . show us where we can find something that will help us win the Game. Can you do that?"

And my penny thrummed once, then pulled straight outward on its twine, out toward the dunes and crags to what I guessed was north.

I opened my mouth to tell him what it meant, but before I could, I heard the unmistakable sound of a gun being cocked.

"You're not going anywhere," said a voice. And when Asa and I turned, we found ourselves looking down the barrels of two pistols.

CHAPTER 14

Asa and I put our hands up and stood, completely taken aback. There were two of them: a tall, slim Black girl in men's clothes and a cowboy hat, and a sturdy, broad-shouldered white girl in a sundress with her brown hair tied up in a bun. The Black girl had two pistols and an air of quiet confidence that told me she knew how to use them. The white girl had an animal energy and a football player's stance, ready to tackle me or Asa or both of us with the ferocity of a wolverine.

"Who the hell are you?" said the white girl. "And what are you doing on our side of Black Mesa? If you're from the Laredo settlement—"

"Do you see that black shit they put on themselves, Judith?" the Black girl said. "They're not from the Laredo settlement." She turned back to me and Asa and raised an eyebrow. "You do look familiar, though."

"Harold Lloyd!" said Judith. "He's the spitting image of Harold Lloyd, Zo!"

"No, you idiot." Zo lifted her weapons. "They're the two who were fighting last night," she continued. "The Witches' Duel. They were part of the trap."

Asa and I glanced at each other. *The thieves.* For a moment I expected Asa to disappear again, leave me like he had in Elysium. But this time, he stood his ground.

"Were you?" Judith demanded. "Is that why that old cowboy came and left that bag you got?"

Mr. Jameson. They'd seen him leave the rations for me and wanted them for themselves.

"Look," I said. "We were part of the plan, but we've been exiled now. We're not part of that anymore, and I promise if you let us go you'll never—"

"We were victims of circumstance!" Asa said. "Pawns in a cruel game! Gifted witches thrust out of Elysium when all we intended was to make things better. And look where it has gotten us! Please, ladies . . ." ("*Ladies*," Judith chuckled.) "Do not give us your judgment. Give us your help!"

They looked at us.

"Frisk them," said Zo.

Judith started with me. "I'll be taking this," she said, yanking the bag of rations out of my hands. She rifled through it as Zo held one gun on me and one on Asa. "Salt pork, biscuits, water. You think this is safe, Zo?"

"Better not risk it," Zo said, a dark, cautious tone in her voice.

Judith shrugged; then she slammed the bag of rations on the ground and when the water from the burst rations leaked into the dust, I nearly cried. *The one nice thing, the only thing I had.*

She patted me down roughly. Then, one by one, she opened the pouches and looked in.

"Just a buncha dust and feathers," she muttered.

"It's one of those witch belts," Zo said, holding her gun on Asa. "Take it anyway."

My stomach lurched. Without that belt I was defenseless, and I knew they had magic too. Mr. Jameson had said so. I'd seen it. But how could I defend myself now with my hands over my head?

Judith took my belt and wrapped it around her chest like a bandolier. "What about this?" Judith said, pulling the Booke out of my pocket and holding it into the light.

"I dunno, see what it is," said Zo.

Judith opened it and skimmed through it. My breath caught in my throat. *Oh no,* I thought. *Not that. That book is my only hope out here.*

"Some Russian book or something," she said.

"You can keep that one," said Zo.

The Booke is written in plain English . . . isn't it? I wondered as she slipped it back into my pocket. Before I could think about that too much, though, she was finished with me, and Zo's gun was in my face as Judith moved on to Asa.

She patted him down completely, even looking inside his hat, and as she did so, an elongated black tooth slipped down over his lip. I raised my eyebrows at him; he twitched and it was gone again.

"Well, what've we got here?" Judith had pulled something from his pocket that I'd never seen before: a piece of paper—no, a photograph with something written on the back of it. She left Asa standing there, arms still up, and showed the photograph to Zo.

"Tie them together and let's get going," she said, her eyes on Asa. "With the trap and now this, there's no way the boss isn't going to want to see them."

Asa and I exchanged looks. With Zo's guns on us and my belt gone, we had no choice but to stand as they tied our hands together with a length of rope from Judith's pack. Then Zo put her guns to our backs and marched us out into the desert, leaving the ruined rations behind. But as we marched, I kept quiet. We were heading straight in the direction my penny had pointed.

• • •

They walked us all day and into the night, stopping once for food. This ended up being a giant grasshopper, which Zo shot through one huge, faceted eye and out the other. ("Surprisingly nutty," Asa said with his mouth full. I had to close my eyes and pretend to be somewhere else to choke it down.) Judith, however, ate what looked like hardtack, and avoided the grasshopper altogether.

"I'm a vegetarian," Judith said when Asa offered her a grasshopper leg. "Thanks, though. You're pretty polite for a prisoner."

Polite or not, as it turned out, Asa was surprisingly bad at traveling. He drank more than his share of water, ate quite a lot of food, and he had the tendency to quietly mimic the things the girls did. He didn't mean it in a schoolyard-taunting sort of way, thank God, or they might have killed us there. It seemed he was genuinely trying to learn things . . . but I could tell it was grating on Zo's and Judith's nerves. Once, Zo snapped her fingers, trying to get his attention; then, for an hour, I had to deal with Asa next to me, trying over and over to snap. When he started to nod off while walking, I whistled short and fast, to keep him from falling in his traces and taking us both down. And then, of course, he had to try to learn to whistle.

"Cut it out, songbird," Zo said. "Or I'll bury a bullet in your back."

That shut him up.

"I don't get it," I whispered. "You can do magic tricks but you can't snap or whistle?"

Asa shrugged. "I was created knowing how to do magic tricks," he whispered. "Learning human things like this is something else. Besides, it keeps my mind off things." He rolled his tongue into a tube. "Can you do this?" he said. "I heard that not everyone can."

"Asa, I swear to God—" I started.

"Y'all got something to say?" Judith said.

"No, ma'am," said Asa.

"'Ma'am,'" Judith snorted. "You gotta stop with all this 'ma'am' and 'miss' and 'ladies' stuff. This ain't 1843, you know."

"Sorry," said Asa. "Old habits die hard, I suppose."

"Well, kill them faster," said Zo.

Old habits, I thought. *He's been a human for, what? A month?*

"What's your deal anyway, Harold?" Judith said, turning and walking backward as she held the rope that bound us together. "I know this one's that old hag's Successor, but what are you? You some kinda preacher or snake oil salesman or something? You Little Miss Successor's boyfriend?"

"Ew, no!" I said, my voice sounding more disgusted than I meant to.

"You sure?" Judith's eyes flickered from me to Asa.

"Our Successor here isn't the boyfriend type, if you know what I mean," said Zo. She looked me up and down, then smiled smugly. "There isn't a man alive who could tie her down."

My insides seemed to crinkle in irritation. "I don't know what you're getting at—"

"To answer your question, I am simply a magician," Asa said, cutting me off before I could get us killed. "Of the street-performing variety."

"And a daemon," I added under my breath, but no one heard me.

"Oh, Cassie will like this, Zo," said Judith, her eyes lighting up. "Maybe the boss'll keep him alive long enough to do a few tricks?"

"Don't give them false hope," Zo scolded. "It's rude. Besides, we don't want any of the kind of nonsense they pulled back in Elysium. You saw all that smoke." She looked back at us and shook her head. "Not worth our time."

"Well, *I* hope you get to do some tricks, anyway," said Judith, patting Asa on the shoulder.

"Thank you," said Asa, growing pale even in the darkness. "I appreciate the sentiment."

There was a noise to our right, and I saw Zo's body tense in the moonlight.

"Quick! Down!" she hissed. She dove behind a massive cluster of tumbleweeds, and we felt ourselves yanked off our feet as Judith slung us behind her.

"Don't make a sound," Zo whispered. "Don't even think of it or I will kill you. Do you understand?"

We nodded. Then we heard the sound of distant voices, loud,

crass. Men's voices. We froze. Zo had her guns cocked and ready. Judith had a big stick in her hand, ready to club someone to death.

A group of men came out from behind a ridge then. There were twelve of them, all big, all shirtless, their once-pale bodies baked pink by the sun, now a mottled color in the moonlight. Some wore what looked like handmade dust masks, all metal and glass, over their mouths; some had old dust masks around their necks. All of them carried weapons that looked like modified clubs and spears and guns, and the ones who weren't carrying guns were carrying what looked like pieces from old trucks and tractors. But what was most striking about them were the black designs painted across their bodies. Biblical designs like crosses and serpents and skulls, painted in something greasy and pungent. Axle grease, I realized when the wind blew their stink our way. Axle grease and—I squinted—yes: blood spatter. They had killed something recently. Or someone. I shuddered and kept still, trying not to breathe.

"The Laredo Boys," Judith whispered, voice thick with hatred.

"And there's Samson out front," said Zo. "I wonder what they're doing all the way out here?"

I remembered hearing about these men before, men painted with axle grease, raining terror beyond the walls. They'd been ranchers once, or so the story went, ranchers who refused to live by Mother Morevna's new laws and chose to take their chances in the desert instead of living in a city where a woman ruled and everyone could drink from the same wells.

"Got lucky today," one of them said to another as they passed us. "What a haul!"

"Too bad about the old man," said another, carrying what looked like the door of an automobile.

"He shouldn't have put up such a fight," said the first man. The top of his bald head was painted with a design of a grinning skull with wings. "But he's buzzard food now."

"So *these* are the people I was supposed to be running from," Asa whispered, a little too loudly.

Judith clapped a hand over his mouth, but it was too late.

"Did you hear something?" the bald man said. He and the other man stopped, took a step toward our tumbleweed nest. Judith and Zo exchanged glances, ready to come up swinging, shooting. Then the biggest one, their leader, turned. His eyes were hard blue, slivers of pale in his sun-reddened face.

"Quit bullshitting," he barked. "We got three miles to go."

"A-all right, Samson," said the bald man. "I was just checking is all." He cast another glance at the pile of tumbleweeds, then fell in behind the rest of the group. They trudged onward until they topped the ridge and disappeared into the dark.

Zo and Judith held us there a few moments more, watching. Then, when Zo saw that the coast was clear, she pulled us from behind the rock.

"Good job keeping quiet, for the most part," said Zo. "It was smart of you. You don't want to know what would have happened to you if they'd caught you instead of us."

"I suppose I should consider myself lucky." I patted dust off my skirt.

"Yeah," Judith said earnestly. "You really should. If they had it their way, we'd all be wives or something. Always pregnant, always getting hit, until we got too weak or sick to take care of, and then getting eaten when hunting or scavenging is bad."

"E-eaten, did you say?" Asa gulped.

"So the stories go," said Judith. "They're our enemies, through and through."

I shuddered involuntarily, thinking of all the stories I'd heard passed around in Elysium. Of all the ones to be true, why did it have to be those?

"Wh-what were they doing with those car parts?" Asa asked.

"Out here, we don't have anything," Judith said. "So when you're building your shelters, making your own machines and stuff, whatever you can strip from old cars comes in handy. They use it to make weapons, shields, things like that. And the more parts you got, the better off you are out here. They've got a pretty good mechanic, but we have the best one out here."

"For now," said Zo, and her voice full of bitterness.

"Is she angry with us?" Asa whispered to me.

But before I could answer, a familiar, dreadful feeling rose up out of nowhere. Nausea, sharpness. The rain was coming, just as it always did, without rhyme or reason. Coming just because it could. Just to show me I'd never be rid of it, never understand it.

Not now! I thought at the rain. *Not now, please!*

"Sal!" I heard Asa say. "Sal! What's wrong?" But his voice sounded far away, muffled as though he were underwater, or I was. I fell to the ground, dragging Asa with me. "Help!" he cried. "Somebody help her!"

"What's the matter with her?" said Judith's voice.

"I don't know, I don't know!" Asa panicked.

"Get out of the way!" Zo flipped me over expertly. Her hands were on me, opening my mouth. "Make sure she doesn't swallow her tongue!"

I was shaking. The darkness was rising.

"Fight it!" Asa was saying. "Whatever's happening, fight it!"

But this time, the rain would not be fought back. It rose in my head, the roaring of it like a train in my mind. I clutched my stomach. But as the darkness rose around me and I felt my eyes roll back, I knew I was powerless to resist it.

"Sal!" Asa cried. But I was gone.

• • •

I was wandering the edges of Elysium as the walls were being built, my eyes on the horizon. It was that day, I knew. That awful day all over again. The first time I saw the rain.

The sound of hammers and nails filled the air, of mud being slapped into frames and made into bricks. Mama was somewhere behind me with the other water pitcher women, going around the perimeter of the wall, offering water to the workers.

But my eyes were on the horizon. In my bones, I could feel something significant, something blessed. Change was coming. But what? And from where?

I looked out over the strange new desert, seeing it not for its danger, but for its splendor. This was a land where a girl could have adventures, just like the ones I'd read about. This was a land where a girl could be the hero she knew she was. I was not afraid.

Out in the desert, the sky was darkening. A ripple of excitement ran through me. I turned back to see the workers' expressions, but none of them looked up. Why didn't anyone notice?

Across town, I heard the choir begin practicing, even though the God we knew was just a comfortable tether to our past. Keeping up morale. They started singing, squeaky soprano voices and altos just off-key.

"I'm pressing on the upward way
New heights I'm gaining every day
Still praying as I onward bound
Lord, plant my feet on higher ground."

I could smell it now: rain. That telltale heaviness in the air, the feeling of sudden, damp wind against my skin. Though if I'd looked closer, I'd have seen that no dust was stirring and that the air was still.

I turned and looked back. Nobody was watching me. Nobody was paying attention.

I took a deep breath. Then I plunged. I ran, over the dusty fields with their nubs of stubbly, dead wheat, out into the desert, out toward the horizon. I could see something rising there, a darkness.

This must be the rain! I thought, ignoring the nausea rising in my stomach. And I'll be the first to feel it!

Behind the eyes of my younger body, I felt like clawing my way out, ripping the husk of myself off me and throwing it into the wind. I tried, with all my effort, all my power, to make myself get up, to run back home. But I couldn't speak, couldn't move, no matter how much I wanted to. I was an observer, shackled to the past.

The wind began to pick up. There was a tingle of electricity in the air.

"Sal!" came a voice.

No, I thought. Not again. Please don't make me live through this again. But when I opened my eyes, there she was: Mama. She was running toward me, through the fields, her dust mask hanging from her neck. I realized then that I had gotten so far from the city, so far from the walls.

"Sal . . . ?" she said. "What are you doing all the way out here, honey?"

It had begun to get cold, far colder than it had been only an hour ago.

"Rain's coming, Mama!" I said. "I can feel it!"

Then a siren blared behind us. We turned, slowly, looking toward the north. On the horizon was a dark line. . . . Rain clouds? No. A dust storm, a mile high, ten miles wide. Sweeping toward us.

"Oh, God, Sal . . . run!" Mama shouted. She bent and reached out to touch me. There was a snap of static electricity and she winced, but kept ahold of me.

We ran, our legs pumping as we ran back toward the walls. I could see the black dot that was Mother Morevna coming out into the center of town, drawing everyone around her to cast the Dust Dome Spell.

"Wait!" cried Mama.

But the dust storm rolled toward us, bigger and blacker and thicker than any storm I'd ever seen. No! *I thought.* I will not see this again. *My head pounded as I tried to wrench myself out of the vision. But the dust was still coming, that black wall still advancing. We ran harder, our chests hurting, dust whipping behind us. But we could not escape the storm. It roared behind us, a great dark monster swallowing everything. We were almost there. Just a little more!*

"Wait!" Mama cried again, but we were too far away.

"PULVAREM FIRMAMENTUM!" Mother Morevna shouted. And the dome spread over Elysium, spreading downward in front of us, into the ground. I felt my body connect with the dome of the spell, hard and unyielding as a glass door. We were too late!

We turned to face the storm, pitch-black and howling. Mama reached for my dust mask, but I'd left it behind like the careless, worthless little girl I had been. Then Mama pulled me to her and wrenched her own mask off.

"I love you," Mama said. "Hold on to me."

I tried to stop her, tried to cry out, but before I could, she fastened the mask—her mask—over my face. Then, as the wall of dust roared above us, she pulled me to her and held me close. Then the dust swallowed both of us, the grit and wind cutting us, hurting us, peeling the skin off anything not covered. The sky went black. And this time, even with Mama's mask on, I felt for all the world like I was drowning.

• • •

"Sal!" Asa's human heart pounded; he crouched, powerless with his hands tied to Sal's rope. "Sal, please!"

But she was gone. As gone as someone could be while still being in front of you. Vomit bubbled up out of her throat.

"Quick!" said Zo. She bent and grabbed Sal's braids out of the widening puddle and pulled her head up, but she was limp. Zo pulled her away from the puddle, checked her pulse.

"Rain . . ." Sal said softly. Then she was gone again.

"I need him out of the way," Zo said.

"If you want to help your friend, don't try anything funny," Judith growled. She untied the rope that bound Asa to Sal and held it in her hand, her grip firm. But she needn't have bothered.

Asa couldn't leave if he wanted to. He was rooted to the spot, watching, worried, and awestruck. Magic practically radiated out from her as she lay on the sand, a strange sort of magic, unelegant, brutal. It was a powerful, unhoned magic that could be anything and everything, good or bad, creative or destructive. He had seen Sal's magic before, but never had he seen anything like this. And suddenly, irrevocably, he knew that Sal had a part to play in all of this as well. But what it was, he couldn't say.

"Come on," said Zo, lifting Sal in her arms. "Let's find some shelter. I don't want to travel until she's awake."

Then Judith jerked his rope and he started walking.

Shelter ended up being a hollow space in a fencerow covered with a thicket of tumbleweeds. Judith tied Asa to a fence post and laid Sal next to him, her hands also tied to a nearby post.

He crouched next to her silently, pondering, for hours. When she finally opened her eyes again, Asa let out a whooshing breath of relief and said, "Oh, thank goodness! You really had me there for a while!"

"Where are we?" Sal asked groggily, pulling on her rope.

"In a ditch," Asa whispered. "Judith is asleep just over there. Zo's keeping watch over us. But never mind that! What *was* that? What happened to you?"

"The . . . rain," Sal said, something like shame rising in her voice. "I see rain sometimes. I've seen it since Black Sunday, but this . . . this was worse than usual. I feel like I've been run over by a tractor."

"I can see why," Asa said. "You have no idea how much magic you were using. It was like . . . It was more magic than I've seen all at once, maybe ever. What is this . . . rain you see? What does it mean?"

"Look, I don't know, okay?" Sal snapped. "It's been the thorn in my side for a long time, and I really wish I could just make it never happen again. But I can't. And I don't want to talk about it. Not right now."

"All right," Asa said. "I'm sorry. Forget I said anything. I'm just glad you're back is all."

"Thanks," she said, and he could tell even through her tone that she really meant it.

They sat in silence for a moment; then Sal said, "Are they still taking us north? Still the same way?"

Asa nodded. "In a beeline."

"Good." Sal lay back and took a deep breath. "That's where the penny was pointing. And it's better to be taken there by them than to blunder our way over alone. For now, anyway."

She seemed so sure of it, but Asa was anything but sure. A sense of dread was growing inside him and seemed to multiply the closer they got to their destination.

"I have a bad feeling about where we're going," Asa heard himself say. "Like it will be the end of me. Maybe it's . . . intuition? If I'm human enough to have that yet."

Sal peered through the tumbleweeds at Judith. She was asleep, snoring gently with that big stick clutched in her hand.

"Did you have this feeling before the duel?" Sal asked.

Asa shook his head. "No, it's . . . different somehow. It feels like wherever they're taking me is the last place I need to be."

"Look," Sal said. "My penny has never steered me wrong

before. It might be that they're taking us exactly where we *do* need to be to find whatever it is that can fix things."

"Maybe," Asa said doubtfully. He slipped out of the rope and scratched his nose free of some dust; then he slipped his hand back into the rope.

"Are you serious?" Sal said flatly.

"What?" Asa said.

"You can get out of the rope!" she hissed. "You . . . you don't even have to be here right now, do you? You could vanish in an instant, just like you did back in Elysium. But you're going along with being a prisoner. Why?"

Asa wasn't sure himself. There were a million reasons, he thought. He wanted to make sure Sal was all right, for one. But even though he dreaded what lay ahead of them, he also felt . . . drawn to it somehow. Drawn as the needle of a compass to magnetic north. He thought for a moment, then said, "I don't know. But I know that the last time I left you, you felt abandoned. And I consider you the first friend I made here in the human world. My only friend. And what kind of a heel would I be if I abandoned you twice in one week?"

"Thank you," Sal said, turning to look him in the face. "Really. Thank you. And we may have gotten off to the roughest start ever, but . . . I do consider you a friend too."

And even though it was dark and Asa was semi-tied to a post, he couldn't help but smile.

"What was that picture, anyway?" Sal asked. "The one they took from you?"

Asa shrugged. "Just a photograph I found and thought was

neat. I don't know anything about it, I swear." He sighed. "For a human, I seem to be incredibly unlucky."

"Welcome to Oklahoma," she said.

"You don't really think they'll try to kill us, do you?" Asa asked after a moment.

Sal turned and peered out of the tumbleweed prison. Through a hole in the branches they could see Zo, her slim silhouette dark against the cold, bright sky, awake and alert, with her sharp tongue and her pistols always, always ready.

"I guess we'll just have to wait and see," said Sal.

• • •

When we woke the next morning, our necks and backs aching, they picked us up, dusted us off, and pushed us straight back into walking. As we traveled, the scenery began to change. Where there had been dunes and gorges and cracked earth before, now there were high buttes and mesas. The ground was spread with an array of cholla cactus, juniper, and scrub oak. Rising upward toward the sky was an expanse of hard, familiar black stone. Lava stone. I *knew* this place, I realized.

This was Black Mesa, the setting of vague, faded memories of a family camping trip when I was four, clearer memories of class trips we'd gone on at school, of getting tiny cactus spines stuck in my hand and pulling them out for days. *The highest point in Oklahoma!* and *Watch out for rattlers!* the signs around it said. I knew Black Mesa, and somehow knowing it made me feel like less of a prisoner, even if just for a moment.

Judith and Zo marched us through the black crags and desert brush of the Mesa, taking a path that seemed meandering and purposeful at the same time. I thought of the Booke in my pocket and how I'd read about illusion spells that could only be broken by walking in a specific path. Was this what they were doing? I wondered. Eventually, Zo and Judith's winding path weaved to a stop in front of a black stone ledge. Zo whistled three notes, and the wall just disappeared.

More illusory magic, I thought as we went through the place where it had been. *And not bad either.* The witch who cast this must be very skilled indeed, someone you didn't want to mess with. I gulped.

We turned the corner, and I felt the penny thrum.

Their hideout was an old, rusted train, or at least part of one, sitting like a snake bitten in half at the bottom of the ravine. It was red-orange with rust, but it was not simply a dead thing fallen into disuse: Bits and pieces of flannel and cloth had been hung over the windows, like our wet sheets back in Elysium. Smoke came from the smokestack, smelling like home cooking rather than coal fire, and every now and then we saw things like cacti or succulents growing out of tin cans and teapots. This was the thieves' hideout. But where were the stolen supplies? In one of the train cars, maybe?

They marched us forward, toward the train itself, and as we turned to walk on the sunny side of it, someone said, "Don't tell me these are the ones who have been prowling around the campground, trying to find us?"

A jolt of shock went through me, and Asa and I turned toward the voice.

In a patch of sun, a pale girl, heavily freckled, was sitting cross-legged on a bit of fabric. She wore her light brown hair tied up in a scarf, cutoff shorts, boots, a man's work shirt with a patch that said "Ralph" with the word "Texaco" just above it. What was strangest was that she was absolutely covered with jewelry, including several bangles and necklaces that looked to be made of things like buttons and bottle caps, teeth and bones, and her nails were long and varnished with purple. A purple crystal hung around her neck, and somehow I knew immediately that it was her imbued object, just like my penny. Was this the girl who cast the illusion spell?

"We'll see," Judith said. "The boss in there?"

"She's out back," said the girl. "Where did you find these two? And why did you bring them here now? You know we'll just have to kill them." (Next to me, Asa gulped audibly.)

"Long story," said Zo. "We'll tell you after they're dead."

"All right," the girl said. She smiled brightly and added, "Nice meeting y'all."

Then we were shoved past her and ushered along, parallel to the train. We passed window after window, our reflections pale in dusty glass panes, interrupted by sheeted windows, and returning in new glass panes. Even our shadows looked frightened.

At the back of the train, the ravine came to a dead end where a landslide had brought boulders down, cutting off the train tracks and half the train. Standing in the sandy clearing, smoking a hand-rolled cigarette, was a tall, slim figure in a battered Stetson, dingy, cuffed jean shirt, and dark pants. As we approached, she turned and pulled down the red bandanna that covered her nose and mouth. I nearly stopped dead in my tracks. She was older, taller, harder-looking, but I would know her anywhere.

Olivia Rosales.

Beside me, I heard Asa make a sound, a gasp of recognition? Of terror? I wasn't sure. But somehow, seeing her was affecting him as much as it affected me.

"What is it?" she said, her voice flat with impatience. Under her shirt, I could see a bit of bandage poking out—and a spot of blood seeping through to the outside of her shirt. I remembered the streak of blood on the wall. Had she been the one who had gotten shot?

"We found these two in one of the caves out on the west side," said Zo. Olivia scanned our faces, then turned away. She didn't remember me, but why should she?

"We thought you'd—" Judith started.

"*No,*" she said, turning away again.

"Liv," said Zo, taking a step toward Olivia as Judith held us in place. "They're the ones. They're the ones who set the trap. They're the reason you were shot. They kept us from getting the medicine for Susanah."

"You must be Morevna's new Successor, then," she said, not seeming impressed in the slightest. She turned to Asa. "And you're the new guy. The one who wandered into this hellhole and got trapped." Her eyes flickered over him. "Hmmmm. You're kinda cute, though."

Zo rolled her eyes.

Olivia looked at us for a moment more, then waved her hand and said, "Take them out back and shoot them. Make sure to throw their bodies far enough to keep the Laredo Boys off our tracks. Keep the components belt, though. Cassie can use it or something."

"But, Liv, look at what they had," Zo said. She held Asa's photograph up for her to see. On the back, I could make out a sentence in Spanish.

Olivia squinted at the photograph. Then she turned white. She snatched the photograph out of Zo's hands.

"Which one of you had this?" she demanded.

"The cute one did," said Zo. Judith shoved Asa forward.

"Well?" she said, looking him in the eye. I held my breath.

"My name is, uh . . . Asa Skander, Miss . . . Olivia, I presume?" he said. "I . . . er . . . I lived in your old house for a brief period. And I found this in—"

"Why did you keep it?" she asked. "You like looking at pictures of dead girls, pendejo? Girls who can't talk for themselves? You some kind of sicko?"

"Whoa, whoa, whoa!" said Asa, putting his hands up. "You've got me all wrong—"

"This is a picture of pain. Mine and Rosa's pain. That's a life we can never get back."

My palms sweated. Things were going downhill fast. My fingers itched for my components belt.

"I'm sorry," he said, blinking. "I—"

"So you set a trap, get me shot, and fawn over a picture of me and my dead sister," said Olivia with venom dripping from her voice. "You know she was slow, right? You know what happened to her? Who I killed for her?"

My heart pounded. I'd never heard anyone admit to murder before. And what did she mean, what happened to her?

"I just thought it was a nice picture!" he said, as though that were a reasonable thing to say. "Really! That's all!"

"That's real easy to say now, isn't it? You know that . . . that pinche gringo I killed made her life a living hell, right? And now you've got the nerve to . . ." Then she turned to Judith. "Let this guy go. I'm gonna fight him myself, right now, hand to hand. We'll decide what to do with Morevna's lackey later."

Panic rang like an alarm in my chest, but I was powerless.

Judith kicked Asa in the back, and he stumbled forward.

"What would it take for you to just let me explain?" he asked, pushing his glasses up the bridge of his nose. He sounded calm, calmer than I would've been if I'd just been challenged to a fight by Olivia Rosales.

"A miracle," she said, pulling a long knife from her belt.

"What if I win?" he asked. "If I win, will you spare us?"

"Pfft," she said. "That's not going to happen."

"But if it does?" he said firmly.

Olivia smirked. "We'll cross that bridge when we get there, chavalo," she said. "But for now, get ready."

She squared off, her legs bent, her eyes gleaming, her knife ready in her hand. Asa stood, slack-shouldered. If I didn't know him for what he was, I'd have thought him a fool. But his eyes gleamed behind the broken spectacles, and I knew he must be up to something.

Olivia began to circle him; then, kicking up dust, she charged him, knife flashing in the sun. And Asa vanished beneath her knife. Olivia's face contorted with rage and confusion. She swung behind her, but he wasn't there. Instead, he appeared beside her, tapped her on the shoulder, then disappeared again as she swung at him again. Time and time she swung, and time and time he flashed away, leaving only a little puff of dust. And as he moved, the dust rose thick around Olivia, so thick that she pulled her bandanna over her nose and mouth again.

"It's not fair," Judith said as Olivia's knife flashed again. "He's being a coward."

"If he was being a coward, he'd have just disappeared completely," I said, squinting through the dust. *Come on, Asa!* I urged him silently. *Come on!*

Olivia stopped. I saw her stand still at the center of the dust cloud as the blur that was Asa flickered in and out of existence around her. Then her knife flashed out—a spray of red appeared in the air. Asa had been hit! He appeared for just a moment, bent over, clutching his arm with a blackened, scaly daemon hand, then darted away again.

"She's got him now," said Zo.

Asa continued to flash, here and there, behind her, in front of her, beside her. But it seemed then that Olivia herself became faster. She was missing him by less and less, and sometimes her knife took on the strange, blurred speed of Asa himself. She was fast, impossibly fast, as though she were copying him somehow, gaining his powers.

With a jolt of shock I realized that was exactly what she was doing.

"She doesn't have any magic of her own," Zo said to me, "but when she gets a little of your blood, she can get a little of your powers. Just for a moment. Your friend is good, but she's as good as anybody. Literally."

Again, Olivia lunged and a spray of blood flew out into the dust.

Asa's disembodied voice said, "Argh!" and Olivia wiped her

knife on her pants and readied herself again. Then she stumbled forward, cursing, as the back of her shirt ripped and a diagonal slash of blood appeared on her back. She stumbled to the side as Asa slashed at her left arm, drawing blood. They were shot for shot now, and we all watched—the oddly dressed girl from earlier had joined us now—with bated breath.

Olivia was breathing hard now, her shoulders heaving as she furiously scanned the cloud of dust and speed, looking for the right moment to strike. Then it came. As the cloud of dust rose around her, we had one final glimpse of Olivia as she pivoted and struck, her blade aimed upward and out. Then, silence. None of us moved. And as the dust cleared, we saw them. They were standing an arm's length apart, spattered with blood, and just as Olivia held her knife to Asa's throat, Asa had a blade to hers—or was it a long, black, infernal claw? Neither moved.

"Like I said," Asa was saying. "You've got me all wrong."

"What the hell are you?" she said, her eyes wide with fear and anger.

"That's one of the things you didn't let me explain," Asa said. "Will you let me now?"

Olivia stared at him, her expression unreadable. Then, together, without blinking, they lowered their blades from each other's throats.

"All right," she said to him. "Explain."

"Olivia!" came a high, desperate voice. "Olivia!"

We turned to see a filthy little white girl no older than ten standing in the door of the nearest train car.

"Mowse!" said Olivia. "Get back inside!"

"She's getting worse!" the little girl sobbed. "I put her to sleep, but I think she might . . ." Her lip trembled and a line of snot slid down her raw, freckled face. "Please come see her!"

Olivia took another look at Asa, then at me. Then she followed the little girl inside.

I turned to Asa. I wanted to tell him how glad I was that he'd held his own and to ask why the hell he had had a picture of the Rosales sisters in his pocket the whole time. But Asa's eyes were on the door Olivia had passed through. He looked oddly intrigued.

CHAPTER 15

The other girls exchanged worried glances after the door slid closed behind her. I felt a cold, almost accusatory silence fall over those of us outside the car.

"What's going on?" Asa asked.

"Like you don't know," said Judith, with her hands on her hips. "You're the ones who set the trap."

"Judith, go fetch some water," said Zo. Judith grumbled, then handed Zo my spell components belt and disappeared into a nearby train car.

"I'm going to go check on Susanah," said the strangely dressed girl, Cassie, I assumed. "To see if I can ease the pain a little . . ." And she too disappeared into the train car.

The air felt electric with tension. But no one could hurt us, not after Asa had won our lives, so we stood there, wondering what to do, where to go.

"If we've done something wrong, please let us know," said Asa. "Because we really have no idea, and the last thing we want to do is make enemies out here."

Zo looked at me incredulously, and I guess I looked blank and confused enough, because she sighed and said, "Remember Mourning Night? The robbery? One of the girls, our mechanic, Susanah Mihecoby, was the one to actually break into the Sacrifice building. She got out with a lot of stuff, but not before she'd already stepped into the spell circle on the floor."

Mother Morevna's trapdoor spell, I thought. *The one that would kill anyone who set it off.*

"She didn't know it had got her until later, after we ate some of the food we stole. She's been sick ever since and getting worse every day. The other times we broke into Elysium, we were trying to find some medicine for her, to ease the pain. But thanks to you two and your little trap, we weren't successful. And now Mowse has to watch the only family she's ever known die before her eyes."

"We didn't set that trapdoor spell, Mother Morevna did," I said, indignation flaring in my chest. "We set the trap, yeah, but if you hadn't stolen from the Sacrifice, none of this would have happened. I'm sorry for your friend, but you can't blame us for something that happened because all of you chose to steal."

Zo looked at me for a moment, her expression unreadable.

"You don't understand what it's like to be out here yet," she said. "But you will. And then you won't be so self-righteous when you see that out here there's no black and white. There's just gray. Just kill or be killed, steal or starve. And without Susanah, it's going to be a lot harder for everybody. Especially Mowse."

I was quiet. A part of me was still angry with them for stealing from us in the first place. But I thought of the girl, Mowse, and another, larger part of me remembered how it was to see someone I loved die. To see Mama waste away and be forced to stand by, powerless, as I became an orphan. As I became a burden. And, thieves or not, I didn't want anybody else to have to know that feeling.

Then I had an idea. I reached into my spell component pockets, feeling around to make sure it hadn't fallen out during the journey. Then I felt it: the smooth white stone, the one that Mother Morevna had given me. The one that would undo one of Mother Morevna's trapdoor spells.

"Wait," I said, "I want to help."

Zo rolled her eyes. "Like I said—"

"I didn't do this, but I think I can undo it." I looked directly into Zo's eyes, challenging her. "I think I can heal her."

Zo was quiet, eyes narrowed, unsure.

"Zo," said the other girl near the doorway, pale and worried. "It doesn't look like she's got long. . . ."

Zo looked at me very seriously, scanning my face to see if I was telling the truth, then nodded. "Come on, then," she said. "But if you fail . . ."

"I won't," I said. Across from me, Asa nodded. Then Zo led me up into the train car.

It was dark inside, and the air was heavy with a feeling I knew well: worry and grief.

Toward the back of the room, the girls were clustered: Olivia and Cassie and the little girl, Mowse, kneeling by a cot made out of what looked like old blankets. On the cot, a young woman, Kiowa or Comanche, maybe, was lying on her back with her eyes closed. Her long hair was spread over her chest and on her pillow in sweaty black strings. Olivia heard us enter and turned.

"Zo, what the hell are you doing? Get her out! Now!"

"She says she can heal Susanah. Says she knows how to break the curse."

"You do?" It was Mowse's voice this time, small and hoarse and hopeful.

"Yes," I said. "I think I can heal her."

"Olivia, please," said Mowse from the floor. "Please let her."

Every eye was on Olivia, but Olivia's were on Susanah.

". . . All right," she said. Then, to me, "Get over here and do it."

I went to the bedside and looked down at the girl on it. Susanah was older than me, in her early twenties, probably. She had plainly been strong once, but now she was sunken-cheeked and hollow-chested. Her lips were dry and flaky, and her eyes had begun to sink inward like a dead person's. *Mama looked like this before she died,* I thought with the shallow pang of old grief. She wasn't long for this world. Mother Morevna's spell had drained her slowly, like a hole in a tire. They were lucky that it had been only her and not all of them.

Feeling the other girls' eyes on my back, I pulled out my stone and placed it on her chest. It barely moved when she breathed. Then I cleared my mind and focused my magic into my hands. The penny on my chest warmed to life. With my eyes closed, I raised my right hand to my mouth and bit into my thumb, hard, until I tasted blood. *Set it right,* Mother Morevna had said. *Setzen Sie es richtig.*

"Setzen Sie es richtig," I said, and as I smeared my own blood on the stone, I felt power throb through my veins and into it. The pulse rocked through the girl lying there, and she began to change like a field when the storm clouds roll away. Her dull skin grew bright and healthy. Her hair seemed to change too, become thicker and blacker almost, and her breathing was no longer a shallow wheeze, but deep and regular. I took the stone back; the magic had been done. The girls were around me, watching. I could feel all of them holding their breath. Then Susanah's eyes fluttered open. She looked up at me in confusion.

"Susanah!" cried a small voice.

"Kahúu!" Susanah said, her face breaking into a wide smile. "My little mouse, come here!" Her voice was weak, but she reached down and pulled the little girl, Mowse, to her side.

"I thought you were gonna die," sobbed the little girl.

"No! No, no, no, no, no," said Susanah, "I'd never leave you. Never in a million years."

Then the two of them hugged, and the other girls huddled close around them. I let out a whooshing breath of relief. I had done it. Neither of them had to know a life without the other. And even if I had ruined Elysium, at least I had been able to do this. To return this. I stepped back from their circle of tears, an outsider again. Then I felt someone standing beside me.

"She gave you one of those?" Olivia said, her eyes on the stone in my hand. Her voice had an odd, tight quality to it that I couldn't place. "From what I remember, Morevna didn't just give those away."

"You knew Mother Morevna?" I asked.

“No, I didn’t,” said Olivia, her voice as flat as a stone itself. She watched the weeping, huddled mass around Susanah’s cot.

“You know, Susanah’s been out here longer than any of us—even me,” said Olivia. She took a drag of her cigarette and blew out a line of smoke. “That’s how she found Mowse—she hid in a car throughout Black Sunday after she broke out of that . . . *school* . . . she was in up north. Mowse was inside under some blankets. Probably an Okie family on the way to California who abandoned her, thinking she’d be one less mouth to feed.” Olivia paused. “Mowse would’ve still had us, but . . . I can’t imagine what she would have done if Susanah . . .”

“I know,” I said, watching Susanah and Mowse, feeling my chest grow tight. “I know what that’s like.”

Olivia turned to me and really looked me in the eyes for the first time.

“You’re the Girl Who Cried Rain,” she said. “I remember you now.”

That name. It was always unexpectedly sharp, always cut just a little. But Olivia said it differently, with—no, not pity in her voice. Understanding. Because who could understand being alone against Elysium if not Olivia Rosales?

“Sal,” I said. “Just Sal.”

Olivia nodded.

“We’re in your debt, Sal,” she said. “Anything you want, name it. You’re one of us now.”

One of us. That phrase felt golden in my mind. To be one of something. I’d never had that, I realized. Not even as Mother Morevna’s Successor. That had been more isolating than anything. One of us. But there were two.

"What about Asa?" I asked. "I can't leave him out there by himself. He's invited too, right?"

"Why, of cour—" Olivia began, but before she could finish, Asa himself appeared in the doorway, looking paler than usual.

"Actually, I think I'll have to decline that offer," Asa said, his eyes darting from me to Olivia, a strange kind of panic behind them. "As kind as it is, I think I need to go it alone for a bit. You stay here, Sal. I'll be fine on my own." He turned to Olivia. "I'm sorry again about the picture misunderstanding and I wish you the best, but I don't think I should be here. . . ."

It didn't make sense. Asa seemed so shaky, so fearful. He didn't even cross the doorway. He stood at the edge of it like a vampire waiting to be let in, his eyes falling again and again on Olivia.

"But, Asa, where are you going to—"

"This is stupid," Olivia said. "It's insane to be alone out there. You won't get another offer like this."

"Maybe not," he said. "But I'd rather be safe than sorry." He tipped his hat, and without another word, Asa disappeared into the desert, leaving me. Again.

• • •

Out in the desert, Asa's brain pounded with panic. His human mask threatened to fall off in bits like pieces of a car in a junkyard. When he was with someone else, he could focus on other things, whistling, snapping, making plans. Playing at being human.

But now he was alone. And better alone than there, with her.

Olivia Rosales, the one who could disarm him, whose nature Death was using to further Her own ends. She was Death's Wildcard, she had to be, though he doubted she knew it. A human chosen by Death wouldn't know; she'd just inadvertently serve Death's cause through her own nature, her own decisions. And that explained even more: As the opposing Card, he was drawn to her, drawn inexorably. That's what he had felt as Judith and Zo led them to the train. That's why the photograph had felt so significant. She was the Card. And if he'd had any doubts, fighting her had alleviated them. It had been an enormous risk to fight her hand to hand, but he'd had to be sure. And now he was. If he wanted to fix things, he needed to stay away from Olivia Rosales.

But Sal. Of course she had to stay there. It was the right thing to do. The human thing to do. Sal's security wasn't his. There was no security for him, not now. And who knew if Life would even allow him the chance to make things right again? Who knew if even now Life was sending Her Sentinels to hunt him, seize him, bring him back for punishment?

Asa shook himself mentally.

"I'm okay," he said, smiling as wide as possible (far too wide). "I've got this."

He took deep breaths, looked up at the cold, unfamiliar stars.

But his smile deflated, and he knew that he was very much not okay and that he definitely did not have this. What would he do out here? Where would he go? Asa wasn't sure.

Now that there was nothing to draw his attention away, Asa could feel the foundation of everything tipping. He could feel the crawl of minutes, maggots over the cooling corpse of this world. Their days were numbered. Death would surely win at this rate. And if She won . . .

Asa shook his head. All the fantasies he'd had about being

human, of living a human life seemed minuscule and foolish in comparison with the gargantuan mistake he'd made. Now he knew he'd give anything to have things go back to the way they were, before he was ever sent down to this dusty piece of hell.

He let his eyes go daemon again, like they'd been trying to do for an hour now. He let his legs bend their natural way, his feet and hands and teeth and snout elongating. There was nothing human about him now. If there had ever been anything really human in the first place. How could he kid himself? He was just as bad a human as he was a daemon. Worse, maybe. And now was he even a daemon anymore? Asa wasn't sure, and that made him feel twisted and bent and impossible. Wrong. Like he was a mistake. That's how he'd always felt, he realized. Like a mistake. Why, oh why had the Mother chosen him? Why had Life agreed? Hadn't They known that his curiosity and impulsivity, his wrongness would be his undoing?

Asa had a sudden, awful thought. Had that been Their plan all along?

"If You were trying to prove a point, that I'm the worst daemon that has ever lived, You've proven it!" he shouted at the sky. "I've learned my lesson!"

Asa waited, but only the lonely wind blew around his ankles. He thought of Death and Her inevitable march. Perhaps Life was so disgusted by his failure that She was leaving him to be torn asunder by Her Sister. Or . . . his heart sank. Or perhaps sending him down here was just a way of getting rid of him, the annoying, human-obsessed mistake always on the fringes, always unsatisfied. Perhaps She had never meant for him to succeed in the first place.

But I was her Card, Asa thought. *Am I still?*

In the distance there was a howl, then nothing more. Once an active player, Asa had fallen off the playing board, and it seemed as though his absence wasn't even felt. It was as though he was nothing. It was as though he was nothing at all.

Asa sat down on the dunes and looked out over the great, alien expanse before him. The shadows seemed to bend and twist the more he looked at them, expanding into the shapes of Sentinels, coming to take him back, to rend him to pieces for his failure. He blinked, and the shadows were just shadows again. *But they will come for me,* Asa thought, the hair rising on the back of his neck. *Maybe not now. Maybe not until the very last day, but they will come for me.*

Far away, a faint sound rose, audible only to his daemonic ears. Singing—mournful, tearful singing. Back at Elysium, a funeral was underway.

• • •

It had taken Lucy Arbor's aunt Lucretia four days to die. For four days, she had wheezed and hacked, spitting up mud and blood as the family looked on, helpless. Some of them had wiped her head with a cool rag. Some of them had ladled Dowsing Well water down her throat. Some had gotten down on their knees and prayed. But it didn't matter, Lucy thought. Despite all of that, she had still died.

The funeral had been a classic Elysian funeral: the family standing at the base of the wall, looking upward, as Aunt Lucretia's frail, white-swaddled body was bricked into the top of the wall. They had wept and hugged, and sung the songs from the days before the walls and the Dust had covered everything. They had prayed once more to a god who didn't exist, a tether to culture and the past, and they had left. From there, everyone had gone back to Lucy's parents' house, where a funeral dinner made of rations—more meager than ever in these days after the Sacrifice building burned—waited to comfort their stomachs even if their souls were still bruised with loss.

But Lucy didn't join them. Instead, in her best dress, with her hair in artful braids, she walked across town to the hospital, feeling lucky that the night was so dark and that no one was out on the streets but her—her and the never-ending march of workmen collecting rations and doing their best to build a new Sacrifice before the Dust Soldiers came. *Squeezing people dry,* Lucy thought, *and for what? It's too late. We're just going to die anyway. We could at least go out with full bellies.*

Even with no one on the street, Lucy could feel the shadow of doom hanging over the town. It was present in the number of guards—doubled since the day Sal and Asa were exiled—stooping, exhausted in their towers. It was present in the announcements and flyers Mother Morevna sent out, telling everyone that now was not the time to panic; it was the time to use less and give to the Sacrifice. It was present in her own face, how her cheeks had begun to hollow.

Lucy thought of Aunt Lucretia's sunken stomach and fought back a lurch of grief. She was almost to the hospital, and she had to hold it together there, if nowhere else.

When she got to the desk, Nurse Ada was waiting. Lucy breathed a sigh of relief. Sometimes the older, white nurses still had a little pre-Elysium meanness lingering in the way they looked at her, the tone they used or didn't use. Nurse Ada wasn't like that. Nurse Ada liked girls, like Lucy did, though Lucy wasn't sure how she could tell. She thought maybe that was one of the reasons they got along. Though most of it was probably that she was a good person—sometimes the only person Lucy could talk to while she was in the hospital.

"Here you are," said Nurse Ada, pulling a bundle from under the desk. "These are all her things, everything she had during her stay with us. And I am so sorry, Lucy. Your aunt was a kind, sweet lady, and a lot like you in many ways." Nurse Ada smiled a sad sort of smile. "Always well-dressed."

"Thank you," Lucy said. "And yes, ma'am . . . she was."

Aunt Lucretia's things included a faded blue blanket, a rhinestone brooch, and a tin drinking cup, the one she had used to drink the Dowsing Well water Lucy had kept bringing her long after she knew it wasn't working.

Customarily, now would have been the time to choose what went onto the platform for the Mourning Night ceremony. (The brooch would have been a likely candidate.) But now there was no assurance of another Mourning Night ceremony. No assurance of life beyond the next couple of months, and Lucy simply pocketed the brooch and wrapped the cup in the blanket.

But getting Aunt Lucretia's things was only part of the reason she was there. Ever since Sal was exiled from Elysium, Lucy had been coming to the hospital and talking to Nurse Ada about Dust Sickness, finding out more about it, how it infected people, and, hopefully, how to keep people from being infected.

"Ruth, could you man the desk?" Nurse Ada asked. "I need to speak with Lucy more in depth."

Reluctantly, Nurse Ruth, a bad-tempered elderly white woman, took the desk, and Nurse Ada took Lucy back to her office.

"Do you have anything?" Lucy asked, pulling her handmade notepad from her pocket and her pencil from behind her ear.

"Not so far," Nurse Ada said. "Only that Dust Sickness seems to be spreading faster now. It's so strange. Unless the little bit of dust that got in when Sal Wilkerson and Asa Skander cast Dust Dome is to blame?"

"Maybe," Lucy said, though somewhere inside she knew that was wrong. "But Aunt Lucretia . . ." Lucy paused, swallowed a lump growing in her throat. "She was inside with the windows shuttered when that dust storm hit. So why did she . . . ?"

"I don't know," Nurse Ada said. "None of us know how the dust is getting to people. None of us know how to cure it. All we know how to do is treat the symptoms."

It was strange. Dust Sickness seemed to swoop down and take some people, like Aunt Lucretia and Sal's mother, and leave others hanging on, growing thinner and paler and less of themselves by the day. Personally, Lucy thought the hanging on was worse.

Just then, the door swung open, and a white man rushed in carrying his wife. She hung limp in his arms, her breath coming in a high, thin wheeze. Lucy recognized him from the food ration counter: Mr. Walker, who always slipped an extra ration to families with kids.

"Help!" Mr. Walker cried. "My wife! She's collapsed! I think she has Dust Sickness!"

Nurse Ada rang a bell under the desk, and three nurses rushed out and took them back to the operating room. Lucy heard someone asking about a tracheotomy and someone else asking about chest compressions; then a door slammed and it was quiet again.

"That's the fifth one today," Nurse Ada murmured.

CHAPTER 16

2 MONTHS AND *23 DAYS* REMAIN.

When I woke, the smell of food was in the air: bread, meat, coffee. My stomach growled painfully. It had only been five days since I'd had a proper meal, but it felt like an eternity.

I thought of Asa out there in the desert, and a pang of guilt went through me. Was it something I did? Something I said that made him leave? *Maybe Asa is okay,* I thought. *Maybe he's out there biting the head off a rabbit or something,* I thought, surprised by how easily that visual came to mind. *He said he'd be all right, so I'm sure he will. Besides, it was his idea.* I told myself this, but even so, I was worried about him. More than that, I was worried about what I was doing here. The penny had pointed in this direction, had buzzed when we arrived as though to say, *Here we are!* But what was it that I was looking for? What was I supposed to find?

My stomach growled again, twisted itself in a knot. Whatever I was looking for, I needed to eat first. I dressed and made my way outside, letting the smell of food lead me onward.

The first car of the train, the engine room, seemed to be the kitchen—that was where the smell was coming from at any rate.

Timidly, I opened the door and stepped inside. It was surprisingly homey in a threadbare, modified sort of way. Desert plants grew in tin cans along the slim windows. In the front of the train, behind the windshield, an array of jars and bags and canisters were spread like they might have been on a kitchen counter in a house. There was an old table with no chairs (they probably ate standing up, like Mama had always discouraged) set with eight rag-covered plates. The firebox had been modified into a stove, it looked like, and on it a frying pan simmered on a rack, smelling so good that my stomach growled loudly.

The girl I had healed, Susanah, was making breakfast. She had sliced some homemade bread and was putting it into an odd woven wire contraption. Then she put the bread in its wire cage and hung it from a hook in the oven, close to the pan. She gave the pan a good stirring with a hand-carved wooden spoon and wiped her forehead. The little girl, Mowse, was in a nightgown—no, a man's shirt that fit her like a nightgown—and was putting a bunch of rocks on the floor in a circle. Beside her was a tattered, well-worn book called *Ways of the Comanche.*

"What is 'black' in Comanche?" Susanah asked the little girl.

"Tuhubitu," the girl said dutifully.

"What about 'sun'?"

"Taabe."

"And 'water'?" Susanah opened the oven and checked the food again.

"Uhhhhh . . ."

"Paa," said Susanah. "Paa is water. Remember that."

Mowse saw me then, and said, "The girl is here! The girl who saved you!" Susanah looked up at me, pushing her glasses up.

"Hello," said Susanah. Mowse stared at me from the floor.

"Don't be rude, Mowse," said Susanah. "Say hello to her—in Comanche."

"Maruawe," said Mowse with a little wave.

"Mar-ua . . . ?" I attempted. Then I gave up and just said, "Hello," back.

"A good try," said Susanah. "Come in. It's going to be dried beef gravy over toast."

"When's it going to be ready?" asked Mowse.

"When I say so."

Susanah took the kettle from the flames with a rag around her hand and poured a cup of coffee.

"I hope you like it black, because we don't have any milk or sugar."

"That's fine," I said, and drank a scalding-hot mouthful, trying not to make a face at how bitter and gritty it was.

"Thank you for healing me, by the way," she said. "I would have thanked you then, but . . . Mowse! Stop it!" On the floor, Mowse had pulled a lizard from the pocket of her shirt and was somehow making it walk on its hind legs, in a weaving line in between the rocks. She snapped her head in Susanah's direction.

"You know what I told you about that stuff," said Susanah. The lizard shook its head and wriggled away.

"Sorry," said Susanah, taking a sip of her own coffee. "She likes to make things do what she wants. Fall asleep, walk in circles. But what do I tell you about that?" she asked Mowse.

"That it's rude and we're better than that," said Mowse begrudgingly.

Susanah took the toast out of the oven, put it on a plate, and covered it with a rag. Then she gave the pan one more scraping stir, took it out of the oven, and placed it on the table. "Wait for it, Mowse," she said. "Give it about five minutes, then you can have some."

Mowse pouted, but said nothing. She picked up a corn-husk doll and began playing with it instead.

"Is she the one who made the soldiers fall asleep whenever y'all . . . ?" I said.

"When we robbed Elysium?" Susanah said. "Yeah. She was excited to finally get the chance to use her powers for something."

"Do most of you have powers, or . . . ?"

"No. Just Mowse, Cassandra, and Olivia—sometimes. She doesn't use magic unless she has to. The rest of us are pretty normal. Judith is the muscle. Zo is a sharpshooter. Those two drive each other crazy, but they're inseparable."

"So you're the mechanic?" I asked.

"I build things," she said. "I modified the train, make all the weapons, fix what gets broken. That kind of thing. All the inventions everywhere? Those are mine."

"Wow," I said. "It must have been a lot of work."

Susanah shrugged. "I always hoped that if I ever got out of here maybe I could be an inventor. I still hope that, though it's looking less likely these days."

"Can I have some now?" said Mowse with her plate in hand. "Or are y'all gonna talk forever?"

"Sure," said Susanah. "Eat up, kid." She looked at me and said, "You too. The rest of them can have some when they get up."

The food was surprisingly good, for being made on the firebox of a train, and when our plates were clean and stacked,

Mowse went out to find more lizards ("I won't make them do stuff, I promise!" she assured Susanah), and I leaned against the wall beside Susanah, pleasantly full for the first time in days.

"I heard that guy you were with beat Olivia," Susanah said. "That doesn't happen much. I think she's a little shaken up by it. She won't stop mentioning him."

"I bet," I said. I remembered the look in Olivia's eyes when Asa had held his claw to her throat. She wasn't used to losing. But there was something else there too, and it definitely wasn't horror.

"Do you know where your friend is now?" Susanah asked.

Your friend. A pang of guilt rippled through me. Were Asa and I friends now? Of course we were. He'd saved my life twice. And once you got past the annoyance of him learning humanity, he really wasn't all that bad. For a daemon. Should I have gone back out into the desert with him?

Suddenly, I became aware of how quiet it was.

"Where is everyone?" I asked.

"Zo's out on patrol with Cassandra. The others should be up any minute. They're heavy sleepers, usually. How about you?" she asked. "Did you sleep well last night?"

"Can't complain," I said. "It was better than in a ditch in the desert, even if I was lying there in all those springs and gears and things."

"She's in the machine room?" asked Mowse, slipping back inside. "Now how are we gonna get our parts?"

"I'm sorry," I said. "I didn't know I was intruding."

"It's all right. Mowse just has a one-track mind when it comes to our project."

"Project?" I asked.

There was a gasp from Mowse. "Can we show her, Susanah? She's one of us now, right?"

Susanah looked at me for a moment, then said, "I guess it wouldn't hurt. Do you want to see our project?"

"Sure," I said. "What else do I have to do?"

"Come on, then," Susanah said. "I'll show you."

I followed her outside, along the back of the train to the place where Olivia and Asa had fought. But she led me beyond it, to the cliffside. She stood with her boot on an odd white rock, and said, "Puuku." Then the side of the cliff was just gone and in its place was the mouth of a high, broad cave. She led me into it, and we walked a little ways into the cliffside, Mowse lighting the torches as we passed them with a pinch of something and a whispered word. A tingle of familiarity went through me. Was this the fire spell I knew? And if so, how had Mowse learned it? Had Cassandra taught her?

But before I could think too much about this, they stopped in front of an alcove that smelled of motor oil, and Susanah said, "There they are: our pride and joy."

I moved forward until Mowse lit a torch nearby, throwing the alcove into light. At first, I wasn't sure what I was looking at. Then, when my brain pieced it all together, I couldn't help but move forward to get a better look.

They were horses. Four life-size horses put together from pieces of metal, springs, gears. Robotic horses, with lightbulbs from old headlights for eyes, rusty license plates and pieces of sheet metal for skin, actual bones covered in metal for jaws, and ropes for manes. Their long, lean legs were pistons. Their backs were broad and strong and plainly well put together.

"You *built* these?" I gasped.

"Yep," Susanah said. "With my own two hands."

"I helped!" said Mowse. "Mostly with that one." She pointed to the one on the end.

"Two people can ride on each one," Susanah said. "Theoretically, I mean. I've never been able to get them to work long enough. Anytime I try to build anything that runs off electricity, the desert just drains it. So they're a work in progress, I guess, until I find another power source. But once they're finished, nobody in the desert will want to mess with us."

"But why horses?" I asked. "Why not cars or something?"

"I'm Comanche," she said. "Numunuu, Kotsoteka. We were horse riders from right here on the Plains. And even if I didn't get to learn much about my people before they sent me off to Chilacco, I'm back home now. I can at least have my own horses if I can't have anything else, you know?" Susanah stared at the horses for a moment more, then shrugged. "Anyway, hooves are more maneuverable on sand and dust than wheels are."

We stood, staring at the horses for a few more minutes, Mowse telling me about this thing and that; then we left the horses slumping in the darkness and went back to the train. There, Olivia and Judith were gathered around the table, Judith with toast in her mouth and Olivia finishing a cup of coffee. There were two plates left, carefully saved for Zo and Cassandra.

"Well, there they are," said Judith. "'Bout time we saw you this morning."

"Good thing I came back too," laughed Susanah. "Or you'd have eaten all of it yourself."

"It's not my fault you cook so much better than Olivia," said

Judith. "Hey, maybe we should find that Harold Lloyd guy. Maybe y'all can have a cooking contest and settle it once and for all!"

"Shut up, Judith!" Olivia flicked Judith with her bandanna.

"What is he, anyway?" Judith asked me. " 'Cause he sure ain't normal."

I took a deep breath. Might as well just tell them, I thought. "He's a daemon, given form by the Goddess of Life and sent to help Life win the Game. He was here on a mission to return a cricket in amber to its owner, and somehow that was supposed to help tip the Game in Life's favor, but we got exiled, so now we're out here together."

Judith and Olivia blinked at me, bewildered.

"What's the difference between a daemon and a demon?" Judith asked.

I sighed. "It's like a . . . like a . . . It's some ancient Greek thing. But not evil! More neutral to . . . be a sort of go-between between people and gods."

Judith and Olivia exchanged dubious glances.

"He's a really nice guy, though," I finished lamely.

Judith shrugged and nodded. "If you say so."

But Olivia wasn't finished. "Whatever he is, why did he have my picture?"

"Look," I said. "I know it looks bad, but if he says he just thought it was a nice picture, that's all there is to it. He's never been a person before, so he's just doing his best." I sighed. "I gave him a hard time at first, but the truth is, he's the most innocent pers—most innocent *being*—I've ever met."

"What, do you want to go find him or something?" Olivia asked.

I wasn't sure. Asa had seemed so shaken, so ready to leave. But we had agreed to fix this together, however we could . . . hadn't we?

"Olivia! Judith!" Zo scrambled to the door with Cassandra close behind her, draped with odd gunlike and bowlike weapons that could only be Susanah's inventions. "Come on, we need everybody today."

"What are you talking about, Zo?" Olivia said.

"There's a big lode of metal out there," said Cassandra. "Two trucks, buried almost completely. We found them this morning on the north side. There are dry goods with them, in the passenger side of each one. Dried beef and pork, and maybe venison. I think there's even some old bottles of cider. And, better yet, the Laredo Boys haven't found it yet. No footprints all around."

"But what's the hurry?" I asked. "Don't you have all those supplies you stole from Elysium? Aren't they fine to eat now that I broke the spell?"

"I guess they *would* be, but we burned what was left," said Judith. "Someone decided we couldn't be too careful." ("Hey!" said Zo. "We're still alive!") "Besides, being low on supplies was the only reason we robbed Elysium in the first place. And we were only low because the Laredo Boys robbed us."

"The Laredo Boys have been really aggressive lately," Olivia said. "Running us away from every stash, robbing us of almost every kill—even grasshoppers. They're trying to starve us out so we'll join them. And if we know about a stash they don't, we need to get to it before they do."

"Well, we're gonna need everybody to haul this," said Zo.

"All right," said Olivia. "Let's go, everyone." Then she pointed at me and said, "You too."

"Me?" I gulped. "But I've never done anything like this before. I just got here!"

"Yes, and you're another witch," said Olivia, "with a loaded components belt. I saw a little of that duel. You're raw, but you've got it. Now hurry up. Time's ticking."

Nervous, kind of insulted, and flattered at the same time, I followed them as they went from car to car until they reached the last one of the train. There, on the floor, an array of weapons was laid out. Olivia took what looked like a modified six-gun. Judith took an old Louisville Slugger. Susanah took a backpack loaded with tools and a long, sharpened chain.

"If the Laredo Boys get any more of the metal out here, they'll have the advantage," Olivia was saying. "And if they get the advantage, we can kiss what security we have goodbye, so we gotta get this while we can." She looked at me. "But you, you've got all you need." She glanced down at my components belt. "Just stay close to me, all right?"

I nodded, feeling my pulse tic in my neck, hoping I was as ready as Olivia seemed to think I was. I shoved the Booke deep into my pocket and checked my spell components pouch, and when everyone was ready, they swept me out the door and we headed into the desert.

• • •

In the cave he had slept in, Asa rolled over and yawned a too-wide, sharp-toothed yawn. His clothes were folded neatly with his hat and shoes and glasses on top of them. Taking the human part off, he expected to feel the way Atlas felt handing the sky to Hercules for a moment's relief. He'd expected to feel sad, of course, taking off the illusion, but as he stretched his limbs in the light, he found that being just *him* felt strange too. Like his daemon form also wasn't the real him.

He sighed. Though this human body wasn't rightfully his, having it, being at home in it for so long had taken a toll on him. He had been changed, irreparably changed, and he knew it. Even if a miracle happened and he was allowed back into Her service, would he ever be the same? Would he ever be himself again? And what was he now? Daemon or human? Ugh, he wasn't sure. But he was sure that he didn't like the emotion that he was experiencing. It felt as though it was dragging him down, spreading from him like blood in water.

He thought of Sal, what she could be doing now. Sal had been nice to him. No, not nice. She had been kind to him, and she hadn't had to be. He'd had a hand in burning the Sacrifice building too, after all. And what about their search for whatever it was out here that could save everything? The search that had led them toward the train, toward the girls. He couldn't leave it all to Sal. He had to fix things too, not just hide out here in a cave, waiting.

Olivia's face rose in his mind then, beautiful and dangerous. She could disarm his plan. But wasn't his plan already disarmed? And what if he was able to disarm her, neutralize her Cardness with his own Cardness? Level the playing field?

The sound of human voices out in the ravine interrupted his thoughts.

He threw on his human form and human clothes and looked out through his cracked glasses.

It was the Laredo Boys, the same ones from before, ragged and tattered, their sunburned white skins painted with those disconcerting black designs. They reminded him of the designs the Picts had painted on themselves before they went to war a thousand years ago. The men had a dangerous coarseness to them, even worse now that he could watch them, their bodies slung with rifles, machetes, axes, clubs. They were far away, but even with his human ears, he could hear words like "metal," and "trucks," and "before they do."

Asa could tell that whatever they were doing, they were up to no good. He started out of the cave after them, then thought better of it. He let his fingers extend into claws, let his back grow arched, let his eyes go daemonic. He tapped his teeth and they went back to the long black needles that they usually were.

If they catch me, he thought, *they're not going home without a nightmare.*

Then, moving as silently as the shadow he so closely resembled, Asa slipped out of the cave and followed them.

CHAPTER 17

Zo led everyone through the craggy pass. Olivia followed her, and the rest of them followed Olivia. I drifted along behind my new associates, expecting any and every terrible thing in the desert to throw itself down on us from the cliffs. The others didn't seem upset in the slightest. If anything, they seemed almost excited, talking about all the things they could use the metal for (a shower system, Susanah suggested, and everyone seemed in agreement). But their hands were never far from their weapons.

"I'm about ready to pay those Laredo Boys back," said Judith, her big arms taut with muscle as she dragged a makeshift sheet-metal sleigh behind her to carry the haul. "I hope they show up. In fact, I dare them to."

"They've stolen from you before," I said. "Aren't you worried they'll go and attack the train? Burn it to the ground when you're not there?"

"Unlikely," said Judith. "When they stole the stuff from Elysium, we'd hidden it in a cave and they just got lucky. As for the camp, Cassandra has a mean illusion set up around it. They couldn't find the train if they tried. Unless you're *brought* to camp, or you're carrying something that belongs to somebody *at* the camp, all you see is cliffsides, no matter where you look."

"*Now* you see cliffsides, you mean," said Cassandra with a pout. "After they got through my first set of illusions and stole all our supplies." She turned to me. "We really are sorry about stealing from Elysium, you know? And when that celebration was planned, we figured no one would notice. If we'd known then what we know now we'd never have tried it, I'm sure."

"It was a mistake, all right?" Olivia said, from up at the front of the group. "How was I supposed to know that she'd changed the trapdoor spell? It used to just set off an alarm."

"How did you know about the trapdoor spell in the first place?" I asked.

"You think you were the first brujita she took on as a student?" Olivia said, looking over her shoulder and grinning wryly. A pang of shock and something like jealousy went through me. "We'll have to talk sometime."

Yes, I thought, my hand on the penny around my neck. *We would have to.* I had a lot of questions, and I had a feeling that only Olivia could answer them.

I would have dwelt on this more, I'm sure, but I had another feeling, a familiar tingle beneath my skin, demanding my attention. Deception—and strong, too. But it wasn't coming from any of the girls. Where was it coming from?

"I just hope they haven't gotten to this place yet," said Susanah.

"Don't worry," Cassandra said. "They haven't found this lode yet. I'm sure of it."

"I wish they would come," said Mowse, pulling the corn-husk

doll out of her pocket and making her dance up Susanah's arm. "I could make them all fall asleep."

Susanah reached out and ruffled her hair. "Hopefully it won't come to that. Hopefully we won't see them at all."

Zo led us through the pass and the desert brush for another mile, until we reached a narrow crack in the earth, where the land had changed and a new ravine had opened at the bottom of the one we were in, like a wound within a wound. At the bottom were three automobiles: two pickup trucks and one sedan, falling apart at the hinges. The hole was big enough for two people to slip into. The sand around the hole was clean, save for Zo's and Cassandra's footprints from earlier.

The tingling under my skin was almost an unbearable itch now. Deception was coming from all around me, bleeding out into the air like ink in water.

"There's something wrong," I said. "I can feel it."

"Oh, don't be a scaredy-cat," said Judith. "If Zo and Cass say they cased the place, they cased the place."

"Let's go," said Olivia. "We don't have that many bullets left after the last run, so we don't want to end up having to use them."

Judith nodded and jumped down into the hole. Susanah followed with her backpack full of tools.

"The rest of you, keep a lookout," said Olivia. "And help them load the metal."

There was a horrible rending sound as Judith and Susanah began tearing the doors off the vehicles, ripping the metal, taking off the handles and hood ornaments and mirrors. It echoed loudly off the cliffs and around the ravine. In a few moments, the seats themselves appeared on the lip of the ravine, and we moved them onto the sleigh, carefully stacking the other pieces of metal. To take the engines (Lord knew why Susanah wanted them), we fixed a rope to one of the car doors and made a second sleigh, which Susanah would pull herself.

I flexed my fingers close to my spell components belt. A bead of sweat rolled down my forehead. Couldn't any of the other witches feel it? Then I saw a flash of movement on the cliffside.

"It's a trap!" I shouted. "Everybody down!"

Gunshots rang out, echoing through the ravine as we ducked and ran for cover in every which direction. Bullets ricocheted off rocks, made holes in the truck and car parts. Olivia ducked behind a nearby rock and drew her guns. Judith picked up the car door, holding it like a shield by the rope we'd attached to it. It was so loud, so fast. Something went whistling by my ear. I balked at a flash of blood in the air as a bullet grazed Zo's arm right in front of me. She shoved me past her, then turned and sent two shots of her own back.

"Quick! Over here!" Susanah grabbed me, and pulled me behind the mountain of parts with Cassandra and Mowse. Bullets rang all around us. My hands shook, and my nerves felt like they were full of fire. I screwed my eyes shut and tried to calm my breathing, to think clearly.

Somebody scrambled around the corner, and Zo ducked in next to me, out of breath and bleeding.

"Damn Laredo Boys," Zo said. "There have got to be at least ten of them up there."

"How many bullets do they have?" I heard myself ask. "Surely they can't have that many out here?"

"In the desert, bullets are whatever you can melt down and shove in your gun barrel," said Zo. She reached into her pack and began reloading her pistols. I saw then that her bullets were nothing more than little pellets cobbled together from different materials. "The Laredo Boys have most of the metal out here." She clicked the bullets into their places. "But even they don't have unlimited ammo. We have to wait them out, however long that takes."

"Well, let's see if I can make it faster, darling," said Cassandra, looking somehow unflustered as the bullets whizzed by us.

Cassandra closed her eyes and grabbed a handful of sand from the ground. She began muttering something in what sounded like French. Suddenly, there were two of each of us: our real, flesh and blood selves and a more transparent version of ourselves that was like looking in a mirror: not quite right. It sent a shiver up my spine to look into my own slightly transparent, reversed eyes.

"Go!" said Cassandra. Our shadow selves darted out from behind the metal fortress, running in different directions, and casting no shadows. The Laredo Boys fired and fired, and soon the gunfire grew thinner and ceased altogether. Our shadow selves flickered out. A silence fell over the ravine. All I could hear were our ragged breaths and my own rabbit-fast heartbeat. Were they out of bullets?

Then a sound rang out over the ravine: the sound of someone clapping, loud and slow.

"Well done, girlies," said a deep, cold voice. "Well done." A man stepped out from behind a boulder, still clapping slowly, sarcastically. I recognized him immediately: the man from before, their leader. He started down from the cliffs, and we could see his bald head—shaved and painted with the black designs—and a tattoo of a cross on his chest. He was frighteningly muscled and his eyes were cold blue.

"Samson," Olivia spat.

"Olivia." He smiled. Two of his teeth were silver.

Just the sight of him made me shudder, and whatever he was coming down to do, it wasn't good. I flexed my fingers next to my components pouch, thinking of all the spells I could throw if I had to.

"When we found that lode, we thought of you girls and how sorry we felt for taking so many of your supplies a little while back. We miss you, you know. So we thought we'd leave this lode where y'all could find it, throw some extra rations in there, and have us an excuse to meet again."

"Forgive me for not being flattered," said Olivia.

He smiled and shrugged elaborately, a terrifying gesture with his broad, shirtless frame.

"Well, you know us. We figured we'd get us some more wives while we were at it." He winked at Olivia. "Though it may take a couple of us each to break you in and that ox of yours."

The sound of many male voices snickering rose all around us. I could see Judith's fist clench behind her car door.

"Shut your filthy mouth, hijo de puta!" Olivia shouted. "You're not getting anything! Or anyone! And the only ones leaving here broken today are gonna be you and your boys!"

"Now, now, now, that's no way for a lady to talk!" said Samson. He was much closer now, almost to Olivia, and he stopped about ten feet away from her. "Especially a lady with no bullets."

Olivia's fingers twitched near her gun. Somehow I knew it was true: Olivia was out of bullets.

"What, you're gonna shoot us now?" Olivia said. "Fight us from a distance when we're out of ammo? That's cheap, even for you."

"Who said anything about fighting from a distance?" Samson said. He whistled, and twelve men came slipping down out of the cliffs, their leathery pink skin painted over with those greasy black designs, their faces hidden behind dust masks, bandannas, and strange metal masks made from car parts and wire. Some of them carried old farm equipment—pitchforks and machetes and sickles. Others carried clubs made of twisted bumpers, wore armor made of rusty chrome rims, like junkyard Sentinels, rust monsters given life.

I steadied my breathing and reached into my pouches with shaking hands, checking my spell components. If we had to fight, I wanted to be ready. I wasn't about to be or let anybody else become somebody's wife or dinner if I could help it. But still, my breath came in gasps and starts.

"Don't worry," Cassandra said calmly, putting a purple-varnished hand on my arm. "There are thirteen of them. Thirteen is an unlucky number." I saw her reach into the many pockets of her vest, gathering a handful of what looked like the teeth of a small animal. Getting ready to cast an illusion.

Samson was right in front of Olivia now. She looked up at him, her shoulders set with defiance.

"Now, we can do this the easy way, and you can give up and come with us voluntarily," said Samson, reaching for the machete strapped to his back. "Or we can do it the bloody way."

My heart caught in my chest.

But Olivia just sized him up, looked him in the eye, and spat on the ground.

He smiled. Then he swung out with the machete. Olivia ducked and kneed him in the stomach.

Everyone charged then. The men on the cliff ran down toward us, their weapons flailing. Judith ran at them, knocking two of them to the ground with her car door shield. Zo pulled the modified bow from her back, nocked in an arrow from her belt, and shot one of them directly in the chest. He fell to the ground and didn't move. Olivia and Samson fought hand to hand, knife to machete, Olivia trying to put distance and objects between the two of them.

"Stay here, Kahúu!" Susanah said, shoving Mowse into the hole with the vehicles. She pulled her chain from her bag.

"NO!" Mowse cried. "Susanah!"

But Susanah was already out in the thick of it, whirling her sharpened chain, holding them back. Zo shouted something to Cassandra.

"I'm on my way!" Cassandra yelled.

Just then, two Laredo Boys spotted us and began making their way toward our metal mountain. *Fire or hurricane?* I thought, bringing the spells to mind. *Fire or hurricane?*

"CASS!" Zo shouted, ducking behind a rock.

"Help her!" I told Cassandra, gathering black roller dust into my hands. "I'll take care of these two."

"If you say so!" she said. Then Cassandra—three Cassandras—darted out to help Zo, leaving me alone behind the pile of parts.

Shaking, I forced my magic into my hands and stepped from behind the mountain of parts. The men saw me and began to run in my direction.

I can do this. I can do this. With a dry mouth, I shouted, *"Hurrikanmauer!"* and blew the dust into the air. The dust thickened into a whirlwind, reaching up into the sky. The two Laredo Boys put their arms up in fear, but I slammed them with my dust hurricane, buffeting them with wind and slicing dust.

They staggered and fell back several paces. But my nerves were shot. My fear was affecting the spell. The hurricane began to grow thin in places, and I knew it wouldn't last much longer.

I sent a stronger surge of magic and let the hurricane lift them off their feet. I gave them one final spin, then pushed all the strength left in the spell through my fingertips and hurled them as far away from me as I could. One of them hit his head against a stone with a stomach-dropping smack. The other rose, shaken, and started forward again, madder than hell, but going for Judith this time and not me.

"Judith!" I shouted. She turned just in time to block his punch with her car door. Then she rammed him with the door and turned to fight off two more.

I looked around for the other man I'd thrown, but he was lying still, his blood seeping into the dust. *I killed him.* The thought pounded in my head as I ducked back behind the metal fortress. *I killed someone. I killed someone. Oh, God, I killed someone.*

I knew I'd crossed some sort of a threshold then. But adrenaline shot through my veins and blood spattered the dust and I couldn't afford a moral dilemma right now. I shook myself mentally and ran back into the fray.

Zo and Cassandra were fighting off three of them, Zo dripping blood from a head wound and Cassandra trying to fend them off with her copies. Susanah was fighting two men with her chain. One other snuck up on a cliff behind her, raised his ax over his head. I almost sent a jet of fire his way, but then he stopped, turned on his heel, and began attacking the others with odd, jerky motions. On a rock nearby, Mowse held her hands out like a puppetmaster's, moving them away from Susanah before discarding them behind a nearby boulder like spent playthings.

They worked together, their magic instinctual, enviably natural, while I fumbled with my pouches. Nearby, Olivia was holding her own against Samson, returning blow for blow. But she was obviously tiring. She kept putting distance between them, ducking behind boulders and trees. I couldn't cast a fire spell or a wind spell, not with all the girls all mixed in with the men. Olivia stumbled, barely ducking a blow from Samson's machete. I clenched my fists, trying desperately to think of something, anything, I could do to help.

"Sal!" she shouted. "Give me your power!"

"How?" I panted. A dagger flew by my head. I stumbled, then threw up a wall of dust around me on three sides.

"Blood!" Olivia ducked under a blow, then gave back one of her own. "Use your blood!"

Frantically I scanned the ground. There was a stone nearby smooth enough to smear my blood on. But how could my magic help her?

"Sal, now!" she cried.

I bit hard into my thumb and smeared my blood across the stone, thinking of every offensive spell I knew. *Fire, hurricane, wind projectile, please, please let this work,* until my penny glowed. Then I took aim and threw the stone to Olivia. She caught it and held it to her chest. I felt a red flash through me and I knew somehow that it was Olivia copying my magic.

"¡Fuego!" she cried, and a tongue of flame shot out at Samson. It caught on his axle grease designs and ignited them. He cried out and rolled. Olivia darted away, shouting, "Come on! Let's go!"

All of us ran for the entrance to the ravine. My feet pounded on the hard ground, my chest hurt. I flew with panic and adrenaline. Then I heard a blood-freezing scream and turned.

"Olivia!" Cassandra screamed. "Olivia! Help!"

One of the Laredo Boys had seen through Cassandra's illusions and grabbed the real Cassandra around the waist and held her to him with a knife on her jugular.

I froze, panting, looking to the others.

"Hold on, Cassandra!" Olivia shouted. She started back toward Cassandra, and we fell in behind her, facing the four Laredo Boys who were left. I caught my breath as, behind them, Samson rose. His black designs were bubbling, red burns now, still smoking from Olivia's and my fire. Shaking with rage, he came to stand in front of Cassandra.

"Like I said, Olivia," he spat, his silver teeth bloodstained. "The easy way or the bloody way. Give up now, before my reinforcements come."

"Take the metal, Samson!" Olivia's voice was carefully steady. "Take the rations, take all of it, just let her go!"

"I want it all," he said. "All the metal. All of you. Or she dies."

I clenched trembling hands. I could see Olivia sizing them up, trying to figure out what to do. But there was no spell I'd learned that she could cast without hurting Cassandra too. I was utterly powerless. Behind me, even Mowse was frozen, too terrified to utter a word.

Olivia swallowed, started to say something; then a familiar voice rang out over the ravine.

"Ladies and gentlemen! Boys and girls of all ages! Welcome to the show!"

The Laredo Boys turned, bewildered. Then one of them pointed.

Asa was standing, fully suited and hatted, on an outcrop high up on the side of the ravine.

"I am but a humble traveler from another land, another realm, another place in time!" He tipped his hat, and a white bird flew out of it and shattered into a million pieces of glittering confetti.

"Who's this clown?" one of the Boys sneered.

"I am Asa Skander, magician at large, and I have come to open your eyes to otherworldly feats, death-defying stunts, and fantastical delights the likes of which have never been seen before. So I ask you: You wanna see a magic trick?"

He pulled the chain of colored scarves from his sleeves and stood, arms outstretched, waiting for applause. The Laredo Boys looked from one to the other, confused. None of us moved.

"No?" Asa said, pulling a comical frown. "What about—" Asa reached up and peeled his face up and off, revealing a hole of black smoke. "*This one?*"

The Laredo Boys screamed as the smoke leaked from the hole where Asa's face had been and filled the sky over the ravine, but Samson stood his ground, grabbing Cassandra himself.

"He's just a witch," he said to his men. "Like . . . like these girls here. All tr-trickery."

"Oh, I assure you," said Asa's voice, a daemonic face appearing in the smoke, all fire-red eyes and arm-length teeth. *"I am something else entirely."*

Blue-white flames shot up all around. The ravine went dark as pitch. The cliffs echoed with the sound of inhuman shrieks and howls and wails. Then Asa himself leapt down into the ravine and moved toward the Boys, toward Samson. Samson held his ground for a moment longer, then shoved a white-faced Cassandra toward Asa and turned to run. Asa stepped past Cassandra and opened his arms. Suddenly they too were black smoke, wide enough to cover the whole ravine. And even though I knew I had nothing to fear from Asa, my knees shook.

"He's pushing them," said Olivia. "He's driving them—look."

He was. The Laredo Boys were gibbering with fear—fear of the gaping daemon teeth, the infernal flames, the great, smoky black arms—huddled together, not knowing that behind them the hole the trucks and car had been in was widening. Then, with a shriek, they fell into the hole, which seemed to have deepened too, rather than just widened.

Immediately the sky cleared, the flames disappeared, and Asa, back to normal, leapt down from the outcrop and tipped his hat to us. "Hello, ladies."

"Asa!" I shouted, running to hug him. He felt vaguely spiny beneath his jacket.

"Come on!" he said. "Let's figure out a way to keep them in!"

The girls exchanged glances, then ran forward to help. Zo

pulled Cassandra to her feet, and as Asa ran by, he said, "Sorry, sorry! *So* sorry! I'll make it up to you!"

"Don't mention it . . ." Cassandra muttered, staring straight ahead, in a daze.

Down in the hole, the Laredo Boys were shouting and cursing, trying to climb out of the hole, but sure enough, it had deepened, and they couldn't quite get a foothold. Olivia looked down into the hole, her arms crossed, her knuckles bleeding.

"So now you've met our daemon," Olivia said. "Don't worry. We wouldn't let him eat you."

"Olivia, you bitch!" Samson shouted up at her. "You didn't say anything about a daemon!"

"You didn't ask, pendejo!" Olivia grinned.

"I'll get you for this!" Samson shouted. "One day that daemon will be gone and I'll—" He launched into a string of obscenities too foul to mention, and we stepped back from the hole.

"Want me to kill them?" Zo asked, coming forward. "They're fish in a barrel."

Olivia glanced backward at Mowse's wide eyes and said, "Not this time. It's not fair this way." Then she whistled and said, "Judith!" She jerked her head toward a nearby boulder.

"Got it," Judith said, her lip split and bruises flowering all over her. She went to the boulder, and with a mighty push, rolled it over the opening of the hole. Their shouts were muffled, and where they had seemed so frightening only moments before, they suddenly seemed no more intimidating than june bugs trapped in a jam jar.

Olivia turned to Asa, and when their eyes met, she smiled as though she were seeing him for the first time. They seemed to drift toward each other for a moment; then both of them stopped as though they realized what they were doing and took a step back.

"Thanks," Olivia said. "That was brilliant. Absolutely brilliant." She was smiling at him like she had forgotten that he was a daemon. It was then that I realized how good yet strange they looked together.

"Well, I do pride myself on showmanship," Asa said, blushing vibrantly.

"I hope this means you're reconsidering my offer," Olivia said, her eyes flickering over him.

Asa hesitated. His smile faltered, just for a moment. Then he shrugged and said, "You've talked me into it. After all, I doubt they'll forget what I've done to them, and if they catch me alone out here and decide to get revenge—"

"We definitely wouldn't want that," said Olivia. "It's settled. You're coming back with us. Deal?"

"Deal." Asa smiled.

They shook. Then, practically drunk with triumph, we loaded the metal on top of Judith's sleigh, and all together, we headed back to the train, listening to the Laredo Boys' muffled shouts fade into the distance.

CHAPTER 18

By the time we trudged back to the train with the metal in tow, the sun had begun to slide toward the horizon. A cot was set up for Asa, close to mine in the machine car, and he flopped down on it and was practically snoring before his head hit his shabby, feed-sack pillow. Outside, the mood was high and electric. I'd hoped to finally get to talk to Olivia about what she'd said before. About Mother Morevna. But before I could say anything, Olivia and Judith were on their way back out to go get something from some secret cache of theirs, something special, for a "special occasion."

"What special occasion?" I asked Cassandra.

"For your initiation, darling." She smiled. "Yours and Asa's. You're one of us now, both of you. So we just want to have a little celebration in your honor. Now why don't you go help Susanah and Mowse with those horses and leave it all to me."

So, after Cassandra practically pushed me the whole way there, I spent the next two hours in Susanah and Mowse's cave, helping them cobble more pieces of metal onto the horses, covering exposed wiring here, patching rusted flanks there. Then Cassandra stood at the mouth of the cave and called for me.

"Everything is almost ready," she said. "Zo is starting a campfire, and Olivia and Judith should be back soon too."

"Y'all really didn't have to go to any trouble—" I started.

"Asa will be joining us, won't he?" Cassandra asked. "I certainly hope so, since I didn't get the chance to properly thank him. But he was looking awfully green around the gills."

"I think he's fine," I said, remembering how sometimes after we'd practiced our duel he'd had to disappear for hours at a time. "I think his daemon magic just needs time to recharge or something."

"I do hope he wakes up soon," Cassandra said. "Zo is planning on grilling a grasshopper especially for him." (I tried not to grimace.)

"I'll go and check on him," I said. "Don't worry. I'll bring him out."

I went to the machine car and knocked three times on the door. "Asa! Come out! They're putting together some kind of welcome thing for us. To celebrate the victory over the Laredo Boys."

"I'm not that hungry," Asa said.

"You don't want to disappoint Olivia, do you?" I said, letting a conspiratorial tone creep into my voice.

A pause, then, "I suppose I'll make an appearance. It would be the gentlemanly thing to do." There was a sound of rummaging and rustling. Then the door slid open. "Do I look all right?" Asa asked.

He looked the same as he always looked, if a bit messier. But from the way Olivia was looking at him earlier, I didn't think it mattered.

"I'm sure she'll be impressed," I said. I couldn't help but smile at how silly he looked when he was flustered.

"Now, to be sure, I'm not out to . . . you know . . . court her or anything—"

"*Court* her? Do people still say that?"

"Olivia and I can never be," he said matter-of-factly. "We're star-crossed. Doomed to unrequited pining at most."

"That's awfully negative," I said.

"Well, I'm just temporary, after all," Asa said, his shoulders drooping just a little. "Besides, it . . . wouldn't be a good idea. For many reasons."

My heart sank for him a little. There was something he wasn't telling me—I could feel it just slightly in my skin. But this time, I didn't press it. He was right, after all. She was a girl, he was a daemon . . . person . . . thing. It was probably best that he was using his head for once. But as we left the machine car, I saw him stop in front of the rearview mirror Susanah had hung for us and smooth his hair.

When we stepped outside, Judith crowed, and all I could do was stop and stare, dumbfounded.

The train and the campfire around it were bathed in light. It looked like multicolored fireflies had settled over the whole train, winking slowly in and out, changing seamlessly from one color to the next.

"Here they are! The heroes of the day!" Judith shouted when she saw us.

Applause went up around the circle. Genuine applause. They really wanted us here, I thought. Wanted *me* here. I wasn't used to this, and for a minute I'm sure I was shaky-legged as a colt, thinking of how much magic I still had to learn before I could cast as naturally as the rest of them. But the warmth of their fire washed over me until I felt something I realized I hadn't really felt in longer than I could remember: welcome.

"Well?" Cassandra said, practically bouncing with excitement. "What do you think?"

"It's the most beautiful thing I've ever seen," I said.

"It's all for you," Cassandra beamed.

"All of it . . . for us?" Asa said, his voice low and awestruck.

"I owe you two my life," Cassandra said. "I had to make it beautiful. And what good are illusions if you can't make things beautiful?"

I wish Lucy could see this, I found myself thinking. *She'd be at home under lights like these, with her bright dresses and kerchiefs.*

"Finally, you're awake," Olivia said to Asa. "You can sit next to me."

"I'd like that very much," he said, pushing his glasses back up the bridge of his nose. He sat down next to her, and within moments, they were talking animatedly. Everything about them seemed to be magnetized to the other. It was a strange, impossible thing, seeing Olivia Rosales, the murderer, flirt and be flirted with. I smirked as Asa reached behind her ear and pulled out a coin. *So much for being star-crossed and tragic, I guess.*

"He's a hero and all," Zo said to me, loudly enough for Olivia to hear. "But I don't get it."

"That's because you don't like men, perra," Olivia called, laughing.

Zo gave me a strange sort of look that was meant to be commiserating, a look that confused me.

"Maybe," she said, "or maybe because I know he's really a daemon?"

"Nobody's perfect." Olivia shrugged. Asa blushed even more brilliantly.

"You're hopeless," Zo said. "Anyway, I gotta tend to the food. It'll be ready in a minute."

On a homemade spit they had a skewered calf-size grasshopper roasting. Cassandra and Judith were sitting by the fire, and Zo was setting up some feed-sack targets to shoot with the slingshot in her belt. Susanah had brought one of the metal horses out and it lay folded at her feet as she tinkered with it. Meanwhile, Mowse chased lizards on the edge of the firelight. And as I stood there among them in the warm glow of the fire, I thought that, with just a few tweaks it could be the world's strangest Norman Rockwell painting. Then I saw Judith pull out a big metal barrel marked *moonshine.*

"I've been saving this for a special occasion." Judith winked. "Olivia and I had to go all the way to our western cache to get it." She carefully poured some moonshine and cactus juice into a few Coke bottles and handed one to me and one to Asa.

"Rookies first!"

I sniffed it. It smelled acrid and dangerous. Everyone watched us, waiting.

I looked at Asa, to see what he'd do.

Asa shrugged and we took a swig together. It was terrible—exactly like I thought battery acid must taste—and everyone laughed as we coughed and spluttered.

"You get used to it." Judith clapped me on the back.

I tried another sip of it, and coughing, I went and took my seat next to Asa. "I've only had one sip and I can't feel my lips anymore," I whispered to him.

"It's not that bad," Asa whispered back. "If you imagine you're an airplane in need of fuel."

He threw back his head and downed another swallow of it. Meanwhile, I discreetly set the bottle down behind me on the ground to give myself reason to "forget" it later.

"Ugh! Electricity," Susanah said across the fire where the horse she was trying to Frankenstein into life refused to cooperate. "It surges with the dust storms, then goes away." She stared down at the horse. "Maybe I need more wiring. . . ."

"Susanah, I can't find my doll," Mowse said. "I looked everywhere and I can't find it."

"You had it with you when we went out today," Susanah said. "Maybe you dropped it."

"Noooo," Mowse groaned. "It took me all day to make it."

Next to me, I saw Olivia scoot closer to Asa. Her eyes were on his lips. His were on hers. They started to lean closer together, just for a moment, then Asa leapt up like he'd been burned and said, "I can get some wiring for you, Susanah. I think there's a radio in the machine room." Then he excused himself with a bow and went to find it.

Beside me, Olivia laughed.

"He's something, isn't he?" she said.

"He's something, all right. It . . . doesn't bother you that he's a daemon?"

Olivia shrugged. "He seems more human to me than a lot of men I've seen in my life."

"Like Samson, you mean?"

"Him, yeah," she said. "But the worst was back in Elysium."

There was a heaviness to that response that took me aback. She had to mean Mr. Robertson, the man she murdered. There had been dark, ridiculous-sounding murmurings about Mr. Robertson shortly after the murder, but what *had* he done to be included with the likes of Samson? For a moment, I wasn't sure what to say—if I was welcome to ask what she meant. But before I could respond, Asa was back, a tiny radio in hand, looking much less flustered than before.

Olivia stood and said, "Let's get this started, shall we?" She clinked her knife against her own Coke bottle for attention and we all went quiet.

"Everyone, today we lived through the toughest fight we've ever had. And we got away with only a few bruises and bloody lips." She looked around the circle at all of them. "We know how Sal and Asa got here. But I think we should each say something about how we got here, and how we found each other: the best and only female-led settlement in the desert. It only seems right."

Around the circle, there was nodding and murmuring. Everyone was sitting by the fire now, their faces illuminated by its orange glow.

"Who wants to start us off?" Olivia said.

"I'll go," said Judith. She cleared her throat. "I started out at the Orange settlement, way out east. My family had had a farm, but Ma left us and Pa got killed somewhere out in the desert. The people at Orange said I needed some kind of job. And I'd always been big, had muscle. More muscle than any boy. So they put me in charge of rabbit slaughtering . . . you know, for the rabbit drives. I hated that damn job."

I remembered rabbit drives. Hundreds of rabbits, herded into pens, then bludgeoned to death with clubs when food was especially scarce. I'd only seen one, a long time ago, before the walls went up, but I remembered the savagery of it, the blood spattering the men's coveralls, sinking into the dust. No wonder Judith was a vegetarian.

"I know I'm big and I know I'm tough, but doing that day in and day out does something to you. I just hated killing them, hearing them squeal like that. What did a little bunny rabbit ever do to anyone? That sound, their squealing, kept me up at night till I was completely numb inside. So then, one day, I just left. I was wandering out in the desert, and Olivia found me. 'You look strong. Can you lift fifty pounds? Eighty pounds? A hundred pounds?' and I said yes, that I was stronger than most men. She said she had need of some muscle around here. Then I asked her if I'd have to kill any more rabbits, and she said no." Judith smiled. "So here I am. And I've never had to kill an animal ever again."

Cassandra was next, and she cleared her throat and adjusted her bracelets before speaking. "I came with a traveling circus," she said. "My dad ran it—it was small. Just one tent and only a few acts: clowns, jugglers, a fat lady, a scrawny lion, and me, the Luminous Cassandra: the One-Girl Ensemble." She spread her arms dramatically and laughed. "It was terrible! The clowns weren't funny, the jugglers were always dropping things, and the lion wouldn't do anything but sleep. I was the only legitimate act, really—besides the fat lady, she was *really* fat—and one day, when we were performing for the unfortunate in Boise City, I was dreadfully bored, and I wandered out into the desert to explore. Ran away *from* the circus! Can you imagine? Then the storm came. When I came out of hiding, Boise City was gone. I stayed with one settlement for six years, until my powers made everyone nervous and I had to . . . er . . . go my separate way when I was sixteen. After a few days in the desert with no water, I thought I'd just *die*. Then Olivia and everyone found me, and now I'm never *ever* bored." She turned to Asa. "It's good to have a kindred spirit here now, one who understands the call of the spotlight. We'll have to collaborate sometime."

"I'd be happy to." Asa lifted his Coke bottle in salute, his voice beginning to slur. I didn't want to imagine what horrifying, infernal illusions the two of them could create.

Zo was next. She cleared her throat. "I was supposed to meet my family," she said. "My dad had been a sharpshooter like me, but when he got a job in California, the plan was for me to stay with my uncle just outside Elysium until my dad called for me. Then, on my way across the desert, hunting . . . the storm came. When it cleared and there was nothing, I found myself face-to-face with monsters I'd never seen before, and all I had was my pistols. I was eight. They ran at me and I fired. I was prepared to die out there, taking them with me one by one. Then Susanah—"

"And me," said Mowse.

"—and Mowse"—Zo smiled—"appeared and fought them

off. Beside me. And then we found the others later, and they've been beside me ever since."

Susanah was next. Mowse came and sat on her lap, and Susanah tried in vain to untangle her hair as she spoke. "I barely remember my real family," Susanah said. "I was taken from my parents when I was three, and given to a foster family. *There was no laundry in the home* was what they said when they took me. Whatever that means." She laughed a hard, bitter laugh. "Turns out, they were just looking for excuses to take Indian kids away from their families and *civilize* them somewhere. So it was boarding school for me when I was old enough," said Susanah. "Chilocco, on the Kansas border. Work and building things and forgetting who you were while the teachers tried to force you to be white. One day I just had enough, so I snuck out. I didn't know much about the Comanches—the Numunuu—except some simple words here and there. I didn't even remember where I had been taken from, I was so young. So I stole a book on the Comanches, found that my band was from the Oklahoma Panhandle, and that's where I went. I hopped trains. I walked, and when I got here, there was . . . nothing but dust. And then the storm came, and when it cleared and everything was different . . . I found a baby, crying alone in that abandoned car, and I named her Kahúu. Mouse. A real child of the desert. We both were, I guess. I was only thirteen."

Mowse listened placidly, wincing when Susanah hit another tangle.

"She was the first part of my family. Then I found Zo a few years later, and then Olivia, and then the others after her, and now there are eight of us together." Susanah paused. "You weren't what I was looking for. But you are what I needed."

Olivia stood with her bottle of moonshine and looked at each of us. "All of us came from pain and dirt and shit and death," she said. "But we are family now. And you have my word, hermanas—y hermano—I will do anything for you. A toast to us!"

"To us!" we said.

We toasted with our Coke bottles, the blue-green glass gleaming in the firelight, and took another swig of moonshine (cactus juice for Mowse). It felt like Communion felt, quiet, reverent somehow. Important. And in the firelight, through the pleasant haze of moonshine, I realized that they *were* what we had needed. I had asked my pendulum to help me find something that could help fix everything and it had led me here. But why? And earlier, what Olivia had said about Mother Morevna . . . what had she meant? Questions seemed to spread over my mind like spilled paint, coloring everything warm around me dark again. Finally, I decided I couldn't wait any longer. These questions needed answers.

"Olivia," I said when she sat back down next to me. "Can I speak to you for a minute? Alone?" My voice sounded flat and somber, contrasting sharply to the jubilant, carefree mood.

Olivia smiled and said, "Sure, kid." She gave Asa an apologetic look. He nodded in return. Then I followed Olivia out of the circle of warmth and firelight and into the dark, toward her.

• • •

"You did good today," Olivia said as she shut the door behind us. "If you hadn't thrown me that rock, I think he might have had me. I think you and Asa will be a great fit with us, especially after today. Here, make yourself at home."

I looked around, expecting to see walls of weapons, maps, maybe bloodstained clothes littered here and there. Instead, Olivia's room looked somehow sad and bare. There was one window, a low, twin-size bed with a plaid blanket on it and a feed-sack pillow. Just above the bed, the picture Asa had given her, of Olivia and her sister, Rosa, was tacked up. Something tingled in the back of my mind, but I couldn't put my finger to it.

"So, what are you thinking about?" she said.

I took a deep breath. It was now or never.

"About what you said earlier," I said. "I have a few questions about Mother Morevna, about Elysium . . . and what happened while you were there."

I braced myself for her reaction, though I didn't know what it would be. Anger? Sadness? Would she tell me to go away? Instead, she simply took a swig of her moonshine, held it in her mouth for a moment, and swallowed.

"Well?" she said. "What do you want to know?"

"How did you know Mother Morevna?" I asked. "Did she teach you about magic?"

Olivia sighed. "It was back in the beginning of Elysium," she said. "When she was starting out trying to make Elysium equal—outlawing hate speech, getting rid of 'whites only' areas and stuff like that. One day, I was being harassed by some white boys. They were telling me I shouldn't be allowed in Elysium because I wasn't 'a real American,' that I should have left like other 'Mexicans.' I told them I was proud to be Mexican, but that I was born here and that I'm just as American as they are. We got into a fight, and I hurt one of them pretty bad. When I was brought before Mother Morevna, I expected her to punish me, but instead, she asked if there had been birds on my house when I was born. I said yes. Blackbirds."

Blackbirds, I thought. *My blackbird blessing. So it had meant something after all.*

"Then she told me to touch her hand. I did, and I felt . . . magic . . . flowing into my mind. Then she said to say 'light' in Spanish, 'luz,' so I did and . . . I made light." Olivia smiled at the recollection, a pained, quiet sort of smile. "I was a witch, she explained. With a talent for copying others' magic. She said that I was different, that that's why I didn't fit in, why I was so angry. I told her she didn't know the half of it. My mother was dying then, and we'd just moved to that house with that . . ."

Olivia paused, decided not to mention Mr. Robertson.

"She said for me to come to her when I was angry. She said she could teach me about being a witch, a brujita. That one day I could even be her Successor, someone she could pass her knowledge to. And so I went to see her once a week, and learned what I could, using her power. And every day, she gave me lessons so that one day, when she was dead, I could take over for her. Funny how things work out, huh?"

Every day, I thought, my heart sinking. *I could barely get Mother Morevna to look at me back in Elysium, and she had worked—really worked—with Olivia once a week?* I shook myself mentally before I could allow myself to feel even worse.

"She loaned me this book," Olivia said. "This little book . . . I wish I'd brought it with me. I left it on the bookshelf in the room I used to practice in, in the very back, behind some hymnals."

My heart gave a weird little twist in my chest. I remembered how I had found *The Complete Booke of Witchcraft* behind all the Cokesbury hymnals. That book, the book that I had taught myself from, was Olivia's. The writing in the margins had been hers. The room itself, the one I had stayed up every night in, teaching myself magic when Mother Morevna couldn't be bothered . . . that had been hers too, I realized now. All of it, my entire position as Successor was just a thin, sad follow-up to Olivia. I was just the placeholder put there by a reluctant leader—and then, only because Mr. Jameson had forced her. *Of course,* I thought. *Of course that wasn't real either.*

"Here," I said, pulling *The Complete Booke of Witchcraft* from my pocket. "I found this when I moved into the church." I held it up so the gold lettering caught the dim light.

"¡El libro completo de brujería!" Olivia cried. She looked at the book the same way I'd seen my mother look at toys she'd had in her youth. "Can I see it?"

"Of course," I said. "It's yours, after all." I handed it to her, my heart heavy and numb. She thumbed through it, her fingers touching her scribbles in the margins.

"Yes . . . this is the book," she said, her voice the sad one now. "But it's not mine anymore."

"What do you mean?"

She closed the book and put it in my hands. "It can only be read by who's meant to have it at the time. It appears as gibberish to anyone else who tries to read it. And my time has passed. It's yours now. It chose you, so treat it well."

I remembered how Judith had flipped through it, saying that it was printed in Russian or some other language. It *had* chosen me. A silly kind of relief flooded through me as I tried not to show how much better this made me feel.

"But Mother Morevna chose *you*," I said. "She only chose me because Mr. Jameson pressured her into doing it."

"Don't take it personally," said Olivia. "After what happened with me, I bet she never wanted to choose a Successor ever again."

Images rose to my mind: Mother Morevna as a smiling, patient teacher, Olivia as a young pupil. Then, jarringly, Mr. Robertson, dead and bloody in front of the church.

"What happened?" I asked. "How did you end up out here? Really?"

Olivia's expression changed. Something like regret passed over her face.

"I used to admire her, you know," Olivia said. "A white lady who seemed to care about *us*. Who didn't frown on our own ways, or make us speak English. A bruja too. We were all sisters after all, brujas, even if our arts were different. And we were in power now after the men failed us. I had faith in her. But she didn't deserve it. She was the same as all the other white ladies, even if she wasn't as obvious."

"I don't know," I said, surprisingly defensive. "Mother Morevna always seemed like she was really proud of Elysium being better for women."

"Better for which women?" Olivia said. "Where are the Latinas she's listening to? The Black girls? Even the other old white ladies? I mean, hell, we were both her Successors. Did she ever listen to you? Did she ever ask you how Elysium could be better?"

No, I realized. She hadn't. I'd never heard Mother Morevna ask anyone for advice, not even Mr. Jameson.

"All she cares about is her own vision for Elysium," Olivia

said. "I mean, women can do more, sure, but y'all have a curfew, rationed meals, assigned housing. Y'all can't even wear makeup behind those walls if you want to. That's not being equal. That's just being under a high heel instead of a work boot, and I like my throat free to breathe."

She was right, I realized. Mother Morevna was so proud of her new, equal, woman-led society. But it had never ever felt free. Not even when I was her Successor.

"What did Mother Morevna do to you?" I asked quietly.

Olivia sighed, a pained, frustrated sound. "When I found out about what my step . . . what that bastard was doing to Rosa, touching her, somebody who couldn't fight back . . . I asked for help. I asked for Morevna to punish him, to go over there and burn him to bits or sweep him away in the wind." She sighed. "But I couldn't *prove* it. Those were very serious accusations, she told me. And they came at a bad time, when the old white men were trying to resist her new rules. It would look like favoritism, she said, to toss Robertson out on the word of a girl—of a Latina—when we had no proof. We had to be careful so the men wouldn't revolt. We had to *maintain the balance of Elysium*."

Olivia's dark brows furrowed. "But I couldn't just wait around for proof. And I couldn't do any magic myself, not without someone to borrow magic from. I had to take matters into my own hands."

"What did you do?" I asked quietly, my stomach in knots.

"I talked to Sister Death Herself," she said. "Not la Santa Muerte, not the Devil or the Grim Reaper. But the Death who set this Game in motion. I didn't expect Her to answer, but She did. 'Follow your own instincts,' She told me. 'Elysium doesn't care about you, so to hell with the balance of Elysium. I will give you the power for this.' Magic seemed to explode in me then. It was like something awakened in me, something dark and terrible. And powerful. It was Her power that let me give him the justice Mother Morevna could have given him but chose not to. Muerte para mi enemigo. Finally, Rosa had peace. No thanks to Mother Morevna. And then Mother Morevna turned on me. I had brought her shame. Imagine: her Successor, a murderer. Then . . . well . . . you know the rest." Olivia paused, looked out the window. Her anger, her sadness was almost palpable. I could feel it on my skin like dust.

"You know, Rosa was the one person I loved more than myself," she said, her voice heavy. "She always knew what I was thinking. She could always tell when I was coming home. Like we were connected by our minds or our hearts or something deeper than that. Magic, maybe. I loved her so much. And now that darkness, the darkness that I asked Death for, is always there. And I think it always will be."

My heart ached for Olivia and her sister. But a crawl went up my spine at the thought of Olivia speaking to Death Herself. I thought about a story I'd read once, "The Devil and Tom Walker," about a man who made a deal with the Devil. But this wasn't the same, I thought. This wasn't a selfish deal. And what Mr. Robertson had done to Rosalita, what Mother Morevna had allowed to happen to her, was unforgivable. . . . *What would I have done in Olivia's shoes?* I wondered. I didn't know.

"Now I have a question for you," Olivia said. "What's your specialty?"

I blanched. Olivia continued. "I mean, the spells you used today were powerful, but . . . they seem kind of . . . directionless."

Directionless. That was the word. That's how I'd always felt, even—maybe especially with Mother Morevna. It could be applied to every aspect of my life.

"I don't know my specialty," I heard myself say. "All my life I've wanted to be special . . . to be something important and help Elysium. I thought when I saw the rain that maybe that would be the way I would help. But then that went to shit. And when I thought I'd be learning magic from Mother Morevna, I thought maybe that was how I would help Elysium. But everything I learned I had to teach myself. I worked and I studied and I tried, all to help Elysium, to make my mark there, and now . . . now I'm out here . . . with nothing."

Suddenly I realized that there were tears on my face. A lump was working its way up my throat. I turned away, embarrassed, but Olivia came forward and grabbed me by the shoulders.

"Hey," Olivia said gently. "You've got a lot more than nothing. You're worth way more than anybody back home ever thought, I promise."

"But I'm not," I said. "I have to fix things or the world will be destroyed. I came here looking for a way to fix everything, to save the world. But the Dust Soldiers are going to come back and judge Elysium and we're all gonna—"

"Wait, wait, wait," Olivia said. "Breathe for a second. Think about it. The Dust Soldiers didn't say anything about the desert *beyond* Elysium, did they?"

I stopped in my tracks. "What are you getting at?"

"I mean that the Dust Soldiers only threatened Elysium,

right? So if they're the only ones being wiped out, why worry? Elysium's problems aren't ours. Let them bring their end down on themselves. Hell, why do you think we're happy out here instead of scrambling to try to get back behind those walls?"

I'd never thought of that possibility before. What if it was true? What if the end the Dust Soldiers promised was just the end of Elysium? It made sense. The people outside the walls couldn't rightly be blamed for Elysium's failures, could they? Maybe Olivia was right. But if she was, what about Mr. Jameson? *What about Lucy?* My heart gave a strange, painful dishrag twist in my chest.

"But there are people there that I love," I said.

"Did the people you love keep you from being thrown out here? Did they stand up for you? Because if they didn't, I say to hell with them too. Stay with us. With me and Susanah and Mowse and Judith and Cassie and Zo. It's a good place to be. And I promise, I will help you find your specialty. Then, no matter what happens, at the end of ten years, we can walk out of the desert as the powerful brujas we were meant to be." She sighed. "And if it's really bothering you this much as we get closer to the ten-year mark, we'll go and see what we can do."

Her voice was sincere, her eyes on mine, and if there was a darkness in Olivia, I didn't see any trace of it then. "You promise?" I asked.

"I promise," she said. "Now let's get back out there and make sure nobody's fighting or blowing anything up." And, feeling somehow lighter and heavier at the same time, I followed her.

• • •

When Olivia and I left her train car, Asa was plainly drunk, and everyone was gathered around, watching him pull his endless rainbow of scarves out of his sleeve.

"Looks like someone's had enough," Olivia laughed.

Movements loose with moonshine, Asa reached out and pulled a quarter from behind Mowse's ear. He went to flip it, but it went over his head, where it turned into a june bug and flew away, much to Asa's confusion. Everyone laughed and applauded, and as Judith took Asa's moonshine away, Cassandra said, "Oh, it's been fore*ver* since I've seen a magic show that wasn't designed to hurt anyone!"

"Thhank you!" Asa said. "Thhhank you! I'll be here till the end of the wwworld!"

Suddenly, there was an odd surge of energy. The girls gasped at him, faces pale and shocked.

"Your face," I whispered to him, and Asa moved to fix it.

But as he raised his arm to adjust the human part of his face over the exposed daemon part, there was another surge of magic. The radio under Asa's arm chittered out some static, then, even stranger . . . it began to play.

A male voice was singing ". . . *got to ac-cen-tchu-ate the positive . . . e-liiim-in-ate-the negative . . . latch onnn to the affir-mative . . .*" then the static rose up again and the words were lost.

"Was that . . . music?" Zo asked, her usually guarded voice soft with wonder.

"Oh, er . . . sorry," Asa said. "Sometimes my . . . hic . . . my magic makes electronic things do that."

"Do it again!" Judith said.

We all huddled around Asa then, and he turned the knob until the music strengthened and returned.

". . . *don't mess with Mr. In-betweeeeen* . . ." the male voice crooned.

"That's Bing Crosby!" Judith said, then, softly, "Ma was always listening to Bing Crosby. . . ."

Then female voices joined the male singer, and we all listened in rapt attention.

As the smooth voice, made dusty and crackly by the radio, crooned out the end of the song and the final note faded into silence again, tears welled in my eyes. All around me, the others were crying too, some sniffling like me, some openly weeping like Cassandra, and others, like Olivia, quietly wiping their tears away before anyone could notice.

Asa was looking at us, plainly confused, wondering, probably, what it was about this very upbeat song that had made us all cry. "Humans are so odd," he muttered.

The radio buzzed into life once more, and we all leaned forward again.

"That was 'Ac-cen-tchu-ate the Positive' by Bing Crosby and the Andrews Sisters," said a male radio announcer. Patriotic music began to crackle in. *"And now it's the daily report with Skip Joiner, bringing you the news from our boys at war. Two days ago, Allied forces dropped bombs. . . ."*

"War?" Cassandra breathed. "We're at war? Again?"

"*They're* at war," Olivia said. "The ones outside the desert."

"Truly, nothing changes," Susanah said.

We sat there then, rapt and unmoving, listening to a report about a war we didn't know in a world we were no longer a part of. The feeling that had hung over the gathering before—warmth, acceptance, reverence—had been replaced by a deeper, sadder feeling that left all our hearts and heads and bones heavier. Then the broadcaster began to wrap it up. *"And we would like to emphasize once more: our boys need your support! Buy a war bond today!"* Patriotic music blared again, then the static rose up and the radio went silent.

"I think that's it, everybody," Asa said.

From our places on the ground, we wiped our tears away, tried to compose ourselves as well as we could. But the music, the radio, had affected all of us. It was contact. Contact with a reality that we forgot we needed, that we forgot we were missing, here in this dusty, hopeless place.

Silence hung over us for a moment; then Susanah slowly stood, a new fire in her eyes, as though she had realized something important, something life-changing.

"Asa," she said. "Give me your hand."

"Er . . . all right?"

She took his hand and put it on the side of the horse she was working on.

"That thing you did . . . do it again," she said.

"All right, I'll try," said Asa. He closed his eyes, concentrated. But nothing happened.

"I don't know if I can," he said. "I think I'm all out of . . . hic!"

There was another surge of power. At Susanah's feet, the mechanical horse lay as still as it had been, but where they once had been dark, the lightbulb eyes had begun to glow, surging with Asa's magic. We all stood around it, looking at, watching as the pieces between its metal ribs whirred and clicked with new life.

"Finally!" Susanah said. "Now we're getting somewhere."

• • •

Lucy Arbor had neither the time nor the materials to pursue her makeup empire anymore. And even if she had, she wouldn't have done so. Not now, when the very air in Elysium seemed to reek with wrongness. Instead, Lucy found herself caring less and less about appearances, going out to do her Dust Sickness research bare-faced, with her hair wrapped in a kerchief. (*Out here looking like Sojourner Truth,* she thought as she looked into the mirror one day.) But in times like these, appearances didn't matter. What did matter was Dust Sickness and stopping it from infecting anyone else.

Every night, Lucy walked completely around Elysium, latching open windows shut, giving away homemade dust masks, helping clean porches and bedrooms and kitchens for people who couldn't do it for themselves. Many people had taken to wearing Lucy's sack-cloth dust masks all the time, dust storm or not. Even now, Lucy wore one as she walked the perimeter of Elysium, looking up at the tops of the walls for new height, new names, new graves, and marking the number and the initials. There had been several a day for the past month, sometimes five or six. It seemed like there were always funerals these days, always men up on the walls, building new graves. Never, in her whole life behind these walls, had Lucy seen Dust Sickness kill so many so quickly. There was something very, very wrong in Elysium.

Lucy looked down at her list. Forty-nine. Forty-nine people in one month—including a girl she had had a crush on only a year ago, Maggie McCormick. She'd been seventeen. That funeral Lucy had watched from a distance, placing a flower at the foot of the wall after everyone else had gone.

She turned and looked out into the city. But all she saw was Mother Morevna's shadow behind the rose window—always alight these days, no matter the hour—pacing back and forth, back and forth like a spider on her web. Watching.

Suddenly, a cough rose in Lucy's throat. She coughed and hacked into her handkerchief until the urge to cough subsided . . . but even when she stopped, she couldn't seem to catch her breath. She gasped, trying to cough again. Quickly, she pulled a water ration out of her bag and drank from it until her throat was clear. With shaking hands, she wiped her mouth and drew back a thin line of mud.

Lucy closed her eyes and pushed her fear down as far as she could and steeled herself. She, better than anyone, knew what this was. And she knew that it wouldn't get the best of her before she solved this for everyone, once and for all.

CHAPTER 19

1 WEEK AND *2 DAYS* REMAIN.

"Again!" said Olivia. "Just one more for today."

I took a deep breath and wiped the blood from my nose, then turned back to the objects laid out on the ground before me: a rusted gas can, a sun-bleached bone, a piece of glass, an old pocket watch that didn't work anymore.

I eenie-meeny-miney-moed, then chose the wristwatch. I grasped it and focused. Nausea struck, darkness fell, and immediately, the memory flared into life.

A young man was following his family to a beat-up old car laden with furniture and luggage and threadbare blankets. There were three children in the backseat, and an older man and woman were urging him to get into the car with them. They were headed to California, to find a new life. He stopped and turned toward the horizon, expecting something.

"Come on, Dwayne, we ain't got all day!" the father was saying.

"I gotta give him this watch," said the young man. "He's wanted it forever."

The young man paused, looked out over the horizon, squinting even beneath the brim of his hat.

"I know he's your best friend," said the young man's mother. "But we can't wait any longer."

The young man looked out over the horizon one more time. Andrew was not coming like he said he would. The young man, Dwayne, looked down at the watch. Then, with a pocketknife, he finished the last bit of the inscription "D.B. + A.D. Always," and left the watch beside the porch. He gave one look back at it, aching with sadness and uncertainty. Then he climbed into the car with his family and they sputtered off out of sight.

I gasped and came back to reality, back to myself.

"What did you see?" asked Olivia.

"Looked like unrequited love," I said, wiping the blood off my nose.

"Ah, the worst kind," she said. "Any improvements?"

"It was as clear as day this time. And I came out when I wanted to."

"Great job!" Olivia said. "You're getting better. Let's go get some water."

I nodded and let her help me up. Over a month had gone by since the incident with the Laredo Boys, and Olivia and I had been practicing every day. Truth dowsing, she called it, which was a good enough name for now. Sometimes Cassandra joined, creating illusions of real things for me to test myself on. "Find the real one," Olivia would say, pointing to two identical bottles or sacks of sand or corn-husk dolls. "Dowse for the truth." And gradually, I improved. I even taught Mowse little bits of magic from the Booke, and soon she was out scorching tumbleweeds with her own fire spells.

In only a short time, Olivia and her girls had gone from

feeling like strangers to . . . friends. It was a strange sensation to be part of a group, one I'd never had before. And after being alone for as long as I had, it felt like being warmed by a hot bath, cleaned, made new. I kept waiting for them to turn on me, to find out something terrible about me that I didn't know myself and throw me back out into the desert. But as the weeks went by it became obvious that it wasn't going to happen. They *liked* me. And, I discovered, I liked them too.

And I wasn't the only one feeling fortunate. Asa was getting on particularly well in the group, despite being male and, well, a daemon. He worked on the horses with Susanah and Mowse, did heavy lifting with Judith, and did elaborate circus-style performances with Cassandra as though he was an old pro ("Pick a card, any card! Oop, not that one! That's . . . an entire sewing machine and six cups of coffee! And now it's going to . . . disappear!"). He halfheartedly kept his distance from Olivia when he could, but more than often, he couldn't. Especially since she seemed to want to be near him whenever possible. They sat together in the evenings, talking about this or that, her laughing at his stupid puns, him looking at her as though she were the only girl in the world. Her dark, wry sense of humor seemed to balance perfectly with his earnest gullibility, and they just didn't seem to grow tired of each other. I never thought I'd say it, but as strange as they were individually, they were . . . cute together, if they'd ever actually get together.

Yes, Asa and I were doing well. But when we looked at each other and remembered our mission, all our comfort turned sour in our bellies. We had been led to this group, I knew that. Something about them had the potential to fix things. But try as we might, we couldn't. The time was almost over. In only a little over a week, the Dust Soldiers would return to Elysium and find the mess that Asa and I had left. I tried my best to distract myself, to think of what Olivia had said, that Elysium could deal with its own problems. But the very air seemed to be thinning, and sometimes panic set my heart pounding even when I was sitting still.

And there were other, stranger indicators of the Game drawing to a close. Earthquakes had begun, subtle ones that rumbled underfoot. Rock formations began changing positions. Fire coyotes swarmed at night, howling and burning along the horizon. The sunsets began to grow more red than orange, as though preparing for the bloodbath to come. Asa, too, was having problems. He was beginning to have trouble holding himself together. More and more frequently, parts of him would go daemon and he'd have to slap himself back in place. The time was weighing on him, and though he never mentioned the golden cricket, he wore its loss like an albatross around his neck, dragging him down when he was caught unawares.

Asa and I didn't talk about the Game. Maybe because we knew that we had failed, hadn't found the thing that could save Elysium. Maybe because we were afraid of what the others would think of us. Maybe because we were ashamed. There was one exception, an anxious conversation that left me feeling unsteady.

"I don't have long," Asa said once when we were alone in the machine room, unable to sleep. "I can feel it growing on me every day. Like . . . like moss or something."

"What do you mean?" I asked.

"I mean, I, personally, am living on borrowed time in this body. There's no way the Goddesses have forgotten about me.

It doesn't make sense. So what lies in store for me? I'll tell you. Either I'll fall apart completely or die like a human or . . ." He shuddered.

"Or what?"

"Nothing," he sighed heavily. "Forget I said anything."

We never spoke of that conversation again, but after that, it seemed that his eyes were always flickering to the horizon as though he were waiting for something to happen. And whenever I asked my penny what to do, what could be done, it refused to give an answer of any kind other than "Wait."

But, like Asa, I too felt time creeping ever onward toward the end. Toward Elysium's judgment. And if I sat still, I could feel the panic eating at me like ants just beneath my skin.

"You still having that dream?" Olivia asked as we drank from our canteens on the steps of the third train car.

I nodded. "The same one. Just like two days ago. This makes three times."

Olivia gave me a sympathetic look and took another drink from her canteen, looking for what to say, probably. She wasn't sure what to think about the dream, and neither was I. But each time I had it, I woke, sweating and shaking, my penny burning on my chest.

In it, I was outside in the desert, facing the gates of Elysium. I caught the smell of smoke, of burning hair and flesh and wood. On the horizon was what looked at first like a sunset, but as I squinted at it, I saw that it was a wall of fire. A wall of fire, miles high, higher than any dust storm. It stretched across the entire horizon. Miles high and miles wide, sweeping toward Elysium, I knew what it was: the end. The end of Elysium Asa and I were supposed to be trying to prevent. I thought of Olivia's promise to me, her promise that we could go and see what we could do. How much longer could we wait?

Just then, we heard a lot of shouting go up from the other side of the train.

Olivia and I exchanged glances; then she grabbed her pistols and I grabbed my spell components belt, and we followed the sound of the shouting. Out in the clearing, two of the mechanical horses were cantering in a circle, light and nimble as live horses, Asa on one, looking thin and drained, and Susanah and Mowse on the other. Everyone had come to watch them, these majestic metal monsters with their piston legs and lightbulb eyes and grinning mouths of metal and bone. Inert, they had been striking; alive, they were somehow both beautiful and unsettling.

"Finally!" Susanah was beaming. "Magic energy can be harnessed like electricity in the desert! We just needed Asa's magic as a catalyst."

"Anytime." Asa grinned, his teeth flickering to fangs for a moment, then flickering back.

"Susanah, this is amazing!" Zo said. "Think how much faster we can be now! Think how—"

"I don't care about all that," said Judith. "I just want one of my own!"

"There's enough for everybody if we double up!" said Mowse. "They're waiting in the stable."

Everyone looked at Olivia.

"I'm not sure about this. It could be dangerous," Olivia said, her voice deadly serious. Then her face broke into a wide smile. "Ay, I'm just kidding. Let's go, caballeras!"

We went to the stable and brought out two more horses. Judith and Zo climbed onto one, Olivia and Cassandra climbed onto another, and I joined Asa on his. Even under the homemade saddle, it felt hard and metallic.

It was so strange sitting on a horse that didn't move and stamp and shake flies from its shoulders. Giggling and shouting, the girls rode their horses around the clearing, experimenting with speed and agility. Twice, Judith turned too fast and Zo almost fell off the back.

"Let's play a game!" Mowse said. "A magic game! Can we, Susanah?"

"Oh, I love that idea!" Cassandra said, clasping her hands together.

"All right." Susanah smiled. "What did you have in mind?"

"Hmmm." Cassandra put a purple-varnished finger to her temple. "How about . . . this!"

She closed her eyes and mumbled something, then lifted her hands, fingers spread, and iridescent flying fish shot out of her fingertips and hung in the air. Suddenly, they darted out and flitted around us in a bright, shimmering school.

"Catch them!" Cassandra laughed, pointing to the illusory nets that were in our hands now, feeling as real and substantial as real nets.

"Let's complicate things a bit," said Asa. There was a thrum of power, and Asa clapped once, then several dark, jagged-looking eels appeared in the air alongside Cassandra's flying fish, dipping and spinning among the illusions, looking somehow comical with their yellow saucer eyes and slack jaws. "Ten points for the fish! Minus five if you catch an eel too! How's that, Cass?"

"Brilliant!" Cassandra said. "Once we get out of this desert, we should go on tour—"

"Last one out is a rotten egg!" Mowse crowed.

With a blur of movement, Susanah and Mowse galloped past us into the flat part of the desert, following the brilliant school of fish. Olivia and Cassandra were right on their tail, lunging this way and that in pursuit of the fish, their nets flashing in the sun. Judith and Zo sprang after them, whooping and hollering behind their bandannas as they left us in their dust cloud.

"Shall we?" said Asa, his teeth going daemon for just a moment then back again.

"If you're up for it," I said. "You look pretty green around the gills lately."

"Eh, I've got enough pep left in me for one horseback ride," he said, his eyes on the horizon. "Besides, I can make sure we don't catch any eels—just don't tell Cassandra!" He kicked the horse in its metal ribs and it leapt forward, following the fish.

The wind rose up as we rode, and when I put my dust mask on, I let all thoughts of the dream lose themselves in the thrill of that fast, regular run. We ran and jumped and careened, following those shining fish and dark eels for miles and miles. The mechanical horses were faster than any horses that had ever lived, and they could turn so quickly and sharply that several times we were almost thrown as we lunged to catch a fish or avoid an eel. When the wind burned our faces, even with our dust masks and bandannas, and some of our horses began to rattle in odd places, we decided to stop for a rest. We settled in a scrubby area beyond the ravine and sat in the horses' shadows. The eels and fish disappeared in plumes of green and pink smoke, respectively. Susanah tinkered with our horses, tightening this and banging on that.

"Well, they held together pretty well," said Susanah. "It'll take me about thirty minutes, but I can have them up and running in time to take us home. Just gotta"—she grunted—"adjust this removable bit in the . . . spine!"

"Whatever, Suze. You're just distracting yourself from your *blistering loss*." Judith laughed. "Right, Zo?"

"Yep," Zo said, setting her hat to a cocky angle and leaning against Judith. "Forty-two fish and only three eels. The reigning champions: Judith and Zo! Put that in y'all's pipes and smoke it."

"Cheaters!" Mowse said. "That last eel had three heads! It counts for three!"

"I hope you don't mind if I take a nap," Asa said, his arm flickering daemonic for a second. He looked even worse than before. "I'm feeling a little drained these days."

"Sure, just be ready when . . ." Olivia started, but in the horses' shadow, with his dust mask still fastened, Asa was already fast asleep. ". . . it's time to go."

"Aww no," Susanah said, looking at her own horse. "It's got a bum eye."

"It's winking," said Mowse, tightening one of our horses' hooves with a ratchet. As they fixed our horses, we all sat beneath them, fanning ourselves, watching the heat bend over the desert. When a small earthquake rumbled beneath us, we pretended not to notice.

"How far do you think we went?" I asked Olivia.

"Like . . . two miles, I'd say." Olivia pulled her bandanna

down and pointed into the distance. "See? You can almost see Elysium from here."

But Zo was looking in a different direction.

From the north, a storm was rolling in, miles high and wide as the horizon. In the distance, Elysium's sirens blared, the echoes rising like birds and getting lost in the roar of dust.

Deep within me, the old fear rose. My blood went cold. My breath began to come in gulps. My heart felt like a canary, clanging against my rib cage, desperate to escape.

"Shit!" said Zo. "Shit! Shit! Shit! We've got to go!"

We sprang into action, pulling bandannas and dust masks over our faces, looking for cover, as our horses stood, eerily still and unspooked by the coming storm.

"Everyone take cover!" Judith said.

"There is no cover!" Cassandra shouted.

With Mowse behind her, tying her homemade dust mask, Susanah worked trying to tighten our horses' screws. "Come on, come on, come on!" she said. There was a spark, and she jerked her hand back. The horses' lightbulbs blinked, then went out completely. "Shit! The static electricity! We're stranded!"

My breath came in short, sharp spurts. My knees shook, threatening to buckle. What were we going to do? What could we do? Dust Dome. It was our only chance. But I couldn't cast that spell. Not like last time. I ran to Asa on the ground.

"Asa!" I shouted. "Asa, wake up! There's a dust storm!" I shook him, but he would not wake. And without Asa, what could I do?

The wall of dust roared closer.

"You know Dust Dome, right?" Olivia said, her voice carefully steady. "Pulvarem something . . . you got the stuff for it?"

"Last time I couldn't do it!" I said. "Asa had to help me, and look at him!"

"We'll do it together, all right?" said Olivia, her eyes on the wall of dust blackening the sky.

"But you don't have any power!" I said, yelling now over the wind.

"I can copy yours!" she shouted. "Come on! We don't have much time!"

I nodded, my throat dry. With shaky hands, I began mixing the ingredients. Hare's blood and fur, seashell dust and eggshells. I gave half to Olivia, and she followed my example, smearing it on her hands. The wall of dust roared closer, the air suddenly cold and full of electricity. The horses' eyes blinked crazily. The girls got down, putting their hands over their heads, securing their dust masks and bandannas. Susanah put her body over Mowse's.

I closed my eyes. *This is it. I can do this. I have to do this.* I reached out a bloody hand to Olivia. She took it, and I felt the magic surge as we raised our joined hands to the sky.

"PULVAREM FIRMAMENTUM!" we shouted, the magic flowing through us and out of us and into the sky. The clear dome of magic rose around us, high and tall and broad, doubly strong with both of our magic, and as the black dust spewed and flowed over everything, all went dark and quiet, the roar of the storm silenced by the dome. Darkness. Silence. I felt for all the world like we'd been thrust underwater, and the only sound to be heard was the frantic, painful beating of my heart, the rasp of my breath, and the endless pleading of my mind. *Please let it hold, please let it hold, please let it hold.*

But then the magic surged between us. Everything went

black—darker than black—and I knew that a vision was happening, just as it had with Asa, just as it had with Trixie. I was seeing Olivia's truth, and I was powerless to stop it.

It was dark, nighttime, in a house that I knew. Someone was very close, and a female voice was whispering in the dark.

"Me lastimó, Olivia . . . no dejes que . . . no dejes que me lastime . . ."

Olivia's voice answered her, shaking with quiet rage. "No lo dejaré, Rosa. Nunca te lastimará de nuevo . . . te lo prometo."

And as Olivia began to softly sing a Spanish lullaby, Rosa began to cry, a pitiful, heartbreaking whimper. . . . My mind reeled. I had heard *this voice before. I had heard this crying only weeks ago. . . .*

And it was over. Just like that, it was over. We stumbled, dizzy, our hold on each other breaking. Then we looked up. Above us, the Dust Dome stood, holding strong and sure, even under the strain of the storm. Despite all my fear, despite the storm and all its howling, it held.

"You *heard* that. . . ." Olivia gasped. "You heard . . . ?"

"I didn't mean to . . ." I panted, my brain hurting with magic and confusion. "I wasn't trying to."

"I know," she said. "I know you didn't mean to. Just forget about it, all right?"

There was no malice in her voice. Still, we didn't look at each other. I had seen something so intimate, so private, that it didn't matter if it was an accident or not. But, more than that, I couldn't look at her, not knowing what I knew, not if what I was guessing was true.

"All right," I said.

The only light came from the horses' eyes flickering on and

off, and in that ghostly glow, the other girls were crawling out of their protective balls, pulling their dust masks and bandannas down and looking up at the swirling darkness overhead.

"This is your magic," Olivia said. "We did it, Sal."

Pride bloomed in my chest where disbelief had been only moments before. We had done it. Exhausted, I sunk to my knees in the dust. And as the dust raged, impotent beyond the shimmering dome of our magic, I let myself smile.

• • •

Asa woke and squinted upward. He could see that they were in what looked like a big fishbowl with howling darkness all around. Dust Dome, he remembered. Sal must have cast it—without him this time. *She must be so proud,* he thought, smiling. Craning his neck, he looked for her and found her soon enough, sitting around a fire with the other girls, looking even more thoughtful and far away than she usually did. Her hands were stained with blood, and so were Olivia's. Olivia must have helped cast it. At that moment, Olivia must have felt his eyes on her, because she looked down at him and smiled. He felt a surge of what he knew by now was deep affection, and did his best to smother it back down. But, he thought sadly, what did it matter now anyhow, now that he'd already been disarmed and blown so far off course that his mission was all but impossible to complete?

Above him, the mechanical horses stood in a row, their eyes glowing uniformly again. In the flickering light, he saw that his arm had gone completely daemon. Beneath his shirt, he could feel that some of his chest had too. He focused some magic and slid the human illusion down over the daemon parts again. It was secure now that he was well-rested, but it felt flimsier this time.

If he was honest with himself, it had been getting less and less reliable, and he knew it would continue to do so as the end drew near. But he didn't want to think about that right now. So he didn't. Instead, he got up, dusted himself off as well as he could, and went to join the girls by the fire.

"Well, look who just woke up," said Judith. "Morning, sunshine."

Zo moved over for Asa to sit next to her, but he stood, looking out the dome of magic at the swirling black dust. Something about this storm was odd. Sinister. It set his human heart beating fast and erratic, but he didn't know why.

"How long has this storm been going on?" he asked.

"Over an hour," Cassandra was saying, casually twirling a ball of light between her fingers. "It's very strange, don't you think?"

"I didn't think there was this much dust in the world, much less Oklahoma," said Judith. "Good thing we're out of it."

Asa gave the dust one last look and sat down next to Zo.

"I'm hungry," said Mowse, leaning against Susanah.

"We're going to have to do something about food soon," Zo said. "But we can't go out in that."

"We'll just have to wait for it to stop, I guess," said Olivia. "There's nothing else we can do."

Around her, everyone looked grave. But there in the dome, Asa's pulse quickened. There was a presence in the darkness beyond the magic. Something was out there. Something was coming. He scrambled to his feet.

"N-no," he stammered. "No, no, no, no, no . . ."

"What's wrong?" said Sal. "Asa?"

The girls rose, looking around them, confused. But Asa's eyes were on the dust outside the dome of magic. Something was moving toward them in the darkness. Something big. And he knew who it was looking for.

Then they saw it: eight feet tall, broad, with empty eye sockets and a wide mouth. All the air went out of Asa's lungs.

A Sentinel, Dust Soldier, sent by the Sisters, just as he'd been dreading. Sent to take back what Asa had been given, because he had failed. Terror seemed to set his every sinew on fire.

Panic filled the dome like poisonous gas. Everyone rose and clutched at their weapons, palms slick with fear.

"We're trapped!" Judith said. "We're trapped in here! What are we going to do?"

"But why is it here?" Olivia asked, coming to stand next to him. "What does it want?"

"Me," Asa croaked, his mind pulsing with dread. "It wants me. To destroy me, because I'm no longer useful." He gulped. "I have to go to it. I have to accept my punishment."

Olivia pulled a knife from her pocket and flicked it open.

"You're useful to us," said Olivia. "And if it wants you, it's gonna have to go through me."

She looked at the other girls. Gravely, they nodded. And, to Asa's amazement, they formed a protective circle around him, a circle within a circle, Sal fumbling with her spell components belt, Zo with her guns, Olivia with her knife, the rest with only their bodies. *They would do this for me?* Asa marveled. *For a daemon?*

Susanah pushed Mowse into the circle with Asa, and Asa picked her up and held her. Her small body was shaking.

"Are we gonna be okay?" she asked.

"Shhhh," Asa said. "Just hold on to me, okay?"

They stood, waiting, as it kept up its steady, silent march toward the barrier of the spell, its curved sword dark and wicked-looking even from its sheath. Then it stopped just outside the dome and looked up as though assessing it.

"M-maybe it won't be able to come inside," Judith said hopefully, but Asa knew better.

It put up its hands against the barrier, looking for a moment like a great, terrifying mime. Then it broke through the dome as if it was no more than a sheet of rainwater, and like water, the dome closed behind it. It unsheathed its sword and came forward. Gunshots rang out as Zo took aim and fired over and over. But each bullet simply disappeared into it.

"Entflammt!" Sal shouted, sending a ball of fire shooting toward it. It stopped for a moment, but only its outsides were damaged. Sal tried another spell, hurling rocks at it with wind, but it deflected them with a frighteningly fast slice of its sword. It marched forward, never quickening its pace, never slowing as it healed from Sal's fire spell.

Mowse clutched Asa tightly.

He saw Olivia tighten her grip on her knife, saw her bend her knees as if to run. He grabbed Olivia's shoulder.

"Are you insane?" he said. "Look at that sword! Look at its arms! You'll be dead before you get within striking distance. Besides, their skin can't be penetrated with magic or weapons alone."

"Well, what *can* hurt it?" Olivia hissed.

The Dust Soldier marched closer.

Asa racked his brains. "Back . . . back in the day, before I was given a body, lots of cultures wrote about great holy wars between the angels or the gods. And a lot of them talk about . . . what was it . . ." Asa snapped his fingers. "Enchanted weapons! We could enchant something . . . something long range . . . of course, it's still eight feet tall, but . . ."

"All we've got is a pocket knife," said Olivia, her eyes on the Dust Soldier.

"No," Susanah said, her eyes full of fire. "We've got just what we need."

Without another word, Susanah broke from the circle and ran to the line of mechanical horses. She leapt up into the saddle of her own horse and began working with her screwdriver, up and down the horse's back.

The Sentinel advanced, its eerie eyes on Asa, its pace steady, unhurried. Asa's palms sweated.

Up on Susanah's horse, there was a metallic *shing* sound, and they turned to see Susanah pull a long, pointed metal pole out of the horse's spine. Already, it glowed with a strange blue light.

"How's this for an enchanted spear?" Susanah shouted.

"My magic . . ." Asa said. "Of course!"

"Yah!" Susanah said, kicking it into action. The horse was rattlier than usual, seeming as though it might fall apart without the piece Susanah took from it, but Susanah paid no mind. It reared in a soundless, mechanical whinny, and they galloped toward the Dust Soldier, Susanah on its back, holding the spear out in front of her like a knight. Asa held his breath, not daring to let himself hope. There was a clang as it blocked her first attack with its sword. She made her horse rear, then turned and pivoted, bringing the spear up. She tried it again, but the Dust Soldier lashed out with the flat of his blade, knocking her horse on its side with an enormous crash. Susanah leapt off as it fell, taking the spear with her, and faced the Dust Soldier down.

"Susanah!" Mowse cried. She struggled out of Asa's arms and ran into the fray.

"We've got to help her! Come on!" Zo said.

They ran forward, Zo, Judith, and Olivia grappling onto the mechanical horses, trying to undo metal poles of their own from the horses' spines.

The Dust Soldier kept on in its dogged pursuit of Asa.

Then Cassandra muttered something, threw some dust, and suddenly there were six Asas, all equally terrified. They shuffled themselves like cards on top of his own image, then flew to different sides of the dome. The Dust Soldier stopped and watched them, confused. The others, glowing metal poles in hand, galloped to join Susanah. They jabbed and thrust at the Dust Soldier as it slashed at Susanah. Susanah swung her makeshift spear at it, and their blades locked.

"Help me hold its sword!" Susanah grunted, her arms straining. "Then get it, Judith! We have to protect Asa!"

The girls charged forward, and Olivia leapt off her horse, adding her spear to the weight of Susanah's, pushing the sword down. From behind them, on horseback, Judith raised her spear overhead, and Asa held his breath as she threw it like a javelin. It flew, spearing the Dust Soldier straight through the chest. It dropped to its knees, clutching the weapon. There was a flare of magic, and then, to Asa's astonishment, it began to come apart, to dissolve, until the Dust Soldier was no more than a pile of black dust on the ground with the wickedly curved scimitar lying like a metallic smile in the middle of it. And all went silent again. Outside, the dust storm thinned and cleared altogether, leaving the day as bright as it had been.

And it was over.

Gasping, Asa fell to his knees, hardly daring to believe what had happened, what had been done for him. They had done the unthinkable. They had destroyed a Dust Soldier, and they had done it for him. A daemon would never, *could* never. They just weren't capable of something like that, not for someone else. That was something completely and utterly human.

That is how I want to be, Asa realized then. *That is* what *I want to be. Human like that.*

And then they were on him, hugging him, screaming.

"You're safe now!" Mowse said, wrapping her arms around his neck. "You're safe, Asa!"

"They're gonna have to try harder than that if they want to take you from us." Olivia smiled at him, and Asa's heart beat so hard he was afraid it would leap out of his chest.

"What's Susanah up to over there?" he heard Cassandra say.

Across the dome, Susanah was standing over the pile of black dust, looking down at it. He saw her spit into her hand, then reach down and mix her spit with the black Sentinel dust.

"What are you doing, Suze?" Judith said.

"We won," Susanah said, a strange tone in her voice. "My horse and I. We won our first battle."

She spread the black dust and spit mixture over the palm of her hand, then pressed it to her horse's flank, leaving a black handprint stark against the metal.

"Black is for victory," Mowse explained softly.

Susanah stood back and admired it, her expression one of deepest pride. "Come on," Susanah said. "Let's head back home."

CHAPTER 20

1 WEEK AND 1 DAY REMAIN.

The nightmare returned again that night, blazing and terrifying and worse than it had ever been before. This time, I had seen the people of Elysium leaving the city and running from the flame. Trixie had been among them, and her aunt and uncle, but the flames had caught them and swallowed them whole. Only Mother Morevna stood between the city and the flames, but as I watched, the flames began to climb her long black dress, and as the skin on her tattooed hands began to blacken and peel away, I heard that familiar, familiar voice: "¡Ella viene! ¡Ella viene hoy!"

I woke sweating, shaking, and when I touched my face, my hands were wet with tears. I kept seeing Lucy's face as she climbed the walls, and every time my heart twisted more and more painfully in my chest.

I couldn't hide from it anymore. I had to do something to keep this from happening. I took a deep breath and readied myself. I had to go get Asa. Wildcard or not, he and I had to figure out what we were supposed to do. We had to figure it out and go back, with or without Olivia. Olivia . . . I had to tell her, no matter what the result. She had to know. But how did I breach such a subject after so much time? So much pain?

I racked my mind as I dressed, brushed my hair, pulled on my boots. But when I went into the kitchen car for breakfast, I knew something was wrong. The room was quiet. Food sat on plates, growing cold. A game of checkers Mowse and Cassandra had started lay half-finished.

"What do you mean, *gone*?" Olivia was asking.

"North of the ravine," Zo was saying. "That whole area of desert . . . it's just . . . gone. Like it had never been. Like it dropped off the face of the earth. Like the earth *ends* there."

"Did you go into it?" Olivia demanded. "Did you look around?"

"There was nothing to go into," Judith said. "Just . . . *nothing*. Like the world is . . . I dunno . . . crumbling away at the edges, starting at the horizon and coming inward like a . . . like a jigsaw puzzle in reverse."

"And what's more," Zo was saying. "They found us. Samson and the Laredo Boys. I don't know how, but they found us. They found the train."

"How can you be sure of that?" Olivia asked. "You didn't see them, did you?"

"I saw their tracks."

"Oh, *tracks*," said Olivia. "Well, let's all panic about tracks in the dust!"

"But, boss, all of them had stopped at the edge of Cassandra's barrier," said Judith. "From the looks of their tracks they stood there for a while before leaving. They definitely know where the train is."

"But Cassandra cast a direction spell on it!" Susanah said. "Even though they've been here before, they shouldn't have been able to find it again! Unless . . ." Susanah's eyes went wide. "Mowse, did you ever find your doll? The one you had with you when we fought the Laredo Boys?"

"No," she said, her voice quiet with guilt. "It's gone."

"Samson must have picked it up," Cassandra said. "That's the only way it would be visible, if he's got something from one of us."

"Mowse, you have to be more careful about—"

Another earthquake rumbled through the ground, shaking the canisters on the train's dashboard.

"Lecture her later," Zo said. "You all heard Samson. It's only a matter of time before they invade. And if they know where we are now, I'd bet on an ambush soon. I'd say tonight, if not sooner, if the world doesn't disintegrate around us first."

"So what are you suggesting?" Olivia asked. "What do you want me to do about this?"

"Olivia, we have to move," said Zo. "Farther in, close to the center of the desert."

"Where?" Olivia said. "We'd be sitting ducks out there. All that's there is dunes and rocks and—"

"Elysium," I said. Everyone turned to look at me. "We can go back to Elysium."

"Now's not the time for jokes," Olivia said.

"I'm not joking," I told her, drawing myself up to my full

height. "You promised that, as we got closer to the end of the Game, we could go back if I still wanted to. I still want to. We need to go back. I need to do what I came here to do."

"What is it with you and Elysium?" Olivia said. "They rejected you! They threw you out!"

"But I did this to them," I said. "Elysium is my responsibility. I'm the Successor. And even if they reject me again, I won't see it destroyed on my account, not when there are people there I care about."

"I'm not going to send everybody to their deaths in Elysium when they're safe out here," Olivia said. "We can go and get your friends out, maybe, but—"

"No one is safe out here," said Asa from the door. "Not if the desert is doing what you say it is." He came into the room, looking paler, more serious than I'd ever seen him. "Everything depends on Elysium. On the Game. The desert is a—"

He bent, coughing, smoke trickling from his mouth and nose. Then he gathered himself and pointed to Mowse and Cassandra's checkerboard.

"A playing board," I said, realizing suddenly, my heart dropping. "It's not just Elysium. This whole tiny world they've created is part of the Game."

Asa coughed again and nodded.

"And when the Game is over . . . ?" I breathed.

Asa bent over the table. With one swoop, he knocked all the pieces off the board and let them clatter to the floor. There was no mistaking his meaning. Doom and dull panic fell around us. The room went quiet.

"So *everyone* will die?" Zo said. She shook her head in disbelief, rubbed her temples. "I'm gonna need some more details on this, daemon boy. What all do you know?"

"He can't," I said. "He's prevented from giving too much away. He literally can't."

"Here," Asa said. He held out his hand to me, and I knew what he wanted me to do.

A shiver of fear trickled through me. I remembered the last time I'd seen into Asa's memory, how painful it had been, the brain-bending voice of the Goddess of Life in my head. But Zo was right. We needed more details, not just for them, but for me too. So I could finally understand. Gulping, I reached out and took Asa's hand. *Show me,* I commanded.

Darkness and nausea rose, and I was back in that boundless, thrumming darkness of the place between worlds. It filled my mind then, all the things he wanted to say. I felt my brain throbbing, threatening to bleed or explode. Then, just when I thought I could take no more, I wrenched myself out and back into reality.

On the floor of the kitchen, I gasped like a diver breaking the surface of the water as I dropped Asa's hand. My head throbbed again, and my face was wet with blood. The feeling of smoke was in my throat and nose and eyes. I wiped the blood away with my forearm as they all stared down at me, horrified.

"Everything relies on Elysium's test," I said. "That's all the Game is. A test to see if people can be good and responsible in the worst conditions. And because of me, we're failing the test right now," I said. "That means Death is winning. And if Death wins, the desert and everything in it will be destroyed." I looked down at the fallen checkers and swallowed with my paper-dry throat. "It's already starting."

"What happens if Life wins?" Cassandra asked. "What happens if we turn it all around somehow?"

"The desert continues," I said as Asa coughed a plume of smoke. "Elysium continues. This world continues forever."

"So even if Life wins, we'll never rejoin the real world?" Judith asked.

Beside me, Asa shook his head sadly.

We looked at each other, all the plans we'd made for what we'd do once the Game was over deflating like day-old balloons. More of this world? Forever?

"Those options are bullshit," Olivia spat. "Ten years of pain and death and suffering . . . for what?" She shook her head. "If only there was another way to win. A way *we* could win and beat the Goddesses at Their own stupid Game."

We were all quiet then, all somber. All angry. And we were right to be. It seemed that every way we turned, death awaited us. Oblivion awaited us. We were nothing but playthings of Goddesses who cared nothing for our own lives, for Their own creation. My stomach churned. My head throbbed. But beside me, Asa's eyes were on the checkers that he'd knocked to the ground.

"What if . . ." Asa said quietly. "What if we . . . break the Game?"

Every head raised. Every eye turned to Asa.

"What do you mean?" Olivia asked.

"Ten years," Asa said, a delirious smile beginning on his thin face. "The terms of the Game were *ten years*. What if we—" But before he could finish, he bent double and retched violently, vomiting more white, sulfurous smoke.

"Break the Game by prolonging it . . ." I breathed. My heart raced, my aching brain whirred, but this new thought rose like the sun in my mind. "It's supposed to be just ten years long, but if it runs past the ten-year limit, both Goddesses will have to forfeit, and then . . . then *we* could win!"

"And how do you suggest we do that?" Zo asked.

My eyes fell on the scimitar Susanah had brought back from our battle with the Dust Soldier.

"We fight," I said. "Fight the Dust Soldiers! They'll come at sunset of the last day to destroy Elysium. If we resist them, keep them from destroying Elysium, just until sunrise, then maybe . . . maybe we'll have a chance. We fought them before—"

"We fought *one* before!" said Judith, exchanging looks with Zo. "One!"

"I think that we can do it," Susanah said. "I'd have to have more horses, make modifications. . . ."

The penny thrummed on my breastbone, warm, full of truth, and my heart trilled in my chest. "See?" I said, holding the penny out. "This is it! This is what I was supposed to find out here. This is what can fix everything!"

"No," Olivia said. "I know I promised to take you back to Elysium, and I will. But I'm not going back there and fighting an army of those things for the people who kicked me out. Elysium is nothing to me. Everyone I loved there is dead."

I thought of the voice, that familiar, familiar voice I heard in my glimpse of Olivia's truth. That voice that cried out whenever Olivia was coming to Elysium. I steeled myself.

"Are you sure?" I said. The room went completely silent.

Olivia's face went ashen. Her mouth was a straight, tight line.

"What do you mean?" Olivia said quietly.

"Are you sure that Rosa is dead?" I pressed. "Because I'm not. Not after what I saw in your memory."

"Don't you dare lie about my sister to get me to go back there." Olivia came toward me, stood tall as though challenging me.

"I'm not, Olivia," I said, keeping my voice steady. "I don't know that it *is* your sister I'm thinking of. But I can let you see what I saw. Decide what you want to do then, but let me show you."

Olivia regarded me for a moment. Then she extended her hand to me.

"Show me," she said.

And never taking my eyes from hers, I did. I took her hand and sent everything I had into her, all my memories of the girl in the room. The closed door. The sounds of things being thrown. The breakfasts half-eaten. Her crying, her laughing, her murmuring to herself. Her crying out whenever Olivia was coming to Elysium. Me trying to talk to her through the closed door late at night. And when it was over, I pulled my hand out of Olivia's and we sat back, gasping.

"Is it her?" I asked.

". . . Yes," Olivia said, her voice raw. "It's Rosalita. Mi hermana. She's alive. After all these years, she's . . . she's alive." Olivia started to cry, though whether the tears were happy ones or sad ones, I couldn't tell.

"What do you want to do, Olivia?" I said. The other girls watched with wide eyes.

The room was quiet. Every eye turned to Olivia and me. Olivia stood and wiped away her tears.

"Well," she said. "Pack your bags, kids. We're headed to Elysium."

• • •

Our bags were few, of course. As we went out to the horses before the sun rose, loaded up with bindles and old suitcases, we looked like hoboes on our way to jump a new train. Judith and Susanah also rigged together a makeshift sleigh that could be pulled behind one of the horses. This would carry the remaining supplies from the train. It wasn't as good as the stolen goods, but any leverage we could get would help us, we thought. Plus, if we left it, it would only go to fill the Laredo Boys' stomachs if and when they actually came after us. So we loaded up the horses, hitched the sleigh of supplies to one of them, and said our goodbyes to the train.

Then Judith and Zo doused all of it in what was left of the homemade moonshine. Olivia lit up a hand-rolled cigarette, took a long, sad, indulgent drag, then tossed it at the foot of the train.

The flames started small, then grew higher, hotter, pushing us back to stand and watch everything that we had had blaze orange in the sunset. The crackling grew to a roar, and the metal buckled and groaned in the heat of the train's funeral pyre.

Asa and I stood back from the others as they stood there before it, silhouetted in the orange light. We were part of the group, yes, but the train wasn't to us what it had been to them. I saw Zo put her arm around Judith as though steadying her. Mowse reached up for Susanah's hand. Cassandra shifted from foot to foot. Only Olivia stood still as it blazed, holding her hat over her heart.

"Come on," Olivia said finally. "Let's get going." And we turned and began the march toward Elysium.

• • •

We set out, winding through the crags and boulders and into the flat expanse of no-man's-land, taking the straightest, most open route we could, lest anything try to attack us. Olivia rode in the lead, her eyes on the horizon as the horses cantered onward, never stopping, never tiring. And as we rode toward the horizon, we could see giant chunks of the land missing, only sky in the places they had been. It was stark and ugly and our brains seemed to reject it, but it was true: Pieces of the world had fallen away—and no matter how unsettling it was, more would follow.

"Are you sure we have to do this?" said Mowse when we finally stopped to rest.

"There will be other kids there," said Susanah. "You want people to play with, right?"

"I wanted to stay," Mowse said.

"Don't pull that foolishness with me right now just because you're scared," Susanah said.

Mowse was quiet for a moment, then said, "What if they shoot us?"

"They're not going to shoot us," I said. "Not with the supplies we brought for them."

Mowse didn't reply, but it seemed to be enough for her. She

finished the rest of her lunch in silence. Susanah looked at me as though to say, *I hope you're right.* I hoped I was too.

Asa shuddered, but kept quiet.

"Let's get going," Olivia said. "We've got a lot of ground to cover."

"Wait a minute," Asa said. "Do you hear that?"

There was a rumbling in the distance, but no vibrations underfoot, no cracking earth beneath our feet. It was not another earthquake. It was the sound of chariots—makeshift chariots made from the skeletons of cars and drawn by strange, scaly, two-legged beasts with no eyes and mouths full of teeth. At the reins were men painted with black axle grease, holding spears and machetes and guns. Men screaming for our blood. And in the leading chariot was Samson, his broad body unmistakable even at this distance.

"The Laredo Boys!" Zo said. "They must have tried to ambush us and found us gone!"

"And now they want to pick a fight when we try to leave," Olivia said. "Typical men."

"We're just under a mile ahead," said Susanah. "We can beat them to Elysium."

"And then what, fight them at Elysium's door?" Olivia said. "Fight Samson while we duck under buckshot from the guards? No." Olivia pulled her horse to a stop and turned to face the oncoming onslaught. "If we're gonna fight a bunch of Dust Soldiers, we might as well practice on these idiots first."

We turned to face them, weapons out, my hands hovering close to my components belt. Beside me, I could feel Asa's strange, daemonic power growing as he prepared something devastating.

"Steady . . ." Olivia said. "Let's let them get a little closer. . . ."

The Laredo Boys charged onward toward us in a V with Samson at their head, leaving a massive cloud of dust in their wake. They were screaming out, voices nearly inhuman with bloodlust mixing with the shrieks of their beasts.

"A little closer . . ." Olivia said, squinting into the dust. They were a little over a half mile away now.

Zo cocked her pistol and raised it.

But she would not get the chance to shoot. There was a rumbling as though the earth wanted to rend itself in two. Asa's face and arm went daemon. We fell back. Then the desert went suddenly silent as their battle cry was cut short. Suddenly, the Laredo Boys and their chariots and the land they were standing on were just . . . gone. Clipped out of existence, leaving only a glaring, brain-bending nothingness where they had been. A hole in a disintegrating world, so close to us we could nearly touch it, if there had been anything to touch.

We sat there on our mechanical horses, staring into it, hardly daring to believe what we had seen, what we were seeing, this nothing that had once been the land our enemies stood on. After all the terror they had caused, all the pain, they were just *gone*, as though they had never been.

"Wh-what happened?" said Judith, squinting. "And what's that?"

"It isn't an illusion." Cassandra's voice quavered. "I don't know what it is."

"It's *nothing*," Asa said darkly. "Like Zo saw earlier."

The nothingness seemed to yawn and expand in front of us. It wasn't a hole or a tear or darkness. It wasn't heaven or hell or even death. It was simply *nothing*, like I hadn't known nothing could be. An indescribable void that seemed to pull at my very blood even as it terrified me.

"This is what happens as the game board decays," Asa said. "More and more of the desert will fall away until all that is left is the land just around Elysium. And then, depending on what happens, the land will either be restored, or Elysium too will become this."

I stared into that emptiness, that nothing, disturbed by its stillness, its unspoken, booming promise of erasure, of the one, true kind of end: becoming nothing. The blood in my veins turned to ice water, and I tore my eyes away from it.

"Let's keep moving," Olivia said finally. And with shaky hands and shaky nerves, we turned our horses and rode until we could no longer feel the pull of the hungry void behind us.

• • •

When we reached Elysium, the sun was setting. I had only seen it from the outside at night, or been retreating from it, and the sight of it sent a strange thrill through me. It looked huge and imposing, like the fortress it always had been. Unforgiving, even in the sunset light. It felt strange to be voluntarily going back to unwantedness. Without realizing it, Asa and I stopped our horse and looked up at it, hesitating.

"Don't worry, it only looks bigger in the daytime," Olivia said.

We approached, moving together, our eyes on the walls. Soon the guards saw us and began to assemble, their rifles trained on us. When we got about twenty yards from the gates, one of them shouted, "Stop where you are!"

"We need to speak to Mother Morevna!" I shouted.

"Y-you're exiled!" The guard looked from me to Olivia. "Holy . . . Is that . . . ?"

"Olivia Rosales, in the flesh." Olivia smiled wickedly. "Get Morevna. Jameson too, if you want. We've got something to offer Elysium. Something that could save your asses from certain destruction, and they need to hear it from us. Unless you want to get hacked up by a Dust Soldier next week."

The guards looked from one to the other, deliberating, then the one who had spoken to us disappeared.

"Do the walls look a little taller, or is it just me?" Asa whispered.

They were definitely taller now in places, the mud brick still drying here and there. New graves. A lot of them. My heart dropped to my stomach. *What has happened since we left?* But aside from Rosa's grave, none of the names had been carved on the outside of the wall. *Mr. Jameson,* I thought. *Lucy.* I swallowed the nothing in my dry throat and waited with the others in front of the great steel door.

A moment later, I saw Mother Morevna's silhouette on top of the wall. She was more stooped than I remembered her, leaning on a cane now.

Her sickness must finally be catching up to her, I thought.

Mr. Jameson appeared beside her in his Stetson, squinting out at us from up on the wall. Then he saw me, and unmistakably, his face creased into a wide, relieved smile—one that I'm sure mirrored the one on my own face. He was still here, with his hat and his gun and his peach can. He wasn't part of the walls yet.

"Hold off, boys," he said. The guards' rifles dropped but remained in their hands.

Mother Morevna's expression, however, didn't change.

"I thought you'd be along soon, Olivia," she said. "Though I must say, this is bold of you. Usually those who are exiled do not return to the place they were exiled from." Her eyes flickered to me, then to Asa. "And now I see not one, but three people I've exiled standing outside my door." (Asa sheepishly tipped his hat.) "All three of you have caused enough problems already. Begone, the lot of you, before I order them to shoot."

The other girls looked at each other. Mowse huddled into Susanah's back. But Olivia climbed down from her horse and took a step toward the door with her hands up. Trying my hardest to calm my nerves, I climbed down from Asa's and my horse and went to stand beside her.

"Listen to me," said Olivia, her voice careful but firm. "We're here to make you an offer, one that could be beneficial to both of us."

"You're not in the position to offer us anything now," said Mother Morevna. "Except extra mouths to feed. And that, we cannot afford."

"We're offering a way out," I said. "We doomed Elysium, and we want to save it now."

"And how do you propose to do that?" Mother Morevna asked. "You think coming in here on those . . . things . . . and giving us a few sacks of supplies will make up for ten years' worth of goods saved up?"

Olivia pulled the Dust Soldier's scimitar from her bag and

raised it over her head, pointing toward the sky. "We can get Elysium out of this mess. For good."

The guards on the walls began to mumble to one another, their heads turning to measure their reactions. Mother Morevna remained expressionless.

"We know how to kill the Dust Soldiers," Olivia said. "We're offering to arm the guards and train them. Because right now, we're past the point of winning and losing. All we can do now is fight."

"Fighting them would be madness." Mother Morevna's voice was like a soft whip crack.

"No, ma'am," I said. "Fighting is our only hope. The Game has a limit of ten years. And when they come for us on the final day, if we fight them from sunset until the dawn of the next day, we prolong the Game. And if we prolong the Game outside the ten-year limit, then we can end the Game on our terms. We can be part of the real world again. This desert, this godforsaken Game, can finally end!"

Silence fell. My heart skipped in my chest. But I didn't take my eyes from Mother Morevna's.

"And how do you know this is true?" Mother Morevna asked.

"Because her specialty is finding the truth," Olivia said. "Not that you helped her figure that out in any way. You let people keep thinking she was a liar instead of what she is: a truth witch!"

My heart stumbled over itself. It was true, I knew. That was my specialty, and it always had been. How else would I know deception for what it was? How else would I be able to see people's innermost pain, their first truths? It felt real, empowering to have a name for it. I looked back up to Mother Morevna, but her face was expressionless. She knew, I realized. How long had she known?

"Is this true?" she asked me this time, only me. "Is all of this true?"

"Yes," I said, drawing myself up to my full height and glaring back at her. "It's true, all of it. Take your pendulum out and ask it if you want."

"Unless you've got a better plan for saving Elysium," Olivia said.

There was a long moment of silence as Mother Morevna's cold eyes bored into my own. But I didn't look away. I wouldn't look away.

"What is it that you want?" Mother Morevna asked.

I couldn't believe it. She was willing to listen, to go back on one of her decisions.

"All we want is to be welcomed back inside the walls and be treated as equals," I said. "All eight of us. We want a place to live, food, a place to train, and as much scrap metal as you can spare. Then we'll help, as we said."

"It can be done," said Mother Morevna. "But I am wary of offerings of horses in this walled city. This will not be Troy. I will not accept this gift on simple trust when my city is at risk. You will be relieved of your weapons when you are not training, including spell components belts, and when the Dust Soldiers come, you will lead your attack from the front lines. Do we have a deal?"

"One last thing," Olivia said, her voice fierce, her eyes flashing. "I know Rosa is alive. Give her back to me!"

A rumble went up among the guards. "Rosa? Rosa Rosales?" "I thought she was dead." But Olivia stared straight at Mother Morevna. Mother Morevna's mouth was set in a thin, straight line. Olivia's eyes narrowed. It was a battle of wills, two wills, each made of steel. But to my surprise, Mother Morevna was the first to look away.

"All right," Mother Morevna said. "She will be returned to you. But you must lead the attack against the Dust Soldiers, should it come to that. You must be on the front lines, ready to give your life for this last-ditch plan."

"Done," Olivia said. She turned to me, and I nodded, though the thought of being on the front lines made me a little queasy. If that was what we had to do, so be it.

"Open the door!" Mother Morevna said.

With a great, ear-rending groan, the steel door slowly opened. Up on the horse, Asa looked tense, his yellowish eyes darting to and fro. The other girls and I exchanged glances. Mowse peeked out from behind Susanah. Then Olivia and I climbed back onto our horses and led the girls through the gates of Elysium.

The feeling of Elysium, a shocking feeling of relief, rushed over me. The weight of watchfulness that I'd carried in the desert was lifted from me as soon as I passed behind the walls. I felt the familiarity of it change my stance, make my movements looser. Elysium was far from perfect, but it was *home*. One by one, the people of Elysium came out of their houses and stood in their doorways to watch. Every disbelieving eye was on us and our skeletal mechanical steeds. All around, I heard whispers of confusion, fear, distrust . . . and amazement. People simply didn't know what to believe as we passed through the streets, the only three people to ever be admitted back into Elysium. But this time, with all of us there together, I didn't feel alone.

"Oh, now she's letting murderers back in," an old white man said loudly as we went by. "Really is the end, isn't it?"

"Don't listen to them," I heard Zo whisper to Olivia.

"Don't worry, chica," she said, her eyes forward, her back straight. "I've been at this for a long time. All I want out of this hellhole is my sister."

"People of Elysium," Mother Morevna's voice suddenly boomed over the city. Up on the wall, she looked down at us. *"There has been a change of plans. As a final attempt to save ourselves, I have permitted reentry to Elysium to three formerly exiled members of our community and their friends. I urge you to welcome them, for as I reassemble the Sacrifice, they will be fighting to defend us against the Dust Soldiers in the event that my attempts are unsuccessful."*

Asa smiled the brightest, most forced of smiles and gave a little wave to a woman in the middle of drying her laundry. She did not return it, but she gave him a somber nod of her head. All was not forgotten, but it was momentarily forgiven. I turned and exchanged nervous glances with the girls, and, wordlessly, one thought beat through all of us. *We're here now. And there's no turning back.*

• • •

From the shadows behind the water tower, Lucy Arbor watched as the doors were opened.

A jolt went through her. *Sal's back!* She started to run forward, to embrace Sal, to tell her how she'd missed her, how none of it had been her fault. But then she saw the mechanical monstrosity that Sal rode in on. She saw others with her, these outlaw girls covered in sweat and grit and blood, and Lucy stopped in her tracks.

Sal was riding next to Olivia Rosales.

Though Olivia was plainly the leader, there was something different about Sal now. A hardness, a toughness that hadn't been there before. Where Sal had once seemed out of place no matter where she was, she seemed at ease, confident . . . accepted completely. No, valued. She was as much a member of the group she rode with as any of them were.

Sal, the outsider who had nothing. Sal, whom Lucy had pitied and protected, had grown up in the short time she'd been away. Grown into someone who didn't need protection anymore. Strength shone in the strands of her hair and the freckles of her skin. This new strength looked good on Sal, Lucy realized. Beautiful, in fact.

A fit of coughing seized Lucy, and she doubled over, hacking mud into her stained handkerchief. She gasped for air, pain blooming out through her chest before she could finally breathe again. How different she was now, the opposite of Sal. Before, Lucy had been beautiful, feminine, fashionable, with her underground makeup empire and coordinated outfits. But things were different now. Lucy looked down at her drab clothes, felt her rough kerchief, touched her sunken, Dust Sick, makeupless face. Sick, like Sal's mother had been before. . . .

Lucy shook herself mentally.

Sal was looking into the crowd, scanning for familiar faces. Before Lucy could help herself, she ducked behind a nearby house. And troubled by this new, unrecognizable feeling growing in her chest alongside the pain, Lucy glanced one more time over her shoulder at Sal and the girls with her.

She can't see me like this, she decided finally. *She should remember me as I was.* Then Lucy stuffed her muddy handkerchief back into her pocket, took a swig of her water ration, and disappeared into the dust and grit of Elysium.

PART THREE:

HOMECOMING

CHAPTER 21

1 WEEK REMAINS.

The guards came and gathered around us, and after they took our weapons and led us through the streets of Elysium, toward wherever we'd be lodging, the changes that had taken place in my absence became starker, more ominous. This was not the Elysium I remembered.

Entire houses that had once glowed with life were empty, boarded up. Everyone was thinner now, and sadder, their clothes more threadbare, their shoes more worn. Even the church seemed to have grown dingy, black around the edges and between the planks of the siding. Decrees from Mother Morevna hung on houses and on windmills: *WE MUST ALL DO WITH LESS SO THAT WE MAY LIVE*, they said, or *NOW IS NOT THE TIME FOR SELFISHNESS*, or *KEEP CALM. PANIC ONLY KILLS FASTER*. And of course, the walls were higher, the worst sign of all.

But it didn't seem that these signs and precautions had done anything. The panic was there, a tic like a pulse beneath the very earth of Elysium. The sense of doom in the air was so thick it was almost palpable. It hung like fog over the whole city, a silent, mortal panic that seemed to swarm beneath the skin of every man, woman, child, and even animal within the walls. You could feel it in the dripping of water into waiting buckets and dippers, in the hammering of workmen nailing the shutters of the emptied houses closed, in the footsteps of people passing, trying to live out their final days with some modicum of dignity. And as we passed with our mechanical horses, the whisperers fell silent.

I heard a familiar set of footsteps fall in next to mine and Asa's horse. "It's good to have you back, kid," Mr. Jameson said, his eyes crinkling at the corners. "I was worried about you out there."

Among all the stares, all the hostility and confusion, Mr. Jameson's gravelly voice felt like an anchor in an unsteady sea.

"I'm just glad we're back on the same side again," I said.

"We are," he said, giving me that hangdog look. "I promise."

"Ah, Mr. Jameson," Olivia said, riding up to him. "Didn't think you'd see me again, huh?"

He touched the brim of his hat. "It's good to have you back too, Olivia."

"Well, we'll see how the rest of Elysium feels about that," said Olivia, looking out at the sunken eyes and sunken cheeks of the onlookers. "Now, where is my sister?"

"Mother Morevna will bring her to you tonight," Mr. Jameson said evenly. "Just let me get you all settled in first. It doesn't make sense to get her back without a place to take her, does it?" He sighed. "So you know, I objected to all of this from the very beginning," he told Olivia. "Faking her death, using her as an Alarm to let us know when you were coming. I'm glad it's over."

I remembered then what I had overheard so many nights ago, when I had first moved into the church. That whispered conversation, Mr. Jameson feeling nearly sick about a girl who was directly above him. Rosa. I could feel all of this from him without even having to touch him. But that didn't excuse it. I stepped away from him, letting him feel the distance between us.

"You still did it," Olivia said, her eyes on his, hard and unforgiving. "You went along with it, what Mother Morevna told you to do. And even if I had trusted you before, I can never trust you completely now."

"I understand," he said, a thread of pain running through his voice. "And I don't expect your trust. But I want you to know this: All this time, I made sure no harm ever came to Rosa and that she had all she needed. And if you want enemies, girl, look all around you, but don't make one out of me, not when I'm trying my best to help you."

Olivia was quiet. She didn't necessarily trust Mr. Jameson—how could she?—but I could tell by the set of her jaw that she would call it a truce for now.

Through the open, sheet-covered windows of a nearby house, we heard the sound of someone sobbing. Loud, racking sobs that sounded like the poor person would surely be broken in two by her own weeping. On the porch, a man sat with a homemade cigarette, too beaten down by sadness to even look up as we walked by.

"I don't like it here," Mowse whispered. Susanah took her hand and said nothing.

"What's happened?" Asa asked Mr. Jameson. "It seems a bit . . . heavier in here since we left."

"A Dust Sickness outbreak," Mr. Jameson said. "The worst we've ever had. And more than that. We've only got one week left. People don't take doom well."

Asa and I exchanged guilty glances. All we could do was what we came to do. To set it right again. To be the saviors we each had wanted so desperately to be. And now we had no other choice.

As we walked, I scanned the crowd, looking over heads, in between bodies. But the longer I looked, the more my heart sank. The face I was looking for was nowhere in sight. I started to look up where the white-clad morticians were laying another body to rest, bricking it up in the walls.

"Where's Lucy Arbor, Mr. Jameson?" I asked. "Is she . . . ?"

"Lucy Arbor?" He thought. "She's all right, last I heard. Been spending a lot of time at the hospital, helping out. I'd have thought she'd come down here to see you. Maybe she's still working with Nurse Gladys."

"I'd have thought so too," I said, my heart sinking painfully, dragging the rest of me down. "Maybe I was wrong."

When we stopped in front of a two-story house with darkened windows, Mr. Jameson reached into his pocket and pulled out a jingling ring of keys.

"The last lady to live here died a week ago, so this one's open," said Mr. Jameson. The house had been white, long ago. White with green trim, it looked like. But now the paint had been almost completely stripped from the wooden planks. The roof was missing more shingles than it had been before, and the windows were caked with dust, but it was a house, and it was big enough for all of us.

We brought our horses to a stop by the side of the house and followed Mr. Jameson to the door, our boots leaving prints on the dusty porch. He opened the door with a creak.

We stepped into the house, which was like any other in Elysium, with newspapered walls, a round wooden table, an old green stove visible through the kitchen door. Though the woman who'd owned it hadn't been out of it for long, it was already almost ankle-deep in dust. The stairs to the right were caked with it, and the windows were so bad that we couldn't see out them.

"I'll get Mrs. Winthrop to send water and rags for y'all in a little while," Mr. Jameson said. "And some brooms."

"Why are there guards outside?" asked Mowse. Sure enough, as we spoke, four guards were approaching, looking nervous. They went to stand outside each corner of the house.

"To make sure none of you puts a toe out of line," said Mr. Jameson, giving each of us our own individual no-nonsense look. "Everybody thinks we're taking a big risk with y'all, and most of them don't even know the half of it. Now, while y'all are here, I don't want to hear about y'all being hooligans, stealing pies off windowsills, writing ugly things on houses . . ."

"What do you think we are?" Zo said, leaning against the doorway.

"Thieves," Mr. Jameson said. "Unless it was some other gang of girls who stole from the Sacrifice building a few months ago."

Zo crossed her arms and went quiet.

"It's nothing personal," he said. "But y'all have a little bit of a . . . reputation. And until it's proven false, we gotta keep the guards out there every night. Now, they aren't gonna bother you as long as you don't do anything stupid. So don't do anything stupid, all right?"

"Yes, sir," Zo grumbled.

"You hear that, Judith?" said Cassandra from the stairs, where she had stuck her skinny head through the railing.

"Shut up!" Judith said.

"Thank you, sir," I said. "I'll take it from here."

"Come on, let's check out the kitchen, Mowse," said Susanah.

"I'm gonna go pick a room!" said Judith, heading upstairs. Cassandra followed her, and Zo disappeared with Susanah and Mowse into the kitchen. Only Asa and Olivia and I remained.

"As for you two . . . Olivia Rosales and Asa Skander," Mr. Jameson said. "Both of you have claim to the Robertson house, which is still . . . vacant. So which one of y'all wants to lay claim to it?"

"Oh, I couldn't possibly—"

"He can have it," Olivia said, and she pushed past me, up the stairs. "Just tell me when I can go get Rosa." And she was gone.

"Well, I guess that settles it," said Mr. Jameson. "I'll arrange for an escort to be sent over in an hour."

In the background, there was a giant crash from the kitchen, followed by "Mowse!" from Susanah and "I'm SOR-ry!" from Mowse.

"I'm going to go check on that," said Asa. Then he too disappeared into the kitchen, leaving me alone with Mr. Jameson.

"Well, I got a lot of preparations to do, so I'll leave y'all to settle in," Mr. Jameson said, pulling the door open. "Be ready tomorrow at sunup. We ain't got time to lose now."

"Yes, sir," I said.

Mr. Jameson turned, then he stopped.

"I really am glad to have you back, you know," he said. "I just wish I could have done more for you all these years. God knows I tried. I guess I just didn't try hard enough."

I felt a lump grow in my throat, and before I could stop myself, I hugged him. He stood still for a moment, shocked, maybe, then returned the hug, and when he did, I could feel the loneliness and pain and loss and hope he felt for his family back in Texas. His daughter, Doris, who must be my age now.

"It's all right, Mr. Jameson," I said. "Everything is going to be all right."

"I sure hope so, kid," he said. Then he turned and walked out of the house, his footsteps echoing as the door swung shut behind him.

• • •

Back in the Robertson house, Asa laid himself out on his old bed and looked up at the ceiling in the dark, trying to quiet the panic that beat along next to his own, temporary heart.

Only a week. They had only a week to prepare, and either way, the same fate awaited him.

Fear reared up in his chest. In his mind, the smell of mercury and petrichor rose.

What would he do now? What did that mean for him? Even if their plan did work, he was still a creation of Theirs, and he doubted either of the Goddesses would be pleased with him when the Game ended.

There was the sound of a footstep, and Asa bolted upright. He climbed quietly out of bed and tiptoed to the hallway. Through the darkness, a figure was visible in the kitchen.

"H-hello?" he said, his mind reeling with images of Dust Sentinels and their gaping mouths. "Who's there?"

"It's okay, it's okay," said the figure. "It's just me."

The figure struck a match and lit an oil lamp on the table.

Olivia's beautiful face flared into light. "Hey," she said simply.

"What are you doing here?" Asa asked. "How did you get past the guards?"

Olivia shrugged. "I borrowed some magic from Mowse," she said. "The ones at Sal's house are asleep. So are the ones outside your door. It was pretty easy, really."

"But I thought you didn't want this house?"

"I don't," said Olivia. "I just wanted to . . . see it again and see if any of our things are left before Rosa comes back. That's all. So she doesn't have to see it."

"They still haven't called for you?"

"Not yet. But they said they will soon. They'd better." Her dark eyes swept over the countertops, the stove, the table, the cabinets. "It's different somehow," she said. "It even smells different."

Something about her had changed. The flirtatious demeanor she usually had with him was gone, replaced by an odd . . . hollowness. She was wearing an expression he hadn't seen her wear before, sort of serious and almost sad, but not quite. He wasn't sure what human emotion corresponded to such an expression, but he could tell that it wasn't a good one. He could tell that it was all that she could do to contain it. And suddenly his worries seemed minuscule in comparison.

"I'm going to give it one final look through, if that's all right with you," she said.

"Be my guest. I'll stay right here."

"Thanks." Olivia lit another kerosene lamp. "I'll just be a second."

Olivia scanned the kitchen one more time, then started down the hallway, her lamp illuminating the dark with a ball of dim gold light, then disappearing again. He heard her walk the length of the hall, duck into the bathroom, her old bedroom, every room except the one with the bloodstained floor. He heard a drawer slide out, then a soft fumbling. The door slid shut again, and he heard her footsteps coming back up the hallway.

"You want a smoke?" she said to him, pulling a cigarette out of her pocket as she came out of the dark. She sat down next to him at the kitchen table.

"Why not?" he said, and took one. But his eyes were on her.

They sat in silence for a moment, sending up clouds of thoughtful smoke.

They had shared cigarettes before. Smoking made Asa feel like he thought a dragon must feel, lungs hot and sulfuric, controllable. She had laughed when he'd smoked his first cigarette, coughing and going green at the gills. But this time, Olivia seemed to smoke without thinking about it or taking pleasure in it. But by this point, he knew that it wouldn't help to ask her what was wrong. All he could do was wait.

"I like what you did with the place," she said finally.

"Thanks," said Asa. "Though I haven't really gone into the one room with the bloodstain. It . . . feels bad in there."

"Yeah," she said. "It always did." She blew another cloud of smoke. Then she reached into her pocket and pulled out what looked like a doll carved from pale, soft stone and a chain with a heart-shaped locket dangling from it. "I had to get these," she said. "Rosa and I had our hiding places in the house. The bathroom, our room. I wanted to give them to her if they were still there. And they were. Thanks."

"No problem," said Asa. "If there's anything else hidden in the walls, feel free. I found a dead rat once. It's probably still there if you want it."

That did it. Olivia smiled.

"You're really something, you know?"

"Yeah," said Asa. "Though exactly what that something is is becoming blurrier by the day."

She glanced back down the hallway, toward Asa's bedroom—her old bedroom.

"You've met Her?" Olivia asked, her voice quiet. "Death?"

Asa's heart thudded once, painfully.

"You could say that," Asa recovered. "I'm more Her Sister's creation, though." Asa paused, decided to take a gamble. "But, of course, you've met Her too. I've seen the wall in there."

Olivia looked down at the table. Let her cigarette burn.

"I didn't know what else to do," she said quietly. "I needed a way to stop it. To stop him."

"She is good for ending things," said Asa. "Of course, She never does anything for free."

"That's what's bothering me," said Olivia. "You know how you were sent here on behalf of Life? Well . . . do you think

Death was helping me so I would help Her win the Game? Help Her end Elysium?"

She seemed younger as she looked at him then. All her toughness and grit had been peeled back, and this is what she was at her core—just a girl who loved her sister—and Asa's heart seemed to swell so much it ached. He knew then that he'd give anything to give her peace. But peace was not what he had to give. Only truth.

"Yes," Asa said. "I believe She did choose you, just as Life chose me. And for the . . ." A wisp of smoke curled up out of his mouth, blending with the cigarette smoke. ". . . the reason you guessed. I'm sorry, Olivia."

Silence fell. Olivia's eyes were on the table.

"But what does it all mean?" she asked, her voice taut. "I'm supposed to . . . to help destroy Elysium? To help destroy all of us?"

"It means that you *could*," Asa said. "It means that you are *capable* of it because your decisions have been given more weight than those of others. But it doesn't mean you *will*." Asa stood. "Look at me! I'm a Card too, and I certainly haven't helped Life's cause at all."

"But everything I do . . . everything I have done . . . it's only helped Her. Death, I mean. When I killed him . . . when we attacked Elysium. All of it only pushed Elysium closer to collapse. Like I wasn't even trying. Oh, God . . ."

"That's how it works," Asa said. "There's likely something She wants you to do, some mission you have that only you can accomplish, like mine."

"But what could it be?" Olivia asked, her eyes on the table, her brows furrowed.

"I have no idea." Asa shook his head.

"Are you sure I'm the one?" Olivia asked.

Asa thought about this. He had felt a growing sense of dread as he had headed toward the settlement, felt a tug of significance on his heart when he had first laid eyes on her, first fought her. But now that dread was gone. Now talking to her was as natural to him as breathing.

"No," Asa said honestly. "But I know that Death's Card is female, and that she uniquely proves the greatest threat to me."

Olivia looked up, her dark eyes on him.

"What do you mean I'm the greatest threat to you?"

"The two Wildcards can . . ." Another wisp of smoke, a burning in his chest.

Thinking fast, Asa made a hand motion of two cars colliding and exploding. Olivia watched with a grim expression. "Do you get it?" he said.

Olivia nodded.

"And if I think about it . . . I think it may be why we're drawn to each other," Asa sighed. "We are each most vulnerable to the other."

"It's more than that, what's between us, and you know it," said Olivia.

"I know," said Asa. "But we cannot ignore what we are, our parts in this. All we can do now is fight."

"Can we fight something like fate?" Olivia asked.

"Of course," Asa said. "Humans do nothing but fight fate

every day. Humans are the most blessed and cursed of all creatures because humans can choose. Humans can *change.* For this reason, they cannot completely be used. That's what I think I've envied for so long: the ability to be . . . not just a person, but my *own* person. Someone who *can't* be used." He paused, hoping desperately that she understood. "Death has positioned you based on your *potential* to be useful to Her. Nothing more. Your choices about what to do are completely your own. And it's not like you, the strong, patient, ingenious girl I know, to bow before something as insignificant as fate."

Olivia turned to him, her eyes so dark and wide and beautiful. Asa found himself leaning toward her, drawn, again, as though magnetized to her and she to him. But this time, they didn't stop. They didn't pull back. Their lips met and it seemed as though an explosion went off somewhere within him. A very un-daemon-like explosion of affection, of urgency, of several thousand other things at once, but this time Asa didn't care to quantify them. He shut his eyes and fell into the moment, into a cigarette-tasting frenzy of kissing, heat, closeness, passion, and he couldn't really tell if this was all one kiss or more than one, but he didn't care, because her hands were in his hair and she was nearly in his lap and—

A knock on the door. Asa and Olivia sprang up as though burned. "Olivia Rosales!" a deep voice said. "Are you in there?"

Adjusting his clothes, smoothing his hair, Asa went to the door and opened it to find two guards standing on the doorstep.

"We're here for Olivia Rosales," one guard said. "We were told she might be here?"

"I'm here," Olivia said, coming to the door beside him. "Is it time?"

"Yes," said the guard. "Your sister is ready to see you."

Asa could see the happiness and apprehension rise within Olivia. He couldn't imagine what she must be thinking, finally being able to see her sister again after so many years.

"Can he come too?" Olivia asked, to his surprise.

"Fine by me," said the other guard after a moment. "But come on. Miss Iba—I mean, your sister—has been making a racket all day."

• • •

The guards led Asa and Olivia to the church and stopped them before the door.

"Wait here," they said. They went to the door and knocked.

Asa felt Olivia slip her hand into his.

The door opened, and Mother Morevna appeared, stooped and sunken. But power still emanated off her like heat from a summer road. She nodded once to Olivia, then opened the door wider.

"Come now, girl," she said. "Your sister is here to take you."

Asa heard Olivia catch her breath.

A girl in a long white nightdress stumbled forward then, hair long and mussed, but clean. She was a thin imitation of the girl from the picture. She looked like Olivia, but pale and sallow from years spent locked indoors, and she was so frail that she seemed nearly insubstantial. She blinked once as though waking from a dream. Then she saw Olivia and light leapt into her eyes.

"*¡Olivia! ¡Has vuelto! ¡Has vuelto!*" she cried, running into

Olivia's arms. The two collapsed there in the dust in front of the church, holding each other and weeping.

"Rosa! Mi hermana, mi hermana . . . ¿Estás bien?" Olivia asked, stroking her hair as she held her close. "¿Te lastimó? ¿Era cruel contigo?"

Asa stood back and watched the two of them there in the dust, so similar, yet so different. Olivia was so gentle with her. There was such love, such tenderness in every weeping syllable the two uttered.

He loved her, he knew then. Completely, irrevocably, with a love so doomed and impossible that he suddenly understood all those Shakespearean characters with their monologues and knives, ready to be plunged into their own hearts. It hurt, terribly. But he knew then that even if he'd known how it would turn out, he'd have chosen this again and again and again.

"Come on," Olivia said, putting her arm through the crook of his elbow. "Let's take Rosa back home."

"Olivia . . . ¿quién es el?" Rosa asked, wary eyes on Asa as she held Olivia's other hand.

"Asa Skander," Olivia said. "Él es mi . . . novio." (Asa's heart gave a fluttery thrill at the last word.)

"Buenas tardes, Rosa. Mucho gusto en conocerte," he said, smiling his friendliest smile. Then he pulled a thornless rose from behind her ear, much to her delight, and handed it to her as she marveled.

"I didn't know you could speak Spanish," Olivia said, tucking the flower behind Rosa's ear.

"You never asked," Asa said. He tried to smile, to keep things lighthearted, for Rosa's sake, but he became aware of Mother Morevna then, watching from the doorway. Her eyes were not on the Rosales sisters. They were on him, scrutinizing him, as though he were a puzzle to be completed.

"Come on," Olivia said, beaming. "Let's go see the others."

And, with a glance back over his shoulder at Mother Morevna, Asa followed the Rosales sisters into the dark, back to the house where the other girls waited.

CHAPTER 22

When Olivia and Asa arrived with Rosa behind them, we weren't sure at first how we should act. I worried that Judith or Mowse would scare her, she seemed so timid. But as Olivia introduced Rosa to all of us and she hugged each of us in turn, we found our voices lowering to match pitch with hers. To my surprise, it felt natural having her around. And to my surprise, when she was close, I could feel magic emanating from her too, faint but present, hanging around her like perfume.

Asa, ever the performer, was surprisingly good with her, for not being truly human. He spoke to her in fluent Spanish and always made sure to communicate with her as clearly as possible without talking down to her like I'd seen nurses do to a deaf man once at the hospital. And whenever he made Rosa laugh, I thought Olivia's own face might split in two, her smile was so wide.

"He's going to take care of her tomorrow, while we train the guards," Olivia told me as we watched Asa entertain Rosa with his sleeves full of colored scarves. "There's no use in him coming until the horses are ready to be powered up. And, anyway, she adores him, don't you think?"

Asa turned a scarf into a doll and handed it to Rosa, who, delighted, held it to her chest, murmuring to it in Spanish.

I met Olivia's eyes. "She's not the only one," I said. "What about you? What are you going to do when this is over?"

"I know," Olivia said, a note of pain in her voice as she watched the two of them laughing together. "I know that whatever happens, the Goddesses won't be happy, and I'll probably never see him again. But we'll cross that bridge when we get there. Until then, I'm just gonna take what happiness I can get, and prepare to give them the fight of my life."

We settled in, putting Olivia and Rosa in one of the upper bedrooms, Asa went back to the Robertson house, and all drifted into slumber, lulled to sleep by the rumbling of our temporary earth.

• • •

The next morning, we were awakened at dawn and taken to a barn on the south side that I had never seen before. It was empty, save for a long table, three feed sacks hanging from ropes, which were probably intended to be used as punching bags, and boxes of ammunition and weapons. It had an acrid, dusty man smell to it.

"All the guards trained in here," a short, pimply guard said to me. "But we cleaned it out as well as we could last night."

"Where's Mother Morevna?" I asked.

But before either guard could respond, Mr. Jameson came through the back door of the barn with fifty men behind him. Some were tall, broad, experienced, and some looked younger and scrawnier than the two who had been our escorts this morning, and they shook in their boots as Mr. Jameson assembled them in two straight lines before us.

"This is it?" Zo said, leaning over to whisper to Judith.

"Good morning, girls," said Mr. Jameson. "These here are all the guards and builders and volunteers I could muster in a day, but I'll try to get some more. They're ready, willing, and eager to learn everything y'all have to teach them about fighting Dust Soldiers, right, boys?"

"Yes, sir!" they said, some more enthusiastic than others.

"We've been here in this desert for as long as any of us want to be here," he said. "And even if this is a long shot, we're prepared to give it all we got to get out of here."

He wasn't just following orders, I realized. He really believed we could do this. For once in ten years, we'd offered him the chance to go back to his family, to make a difference, and he was going to pursue it with his whole heart.

"Now let's get started," he said, and with a gesture, he gave us the floor.

We exchanged glances. Then Olivia pushed me forward.

"Um . . ." I said nervously. "So as it is, the plan is to build a bunch of horses like the ones we have. The magic in them—Asa's magic mixed with some of our own—is deadly to the Dust Soldiers when combined with weapons, so . . . we're going to power the horses up with magic, and, when—if!—the Dust Soldiers come for us, we shut the doors of Elysium behind us and fight them as long as we can. If we can extend the Game to ten years and *one day*, we'll break it, and . . ."

I swallowed. It was strange to be in front of everyone again, speaking to them like the leader I'd always hoped to be. I felt my heart had begun to speed.

"And we may have a chance to finally get out of here," Olivia finished, coming forward to stand next to me. "So the plan is: While the builders build the horses, the soldiers learn to fight and the witches practice magic so they can serve as an artillery, kind of. So . . . builders! Come forward."

About fifteen scruffy, hard-looking men came forward, and I could see how rough their hands were. Many of them had burns on their forearms from working with hot metal.

"I'm Susanah Mihecoby, inventor of the horses," said Susanah, going to greet them. She was almost comically short compared to the tallest of them. "If you show me where the metal is, we can get started right now."

Mowse ran out from behind Judith and came to stand by Susanah.

"I'm going too," Mowse said. "I know how to build these."

"Sure you do," Susanah said. "But I had something different planned for you." Susanah turned to Mr. Jameson. "Hey! Do y'all have a school here?"

"Sure we do," said Mr. Jameson. "It'll start up in about thirty minutes."

"School?" Mowse blanched. "What?"

"I want to send Mowse to school today, just to see how it goes," Susanah said.

"I can arrange that," said Mr. Jameson. "Tommy, why don't you take her down to—"

"I can't go to school!" Mowse said. "I *won't* go to school! I'm going to build the horses with you!"

"Mowse, please," Susanah said. "I know I'm not your mother, but I'm the closest thing to a parent you've got. And now that there's a school around, I want you to at least *try* to get an education. A real one, not just me teaching you ABCs and simple math. Real stuff I can't teach you."

"But what if they make me forget everything, like they made you?" Mowse asked so quietly I almost couldn't hear her. Her eyes were big and wet and frightened.

Susanah blinked in surprise, and when she spoke again, her voice quavered. "They won't, Kahúu," she said gently. "It's different for you. I promise. And if they do, I'll pull you out, no questions asked. Just go and give it a chance, okay?"

Mowse looked at her, then back to the rest of us.

"It really will be fine," I told her. "You'll get to do all kinds of things. Read books, learn math, play on the playground, study maps of Europe and Asia and Africa—"

"What's the point if we're all going to die?" Mowse said.

"We're not," Olivia said. "I promise. Right, Susanah?"

"Right. You know I wouldn't let you die. Now, go on, okay?"

With one final hug for Susanah, Mowse went with Tommy, the pimply guard from before, and headed across town to school.

"Okay," Susanah said. "Where's the metal?"

"Out back," said Mr. Jameson. "Behind the building."

"Great," said Susanah. "Builders, come with me!"

And without another word, Susanah led them, unsure and shuffling, out of the church.

The others looked at us expectantly.

"Um . . . Judith! Zo!" Olivia said. "You think you can teach them how to fight Dust Soldiers?"

"We got it, boss!" Judith said. "Come on, y'all, let's go." And she and Zo led them to the back of the barn to begin sparring.

Only Cassandra, Olivia, and I were left. We turned to each

other, bewildered. It seemed unbelievable, Mother Morevna trusting us with this responsibility and not being here, breathing down our necks.

"What are we going to do?" asked Cassandra. She looked at all of us, then at Mr. Jameson.

He put up his hands. "That's completely up to you witches," he said. "Though I wouldn't say no to an enchanted rifle or something. Maybe a bunch of 'em for the artillery, if, as y'all say, enchanted weapons are what gets 'em."

"That's . . . not a bad idea, actually," said Olivia.

"What's Mother Morevna doing now?" I asked.

"She's handling the Sacrifice, trying to get a new one built up before the Dust Soldiers come back," said Mr. Jameson. "Been working herself to the bone these days. I'm surprised it hasn't killed her, to tell the truth. I know she doesn't expect to live through this, whatever happens, but she'll never stop trying."

But before I could say anything, Mrs. Winthrop, Mother Morevna's housekeeper, appeared in the doorway, lugging a huge rucksack.

"These are for all of you," she grunted. "Sent by Mother Morevna."

She emptied the rucksack onto the table before us. Books scattered to and fro, pages fluttering.

"Spell books?" Cassandra said.

"And some kind of witch belts," Mrs. Winthrop said, opening a pouch and pulling three spell components belts from the rucksack and throwing them onto the table. "One for each of you."

The others took the belts nervously and buckled them on.

Mrs. Winthrop's eyes flickered over all our faces and lingered on mine.

"Let's hope it doesn't come down to you. But if it does, then, for all our sakes, make use of this time. Lord knows we've had enough funerals around here as it is." She looked up at Mr. Jameson. "Come with me, Jameson," she said. "Mother Morevna wants to speak to you."

Mr. Jameson nodded to us and followed Mrs. Winthrop back to the church.

I looked from face to face. "Are y'all ready?"

Everyone nodded.

"Good," I said. "Let's get to work."

As if on cue, the sounds of hammering, sawing, metal rending rose in the air.

"Hayloft," said Olivia, jerking her head toward the ladder. "Let's go. Maybe it'll be quieter up there."

We each grabbed a stack of books and headed up to the hayloft. There among the hay and dust, we laid everything on the floor and sat in a circle, dividing the books among ourselves.

"Well . . ." I said. "Let's get started, I guess. We'll . . . focus on offense first. Illusions, projectiles, things like that. Then . . . then we can move on to the defensive spells. Does that sound okay?"

Everyone nodded.

For three hours we studied, we discussed, we tested sigils and runes, drawing them in the dust with our fingertips. We made lists of the spells we could perform, and ones that might be useful for Olivia to copy.

I had never seen Olivia like this. She always seemed so

confident, so sure. Now she paced like a tiger in a cage, muscles taut, full of energy, but with nowhere for it to go.

"Do y'all mind if I get some air?" she said.

"Go ahead," I said.

Olivia pushed the door to the hayloft open. Then she gasped and stepped back.

"Holy shit, Sal," she said. "Come look at this."

I went to the window and looked out. From the hayloft, most of Elysium was visible, the church, the jail. But from this height, the differences were even starker. Where the Sacrifice building had stood before, there was a new, crudely constructed platform on wheels. The fruits of Mother Morevna's labors. There were guards all around it, watching as men moved boxes and bags and sacks onto it, trying to scrimp what they could from everyone in the vain hope that it would be enough. No wonder the food rations were so much smaller now. Only one meal a day, instead of three. But the pile of goods was only a third of what it had been before—and Mother Morevna was lucky to have gotten that. The sight of it made my head pound and my pulse begin to tic faster.

"What's that line for?" Cassandra said behind me. I turned in the direction of her pointed finger. The Dowsing Well. A long, snaking line had formed from it. Men and women standing in line with their water rations in hand, waiting, blank faced and quiet, as two stern-faced guards ushered them forward with their buckets.

"The Dowsing Well," I said. "Looks like it's been opened to everyone at all hours. I've never seen it so bad."

An earthquake rumbled under us, and dust shook from the rafters.

The hospital was full to bursting, full of unconscious people being carried on stretchers, anxious farmers waiting to see loved ones, nurses running from the hospital to the jail next door with buckets of water. Mr. Jameson hadn't exaggerated. Dust Sickness was tightening its grip on Elysium, squeezing, choking, suffocating, and somewhere, I knew that Lucy was out there in the thick of it.

• • •

By the end of the training, our brains were fried and our fingers were covered with dust and ash, but I still felt numb with worry. We came down from the loft and met Zo, Judith, and Susanah, who had had quite a day as the de facto head of the "Scientific branch" as she called it.

"—they started out by talking over me," Susanah was saying. "Me! The inventor of the only weapon that works against the Dust Soldiers!"

"Next time, tell them you'll slit their throats." Olivia winked. "Always worked for me."

"I ended up saying, 'Do you want my help or not? Because with you talking so much, we may as well start making our peace.' "

But I barely heard any of it. Again, I took my penny from my neck and held it in my hand.

"Find Lucy," I whispered to it. "Please. I just want to make sure she's okay."

But once again, my penny was still.

"Are you ladies ready to head home?" said a guard, coming down to us. He was a different guard this time, an older one, with graying hair at his temples.

"What about Mowse?" said Susanah.

"Your little girl? She should be back at the residence by four," said the guard. "But I'm supposed to take y'all to get your water rations before I take you home, so let's get going."

The other guard, the one I was waiting for, met us at the door, and we began the silent walk home. The crowd parted like the Red Sea for Moses.

As we neared the Dowsing Well, the line had wound its way several times in front of the church, and nearly all the way back to the windmill.

"Is there another place we can get water?" Cassandra asked as the guards led us toward the line.

"You can go to a different windmill," said the older guard. "But this water is the cleanest in town."

"Let's risk it for now," said Olivia, her eyes on the shuttered windows of the church. Up behind the rose window, I couldn't see her, but I could feel Mother Morevna's presence looking out, watching over all of Elysium.

The guards shrugged and led us to the much shorter line at the next well over.

Desperately, I scanned the tops of the walls, looking at the new graves, squinting for names. But I didn't see Lucy's name, not on this side of the wall.

The crowd parted, and in front of us, four men in dusty white uniforms, with dust masks, carried a stretcher across our path. There was a man on it, lying still, mud-vomit on his shirt. But they were headed toward the jail, not the hospital. *There must be too many people in the hospital now,* I thought, worry reaching up and squeezing my heart.

"Can I go?" I whispered to the guard. "To the hospital? I think my friend is there."

The guard looked at the line, then across to the hospital. He looked over his shoulder to make sure no one was watching, then gave me the nod to go ahead.

I ran all the way to the hospital, and when I got there, the waiting room was so full that there was no room to stand, let alone sit. Fear rose over everything, so thick I felt I could almost touch it with my hands. People of all ages, all colors, all genders sat or stood or leaned against the walls. Guards, factory workers, farmers, cowboys, all wearing cloth dust masks. In a sad, sick way, I thought, *Here's our equality.* Here, our fear made all of us truly, horribly equal. Who could escape Death, after all? Who was immune to this outbreak?

"Excuse me," I said, approaching the desk. The nurse was one I'd never met before and she looked at me with tired, rheumy eyes over her dust mask. "Lucy Arbor . . . is she here?"

But the nurse cocked her head to the side and looked at me, confused.

"Lucy Arbor? Our nurse in training?" she said. "You just missed her."

My heart leapt. I ran outside and looked around, scanning the crowd for her colorful kerchiefs, her bright dresses. But all the faces, kerchiefs, dresses were drab and dust colored. My heart sank. Surely she had seen me coming, or else why wouldn't she have used the front door? It was as though she had just vanished. Worse, like she was avoiding me.

• • •

By the time the girls came back from training, sweaty, tense, and covered in dust and ash, Asa too was completely drained. He had spent all day with Rosa. He had made her breakfast, read to her, done a few magic tricks, made her lunch, read a few passages from a book, and assured her that, yes, Olivia would be coming back today.

"Olivia!" Rosa shouted, running into Olivia's arms.

"Thank you," Olivia mouthed over Rosa's shoulder. "So much."

"You all right, Asa?" Sal asked, though she didn't look all right, herself.

"Yeah," he said. "Just . . . glad y'all are back. Taking care of her full-time is hard work."

"Looks like you did great." Olivia beamed. She came over and gave him a peck on the cheek while Rosa wasn't looking. ("Ooooooooooh!" said Judith.)

Asa sighed, went to the washroom, closed the door, and locked it. Then he let his human form unravel, conserving as much magic as he could. He looked down at his daemon arms, hands, claws. They were as alien to him now as his human hands had been only a short time ago. He would miss living.

Suddenly, Asa smelled the familiar, unmistakable scent of mercury, and a dark, familiar voice wrapped itself around his brain.

Having a little trouble, are you, O great one chosen by my Mother? Death said.

"I'm fine," he said under his breath. "No thanks to You. I know what You did when Sal and I fought. You destroyed the Sacrifice building, didn't You?"

You can't prove that, She said. **And even if you could, it wouldn't change anything.**

"Are You just here to gloat?" Asa asked. "I thought Death would have better things to do."

My, my! Your time as a human has made you awfully saucy! said Death. **But no. I am here to make you an offer—a very good one, I might add.**

"I doubt I'd be interested," said Asa.

Oh, I don't know about that, said Death. **It wasn't so long ago that you were out in the desert, crying out for my Sister to hear you. Well, I am not so hard-hearted as She is. I am offering you a chance for humanity. Leave this temporary realm and go to the real world, the human world, as the human you have learned to be. Untouched by the grit and ugliness of this place. Untouched by my wrath.**

An earthquake roared beneath him and Asa steadied himself against the sink.

Well? She said.

"What do You want?" Asa said. "I know now You'd never offer something like that for free."

All I want is for you to leave, Death said. **Leave now and let all thoughts of this little rebellion, this little war fall behind you. You realize how much of a long shot it is, right? How little of a chance you have? Do not use the magic inherent in your form to power those . . . machines! It isn't worth it. Not compared to a real human life.**

An image rose in his mind. Asa saw himself—his human self, around twenty-five years old—walking the streets of Paris. He saw himself sailing on a boat, out over the rich blue Mediterranean, drinking champagne at a party on New Year's Eve, being kissed by a woman whose eyes sparkled like blue diamonds. He saw himself aging, becoming middle-aged, then old. He saw his hair whitening. He saw himself reading a story to dark-haired children who could only be his grandchildren. *The Velveteen Rabbit*, he read on the cover.

A beautiful dream. A beautiful life. It was everything that Asa had ever wanted, everything he'd ever dared to dream of, and when he reached up to touch his daemon face, he felt human tears on his claws.

But he thought of Olivia. And Rosa. And Sal. And Susanah and Mowse and Judith and Cassandra and Zo. He thought of the people of Elysium with their dust masks and their sunken cheeks and muddy lungs.

"I can't trade their lives for one I was never meant to have," Asa said, a note of iron in his voice that surprised even himself.

So you mean to declare war on Me, eh? Death said. His mind spasmed painfully with Her laughter. **Then war you will have. Farewell, little daemon. See you on the battlefield.**

And Death trickled out of his mind, leaving Asa gasping against the sink, a fire in his brain. But he was more sure than he had ever been before. If She wanted a war, then She was going to get one. And if She was offering him a way out, that could only mean one thing.

They could win.

CHAPTER 23

6 DAYS REMAIN.

I sat in my room all through dinner, feigning a stomachache. Why didn't Lucy come see me? I kept asking myself. What did I do to upset her? Surely she didn't blame me for the Sacrifice building burning down. What had happened while I was away? I lay down on the creaky old bed, looking up at the ceiling.

"I told you!" Mowse's voice said in the hallway. "The teacher let us out early!"

"Because you used your mind control on her!" Susanah was saying. "I've told you about that stuff, Mowse! You can't just *do* that to people. You're in big trouble!"

"Only if you can prove it!" Mowse said. There was a sound of running and a slam of the upstairs bathroom, then the click of the door locking.

"Ugh," Susanah was saying to herself. "This school's a bad influence on her. So what if she learned all forty-eight states in a day?" She knocked on my door. "Sal? I brought you a plate of greens."

"Thanks, Susanah, I'll get it later," I said. She paused in front of the door as though she was going to say something; then I heard her footfalls disappear down the hall. I toyed with the penny on my chest. Then I sat upright. If Lucy wouldn't come find me, I would go and find her.

I went out onto the porch, looking out into Elysium for a moment, into the dusty streets and dusty roofs and dusty shacks. I took a deep breath and took my penny into my hand.

"Here goes nothing," I said.

I closed my eyes and thought of Lucy, of her bright dresses and kerchiefs, of her smile, and her voice, fierce and feminine still, even in the grit of Elysium. Slowly, the penny in my hand began to glow, and pulled straight outward, hesitantly, pointing into the rows of clapboard houses on the west side. I began following it, following its pulling, jerking movements through the winding footpaths between the houses, my heartbeat rising to match pace with my footfalls. Some people closed their windows as I walked by; others stared, but I kept moving. I walked by a porch where two grim old men were playing dominoes, passed three shuttered empty houses, and even as another earthquake nearly shook me to my knees, the penny never ceased its insistent, glowing pull.

It led me around a sharp corner, and dragged me straight toward a clapboard house with a dusty vase of dried daisies in the window, the windows shuttered forever, a mount of dead flowers covered in dust at the doorstep. Lucy's aunt's house. The penny went still and dropped limp in my hands. I took a deep breath, trying to still the fear that rose in my chest. *This is it,* I thought. *Just talk to her. Try to make it right, whatever it is. You've got to do this.*

"Sal . . ." said a voice.

I turned to see her standing behind me. Gone was the brightly colored dress, the bright, coordinating kerchief. Gone was the subtle lipstick, light mascara. I hadn't seen her like this in years, but she was still beautiful, and the sight of her sent a jolt of warm electricity through me. A feeling I didn't understand. I wanted to run to her, to hug her and thank whatever gods there were that she was all right.

But Lucy didn't want to see me. I stood still.

Silence built between us. And something like anger, like hurt, grew in me.

"I looked for you, you know," I said. "I had to dowse to find you. Why didn't you come to see me when I came back? I thought you were dead. . . . I thought . . ." My voice cracked. "Are you mad at me? For burning down the Sacrifice? Is that it?"

"No," she said. "I'm not mad at you."

"Then why—"

"I'd rather not, Sal," she said.

"Lucy, no matter what happens, you're my friend," I said. "I've admired you for so long, you know? I went to the hospital. I know you're becoming a nurse. And those dust masks that people wear now? The cloth ones? I know they were cut out of your old dresses. You're such a kind, good person. I'd hate for our friendship to end for any reason—especially if I don't know what I did to end it."

"You didn't do anything, Sal," she said, her voice weary. "Trust me. It's not you."

"Then what . . . ?"

"The finer fabric is harder for the dust to get through," Lucy said. "But even with the masks, people are still getting Sick." She sighed and pulled a handkerchief out of her pocket, one covered with mud and blood. "I'm Sick, Sal."

It seemed then like all the sound went out of the world. The only thing left was that heavy, doom-ridden word. Sick. Sick. Sick.

"How long . . ." I started. I let the terrible sentence end there, unfinished.

"Not long," Lucy said softly. "That's why I didn't come and see you sooner. I didn't want you to see me like this." She summed up her drab dress and rough kerchief as though they were supposed to be ugly, as though anything could be ugly on her. "I didn't want to distract you when you have such an important job. Not when your mother . . ."

"Lucy," I said. "You are not a distraction. You're one of the reasons I'm fighting in the first place. And I'm going to be with you every step of the Sickness . . . if you let me."

She came to me then and hugged me tightly, and just for a moment, I allowed myself to relax in her arms, to just be.

"Sal," she whispered when the hug broke, "something's wrong. Something's wrong in Elysium."

"What do you mean?"

"The outbreak came as soon as you two were exiled, and it's only gotten worse," she said. "It's still getting worse, the closer we get to the day the Dust Soldiers come back. Sal, Trixie's dead," said Lucy. "So are her aunt and uncle. And so many other people."

My heart did a strange thing in my chest before dropping down into my stomach. I couldn't pretend that I hadn't imagined what Trixie's face would have looked like when she saw me come into Elysium on my mechanical horse, with Olivia and the others by my side. But now our petty squabbles were meaningless. Shame crept over me and hung on my shoulders like a cape. But Lucy wasn't finished.

"After Aunt Lucretia died, I started helping out at the hospital, trying to figure out where it was coming from, looking at patterns of who's gotten it and who's been safe. But it all seems so random. Even people who were inside on the day that that dust storm came and broke through the Dust Dome for a second . . . even some of them have gotten Sick, while other people who were right out in it are okay. It's like names are being drawn out of a hat or something." She paused, seemed to measure her words. "And I think they might be."

"What do you mean?" I asked.

Her eyes darted, looking into shadows as though someone was watching her. "I think Mother Morevna's doing it."

"What?" I breathed. This seemed so far-fetched, so insane. Mother Morevna was fierce, sure, but she loved her flawed creation more than life itself.

"Think about it," Lucy said. "Another outbreak, just when we need to conserve resources? Then there's the list."

"List?"

"The rations you gave me," Lucy said. "There was a list with it. It looks like a list, anyway. A list of weird symbols."

She reached into her pocket and pulled out a folded slip of paper. Even half-folded, I recognized it. It was that piece of paper of Mother Morevna's, the one I couldn't make sense of. I saw the familiar, alien symbols—sixty symbols at least—and, under the columns, what looked like a few sentences, also written in the odd symbol language Mother Morevna had never taught me.

"I just sort of held on to it hoping somebody could tell me what it meant. It feels . . . not right too, like it's important. I thought it might explain something. But then I ran out of time."

I took the paper and looked it over, scanned my finger down the column of symbols. It did feel important, I realized. It practically thrummed with Mother Morevna's magic, and another familiar feeling too . . . a dark one. One that I couldn't quite place . . .

"There's something wrong here," she said. "And Mother Morevna is responsible. I know it."

I wanted to deny it. But I knew exactly what she was talking about. I felt the panic and the fear and the sense of doom, but there was something else, something sinister lurking beneath the very ground of Elysium. Something that set my skin tingling and my head aching. Deception. I recognized it now. But who was the deceiver? And what was the lie?

"Let's take it to Jameson," I said. "He's the closest to Mother Morevna of anybody. Maybe he can tell us what it is."

"Will you come with me?" Lucy asked. "He'll pay more attention to you."

"Of course," I said.

• • •

Mr. Jameson was sitting on his front porch, just as he had so many nights before, his peach can in his hand, stark against the dark, supernatural sky. He looked sadder than ever, and more determined somehow. The set of his jaw reminded me more of a bulldog now than a hound dog, and he sat with his rifle next to him. The gravel crunched under our feet as we approached and he turned.

"Sal Wilkerson and Lucy Arbor," he said. "The two most likely to be out after curfew. What can I do for you? No problems, I hope."

Lucy and I exchanged glances. "We just have something we want explained. We were wondering if you could take a look at it."

"I'll do what I can," he said.

Lucy pulled the list out of her pocket and unfolded it.

"This is Mother Morevna's," she said. "I just want to know what it means. That's all."

Mr. Jameson took the note and looked at it, squinting in the dim light that streamed from the window behind him. His brows furrowed.

"What in the . . . ?" he breathed.

Suddenly, he heaved himself up and went inside, leaving the door wide open behind him. Inside there was a sound of rustling papers.

"Mr. Jameson?" I said. Lucy and I followed him inside.

"This just don't make sense," he was saying, shuffling through a stack of papers all in Cyrillic code. "It don't make sense at all."

"What?" I asked.

"Usually, we use this as a code, but these symbols are initials," he said.

"Initials?" I asked. "Whose initials?"

Mr. Jameson got a pencil from his desk and began translating beside the list. We watched as he went down the list, his pencil leaving a list of initials behind.

"A.D. . . . J.M. . . . L.D. . . . A.S-R. . . ." Lucy read. "Wait . . ." She reached into her bag and pulled out a small notebook. She flipped several pages to a long list of names and skimmed it, her eyes flitting from the page to the Cyrillic list and back again. Her eyes widened. "These are initials of people who died of Dust Sickness. Starting a long time ago."

"What?" I said. "What do you mean?"

"Look!" she said, pointing. "T.H. That's Trixie Holland. And then, a column later, R.H. and D.H. Her aunt and uncle . . ." Lucy paused. When she turned back to me, her face was grim. She pointed to a set of initials close to the very top. M.W. My heart thudded.

"Mama . . ." I breathed.

Lucy looked back to the list, scanning it. Then she pointed again, to a set of initials on the very bottom.

"L.A." she said softly. "Lucy Arbor." She turned to me and smiled a pained smile. "I was right. I was right all along."

It felt as though all the air went out of my lungs.

"But this paper is so old it's almost falling apart. And the date . . . !" Mr. Jameson pointed to three symbols up near the left-hand corner. "The date for this last section is the day after you were kicked out of Elysium, before fifty of these people even got Sick. There's no way she could have known. . . ."

"She caused it," Lucy said. "She's the one making people Sick. She's the one who made me Sick. She's killing us so she'll have more resources to sacrifice. Just like I thought." Lucy bent then and coughed into her handkerchief. She braced herself against me, and I held still to support her. Her rattling wheeze made my breath quicken, brought back images of the hospital, of Mama on her bed. "She's doing this on purpose," Lucy finished weakly, putting her muddy handkerchief back in her pocket.

My mind reeled. All this time. All this time the woman I had lived with, learned from, idolized, had been the one who killed my mother. Had been the one who caused the death I'd blamed myself for since I was young. And now she was killing Lucy.

"Mother Morevna wouldn't do that," Mr. Jameson said shakily, eyes on the backs of his hands. "She's a hard woman, and not easy to understand, but I know her." Then he shook himself and said, weakly, "She loves this town. She loves these people."

I stared at him, daring him to look away. "Do you really believe that, Mr. Jameson?" I demanded. "After she didn't listen to Olivia about Mr. Robertson? About Rosa? About me?" I kept my eyes on his. "You know it deep down. You know that she did it. You know that she's responsible for so much suffering in Elysium. Don't you?" I breathed. "But you don't want to say, because if she's done this, that means that by not questioning her, you . . ."

"That I've helped her," Mr. Jameson's voice broke. "Oh, Lord, I've helped her the whole way."

Mr. Jameson's voice was as hollow and empty as a tomb.

"But I still don't know how," said Lucy. "Surely we'd know if she cast a spell over all of us."

Mr. Jameson shook his head in disbelief, leaned closer to the fire to scrutinize the list again, looking for anything that would absolve the woman he'd been working with all this time. Anything that would absolve himself of his passivity.

"Wait . . ." Lucy said. "What's that on the back?"

I squinted. On the back of the paper, more Cyrillic letters were slowly appearing in a paragraph at the bottom.

Mr. Jameson flipped the paper over and read the paragraph on the bottom.

"It's code . . . but it's . . . it's talking about spells. Trapdoor spells laid a long time ago, at the beginning of Elysium." He squinted. "It's talking about a stone . . . put somewhere far away."

"The Master Stone," I said. "She must have made one a long time ago and put it somewhere safe. That's what she was talking about when she told me about taking precautions. There might be layers and layers of spells. Major ones that can't be undone by any white stones. We'd need the Master Stone for that." I shook myself mentally, focused on the task at hand. "But what about this one? What's tripping the spell for Dust Sickness?"

Mr. Jameson read on. Then his face went white as a sheet. "The Dowsing Well," he said.

"Sal," Lucy said. "The water rations . . ."

A jolt of horror went through me. Suddenly I remembered Trixie's memory, the water rations under the table, how they'd all had a black smudge on them. I thought of all the Dowsing Well rations I'd given Lucy for her aunt. All of them had had the same black markings.

"So that's why only certain people were allowed to drink from the well in the first place," I said. "She was controlling who gets it and who doesn't."

Across from me, Mr. Jameson's face was pale. The paper hung limp in his hands.

Mr. Jameson put his head in his hands, his shoulders shaking. Lucy and I stood by in silence.

We had never seen a man cry before. Not a man with experience and power, like Mr. Jameson. He was the one who handled things, who fixed things. And to see him like this made me feel a kind of helpless I'd never felt before.

Then Lucy began to cough. She coughed and wheezed, clasping her handkerchief to her mouth. She swayed on her feet, a rattle sounding in her throat; when she finally caught her breath, her lips were flecked with blood and black mud. My heart sped painfully. Not Lucy . . . not now . . .

At that moment, Olivia walked through the doorway, stopped and regarded the scene unfolding before her.

"Sal," she started. "What did I miss?"

"I'm going to the church," Mr. Jameson said, rising with a steely look in his eye. "I have business to discuss with Mother Morevna." He turned to us and said, "You girls coming?"

"Of course," I said. "Lead the way."

• • •

Mr. Jameson burst through the sanctuary door, and we followed him.

"Marike!" he said, boots thudding as he strode across the empty sanctuary to the bottom of the stairs that led to her room.

"What is it, Jameson?" Mother Morevna said, coming down the stairs, stooped and frail, in her nightgown and shawl. "What's all this ruckus?"

"How could you, Marike?" Mr. Jameson said, his body tense as a coiled spring, his voice harder than I'd ever heard it. "After all we did to build this town and protect these people. How could you?"

"What are you talking about, Jameson?"

"We know, Mother Morevna," I said, my voice hard and sharp as flint. "We know that you've been causing the Dust Sickness. We know that you killed my mother, and Lucy's aunt, and everybody who's ever died of Dust Sickness."

Mother Morevna blinked. A shadow seemed to pass over her face.

"Everything I've done has been to save us," she said. "Even now, I am trying to satisfy the Goddesses."

"This is sick, Marike," Mr. Jameson said. "All the suffering, all the pain within these walls . . . you've caused it. And I'm done helping you."

There was a crackle of power around her, of anger. But she remained calm.

"And what will you do, Lloyd?" she said, her voice soft as the hiss of a snake. "Expose me? Cast me out of Elysium when everything is unstable as it is? When I am the only thread holding the people together in this sea of uncertainty?"

Mr. Jameson hesitated. It was true. The thought of it felt slimy and disgusting in my mind, but it was true. Casting Mother Morevna out right now, or exposing her role in the Dust Sickness epidemic would only throw the people into a panic. And we couldn't afford that. Not when we needed to build their trust, rally them against fate itself.

"No," said Olivia, coming forward, her eyes on Mother Morevna's. "You're dying, right? Well, pretend to be ill. Stay here in your church and gather supplies for the Sacrifice or something. But give up your authority." Olivia paused, stepped forward. "Give it to us. It's about time this city had women who deserved to lead it."

Everyone was quiet. Never did I expect Olivia to show mercy, or to make such a demand.

"Lift the spell," I said, my voice shaking. "Lift the spell so the people with Dust Sickness can get better." I glanced at Lucy.

"I cannot do that," Mother Morevna said calmly. "The Master Stone that I used to cast the spell is lost, placed out in the desert long ago and buried under an ocean of dust."

Mr. Jameson seemed to stiffen beside me. "That stone . . ." he said. "The one you had me take out into the desert and toss . . . that was . . . ?"

Mother Morevna nodded. "So you see, I simply must let the spell run its course. We only have six days left."

I thought of the desert, how new chunks of it turned to nothingness every day, taking anything buried in the dust with them, never to be seen or felt or exist again. Beside me, Lucy held in a cough. I took her hand and clasped it tightly in my own as though to say, *I'm sorry, Lucy. I tried.* And I felt her squeeze back. *I know. But it isn't over yet.*

The magic crackled around Mother Morevna, power, nearly visible. But we stood tall before her, telling her with our stances, our eyes, our magic, that we refused to back down. Then, slowly, her magic receded, pulled back.

"I will agree to your terms," Mother Morevna said, her eyes flickering from Mr. Jameson's surprised eyes to mine, Lucy's, and Olivia's, then back to mine, where they stayed. "I have done what I can for this city, whether you realize it or not. Now I wash my hands of it. Leave me." And Mother Morevna turned then and crept back up the stairs, shutting the door behind her.

Olivia and I blinked in astonishment. We'd expected a fight—my hand was never far from my components belt. We didn't think it would be that easy, that she would just withdraw.

Anger welled inside me, dark and rolling as the mightiest dust storm. *How ill is she?* I thought, looking up at the closed door to her room. However ill she was, it wasn't nearly cruel enough of a fate for someone who could set something like Dust Sickness loose on her people. I wanted her to hurt. I wanted her to suffer as my mother suffered, as Lucy suffered beside me right now.

"What's the first order, Sal?" Mr. Jameson said. A jolt went through me. That's right. We were in charge now. The safety of all of Elysium was on our shoulders.

"Um . . ." I started. Then Lucy squeezed my hand, and I stepped aside as she came to stand beside me.

"Let's shut down the Dowsing Well first," Lucy said. "That way we can at least slow the spread of the Dust Sickness."

"Right," Olivia said. "And we'll get the horses finished as quickly as we can. I'm Olivia, by the way."

"Lucy Arbor," she said.

"So you're Lucy!" Olivia said. "Sal's told me a lot about—"

"And we'll set up another line of defense," I said. "Magical defense. So if they break our lines, we can still have a chance of holding them off."

"Sounds like a plan," Mr. Jameson said. The ground rumbled beneath us and almost threw us off our feet. "And now we don't have a moment to lose."

CHAPTER 24

5 DAYS REMAIN.

The following day, the sky had already begun to darken. It was a dry, unnatural sort of cloudy that rumbled like stones sliding together, just as the earth rumbled below us, making the cattle nervous and setting the chickens into flight.

The Dowsing Well was closed, as per our orders, and people milled all around the other wells, carrying buckets and Coke bottles brimming with clear, un-cursed water.

In the barn, we separated ourselves into witches and fighters. Downstairs, Susanah and the builders hammered and sawed, welded and soldered, and we could see each horse being finished and put in a line behind the barn. Almost fifty now. Half of the hundred we'd need.

On the walls, Zo was with Mr. Jameson and the other sharpshooters, practicing with rifles we would try to enchant later. Their gunshots sounded rhythmically, *bang bang bang bang*, then stopped for them to load their guns full of whatever shrapnel they were using for bullets. Then again, almost loud enough to drown out the sounds of Judith teaching the guards to use javelins.

"You gotta hold it like this, see?" she was saying. "No, no, no! What are you, a grandma?"

And up in the loft, Cassandra, Olivia, and I pored over our books as, back at the house, Asa watched Rosa and gathered spell components for us.

"This isn't any good, and neither is this!" Olivia said, pushing another book to the side. "We need something they can't break through if they get past our line!"

"Here." I handed her a napkin marked with my blood. "Try out whatever you want."

Without looking at me, Olivia took the napkin, mumbled something from under her folded arms, and sent a whirlwind scattering papers and dust all around the room.

We spent the rest of the afternoon studying. But no matter what we did, no matter what we tried, the spell we needed seemed to elude us. We simply couldn't find anything big enough, anything that covered the area we'd need. And what could stand up to a creature sent by the Goddesses to destroy us?

"What about Dust Dome?" Cassandra said suddenly.

"Uh, were you not there last time we cast that?" Olivia asked. "The Dust Soldier walked right through it."

"Well, I just thought that it covers the right area," Cassandra said.

"You have to be inside it to cast it," Olivia said. "We're looking for something we can cast behind us that can keep them from getting past us."

"But what about Asa?" Cassandra said.

"Asa?" Olivia cocked her head. "He's already set to power up the horses."

"Last time we did Dust Dome, he was unconscious," Cassandra said. "But his magic is like theirs, right? Because he's a . . . you know . . . a daemon, darling."

I thought of the spears Susanah was creating, the spears that snapped out of the sides of the mechanical horses, sharp and deadly, glowing with Asa's otherworldly magic, the only defense against the Dust Soldiers. "It does make sense," I said.

"What if his magic is the key to keeping them out?" Cassandra said, her eyes alight in her exhausted face. "What if we just . . . did Dust Dome, but used Asa's magic too?"

We looked at each other. There was something to this idea, we thought. Certainly none of the old, established spells were much help.

"I dunno," Olivia said. "Dust Dome requires a lot of magic at once, and . . . at this point I don't know if he can do it by himself and power the horses and have power left to fight. He's falling apart as it is."

It was true. With every earthquake, every change, Asa seemed to flicker. His mouth and arms and eyes had begun to go daemon far more frequently than usual. Was his magic a finite resource? I wasn't sure.

There was a sparking in my mind, a sudden kindling into flame. I reached into my pouch and pulled out a black stone.

"We need to write our own trapdoor spell," I said. "One that uses all our magic. One that can be activated by anyone with the stone. I can use Dust Dome as a model, I think, but instead of the coyote blood, we could use Asa's. Maybe that will keep us from having to take so much magic from him."

"Are you sure this will work?" Olivia said, her expression somewhere between impressed and wary.

"It's going to take some time, but I think . . . I think it could."

We sat in silence for a moment, considering this.

"A trapdoor spell," Olivia mused finally. "How appropriate."

I looked out the window to the rose window of the church, but it was dark. Mother Morevna was nowhere to be found.

• • •

That evening, after we dragged ourselves back, our hands burned and bloody, our pockets full of stones, we were sore, brain-tired. We sat around the kitchen table, watching Judith and Mowse play Go Fish. Olivia was sitting in a chair, brushing Rosa's long black hair as Asa read to her from *The Red Badge of Courage.* The earth rumbled beneath us, and we were silent for a moment. Then we shook ourselves and let it pass.

"You did it again, Mowse!" Judith said. "Fantastic! You're real good at Go Fish!"

"Or she's mind-reading," said Susanah from her chair by the stove.

"What's the capital of North Dakota, if you're so smart?" Mowse asked, her nose in the air.

"Bismarck," said Susanah. "Don't forget, I went to school too."

"You okay, chica?" Olivia asked, coming to where I stood by the window, leaving Asa to finish braiding Rosa's hair.

"I'm all right," I said. "Just . . . thinking. There's just so much wrong and . . ." I sighed. "I . . . I can feel it all the time."

"Thinking about your friend, huh?" Olivia said. "The one from last night? With Dust Sickness?"

I nodded. It was true. The news of Lucy's Sickness had been weighing on me. Sometimes I felt like I'd fallen in a grain silo, like I'd just struggle in it, the unfairness of it, until it swallowed me whole and left my corpse suspended and irretrievable. It was evil, nefarious, but I refused to believe it was unstoppable, not now that I knew it was a curse. Surely there had to be some way to lift it without the Master Stone. But with so few days left . . . would it even matter?

"I know," Olivia said. "And I'm sorry. It's a hell of a thing to get, especially somebody as good as her."

"How do you know how good she is?" I asked.

"If you like her so much, she must be," said Olivia. She turned to me. "But look at the hand we've been dealt. We've got more power now than we ever had and we've done what we can. We'll solve it. The defense spell, the Dust Sickness. All of it. But right now we have to focus. We have to break the Game."

She was right, I knew. But how could I focus on one enormous thing when another loomed in my sight, darkening everything with its shadow? The earth rumbled underfoot then, as if in answer to Olivia, sending dust drifting down from the rafters. I could hear Asa saying, "Shhhh, shhhh, it's going to be all right," as he braided Rosa's hair.

"I just wish I could see it that way," I said quietly.

Olivia regarded me for a moment. "You know what I like to do when everything's getting to me and it feels like I'm going to explode?"

"Smoke thirty cigarettes."

"No, even better." She turned to everyone else, cupped her

hands around her mouth. "Hey!" she shouted. "Who's up for a boxing match?"

• • •

"How about up there?" Judith asked, jerking her head upward, her arms full of the homemade boxing gloves we'd sewn from feed-sack fabric and pillow stuffing.

We all looked. Up on top of the Blue Moon Diner was a wide, flat area perfect for setting up a makeshift boxing ring. My heart seemed to constrict. The man who owned it had died two weeks ago, according to Lucy. Another victim of the Dust Sickness spell.

"There's a ladder back here!" Mowse said, pulling at a stack of crates behind the building.

As we climbed the ladder up to the roof, my heart twisted in pain as I thought of the pies the Blue Moon man had given me only a short time ago, how Lucy and I had eaten them on her porch back before everything had gotten so bad.

Susanah and Asa moved the crates out of the way, and one by one, we climbed up onto the flat, dust expanse of the roof.

"There's just something liberating about looking out over it all, isn't there?" Cassandra said, her bracelets and necklaces clattering as she opened her arms and spun in the dusty night air.

We went to the edge of the roof and looked out, Olivia and Asa with Rosa between them. The whole of Elysium stretched out before us: the animal pens, the factories, the church with its steeple and stained glass. We looked out over the roofs, both flat and pointed, the jail with its barred, dark windows, the hospital, ever bustling no matter the time. And despite all of the doom and gloom, the death and hurt and magic that surrounded us like an ocean, the windows of the houses still glowed with warmth and light, and the smell of home cooking rose over the smell of dust and Sickness. And as we stood there, looking out, a woman calling her children in for the night looked up at me and smiled. The people of Elysium were doing what they had always done, even back when we were just farmers living through the Depression: surviving, despite everything. I couldn't fail them.

"All right!" Judith said, weighing down the blanket that would serve as our ring with bricks. "Let's get this started!" She threw us each a pair of gloves. "Come on, Zo! First one to twenty hits wins!"

"That'll be way too fast," Zo said, pulling on her gloves. "I'll be done with you in five minutes."

"Put your money where your mouth is!" Judith said with a wink. "Let's go, champ!"

We gathered, sitting around the ring, drinking our Coke bottle water rations as Judith and Zo ducked and weaved and dodged, throwing punch after light, jabbing punch. Rosa clapped in delight and Olivia and Asa stood back, holding hands.

"Twenty!" Olivia called, Rosa waving her hat like a flag. "That's it! Judith is the winner!"

"One point! Just one point!" Zo said. "Or I'd have had you, Goliath!"

"Come back with a sling next time," Judith countered, sticking her tongue out.

"I'm going next!" said Mowse. "Get ready, Judith!"

"You're not even half my size, pipsqueak," Judith said.

"I'll fix that," said Susanah. "Come on, kid."

And we all laughed as Susanah hoisted Mowse up on her shoulders and squared off against Judith. Mowse swung like a kitten batting at a string, and as Judith made face after face, I allowed myself to just sit and enjoy the spectacle of it.

"Oh nooo!" Judith shouted, throwing herself to the ground when Mowse landed a punch.

"You're faking!" Mowse shrieked, giggling. "You're faking, Judith!"

"No I'm not! You're just too strong!"

"I guess it'll have to be me next," Cassandra said, taking off her bracelets. "Do your worst, Mowse!"

"I'll never understand humans," said Asa next to me as Olivia talked to Rosa. "How are we doing? How are the horses?"

"They're almost ready for power," I said. "Once they finish building that last batch tomorrow."

"I'll have enough magic for that," Asa said. He paused. "But I might start looking a little . . . daemony."

"It's okay," I said. "We get it."

"I just hope Rosa gets it," said Asa. "I'd hate to scare her."

He meant it, I could tell. But as I looked at him then, watching Rosa and Olivia, he'd never seemed more human.

"Olivia and Sal!" said Judith. "You're up!"

"Just in time," Olivia said. "Come on, Sal. I'll go easy on you, I promise."

"Speak for yourself," I said, pulling my gloves on.

"That's what I like to hear!" Olivia said. "Come on! Give it all you got! Asa, watch Rosa for me!"

"Of course!" said Asa. "¡Rosalita! ¡Ven conmigo!"

And we dove into the ring, not caring who won, the lightness of adrenaline and fun and being young breaking the surface of our gloom, our troubles momentarily forgotten.

• • •

Lucy Arbor left the hospital after midnight, her shoulders sagging, her heart sinking. Three more Dust Sickness deaths. Three more bodies to be added to the wall, despite the closing of the Dowsing Well.

Above her, there was a sound, and darting into the shadows, Lucy watched as Mother Morevna opened the rose window, pushing it outward.

That thing can open? Lucy thought, pressing herself against the wall of the jail.

Mother Morevna leaned out of her window, her tattooed hands full of something Lucy couldn't see. Pebbles? Marbles? Mother Morevna looked up at the sky. The moon was full and round and reddish. She stared at it for a moment, then put the handful of whatever it was to her chest and closed her eyes. Her lips were moving as though she were praying, but Lucy couldn't hear her words. The tattoos on her hands began to glow in the darkness like lines of flame, brighter and brighter until suddenly they stopped. Then Mother Morevna laid the small things in a row, one by one, on the windowsill and turned back inside. Down on the ground, Lucy just kept looking up at the window, trying to still the beating of her heart, trying to tell herself that the feeling growing in her chest wasn't what she knew it was. Dread.

CHAPTER 25

3 DAYS REMAIN.

Every day we saw the world around us change. We felt the ground pitch beneath us, roaring like the great stomach of a hungry titan whose bonds were ever loosening. The sky took on the permanent darkness of a thunderstorm, swirling angrily overhead, promising nothing but divine wrath.

Our every moment was consumed by training. We came home from the barn, dusty and burned and exhausted, smelling of smoke and sulfur and magic. I rarely saw Lucy, as the hospital kept her busy day and night. But when I did, our conversations were grim, and her beautiful face was more sunken and ill than ever. Gradually, it became more and more real to us: We were really going to have to do this. We were really going to lead a war for our survival.

Three days before Judgment Day, the horses were ready to be brought to life, and we headed to the barn, walking slowly as the ground writhed beneath us. We split off into our respective groups: fighters, sharpshooters, inventors, and witches. Up in the hayloft, Asa was waiting, and he gave us a somber nod as we returned to the row of rifles and shotguns and cases of home-made magical bullets sitting on the floor, glowing softly with enchantments. We passed through the barn and out the back, into the lot behind it. There, ten rows of metal horses were waiting, still and frightening, a silent mechanical army. The guards were there as well, standing quietly, their eyes on Susanah, awaiting instruction.

"So what do we do?" Cassandra asked.

"Sal had the idea of creating a kind of spell that would allow us to power all of them up at once," said Susanah. She pulled small five white stones from her pocket and handed one each to Cassandra, Olivia, Mowse, Asa, and me.

"These stones are connected to the others around the horses," Susanah explained. "It's a trapdoor spell, basically, or so Sal said. So what you do, theoretically, is just . . . uh . . . Sal, could you explain this?"

"You just will all the spells you've learned into your stone," I said. I reached into my pocket and pulled out another stone that was almost identical, but a bit larger. "This is the Master Stone," I said. "It channels all the magic from each of you . . . hopefully. I'm going to give it to Asa, and after you all . . . do your thing . . . Asa should be able to power up the horses."

I put the stone in Asa's hand, and he held it like a boy about to skip a rock over a pond.

"What do I do?" Olivia said.

"Copy Sal's magic, if you can," Susanah said. "Maybe we can get a double dose of it."

"Well, here goes," I said. I stepped forward and, with the

stone in my hand, chose all the spells I'd memorized, all the ones that would power the horses and their weapons. I felt a glow, a buzz, a thrum as the magic flowed from me and into the horses. And then it was over. I stepped back, feeling drained. The horses' eyes had begun to flicker.

Cassandra went after me, Olivia third, and Mowse last, powering what seemed like an almost explosive amount of power into the horses. But still, their eyes flickered. We needed Asa's magic to anchor our magic to the horses.

Asa took a deep breath and stepped forward, juggling the stone from hand to hand. He clapped his hands together over the stone and closed his eyes. I felt a wave of power surge from him, making my ears ring. It rumbled out in a dark blur, wrapping around the horses like fog, and disappearing into them.

Asa sank to his knees and flickered for a moment, as though he'd disappear. But he stayed whole, and when he rose and came back to us, the horses' eyes glowed so brightly it almost hurt my eyes.

The guards stood back in awe at the monsters they'd be riding. They looked like an apocalyptic cavalry from machine hell, silent and spear-spined, living metal weapons brimming with infernal magic. But they were ours. And looking at them there, so quiet and formidable, I could feel in the very cells of my blood that these were our best chance of winning. Of breaking the Game once and for all.

• • •

Lucy Arbor took another bucket of rags to the fire out back and tossed them in. They had been white but were now covered in mud and blood. All day she'd been running back and forth from the hospital to the jail, to the wells for water rations, and back to the hospital, trying to keep her own symptoms at bay. But now, she allowed herself to sit and breathe just for a moment, shakily and carefully, praying she didn't cough.

"Oh, there you are!" said Nurse Gladys, pushing open the back door of the hospital. "You'd better come back in. We've got another one."

"More Dust Sickness?" Lucy asked. "Because I already got the water. It's on the back desk."

Lucy had not told anyone about the spell, that Mother Morevna was behind it, though in every part of her, she ached to do so. It would only cause panic, outrage, and that was the last thing Sal and the girls needed. But seeing the Sick every day, watching herself deteriorate, feeling the sense of doom grow inside her, the seed of anger and injustice had taken root and would grow out of control if she let it. And she couldn't allow herself to become that angry. Not yet. Not when so many people needed her.

"No," said Nurse Gladys. "Another one of those marks."

Lucy nodded. "I'll be in in a minute." Coughs racked her body. She bent, double, wheezing, unable to catch her breath. Nurse Gladys ran to her and pounded on her back, shoved a glass of water into her shaking hands and forced her to drink until the coolness of the water drowned the pain.

This will kill me soon, Lucy thought. *This is going to rise up in my chest and fill my lungs with mud and I'm going to die.* Panic flared inside her and set her heart racing. It seemed that the huge, unbearable darkness of mortality opened before her like a gate and Lucy stood in front of it, waiting to be swallowed whole. And for what? Because the leader of Elysium saw her life as worthy of forfeiting.

"Lucy!" said Nurse Gladys.

Lucy shook herself. "I'm all right," she said, wiping the bloody mud from her lips. "Give me a minute. I'll be in in a minute."

"God bless you, child," said Nurse Gladys. And she closed the door.

Lucy stared into the fire again, feeling the pain in her chest die down. Lately, there had been seven cases of strange, bloodred bumps appearing on the backs of people's hands. Probably some new desert malady brought by the changing winds or the dark, groaning sky here in the final days of Elysium, or so was the consensus among the doctors and nurses. They were painless and didn't seem to cause any harm (Nurse Ada herself had one), but they appeared so quickly and looked so strange that they frightened people. So several times, Lucy had been sent to calm people down, do a quick examination, and send people on their way, telling them to thank their lucky stars that it wasn't Dust Sickness.

Lucy felt another cough coming in her chest, but she took a gulp of well water, wiped the mud off her brow, and rose, thinking, *This might kill me. But it sure as hell isn't going to kill me before all of this ends.*

• • •

The defense spell consumed us all day and all night. And by the time Olivia, Cassandra, Asa, and I had finished writing it, the sun had set and we followed the light of the torches back home.

We walked in silence, none of us talking about the spell that filled us with dread, the spell we'd tried for what seemed like ages to avoid. But it loomed in our thoughts anyway. And how could it not when the spell required such sacrifice? Now all there was was to tell the others. To see what they said.

The rest of the girls were already eating dinner (corn bread and beans) and Mowse was trying to explain to Rosa about the difference between a kingdom and a phylum, but when we came in, everyone turned to us as though they could tell the weight of the news we had to bear.

"Um, can I talk to everybody for a second?" I said, and the room grew even quieter than it already was. I gulped and continued. "We created a spell today, a last-ditch spell that can protect the city from the Dust Soldiers if the cavalry lines are broken. It can be cast by any one of us, no matter if we have magic or not."

"That's great," said Judith, looking to each of us in turn. "So why doesn't it feel great?"

"There's one problem," I said. "If we cast it, there's no way all of us will get out alive."

The girls went quiet, their faces emptied of the humor that had been there only moments before. I continued.

"Unlike Dust Dome, it can't be cast with the caster in the middle of it. It's designed for keeping things out . . . and we couldn't figure out a way to make it accept the caster after it had been cast, or for the caster to cast the spell from inside the range it's meant to cover."

"What does that mean?" Zo asked, leaning forward in her chair.

“Someone has to remain outside the gates in order to cast it,” I said. “And once it’s cast, the caster will be stuck outside with the Dust Soldiers, unable to get back in.”

“So dead, basically,” said Zo, her voice loud in the quiet kitchen.

“There was no way around it,” Cassandra said, even her airy-fairy voice serious and flat as a stone. “It won’t work unless someone agrees to be left behind.”

“Well, who’s it going to be?” Judith asked. “We gonna draw lots or something?”

“There’s no use deciding now, since there’s no telling where any of us is going to end up in the battle,” I said. I reached into my pocket and pulled out seven black stones, each with a smear of Asa’s blood on it. “These are for each of you. This means that, if it comes down to it—and I hope it won’t—any one of us can close the spell over the city. All you have to do is place it at the gates and say ‘Pulvarem spiritum.’ ”

“Pulvarem spiritum,” they repeated quietly. Each girl looked at the stone for a moment, then put it in her pocket, hoping to never have to bring it out again.

“There’s no guarantee we’ll use the spell,” I told them. “Hopefully the cavalry and artillery will be enough.”

Susanah nodded. “They will. I’ll do everything in my power to make sure of it.”

The kitchen went quiet again, and I knew we were all pushing the spell to the back of our minds, hoping that it would not surface again. I saw Olivia put her arms around Rosa and kiss her forehead. I took my plate and ate quietly, my brain aching from the long day of spell writing.

"Mowse, what's that on your hand?" Zo asked.

"I dunno," said Mowse, showing a bright red bump on the back of her hand. "But it doesn't hurt or anything. Three other kids at school have it."

"Looks like you gave it to me already," Judith said, raising her own hand, where a similar red bump was already forming.

"And Rosa," said Olivia, taking Rosa's hand into her own. "This better not be ringworm, Mowse."

"Schools," Susanah said, shaking her head. "I forgot what disease factories they can be. Don't go wiping that on anybody. Keep that to yourself. Now what were you telling us about school today?"

"I played five games of marbles against George Arbor and won all of them," Mowse was saying. "And for all of that I won this!" She pulled something small and golden out of her pocket, and behind me I heard the sound of a glass breaking on the floor. Asa stood over the glass, white-faced and ashen.

"Wh-what?" Asa said, stumbling toward the table. "Let me see that!"

Confused, Mowse handed her small trophy to Asa. With a crazed look on his face, he held the tiny golden thing into the light. It was a small piece of amber with something suspended inside it. I squinted. Yes, a cricket. The thing Asa had been sent to return. The thing he had put from his mind forever, or so he'd thought.

"George Arbor?" I asked Mowse. "Lucy Arbor's little brother? How did he get this?"

"He said he picked it up when y'all were kicked out of Elysium." Mowse shrugged.

"Of course," Asa said, his voice sounding strange in the silence of the kitchen. "Of course this would come to me now, when I am bound to be ripped apart in a matter of days."

Suddenly, maniacally, Asa started to laugh.

He laughed and laughed, a cold, harsh, hopeless laugh, and we all turned our eyes away until he stopped.

"Well," he said bitterly. "I suppose no one can accuse the Sisters of not having a sense of humor."

CHAPTER 26

1 DAY REMAINS.

By the evening before our judgment, the sky was so dark that there was barely any difference between day and night. But the clouds that rumbled and threatened overhead were not lined with blue, but an angry, supernatural green. The pile of supplies for the substitute Sacrifice had grown to nearly the height of the first one, and the great clock of panic was ticking faster and louder.

It was on the last day that I went to see Mama for the first time since I'd been back.

"Hey, Mama," I said to her name on the wall. "I guess I've got a lot to tell you about."

I reached out and brushed the dust out of the engraved letters, wondering where to begin. I could start with the witchcraft, how I'd been a witch the whole time and not known it. I could talk about the Sacrifice and how Asa and I had destroyed it. I could talk about Olivia and the girls, Mother Morevna, the Dust Sickness that had killed her and would soon kill Lucy. I could talk about our plan to fight our way out, to defy the Goddesses. But what I said was, "I don't know if I'm ready, Mama."

Saying it, hearing how easily it came, surprised me. And it was true, I realized. Sure, we'd practiced every day. Sure I could call down lightning, summon a whirlwind, breathe fire, but when I thought of the Dust Soldiers, my heart still beat like a rabbit's heart must beat.

"Everyone is counting on us," I said. "*We're in charge.* And . . . it's just . . . so much."

Once I said that to her name there in the wall, it seemed like the words wouldn't stop, couldn't stop. A dam of uncertainty had burst somewhere inside, and everything threatened to flow out of me and into the dust at my feet. Tears came then, hot and stinging, and I let myself cry them there in the silence.

As my tears began to cease, I reached out and lay my palm across her name, wishing she were there to hold me, to stroke my hair, to help lessen everything for me. At that moment, so faintly in the back of my mind, I felt a sense of warmth, smelled a familiar but unplaceable scent. And as I closed my eyes to try and keep it just a moment longer, I could hear a sound like black feathers falling.

When I finally took my hand off the wall and wiped the muddy stains from my face, I took a deep breath, clearing my mind, readying myself for the task that awaited us tonight.

"Goodbye, Mama," I said. And I rose and left her for the last time, knowing finally what I'd always known: No matter what happened, I was born for this.

• • •

Asa sat at the kitchen table in the Robertson house, holding a cigarette between his teeth. They were long again now, pointed and black, and his spines protruded between the spokes of the chair he sat in alone, trying his best to conserve a last, small amount of magic for the fight. The cricket in amber sat on the table, throwing a small amount of honey-colored light on the wood around it.

Suddenly, for the first time since She sent him down to Elysium, he felt Life there with him, a trickle like a bright stream through his brain. **There is still time for you to be the Card I needed! Don't just sit there! You are letting Her win the Game!**

"I have a new strategy now." Asa lit a cigarette and took a long drag.

And it is madness! She said. **She will win! Especially now that M—**

"You don't even care about them, do You?" he said, sending up a long, thin cloud of smoke.

What do you mean? She asked with an edge to Her honeyed voice.

"I mean, why put the people through this?" Asa said. "Why use Your power to create a world like this? Do You care about the beings You've trapped here, who could be living lives with dignity and health? Do You care about the creatures You created who will be destroyed when the Game ends, one way or another? Or do You just love to gamble?"

How dare you speak to Me so! She said. **I knew I shouldn't have listened to Mother. I gave you life! I gave you everything you have, and I can take it away in an instant!**

"I don't think You can," Asa said. "I'm already on the board. If You could, You'd have done it already. No. This time, we're making the decisions. And we are going to win."

What has happened to you? She asked. **Why are you like this? Because of the girl? You know that a human could never**

truly love a daemon, Asa. And a daemon can never truly love a human.

"Maybe," said Asa. "But as far as I'm concerned, I'm not a daemon anymore, no matter what I look like. I am more than that now."

No daemon has ever done this before, She said. **You have broken from Us completely. You know that the punishment We will arrange will be spoken of for eons to come. The very atoms of the universe will weep for you.**

"I know," said Asa. He took another drag on his cigarette and let out a long, indulgent cloud of smoke. "But it's been one hell of a ride while it lasted."

Angrily, Life trickled out of his mind like a flow of diamond dust and was gone.

Asa finished his cigarette as the ground rumbled and pitched beneath him, knocking over a vase nearby. *Not long now,* he thought. He closed his eyes and thought of Olivia, of Rosa, of Sal.

Asa put his cigarette out in a dish. Then he slipped back into his human form—what of it he had left, anyway. He flexed his fingers and pulled on his gloves.

He pulled the cricket out of his pocket and looked at it.

"Too late now, I'm afraid," he told it.

And as he slipped out into the streets of Elysium, he let the cricket drop into the dust outside the Robertson house. He didn't even look back.

• • •

When I returned to the house, the other girls were in the kitchen, sitting around the table, already holding their weapons. They were completely silent, feeling the gravity of tonight pull at them like the moon.

An earthquake sent us grabbing for chairs and walls. The lights flickered. Rosa had been so frantic that Mowse had had to put her under a sleeping spell, and Olivia sat, holding her hand for hours, smoking cigarette after cigarette.

"What time will they get here?" Judith asked.

"After sunset," Zo said. "Like an execution."

"Don't think of it like that," said Cassandra, her usual dreamy voice suddenly serious.

"I'm just being realistic," said Zo.

"No you're not," said Cassandra. "You're being gloomy and a pessimist, and that is the very worst thing to be right now." She took a deep breath and let it out. "We can't afford to think we'll lose, or we will. All we have to do is hold them off until morning. And the horses are splendid. We *will* win. And none of us will die."

"Okay, then, Pollyanna," Zo said, but there was a softer, more apologetic tone in her voice that hadn't been there before. "You're right. We're going to be fine. We at least got a fighting chance."

"Hell yeah we do," said Judith, forcing lightness into her voice. "I'm gonna take out at least ten by my damn self. How about you, Zo?"

"Probably more," she said. "Having a gun and all. I set the goal for a hundred."

"See?" Cassandra said, gesturing with hands so picked clean of nail polish they looked almost unpainted. "The power of positive thinking."

"How many of them were there supposed to be again?" Mowse asked, even her voice sounding quiet and meek.

"A hundred," I said. "One hundred soldiers including the artillery. But we've got this. We do."

No one said anything.

There was a knock at the door then. Cassandra answered it, and Asa stepped in with a coat over one shoulder. His eyes were bloodshot. His teeth were sharp, and his hair looked wilder than ever, but at the same time he looked sure of himself, calm. Like a man making his peace before being taken to the gallows. Olivia went to him and put her arms around him, and they stood there, holding each other for a long time before he turned to me. "Tonight's the night," he said. "Are you ready to make it right again?"

"Ready as I'll ever be," I said, conscious of the weight of the black stone in my pocket. "How about you?"

But before Asa could answer, there was another knock on the door.

"My, we're popular today," said Cassandra. She opened the door.

"Is Sal here?" said a voice, and my heart leapt. Lucy stood there, makeupless and kerchiefed, but somehow she was the most beautiful sight I'd ever seen. I wanted to run to her and hold her close, but something about her manner held me back. She seemed so fragile she might break in two.

I knew she'd been spending more time at the hospital lately. The two days in which I hadn't seen her seemed like weeks. But she had come to visit tonight, and when she saw me, she smiled, and that's all that mattered. Across the room from me, Zo made a confused *Who is this?* expression, then winked and gave me a thumbs-up. I ignored her.

"I just came to say good luck," Lucy said, coming into the kitchen. "Y'all are the bravest girls I've ever met. And you too, Asa."

"Thank you kindly," Asa said from his place by Olivia and Rosa. "Though with all your work at the hospital, I think you're pretty brave yourself."

Lucy smiled a tired-looking smile. I pulled out a chair for her, and she sat.

"Not long now, huh?" she said.

"Nope," I said, taking a seat beside her. "About three hours left."

"Wait a minute." Judith squinted at her. "You're the one Sal was talking about. The one who sells makeup."

"Not much these days," Lucy said. "But I still got this." She opened her sack and put it on the table. The girls gathered around to see inside.

"This is mascara?" asked Cassandra, with a hand on her chest. "Oh, I never thought I'd see mascara again!" She held up an eye shadow palette. "Judith, this would look striking with your blue eyes."

Mowse reached for a tube of lipstick and Susanah gave her a look. "Not till you're older."

"I might not get older," Mowse said. Susanah nodded, and Mowse took a corncob-disguised tube of coral lipstick and smeared it over her lips.

"None for you?" Lucy said when she noticed Zo sitting back, completely away from the makeup in her suspenders and boots. "You have great bone structure."

"It's just not my style," she said, smiling. "But thanks."

Zo looked at Lucy in a slow, appraising sort of way, and something strangely like envy rose in me, but I pushed it back down as well as I could.

"Oh, come on, Zo," said Judith, swiping fawn eye shadow over her lids. "You'd be pretty."

"Yep," said Judith. "The prettiest sharpshooter I ever did see."

"Aww, don't make me blush," laughed Zo. The girls milled around the spilled contents of the bag, trying this, considering that. And for a moment, I saw them as they could have been back in the real world: just teenage girls living their lives as they were meant to.

"You scared?" Lucy said quietly as she watched them. She extended her hand to me.

"Not as scared as I thought I'd be," I said. I took it.

"I'm not scared at all," said Mowse unconvincingly through her coral lips. "We've fought them before, you know."

"I heard," said Lucy. Then her eyebrows furrowed. "That mark," she said, pointing to Mowse's hand. "You have one too?"

Mowse nodded. "Half my class has them," she said. "The teacher says it's probably ringworm."

"I knew it," muttered Judith, scratching at the spot on her hand. "Dammit, Mowse."

"Those marks are spreading fast—nearly as fast as the Dust Sickness," said Lucy, concern rising in her voice. "Seems like a fourth of the town has them now."

"I think we have bigger problems to worry about than a ringworm outbreak," Olivia said soberly, looking out at the sky. Beside her, Rosa twitched on the couch, the red mark on her hand vivid in the low light.

"I know, I know," said Lucy. "Still . . . this just . . . doesn't feel right somehow."

Lucy bent suddenly with her handkerchief over her mouth, coughing a deep, muffled-sounding cough that sent ice down my spine and a knife through my heart. I reached over and held her to me, held my forehead against hers, feeling her ragged breathing steady itself, hearing the telltale rattling in her throat, hoping that somehow I could take some of it from her, wishing I had the magic to do just that.

"I'm going to make this all right," I whispered to her. "We're going to win. I promise. Then the Dust Sickness and everything else will be over."

On the couch, Rosa whimpered in her sleep. At that moment, Judith and Mowse both clutched their hands in pain.

"Ow!" said Mowse. "That spot hurts!"

"Mine too," said Judith, turning her hand over to look at it more closely.

"How did it hurt?" Lucy asked. "Burning? Sharp? Dull?"

"Burning," Judith said. "Like a . . . a pulse. Kind of a . . . a thrum."

"Let me see," Asa said. He took Judith's hand and scrutinized it. "There's magic in this. Dark magic." He turned to me. "And I'll give you one guess whose it is."

Olivia and I exchanged glances.

"Mother Morevna's," growled Olivia.

Lucy's eyes widened in realization. "You know, I did see her doing what looked like a spell the other night . . . with stones, looked like. Looking out over the city."

A trapdoor spell.

"I knew she wouldn't give up her power that easily. She's behind this," Olivia spat.

"But what is it?" I asked.

Olivia rose from her place by the couch. "Whatever it is, it can't be good. We're going over to the church and shutting it down."

"We report to the walls in two hours!" said Susanah. "We can't just—"

"I don't want the rest of you to do anything," Olivia said. "You all go to the walls as planned and fight. We've come too far not to. But this . . . this is a matter that concerns the people of Elysium. And as an Elysian, this is my responsibility."

Asa reached into his ear and pulled out a green silk handkerchief. Then he bit his finger and let the blood soak into it, muddying the green silk.

"Take this," he said, handing the handkerchief to Olivia. "I'll be most effective on the walls. But take my power with you. Just be careful. Please."

Asa's face flickered daemon for a moment, one eye his usual odd yellow and the other black and terrifying above a still-human nose and mouth. Then he was himself again.

"You know how important your decisions are now," he said. "Don't play into Death's hands after all this. We still have to fight."

Olivia put her arms around him and kissed him deeply.

"I'll be back," she said. "I'll be back in time to fight the

Dust Soldiers, right beside you. Beside all of you. I promise. But Morevna has to pay for this."

"I'm going too," I said, and Olivia turned to me. "I've got to get her to lift the spell. Besides, even if she's dying, Mother Morevna might put up a fight. You'll need my help."

Lucy came to me and held my hands in her own. She looked at me for a moment, as though she was unsure what to do. My heart sped. Then, quickly, she reached out and kissed me on the cheek. "You can do it," she said. "I'll see you soon." Then she went to the door and disappeared into the night, leaving the place she had kissed me burning on my cheek. Without thinking, I reached up and touched my face. ("I knew it!" said Zo's voice somewhere in the background. "Pay up, Judith!")

Then Olivia, looking amused despite herself, snapped her fingers and brought me back into the real world.

"We only have two hours until nightfall," Olivia said. "Come on. Let's put an end to this once and for all."

CHAPTER 27

2 HOURS REMAIN.

The ground rumbled. The sky churned green and black, making the setting sun look queasy through it. Already, the guards were pulling the platform the new Sacrifice rested on, all of it, out the gates and into the desert. This way, the Dust Soldiers would have to judge our sacrifice outside the city walls, giving us time to fight back. The horses were already outside, a mass of spectral glowing eyes, skeletal metal frames, waiting to be spurred into battle. Olivia and I watched as the guards shoved the doors shut behind the Sacrifice. The place where it had been sat as bald and empty as an abandoned nest.

"Come on!" Olivia said. We sprinted across the square to the church. All the windows were dark. Even the round, spying-eye window in Mother Morevna's room. We looked at each other and nodded, prepared to pick the lock or bust the door down. But when we turned the knob, the church door opened without resistance.

We crossed the sanctuary, nearly soundless on the wooden floor, then another earthquake sent us stumbling and brought dust floating down on us like snow. From above us, stained-glass

Jesus paid us no mind, eternally sweating His blood in the Garden. But there was no sign of Mother Morevna.

"The stairway!" I said, moving as quietly as possible.

We went up the stairs, to the sliver of light beneath Mother Morevna's door. We halted before it, for a moment, thinking of her fiery spells, the power that emanated from her at all times. Then Olivia took a deep breath and turned the knob.

"*¡Ah, mierda!* It's locked! And I don't have anything to pick it with!"

"Don't worry," I said. This time I was prepared. I pulled a hairpin from my hair and inserted it into the keyhole. A wiggle here, a push there. *Click.*

Then, with a final glance at each other, Olivia and I plunged through the doorway and felt the door close behind us.

• • •

When the clock struck, Asa and the girls left for their places at the walls and hoped that Sal and Olivia would catch up to them. From his spot on the wall above the doors, Asa could see the whole desert, what was left of it, anyway. It looked strange out of two different eyes.

The human eye perceived the dark, jagged, puzzle-like expanse of the desert, all shadows and spots of foxfire glowing here and there between the nothingness.

His daemon eye saw what the desert really was, the magic that flowed through every stone and twig and grain of dust and disappeared at the places that had disappeared. With his daemon tongue, he could taste the mercury and petrichor in the air. And far out in the desert, he could feel the rumble of Their coming.

They were very close now. And above it all, he could feel Her watching, the Mother, the one who had chosen him in the beginning. She would be the arbitrator. He tried not to think of having also failed Her, the highest power in the universe. That was all over now. All that mattered was drawing this battle out as long as he could, no matter the cost.

Asa took a deep breath and looked out. The cavalry had begun to assemble now, rows of glowing-eyed metal horses, and men and girls and pimpled teenage boys astride them. Susanah and Mowse were on Susanah's horse, standing in front of the others, painted with black Dust Soldier ash, ready to lead the cavalry into battle. Judith was on another nearby, her big hands lingering above the spear that glowed in her horse's spine. Neither she nor Mowse had had another problem with the marks on their hands, but Asa could feel something sinister coming from the marks, feel it like a fever spreading, and he kept his eye on them, hoping that whatever it was, it could wait until the battle was over to rear its ugly head.

All around them, along the tops of the walls, between the humps of drying graves, were sharpshooters, waiting with their enchanted rifles. Zo was among them, her expression calm and serious, her holsters glowing.

Cassandra was on the wall to his right, on the other side of the great doors. She looked at him and nodded gravely, her airy-fairyness replaced by steely resolution. They each knew their roles: projectiles and offensive spells from him, illusions from her.

But Sal. Olivia . . . Their absence felt like a hole in their defenses, a chink in their armor. Asa had a sudden thought. It didn't take all of them to cast the final defensive spell that the girls had created. All it took was one person. And if that person had to be him, Asa was all right with that. *That person,* he thought with a smile. *That's how I think of myself now. I don't even have to try anymore.*

Another earthquake sent the mechanical horses stumbling, but when it passed, they stood upright. The guards and militiamen shook in their saddles. There was a moment of calm as the first sign of light appeared on the horizon. Out in the desert a whip-poor-will called, its plaintive cry echoing through the darkness.

Then, on the horizon, a dark cloud began to rise. Miles wide, miles high, black and billowing, sweeping toward Elysium with the speed of a thousand freight trains. But this time, everyone knew it for what it was: the army of Sentinels, sent to judge Elysium. Asa could feel the weight of them in the air. The cavalry stood their ground—how could anyone run from something that was as wide as the sky?—and as the black dust cloud neared, it slowed and came to a stop about thirty feet from the Sacrifice. The cloud began to condense, to shrink, until all of it somehow was contained in the enormous, terrifying forms of one hundred Sentinels, one hundred Dust Soldiers, waiting for instruction. Asa could feel the fear emanating from Elysium's soldiers, but, true to Susanah's instruction, they did not falter.

A lone Dust Soldier broke from the others, moving toward the Sacrifice. It examined the pile of crops and sacks of liquor and dry goods, summing it up.

Then it snapped its fingers.

The entirety of the Sacrifice began to blacken and shrink before his eyes, like ashes without a fire, until all of it, everything, was swept away by the wind. Then a great voice that sounded like all the cosmos speaking as one shouted, **DEATH HAS BEEN JUDGED THE WINNER**.

Asa swallowed the bile in his throat. Just as he thought. Now all She had to do was claim Her win. The Dust Soldiers unsheathed their scimitars. It was time. Time to break the Game.

"Charge!" cried Susanah, holding her spear aloft. She and Mowse lurched forward, their horse leaping into battle. The cavalry surged after them, shouting out their war cry, their spears held like knights' lances. On the wall, Zo gave the command. Fifty shotguns went off, aiming for the Dust Soldiers in the back. He heard Cassandra cry out a command, and the cavalry suddenly looked twice as massive, copies of each horse and rider exploding into life, launching themselves toward the Dust Soldiers. There was a resounding clash of swords and spears, of clanging metal and screams of the wounded and the roar of dust over it all.

Asa's palms sweated. He had seen wars and conflicts before. They were half of human history, it seemed. He had thought he was sure before, but being here in it, officially part of it, was something different entirely. To fight now meant fighting against all that he had ever been. To raise a hand against these Dust Soldiers now was to defy the order of the universe. It was choosing a punishment at the end of all of this, greater than any that had befallen any daemon in history, all so these humans could have the chance to live.

But that was what Sal would do. It was what Olivia would do. And it was what all these rushing human soldiers were doing now: risking everything on the off chance that they could make a better life for their friends even if they, themselves, never lived to see it. And, Asa realized, it was what he wanted to do. His heart *was* human now, through and through. And humanity, true humanity, he realized, was sacrifice.

Asa cracked his knuckles, stretched his hands, and sent an arc of infernal flame down at the rushing Dust Soldiers. He had never felt so sure.

• • •

Lucy left the hospital and went house to house, bringing water rations to the people huddled under tables and praying beside beds. Every so often she stopped and collapsed against the side of a building, wheezing, spluttering blood, wondering each time she gasped for air if it would be her last breath. The ground seemed to roll beneath her feet, and beyond the wall, she could hear the screams of the soldiers and the infernal shrieking of the Dust Soldiers. Mud rose in Lucy's chest. She fell against the side of the Robertson house, pounding her burning chest, trying to shake loose the mud before it choked her completely.

She felt a firm hand clapping her on the back. It thudded against her again and again, until finally, the clod of mud came loose and she vomited it into a bloody pile on the ground and gasped and gasped the hot, dusty, life-giving air.

"Thought you were a goner for a minute there, girl," Mr. Jameson said, kneeling beside her with a bucket. She had seen him, going from house to house, taking the last of the rations to the Sick before heading up to the wall to fight.

"Th . . . thank you," Lucy managed, wiping the gritty blood from her mouth. More blood than mud now. It wouldn't be long. The curse would have its way with her yet. She looked at Mr. Jameson, prepared to thank him, but his brows were furrowed in concern and his eyes were on the ground between them.

Something golden and small sparkled in the dust near her bloody vomit pile.

"My brother's cricket thing," she said, picking it out of the dust. "What's it doing here?"

"That's no trinket," Mr. Jameson said, eyes on the golden thing in her hand. "That's . . . that's the Master Stone! The one I took out into the desert back when the walls went up."

"The stone that can end the Dust Sickness," Lucy breathed.

When her brother had picked it up the night Sal and Asa had been exiled, it had seemed nothing more than an oddity. But now she could feel its power, its darkness, radiating like heat.

Mr. Jameson took his rifle from its spot and put it on his shoulder. "Come on," he said to Lucy as the war raged beyond the wall. "Let's go make this right."

CHAPTER 28

THE END OF THE WORLD.

In Mother Morevna's room, the smell of sickness, of blood and soap, hit us like we'd run into a brick wall. Her cane leaned against the dresser. The low doorway to the roof was open.

We ran to it and climbed the narrow stairs beyond, through the dark, until we saw the swirling sky overhead. We climbed out onto the roof of the church, that flat area behind the steeple, and for a moment, all I could do was stand and watch.

Death had won the Game, and now She was trying to claim Her prize. The Dust Soldiers' speed and strength was terrifying as they lunged and swiped with their enormous black scimitars. But every so often, we saw an explosion of black dust as one of them was run through with a spear or shot by an enchanted rifle.

Out in the middle, we could see Susanah on her painted horse, jabbing this way and that with her spear—chopping one Dust Soldier to the ground and then another as Mowse hung on to her waist. And on the wall, just above the doors, I could see Cassandra casting her copies, and Asa, nearby, hurling blue flames down from the heavens. Another and another Dust

Soldier exploded in bursts of black sand. He was fighting with everything he had. *Hold on, Asa!* I thought. *We're coming!*

"There she is," Olivia said, pointing.

Mother Morevna was standing by the steeple, her shape a dark, bent outline against the swirling sky. She was laying something down, pebbles maybe, to prepare some sort of spell. When I saw her, all the anger I'd been holding began to simmer in my belly. Everything had changed for me now. This woman with all her dreams of equality, with her perfect society, whom I had once wanted so desperately to be like, was the one who had killed my mother, who had cursed Lucy.

I have to make it right again, I thought. *I was her Successor. Her mistakes are my responsibility to fix, or what am I fighting for?*

I secured my components belt. My penny glowed hot around my neck.

She must have felt our eyes on her somehow, because she turned. When she saw us, she didn't seem surprised or frightened or angry. Her face was expressionless, and up close, I saw how hollow her cheeks had become.

"What are you doing?" she said. "You should be down there, fighting, as was your own idea. Leave me. This spell may still win Life the Game!"

She bent again, put another small something at the end of the row she was making.

"But Death has already won!" I said. "That's why we built the horses!"

"We were just buying her time," Olivia said darkly. "What are the marks, Morevna?"

"Precautions, set in place long before I took either of you under my wing."

"Precautions?" Olivia stopped in her tracks.

"When you lead, you *must* be able to choose between the many and the few. And I have. Now go back to your horses and pray that the Goddesses accept the ones I've marked."

"Marked . . ." My stomach lurched. "The red marks! She's going to offer the people who have them as a sacrifice!"

Olivia's face seemed to lose all its color and I knew what she was thinking. *Rosa.* She buckled for a moment as though she'd been punched. And when she looked at Mother Morevna again, her eyes blazed with a dark fire that would make the Devil quail.

"So killing your own people with Dust Sickness wasn't enough?" Olivia spat. "How much blood have you got on your hands, Morevna?"

The old woman's eyes flashed. "Don't you dare judge me as though your own hands were clean. We do what we must to save what we love. And I love this town more than you can possibly imagine." She turned to me. There was a glint of gold in her hand. "If you and that magician hadn't ruined the Sacrifice, we could have gotten by! But this spell was laid long ago in preparation. And there isn't an Old Goddess in the world who can resist blood."

My stomach threatened to bottom out. I stared at the woman whom I had once seen as an idol, a mentor, and in her place all I saw was a monster.

She took a step away from her line of pebbles. I glanced at Olivia. She nodded almost imperceptibly. It was now or never.

"Entflammt!" I shouted. Streams of fire billowed out, enveloping Mother Morevna in a great, white-hot fireball. For a moment, I was blinded. But then I saw her moving in the center of the fire, tall and thin, a shadow at the center of the brightness. As she moved forward, the flames fell from her like sand. Not even her dress was singed.

"You leave me no choice, Sallie," Mother Morevna said.

She raised a tattooed claw and threw a handful of black dust. It became hands, grabbing my legs, pulling me down. It dragged me across the hard, dusty shingles of the roof. I felt the hands connect around my throat, choking, choking. . . .

Olivia had Asa's handkerchief in her fist, holding his blood against her palm, absorbing his magic. She shouted something I didn't understand, voice harsh against the howling wind, and the magical, painful hands crumbled away like flakes of rust.

Mother Morevna reached into her pocket and hurled a handful of salt. The grains became needles as they flew toward us.

Olivia shouted again, something in an infernal language that made the marrow of my bones feel hot. A great spiky black shield rose in front of us, smelling of mercury and rain, and the needles glanced off it and away.

I pulled myself to my feet and reached into my pouches, fumbling for the crushed seashells and chicken feathers I'd planned to use on the Dust Soldiers. I raised my hand and shouted down a new spell, a fork of lightning. It came blazing down at her, but Mother Morevna caught it in one tattooed hand and threw it back at me, a ball of light I barely had time to dodge before it flew past me and blackened the wall at the other end of the city.

Olivia was moving forward, her hand extended, wind rising at her back. She shouted into the wind in what I knew now was the language of the world beyond ours. Shadows rocketed past her and pinned Mother Morevna to the steeple.

"Stop this now, Morevna," Olivia growled, moving forward, the shadows still swarming.

But Mother Morevna closed her eyes. I felt an enormous surge of magic from her, and the shadows retreated. She rose to meet Olivia. She extended her hand and made a slapping motion. Ten feet away, Olivia was knocked to the ground as though by the slap of a massive hand. She crawled back to her feet, her lip bleeding.

An earthquake roared under us, so strong it nearly threw us from the roof. Beyond the walls, the battle raged on, showers of blood and black dust. More of the desert fell away into nothingness.

Mother Morevna bent, clutching her stomach. She winced, then hobbled to her line of stones—I could see them now: small golden stones all in a row.

"Goddesses!" she shouted, her voice magically magnified, booming out over the din of battle. "I speak as the leader of this settlement! Accept this sacrifice for my society, a good and responsible society of equals!" She raised a hand over them, and they began to glow. I felt a surge of dark, smoky energy, could feel its drain all around me. She had set her curse in motion.

A dagger whistled by my ear and lodged in Mother Morevna's shoulder. She turned toward us, her eyes alight with cold fire.

"This isn't *your* society," Olivia said, wiping the blood from her mouth. "It's ours."

“No, my dear,” Mother Morevna said. She pulled the dagger from her shoulder, waved a tattooed hand over the wound, stopping the blood. “This city has always been mine.”

Blue-black flames began to rise around her, licking at her dress, her sleeves, but not burning her. The flames grew and surrounded her, covering her. The column of flames grew taller. Her arms lengthened, multiplied, until she was a great, eight-armed beast of fire. Her frailty was gone, replaced by a fierce, almost feline fluidity that spoke of unfathomable power. The black teardrop pendant was the only thing that did not blaze as she rose, beautiful and terrible before us. We tried to run, but all around us a glowing circle of flames was rising. We couldn’t move our legs; they stuck fast in the circle as though embedded in concrete. Then I saw the white stones placed around the edges of the roof. One final trapdoor spell.

• • •

Asa felt an enormous thrum of power from behind him. Then the sound of hundreds of voices screaming in pain rose from Elysium. Twenty meters down on the battlefield, Mowse and Judith sunk to their knees. “Susanah!” Mowse screamed.

“Mowse! No!” Susanah cried. Then she turned just in time to duck the blow of an oncoming Dust Soldier. “Asa!” she shouted up to the wall. “Take her!”

Without another word, Asa disappeared and reappeared on the battlefield. He ducked a blow from a Sentinel and gathered Mowse in his arms, then flashed back to the wall. Her color was going, draining as though being sucked away by a leech. The red mark on her hand looked bigger and angrier than ever, and Asa understood immediately what it meant, what Mother Morevna was trying to do.

"What's happening to me?" she whimpered.

Down on the ground, Judith was suffering too but powering through it. Still, her movements were slowed by pain, and her skin was gray as old bones.

"You're gonna be all right, okay?" Asa said to Mowse. He put her on the flat part inside the lip of the wall.

There was a surge of heat, a smell of sulfur. Asa turned toward the church. There on the roof, Sal and Olivia were fighting an enormous, fiery beast. Mother Morevna, he realized. But why weren't they moving? His heart seemed to stop beating. Something was wrong. It seemed as though they were stuck there as in the web of a great fiery spider. Asa had to go to them. He had to help.

Then the crack of a magical rifle rang out from somewhere on the ground beneath the church.

Mr. Jameson was standing beneath the church with Lucy Arbor beside him. He hung his rifle at his side and held something in his hand, something small and golden.

"Marike, stop!" Mr. Jameson shouted. "It's over! I have the stone!"

Asa gasped. *No . . . it couldn't be.* But it was. And looking up at the beast Mother Morevna was, the beast she had always been, he finally recognized her for what she was, and what his true responsibility had always been: Death's Wildcard. She was the one who had been working against Elysium, unknown even to herself. She was the one who disarmed him by throwing him out of Elysium. She was the one he had been sent to disarm. And there was still time.

"Don't make me do this, Marike!" Mr. Jameson shouted. "You've gotta make this right again!"

"Mowse, I need you to listen to me," he said. "Stay here behind this wall and do not move, okay?"

"But where are you—"

"I'll be back, I promise. Just do not move."

And without another word, Asa blitzed away.

He reappeared next to Mr. Jameson, who nearly fell back in shock.

"Jesus!" Mr. Jameson said, throwing a protective arm in front of Lucy. "What the—"

"Daemon," Asa said. "No time to explain. But the cricket! Give it to me! I can take it to her."

Still standing between Asa and Lucy, Mr. Jameson put the cricket in Asa's hand. Without another word, Asa blitzed to the roof, placing himself between Olivia and Sal and the beast that was Mother Morevna.

Mother Morevna looked confused for a moment, faltered.

Olivia stepped forward, her hands blazing with deadly magic, ready to aim the killing blow.

"Olivia!" Asa said, holding the cricket in amber up. "Olivia, it's hers! You're not Death's Card! She is! This can disarm her!"

Olivia shook herself and stood down, the magic fading. Asa stepped forward.

"Mother Morevna," he said, holding the cricket out in front of him. "I think I have something that belongs to y—"

A giant, flaming arm caught him in the stomach and knocked Asa off the roof. As he fell, he threw the cricket upward.

"Sal!" he cried. "Catch it!"

And he fell directly on top of Mr. Jameson, sending another magical shotgun blast into the sky.

• • •

I saw the cricket glint in the firelight. It fell at my feet, and I scooped it up, realizing for the first time what it was: the Master Stone, the one she had laid in the desert so long ago. The one that could end the second sacrifice, the Dust Sickness, all of it. The Dust Soldiers roared beyond the walls, and suddenly, I understood all of it. The truth of it all filled me like light, like wind, and I knew what I had to do.

She was so close now that her heat was singeing my hair, wrinkling my clothes. She reached out, and with the cricket in amber in my fist, I grabbed her fiery hand, and as my palm blistered, I pressed the cricket into her hand.

"No!" she roared, her voice crackling like timber. "Put this back!"

"Don't you see?" I said. "The whole time, you've been helping to destroy us. Helping Death. She's been using you!"

"That's not true!" she roared. "I have done only what is good for this city!"

"It is," I said. "And I'll show you."

I willed my magic into our hands. The nausea and darkness rose and took us. I felt the truth of it rise around us, all the mistakes, all the deaths, all the blood. Truth that couldn't be turned away from or ignored. And as it enveloped us, held itself over our minds' eyes, I felt Mother Morevna try to look away. But she could not. And as it burned itself into our souls, I felt her absorb this truth. I felt her absorb every particle of the pain she had caused. The wishes of Goddesses, the wants of witches, and all the misunderstandings of a society built to be equal, gone terribly, terribly wrong. I felt it begin to dim and recede, and when the darkness fell away, instead of a monster, I was holding the frail, tattooed hand of an old woman, an old witch who had finally seen the truth.

She let go of my hand, and as she did so, my blisters healed themselves. I stumbled, then righted myself. Our feet were no longer stuck in her web of magic.

Mother Morevna swayed on her feet, a look of hollowness, of brokenness making her appear far older than she'd ever looked before.

"It's too late," Mother Morevna said quietly. "Oh, God, now it's too late."

She had seen her utopia for what it was, what she herself had made it. She heard for the first time the pain in the cries of her people, and the knowing was the heaviest burden.

"Sallie . . ." she croaked desperately. "Here."

She raised her hands and closed them over the cricket in amber. There was a deep thrum of power, more power than I'd ever felt at once. A feeling of leaving, of draining, of never going back. As I watched, the tattoos faded from her hands until they could have been the knobby, gnarled hands of any old woman. She heaved a great, weary sigh. Then she held out her hand. The cricket in amber glowed in her palm, power radiating from it. But no longer from her.

"I am not fit to wield this power," she said. "But you . . . you saw the truth. You saw it the whole time." She gritted her teeth in pain. "Take my magic! Add it to your own, and set it all right, once and for all. And when my spells have been lifted, use it to fight them. You are our only chance now."

I hesitated. Beyond the gates, there was a roar, the screech of metal, the sound of many men screaming.

"They're gonna break the lines!" shouted a guard. "We need help!"

"Sal!" came Olivia's voice from behind me.

"Go," said Mother Morevna. "Go, now!"

I started to say something—what, I didn't know. Then Olivia shouted for me again, and I took the cricket and clambered back down into the church. We ran across the quaking sanctuary, out of the church, and out into the street where Asa and Lucy and Mr. Jameson waited.

"Go to the house!" Olivia said to Lucy. "Take care of my sister! We've got one last chance to win this!"

"Don't worry," Lucy said. "I've got it!"

"We've got to get to our posts!" I said. "Come on!"

Olivia and I ran to the walls and climbed our ladders. We stood, hands over our components belts, twenty feet between us, in our crow's nests over the battlefield. Asa blitzed to a section of the wall where Mowse lay, crumpled and hiding. He stood over her and looked out over the battlefield.

The scene before us was a bloody one. Through the clouds of smoke, we could see glimpses of the cavalry, rushing, striking, rearing on mechanical limbs. The ground was splashed with dark blood. And through it they fought on.

Zo had come down from her tower and was fighting hand to hand with a Dust Soldier, her spear pulled from a fallen mechanical horse and rider. Judith, bleeding from multiple wounds, held two spears, fighting a Dust Soldier back with one while she threw the other like a javelin, skewering another Dust Soldier in the chest.

Susanah was still out front, fighting two and three Dust Soldiers at a time. And just as three Dust Soldiers were bearing down on an unsuspecting guard knocked from his horse, I saw his eyes go white. Moving like one possessed, he turned and sliced the three of them through the belly with his spear. Then he blinked as Mowse let him back to himself.

From her spot behind Asa, Mowse was doing her best to cast, even though her skin too had taken on the gray of death and the red mark on her hand had deepened to the dark red of blood.

Up on the wall, Cassandra sent illusion after illusion, turning one horse into five, one soldier into ten. She was fading fast. And she had been carrying our weight for too long.

Olivia and Asa sprung into action, throwing down every spell they knew into the jigsaw puzzle stretched out before us. Flames, wind, light, shadow.

Mr. Jameson climbed up the nearest tower and pulled out his enchanted rifle. Dust Soldier after Dust Soldier exploded with his every shot.

I hesitated, holding the Master Stone in my palm. Then I closed my eyes and closed my hands over it. *I accept.*

The amber grew warm, melting in my palms like honey. Then there was a powerful surge, an unspeakable wave of power, rocketing through me. It filled me up, full to bursting, so full of magic that the very follicles of my hair seemed to glow with it. There seemed to be no end to the well of magic inside me, Mother Morevna's magic. *My* magic. And I saw for the first time, the memories that were in the cricket. Mother Morevna's memories.

I saw two Mennonite girls: an older girl, Greta, and the other, a young Marike Morevna herself, running away from home. Home, where their strange ways were ways to be hidden or punished away. For there was no room in the community for girls who could keep the bees from stinging and make the plants grow just by whispering to them. Greta had been thrown out, excommunicated, and Marike's punishments had gotten so harsh that she thought she would rather die than live another day being punished for being who she was. Then Greta had returned with spell tattoos under her gloves, returned and whisked Marike away into the safety of the night, to the safety of the Russian coven. I saw the amulet Mother Morevna had made as her first object, this very cricket in amber itself as she learned to use it. I saw the tattoos rise on her hands. I saw the hands beneath the tattoos begin to age. I saw the coven rise in sisterhood and fall to bickering, to competition, to spite, until every witch in it splintered from the group, certain she alone knew what had gone wrong.

I jerked myself back into the real world, a lump of sorrow in my chest that was not my own. There was a wiggling in my hands then—the cricket had come back to life. It jumped out of my hands and down onto the battlefield.

I took a deep breath, mustered as much magic as I could into my voice.

"Setzen Sie es richtig!" I shouted, willing power into every syllable. *Set it right.*

A thrum of power knocked me to my knees. Magic spread from me, and though I couldn't see it, I felt a sensation like fog clearing, like an enormous flock of birds rising, like Atlas sighing in relief when the sky was lifted from his shoulders. And I knew that I was feeling the smothering heaviness of Dust Sickness lift. And then I felt the air move, a great simultaneous gasp of air, as though everyone who had had Dust Sickness suddenly breathed deep. Farther down the wall, I saw Mowse rise to her feet again, her color restored, the red mark on her hand gone.

Had I done it? I wondered, the beating of my heart drumming in my ears. I had stopped the curses, stopped the second sacrifice. We'd removed Death's Wildcard, because that was what Mother Morevna had always been, wasn't it? It was over now, I told myself. It had to be.

But the Dust Soldiers were still coming. Our world was still ending. My heart lurched. Our work wasn't over.

I reached into my pouches for powdered seashells. Then there was another earthquake, bigger than any that had come before, so big we nearly fell from our places on the wall. The mechanical horses toppled to the ground, throwing their riders. And though the Dust Soldiers marched ever forward, the mechanical horses didn't rise again.

Susanah, Judith, and Zo ran to the front, holding the Dust Soldiers back as Mowse watched, pale and shaking, from the wall.

"Come on!" Susanah shouted at the guards, her mouth bloody. "This isn't over yet! We have to hold them!"

The guards and militiamen hesitated. Then, as the Dust Soldiers marched their death march toward them, each of the bodies of the soldiers they had killed turned to dust and blew away on the wind. And in this moment, I saw the remaining guards falter, as though each one realized that he was no soldier: only a rancher, a cowboy, a wheat farmer. One by one, the guards broke and ran for the door. Susanah, Judith, and Zo stood firm, facing the soldiers.

"We have to help them!" Olivia yelled.

"Asa!" I shouted. "Blitz us down there!"

Asa nodded. He blitzed to Olivia first, then to Cassandra, taking each of them down to the others. Then he was beside me. He grabbed my arm, and I felt myself disintegrating into nothing. I felt speed and darkness and light, and then Asa and I were there with the others.

Side by side, we stood, some of us drained, others bloody, all exhausted. The Dust Soldiers loomed just beyond the reach of Susanah's spear, coming forward, a high dark wall of destruction.

"Let's finish this!" Olivia shouted. And we charged. Susanah and Judith spun and jabbed and twirled. Asa and Olivia threw their brain-bending, infernal magic, and Zo fired her magic-laden shots, and Cassandra and I cast spell after spell. Fire, wind, earth, all at my command. We leapt and ducked, slid and dodged, great black scimitars slicing into our arms, grazing our ribs. We fought like animals. And one by one, the Dust Soldiers exploded. And as Judith ran her spear through the final Dust Soldier, black dust blanketed the battlefield, hung in the sky like cannon smoke.

Then there was silence. A hush fell over the battlefield, and where there had been slashing and hacking and screaming and running, now there was only silence, hazy clouds of dust, and the blood of the fallen soaking into it all.

We came back together, each of us bleeding, gasping for breath.

"That's all of them," Zo said, wiping blood from a slash on her cheek. "Finally."

"I think . . . I think we did it," said Cassandra.

But something felt wrong. The air felt tight and close, and my pulse wouldn't stop drumming in my veins. I turned to Asa for comfort, for reassurance that we had done it. But Asa's face was pale as chalk. He pointed out into the clouds of dust thinning before us. Among them, the dark, dust-covered ground began to move. To rise.

From the fallen dust, the Dust Soldiers were building themselves once more, all of them, all one hundred, re-forming themselves completely. They solidified into their previous shapes, huge, and terrifyingly whole again, and as one, they began to move toward us.

"No . . ." Judith said. "Oh, God . . . no . . ."

They were not running, not charging, but walking slowly, as though they already knew they'd won. And they had. Eight against one hundred regenerating Dust Soldiers was not just bad odds; it was suicide. And as I looked at the others' faces, I knew the same thought was running through all of our minds. *This is the end.*

"The defense spell," Olivia said. "We've got to do it now."

I pulled the black stone from my pouch. "I'll do it. I wrote the spell."

"Whoever sets it off will be locked outside the city!" Cassandra said. "We can't ask that of you!"

"And I can't ask it of anyone else!" I said. "This spell is the only chance we have of holding them off until morning. Get into the city and let me do this!"

"No," Olivia said, putting her hand over mine. "It's all of us or nobody."

I looked at the others, their bleeding, bruised faces; Susanah, her nose broken, staring defiantly; Zo and Judith, bleeding from scores of wounds, side by side; Cassandra, her face the calm mask of one who has accepted her fate. Asa nodded. Then Olivia took the black stone into her hand and went to the door and closed it.

"I'm sorry, Rosa," she whispered. Then she placed the stone in its spot.

She bit her own finger and let the blood flow. "PULVAREM SPIRITUM!" she shouted.

And a great dome of magic, pulsating with Asa's energy, rose around the city. Where Dust Dome had been completely transparent, this looked like a globe of lacy runes written in chalk upon the very air itself, and it felt like protection and doom all at once. It rose above the walls and closed, seamless, over all of it, a great patterned bowl of magic. We had inherited this problem. We had fought like hell for it. And at least Elysium, and humanity, would be protected.

We turned to face them then, a high black wall of destruction. *What will dying be like?* I thought. *Will it be fast? Will there be light? A tunnel? Or only darkness?*

The Dust Soldiers began their charge then. Scimitars

unsheathed, they ran, ready to cut down this chain of girls who dared to stare down the apocalypse.

Beside me, I saw Olivia clasp Asa's hand. Then she reached out for Susanah's. Susanah took Olivia's and reached out for Judith's. I reached for Zo's. We were forming a chain, all of us, save for Mowse on her safe place on the wall. Defiant, even in the face of Death. And as my penny burned against my skin, strong and hot, I thought of what was written on it: *E pluribus unum. From many, one.* I closed my eyes. *All of us or nobody.*

There was a smell then, just a whiff of something green. Something achingly familiar.

A clap of thunder, a blinding flash of light.

And the rain fell.

It rolled in like a dust storm, covering the horizon. It fell in torrents, in buckets, in waterfalls, and as it fell on the Dust Soldiers, they collapsed in upon themselves like sandcastles at our feet.

It fell on roofs of families holding each other close, ready to die until they heard the unbelievable sound of it beating on their windows. It rushed in rivulets over the strange, unholy desert, blurring it like an oil painting, washing it clean and revealing the fields and prairies we had known before.

It felt as I had always, always known that it would. Because this had always been the truth, I realized. We had only had to make it so.

"I don't believe it . . ." Asa breathed. "I never in a million years would have believed . . ."

"What?" Olivia said. "Did Life win?"

"No," Asa said, a smile spreading across his exhausted face. "We did it. *We* won."

Out in the desert, the world was ending. But it was not ending like it had before. This was no grave. Instead, it seemed we were being born. Patches of nothingness were filling in, but not with the desert that had been there before. The nothingness bloomed into fields, scrub, cacti. Back into the Oklahoma we hadn't seen in ten years, and one word echoed through the marrow of our bones. *Home. We are home.*

The dome of our spell flickered and disappeared. Then we heard a groaning of metal as the doors opened behind us.

"Olivia?" said a small, weak voice. "Asa?" We turned. There was Rosalita, awake and blinking against the rain.

"Rosa!" Olivia shouted, running to her and embracing her. "¡Mi hermanita! You're all right!"

One by one, the Elysians ventured out of the gates, gasping at the new old world unfolding before them, all of them hugging and thanking us over and over and over again—even Asa in his daemon form. "You're heroes!" they told us. "Heroes!"

"It was never about the crops at all," I said. "Was it?"

"That was just a factor to add difficulty," Asa said, able to speak freely now that the Game was over. "The real test was to see what you humans would do, what you'd make of the situation the Sisters put you in. I must admit, it was slick of Death to make Mother Morevna her Card. I only wish I'd seen it sooner."

"But Death . . ." I said. "She had won."

"Until you all beat Her," said Asa. "All of you proved what humanity could be. Good and responsible—unlike the

Goddesses, it seems, who were neither good nor responsible with Their creation."

I turned to respond, but my words caught in my throat.

Asa was changing. A glow was traveling over his body, and the strangeness, the energy that he'd carried since the moment I'd met him, was dripping from him like oil and disappearing into the air. He levitated for a moment, then thudded back down to the dust . . . different. New.

"What happened?" I asked.

"I completed my mission," Asa said, turning to look at me with newly hazel, unmistakably human eyes. "This . . . this must be my reward. From the Mother. I . . . I understand why She chose me now. To give me a chance to become what I always felt I was." Asa put his hands on his chest, pressing as though he were afraid he'd disappear under them. "And now I am . . . I'm *human*! One hundred percent human! With a pulse and blood and eyelashes and intestines and a-a-a pointless appendix and everything!"

"One hundred percent human?" Olivia said, coming to stand beside him. "So that means I can do this now and we won't have to think twice, huh?" She took his glasses off, threw her arms around his neck and kissed him, the rain rushing over both of them until the kiss broke, and they stood, grinning at each other through the downpour.

"Oh, you can do that whenever you want," Asa said. "Though this kissing in the rain business is a lot less romantic than everyone makes it seem." Then he said, "I'm sorry I thought you were Death's Wildcard. I'm just so drawn to you that I thought—"

"I'm just glad it was all right the whole time, you and me," Olivia said. "But why are we drawn together?"

"Love, I guess." Asa grinned.

Just then, a guard shouted, "On the horizon! Look!"

Everyone turned. A line of vehicles was coming toward us through the rain. There was a sound of ambulance sirens. Rescue vehicles. All the people of Elysium started running then, running toward that line of cars, splashing and waving and shouting and dancing. The guards were running and tackling each other and sliding in the mud. Judith had an injured Zo on her shoulders, and they were squabbling as usual with wide, rain-soaked smiles. Behind them, Cassandra, Susanah, and Mowse were catching raindrops on their tongues and laughing. Olivia and Asa and Rosalita were walking together, already a family. Even Mr. Jameson was striding out, his head held high, ready to go back to Texas, to the family that I knew somehow still waited for him there. He turned and waved to me to come on, to join them.

I stood back for a moment, watching all of them, my heart filled hurting-full with an emotion I couldn't begin to describe.

"Sal," said Lucy. And when I turned, the sight of her—her skin clear, her cheeks unsunken, her eyes bright again—made my breath catch in my throat. "You coming?"

She extended a hand to me, and I took a step forward to take it.

Then a shadow in the doorway caught my eye. Mother Morevna, just inside the doors, watching as usual with those cold, gray eyes. Watching her people rush out of the city she had built for them without looking back. Leaving her.

I stood there for a moment, feeling her magic in my veins alongside my own, as I would forever.

Then she held up a hand as bare and unmarked as any old woman's.

I nodded to her. And slowly, with one final groan of metal, the great steel doors of Elysium closed forever. Soaked to the skin, I took Lucy's hand and joined the others walking toward that bright horizon, toward the world that waited for us. And somewhere behind us, we heard the solemn song of a single cricket fading into the distance.

ACKNOWLEDGMENTS

The world of children's books is a vibrant, many-splendored one that I've dreamed of joining since I was about eight years old, creating my own versions of the great American fantasy novel in spiral notebooks on car trips. And though I put in a lot of hard work in order to get here, this sometimes seemingly deity-defying mission would not have been possible without the community of people I met along the way (or knew all along) who have been every bit as dedicated to my success as I was.

First, of course, I'd like to thank my agent, Sara Crowe, who is phenomenal in every way and who cannot be lauded enough. You believed in me despite everything, and I hope I make you and the other Pips proud! Thank you also to my editors, Laura Schreiber and Hannah Allaman, who saw the potential in this extremely odd story and decided to take the gamble on me. You're both fantastic, and even if you have to hand the phone back and forth during phone calls from your tiny office, I can always count on your feedback to be brilliant and inevitably exactly what my work needs. To my film agent, Addison Duffy at UTA, thank you, also, for believing in *Elysium Girls*! It's a weird book, but I'm glad all of you love it as much as I do. Thank you to the Cimarron Heritage Center museum in Boise City, OK, for providing me with invaluable information about the Dust Bowl, and letting me touch that extremely fine, terrible Dust Bowl dust. The museum is excellent, and was one of my best resources. Thank you also to my sensitivity readers, poet Reyes Ramirez and Linda Medina Martinez, who provided feedback for my representation of Mexican American characters and Spanish, and to Tiffany Morris, my Comanche sensitivity reader, whose advice on the language was spot-on. Your services are necessary and I'm so, so grateful to you.

Thank you to my friends, too: Ramsey Knighton, my dearest friend and fellow artist, who grew up in East Texas alongside me and was witness to both my highest highs and lowest lows. I love you. To JoJo, too, my biggest fan, who was always there to bounce ideas back and forth and to be my first reader. You are invaluable. The DnD crew—Lauren, Edwin, Kirk, Heather, and Matt—are also to thank for the weekly creative ventures that keep me sane. And, in faraway Dallas, Brandon Stewart, my fellow home-cooking enthusiast, whom I hope is still using so much garlic he wakes his roommates with the smell of it.

To my VCFA family, the MAGIC IFs (graduating class of winter 2014), YAM and I love you. A special thanks to Autumn Krause, Aimee Payne, and Jenn Barnes (Jenn Bishop) for reading draft after draft of my work and always listening to me complain about how writing is HARD. Other VCFAers, too, deserve thanks. My advisors, Mark Karlins, April Lurie, Susan Cooper, and Louise Hawes, taught me invaluable lessons about writing and children's books and trusting both myself and the process (somehow). Vermont College truly is the Hogwarts of writing for children and I will treasure it in my heart always.

And finally, to my family. My mother and father easily could have pressured me toward a different, more lucrative pastime and eventual college major and career, especially since we never had much money. But they didn't. They did nothing but encourage me throughout all of the pitfalls and pools of quicksand I encountered along the way, whether artistic or financial. My brother Matt, my aunts, uncles, grandparents, and cousins were all equally supportive, and took me seriously even as I was a twelve-year-old memorizing passages of *Children's Writers and Illustrator's Market* like a weirdo. I wish Granna and Granddad could have lived to see this, and I'm glad that my niece and nephew, Bonnie and Finn, are young enough to never know a world in which Aunt KayKay isn't an author.